Under the Light of Darkness
Love and Marriage in Antebellum South for the Slaves

By Victoria A. Casey McDonald

Catch the Spirit of Appalachia, Inc.
WESTERN NORTH CAROLINA

First Edition 2013

Books by Victoria A. Casey McDonald
The African Americans in Jackson County, 2008
Just Over the Hill, 2012

Layout by Amy Ammons Garza

Publisher:
Catch the Spirit of Appalachia, Inc.—Imprint of:
Ammons Communications — SAN NO. 8 5 1 – 0 8 8 1
29 Regal Avenue • Sylva, North Carolina 28779
Phone/fax: (828) 631-4587

To order additional books, go to CSAbooks.com

Library of Congress Control Number: 2013942445
ISBN: 978-09853728-9-7

Dedication

This book is dedicated to my sisters,
whose shoulders I stood on for they are my heroines:

Sadye Geraldyne Casey, Lorinda Opalee Casey,
Floretta Joann Casey Graham

and in memory of my oldest sister
Permelia Evon Casey, 1938-2000

and my baby sister
Irma Melvynie Casey, 1949-2013

Prologue

My great-great grandmother Martha and her daughter Amanda were both slaves of William Holland Thomas. On Amanda's death certificate, William Thomas is listed as her father. The Casey family's oral tradition relates that Thomas bought Amanda's mother, Martha, from an auction block in Virginia in the early 1820s. At the time of her enslavement, Martha was about eight years old and fresh off of a slave ship from Africa. She was brought to the mountains of Western North Carolina by Thomas to his new home at Stekoa Fields. Thomas had acquired that land from Abraham Enloe and his brother for unpaid debt. Amanda was born at Stekoa Fields near present-day Whittier. On US 74 at US east Whittier a highway historical marker reads.

> William H. Thomas
> White chief and agent of N. C. Cherokee
> Secured reservation for them. Confederate
> Colonel. State Senator. Home "Stekoa
> Fields" stood ¼ mi. S.

Thomas was born at the Forks of Pigeon near the present day Bethel in Haywood County. His father, Richard Thomas (from Virginia), drown shortly before Thomas' birth. His mother, Temperance, raised and educated him. When he was sixteen, he was hired as a clerk in Felix Walker. Jr.' store at Quallatown on Shoal Creek. Eventually, Thomas became owner of that store and three more. One of these stores was in the Scotts Creek area. He became friends with the Qualla Cherokees and was adopted by the principal chief Yonaguska (Running Bear) and succeeded him as chief when he died. Among the property he inherited from Yonaguska was a slave name Cudjo, who was considered a brother to Yonaguska instead of a slave.

When the Great Removal of 1838 (the Trail of Tears) occurred, Thomas fought the powers that be (including Washington, DC) to allow the Qualla Cherokees to remain in their homeland in Western North Carolina. Therefore, Thomas's personal life was on hold as he traveled to Washington to defend the Qualla Cherokees. In 1848, he was elected State Senator on the Democratic ticket and remained there until 1862. During that time he married and built a home for his mother, who lived to be 99 years old. In the 1860 Census of Jackson County, a T. Thomas is listed. She lived in the Qualla area and was the same age as Thomas' mother. Therefore, I concluded that T. Thomas was Thomas's mother, since she was not listed in his household.

My great-grandfather, William Hudson Casey was born a free man to Harriet Casey of Waynesville. Harriet and her children are listed as mulattos in the 1859 Census. However, Harriet and her children are not listed in 1860 Census. And yet in household of James R. Love there were several young black and mulatto men listed as slaves. It is a known fact that George and James Casey, William's brothers, were conscripted to Love for ninety-nine years. Therefore this writer surmised that William and his other brothers were among the young black slaves listed in the Love household.

Love and Thomas had many business deals and were partners in a commodity store in the Scotts Creek area of Jackson County. Not only did the two slave owners conduct business between themselves, but Thomas married Love's oldest daughter, Sara J. B. Love. Naturally, Amanda and William probably met through these two slaveholders. Therefore this book, "Under the Light of Darkness," is a historic fictional account of my great-grandparents' romance. It is an attempt to share with the reader that a slave's life was never his/her own...for a slave worked from sunrise to sunset. Only after dark was a slave's life his/her own. Hence, this book relates the events of the slaveholder with the slave's life being the main objective.

Slave Marriage Ceremony Supplement

Dark an' stormy may come de wedder,
I jines dis he-male an' dis she-male togedder
Let none, but Him dat makes the thunder
Put dis he-male an' she-male asunder.
I dar fore'nounce you bofe de same.
Be good, go 'long, an' keep up yo name.
De broomstick's jump'd, de world's not wide
She's now yo' own. Salute the bride!

-Thomas W. Talley

Chapter 1

On this June morning, in 1857, in the shadow of the Great Smoky Mountains on the backside of Tennessee, the gentle summer breeze caressed the face of the slave girl, Amanda. She stood watching a wedding party preparing to leave Stekoa Fields. Wild flowers swayed in the wind, as the sun coming up over the horizon greeted the day with the assurance it was going to be a hot one.

Amanda looked up to the heavens, and then turned her attention to Miz Temperance Calvart Thomas. The aged mother of the groom was being helped by Sam, the trusted slave, as she got into the elegant carriage the bridegroom had built at his wagon shop in Quallatown. Amanda knew the carriage was something special. She gazed at the painted red trims on the wheels of the carriage and the boxed-like compartment of the body with its brown door fasteners flashing gold in the sun.

The bridegroom, Senator William Holland Thomas, was mounted on his horse. Amanda looked at his black cut-a-way coat and bleached white dress shirt, ruffles running down the front. Peeking out of the sleeves of his coat were white shirt ruffles, and on his feet, he wore shiny black boots which were folded just beneath the knees, revealing the golden lining. The look on Master Thomas' face was the same as the horse's mood, as the steed anxiously pranced in a circle.

It was a disquieting moment as Amanda, who was in

her fifteenth year, wished she could join them. Her friend, Cudge, the ten-year-old son of Sam was accompanying the party as Master Thomas' personal servant. Looking at him, she saw he was dressed in fancy clothes also. He wore black knickers with a black jacket. She wanted to call to him as he stood by the carriage like a little toy soldier, but she didn't want to put a curse on this solemn event. It was a moment she knew would never be hers.

Spying into the large carriage, she could see Master Thomas's two adopted children, Miz Angelina with her husband, and Mister Andrew, who were among the wedding party. Looking around she found most of the other slaves had stopped their work to wish Master Thomas farewell and good luck on his upcoming marriage. That afternoon Master William Holland Thomas was going to marry Sallie Love, the daughter of one of Master Thomas' business partners. The fifty-two-year-old slave owner was about to settle down after being a bachelor for all these many years. He was the State Senator from Western North Carolina and had been instrumental in allowing the Oconaluftee Cherokees to remain in their ancestral home in these mountains. With pleading from his aging mother, Maser Thomas finally was acquiring a true mistress for his home. All around him were primarily slave women and Cherokee women. Amanda had overheard his mother, Miz Temperance, say, "Being a state senator and lawyer, you need someone who can help you further your political career."

Amanda put her hands over her mouth and sniggered as the other slaves waited silently for the wedding party to depart. She was just a field hand who desperately wanted to be a house servant as her mother had been. Now ulcers were consuming her mother's legs and she was relegated to take care of the little children while their parents slaved in the cornfield. To Amanda, the hard work of being a slave was shortening her mother's life. For many years, Master Thomas had depended on her mother to assist Miz Temperance with the household chores, and also labor in the field.

This demanding drudgery for Martha—the woman whom Master Thomas had bought at a slave auction in Richmond, Virginia at ten-years-old—had taken years off her life. Amanda had seen this happen too many times to older slaves whom Master Thomas owned and she knew her fate would be the same. In a few years she surmised that all the hard laborious sweat of her brow in the field would be too much for her physical body.

Closing her mind to that prospect, she turned her attention back to the wedding party, which slowly rolled out of the driveway to traverse over the rugged mountain terrain to Waynesville. Under Sam's direction the other slaves began cheering and shouting. Cowbells clanged as the children squealed with laughter running alongside the carriage. The men waved their worn straw hats in the air, while the women beamed with pride. For Amanda, time seemed to stand still, although the squealing kids continued to chase the carriage until the party disappeared down the dusty road.

Now Sam took charge. "'Alright," he demanded, "Let's git back to work. Youse knows dat Maser Thomas 'pects us to work whiles he's gone."

Amanda watched as the other slaves slowly meandered back to the fields. After ordering the slaves back to work, Sam ambled off down the road. Likewise, Amanda turned and headed toward the kitchen, which was about fifty yards from the main home. Suckey was now the boss of that domain. When her mother was the cook, Amanda always found the kitchen to be her haven. However, when she entered, she realized she'd made a huge mistake.

"Youse still here?"

"Yeah."

"Maser Thomas didn't take youse with'em!"

"Why sho'ld he?" Amanda demanded.

"I jest fig're he let youse."

"Wat do youse mean?"

Suckey just laughed.

Angrily Amanda left the kitchen and headed for the

slave cabin she shared with her mother. She looked back at the modest five-room log cabin that all the slaves called the big house. Amanda thought Master Thomas should have put an addition on the place, but there was no hint of any changes. The house was situated on a ridge overlooking the Tuckaseegee Valley. Behind the house, a cold cellar was cut into the hillside. Water was piped into the house through hollowed-out logs from a nearby creek. From the rumors that had circulated, the five-room house was very modest compared to Miz Sallie's home at White Sulfur Springs. Amanda wondered how the young Miz Sallie would adapt to Stekoa Fields.

As she went toward the slave quarters, she thought of her mother and Master Thomas. One night not too long ago, she heard the flimsy old door of their slave cabin creak open. Lying on her pallet in the far corner of the room, she had seen a shadowy figure step slowly through the doorway. To her surprise, it was Master Thomas. She watched as he quietly tiptoed to the bed where her mother slept. Gently, he shook her on her right shoulder and quickly Martha sat up prepared to fight.

She gasped. "Wat are youse doin' here. Amanda is. ..."

"I know," Master Thomas assured her. "I just came to tell you that I'm getting married.'

"Dat's good."

"You're not angry."

"Why should I?" Martha responded. "After all youse need a good mistress to tend to yo' household while youse is gone."

"You could do that."

"Wil-Usdi, youse need heirs to Stekoa Fields." She put her hands over Master Thomas's mouth and continued. "It's impor'ant that youse have your own kind. Yer mother a' been tellin' youse dat fer years."

"I know," Maser Thomas kissed Martha's hand. "Just couldn't find the right girl."

"Youse is jest too busy he' pin others orphans. Miser Andy is grown now. Dat orphan Miz Angelina done got marri'd."

Maser Thomas sighed, "I know. I just know how it is to be an orphan. My father died before I was born."

"Wat bout William?"

"You mean Kanaka's child?"

"Yeah."

"He's taken care of".

"Good. Now who be her, Wil-Usdi?" Martha laughed. "I knows who she be. She's dat daughter of Miser James Love of Ways'ville. He's one who's got all den niggers boys a trainin' to be soldiers."

Master Thomas laughed. "How do you know all of this? "

"Jest do."

"If you know that, then you know he believes that the North is trying to change our way of life."

Martha didn't say any more. Amanda felt her mother had more to say, but she didn't want to share her thoughts with Maser Thomas. Turning to the wall, Amanda tried to go sleep, but couldn't. She tried to listen as Thomas' voice dropped to an inaudible mumble.

Now, Amanda found herself at her mother's cabin. Before she entered, she looked up at the sky. Just over head, the sun seemed to stare down at her, trying to drive all her energy away. Therefore, she knew it was noonday and her work was not finished for the day. Amanda knew Sam would come looking for her if she was not in the fields. Hence, she declared that this was a holiday. She went into the cabin and found her mother sitting on the side of the bed. This was the only cabin with a real bed. Most of the other cabins just had pallets to sleep on. Amanda looked around the one-room cabin and marveled at the neatness of it. The floor was packed red clay, but it had been swept clean. The open hearth was burning coal embers, for slaves never extinguished their fire.

Martha looked up when Amanda came in.

"Has dey gone?"

"Who?"

"Maser Thomas an' his weddin' party."

"Yes."

"Why ain't youse workin'? "

"I s vacationin'.."

"Dere's a lot to be done girl." A gleam seemed to sparkle in her eyes. "I 'member when me an' Maser Thomas work'd side by side in de fields. Even his mother help'd."

"I ain't no work hoss."

"Youse is a slave."

"Sam don't act likk a slave?"

"Now girl, he dinks he be diff 'rent." Martha sadly shook her head. "Dat fool Injurn Yonaguska learn'd him some foolish dings."

"Likk wat?" Amanda demanded, "Maser Thomas be a law'er and got'em Luftys to stay here. How comes he ain't givin' us our freedom?"

Instead of answering Amanda, Martha countered. "Wat' s youse worri'd bout? Youse dink dat de new mistress is gonna change dings?"

"She could."

"Jest do yer work. Go!"

Martha and Amanda stared at each other.

"Girl," Martha finally said. "Youse need a man. Miz Temperance finally got Maser Thomas to marry. She's gonna have grandchillen.

"I ain't a wantin' my chillen to grow up as slaves to serve Miz Temperance's grandchillen." With these hoarse words, Amanda ran out of the cabin. She didn't want to hurt her mother, but she had no desire to remain a slave all her life. Yet, she knew there was nothing she could do about it. She could run away, but where would she go.

As she ran out of the cabin and started toward the fields, she ran into Mister Charles Bumgarner, a neighbor of

Master Thomas. He caught her by the shoulder and swung her her around until they were face-to-face. Although she knew it was forbidden to look a white man in the eye, she stared defiantly at him.

"Nigger, what are you doing? This is no time to idle. Where's your master?"

Amanda didn't answer, but turned her face away from him. She didn't like him. She felt he treated his slaves badly. There was no gentleness in him. However, she surmised Master Thomas would not allow him to take advantage of his chattel property. And yet, she also knew she was at the mercy of Mister Bumgarner.

"Where, nigger?"

Mister Bumgarner pushed Amanda and she went sprawling on the ground.

She kept her eyes on the hard ground and mumbled, "He's a went to White Sulphur Springs to git marri'd."

Mr. Bumgarner laughed heartily. "That 'right, Mama's boy is finally getting' married."

"Yes sum." Amanda scrambled to her feet and slowly started backing away from him.

"Seem to me...." Mister Bumgarner spat tobacco juice toward Amanda, "That he would've married one of you niggers or a Cherokee squaw. That boy thinks he's a Cherokee anyways. He's always taking up for'em."

"Yes sum," Amanda agreed.

Wiping the tobacco juice from his bearded chin, he shook his head. "I guess being a senator; you gotta have a wife that is socially 'ceptable. Not a nigger likes your mammy or a squaw like Kanaka."

"Yes sum."

Amanda knew her gallivanting was over. Swiftly she turned and ran toward the cornfield. As she neared the cornfield, she glanced back to see him go into her mother's cabin. Instinctively, she started to go back, but Sam's voice stopped her.

"Girl, youse best git to work."

"Yes sum."

As she ambled on down to the cornfield, Sam also caught her by the shoulder and spun her around.

"Girl, where's yer hoe?"

"I forgot it with all de 'citement."

"Well," he pushed her toward the barn. "Go git it an' hurry."

Without answering him, Amanda sprinted to the barn. She glanced at her cabin. However, neither Miser Bumgarner nor her mother was visible. Desperately, she wanted to check on her mother, but she knew she better fetch the hoe and get back to the cornfield before Sam came after her. She had never been whipped, but she did not know what Sam would do if she disobeyed him. Therefore, she hurried on to the barn, picked up a hoe, and scampered back to the cornfield.

When the sun disappeared behind the mountain and darkness slowly crept on the horizon, the field hands wiped their brow, shouldered their hoes and headed for their cabins. Amanda walked among them. Tiredness engulfed her body and perspiration wet her clothing. Row after row, she had cultivated the garden. There seemed be no end for tomorrow would be the same. She thanked the sun for going to sleep and allowing darkness to invade her world. Hunger gnawed at her stomach and she hoped her mother had cooked something. She wanted anything to fill the emptiness inside. The days were gone when she could go to the kitchen and eat.

Leaning the hoe against the cabin, she dragged her-heavy feet inside. Her mother was bent over the open hearth, stirring something in the old cooking pot. Amanda smelt the familiar supper of wild greens and dough bread. However a different scent pervaded the air, like cooked meat.

"Wat's cookin'?"

Her mother turned and faced her. "Rabbit."

"Where's git it?"

"Miser Bumgarner."

"Oh, I see."

"He says it was too littl' fur him."

Amanda said nothing more. She dropped in the chair by the rickety table and waited for her mother to serve her.

Her mother looked over at her and saw the tiredness that captured her daughter's body. Sadly, she shook her head. And yet, Martha knew that Amanda needed to know the real plight of being a slave. Maser Thomas had been too good to her. It was time she should know her days of flitting around were over.

Sighing, she said hoarsely, "Girl, I ain't gonna serve youse. I ain't yer slave."

The two looked at each other. Martha had a stern look on her face. Her eyes seemed to pierce through Amanda. On the other hand, Amanda was shocked. Her eyes seemed to come out of their socket.

"Don't just sit dere." Martha demanded, "Git yer food."

Amanda lowered her head and quietly got up and served herself. She went to the table and sat down to eat the meal her mother had prepared for her. As she ate, there was an eerie silence in the room. Martha came to the table and sat opposite her daughter.

"Child, youse jest gotta know. Youse a nigger slave. Dat means that Maser Thomas owns us."

Between bites, Amanda replied, "I's know, Momma."

"Does youse really know?"

"Yes'um."

"It's jest me an' youse, child."

"I know."

"Youse ain't got no daddy."

"He be gone."

"Look, child, Maser Thomas be yer daddy."

"What?"

"Child, youse has to know. With Miz Sallie comin' to live here, youse needs to know. Maser Thomas says she be a nice kind gen'le lady, but she's gonna be the Mistress of dis place. An' I's sure dat some folks 'round here are gonna tell her that youse Maser Thomas' child. Some white mistresses don't like to look at one of their husband's niggers, knowin' dat he be de daddy."

"He'd sell me."

"Maser Thomas is kind an' gentle. It's be most lik'ly dat he's gonna pair youse up with one'em boys from Georgy."

"Wat does youse mean?"

"Youse jest right fer marryin'."

"Marryin'?"

"Yeh, child."

"Marryin'...I ain't marryin'."

"Youse will ifen Maser Thomas say so."

"Why's ain't youse neber marri'd."

Her mother didn't respond. A silence filled the room as Amanda finished her supper. She got up and went outside. She needed some fresh air to think about the situation. Slowly, she walked down toward the Tuckaseegee River. As she walked, she hummed a song. She now knew with the coming of a new white Mistress to the house, things would change. Now, she understood Suckey's sarcastic remarks. The night air was cool and refreshing. Amanda did not know someone was following her. When she got to the bank of the river, she sat down and put her feet in the slow moving water.

"Water's cold?"

A male voice reached her ears. Slowly, she turned around. She knew it was not Mister Bumgarner. As she looked up, she saw a black face come out of the darkness. The smiling face told Amanda it was one of the slaves Master Thomas had bought from Georgia. Rumor had it that Master Thomas had bought a whole family.

"Who are youse?" Amanda asked.

"Dave," he smiled. "I ain't been here long, but I's herd 'bout youse."

"Youse with dat family from Georgia dat Maser

Thomas bought."

"Dat, I be one of'em."

Amanda laughed. "So youse the one dat been a givin' Miz Temperance a heap of trouble."

Dave sat down beside Amanda on the bank. "So wat ifen I am."

Amanda threw up her hands. "Hey, youse don't hafto quarrel with me."

"Jest like t'day, Sam a tryin' to tell me wat to do. He's a nigger hisself." Dave picked up a rock and skipped it across the water. "'Fore our Maser died in Pauldin' County, Georgia, he promis'd that we be free. Master Thomas done gone an' bought us. It ain't fair."

"Guess not." Amanda agreed. "I guess not."

She thought about things her mother had said. Looking at Dave, who was about in his sixteenth summer, she knew she didn't want to marry him. She'd heard he was always upset about something. She knew they were slaves and Miz Temperance had told her that the Bible had said blacks were born to be the servants of the white man. It was quite apparent that Dave did not understand. Well, she longed for freedom, too, but she felt she had to try to be satisfied for her mother's sake. All the rumors had said the North were going to free them. It had something to do with a man named Lincoln. He had to be her savior, but she was not relaying the message to Dave.

"Girl, youse can be free yerself."

"How's?"

" Ain't Maser Thomas yer daddy?"

"How does youse know?"

"Everybody 'round here knows dat."

Amanda sighed, "I 'pect so."

"Youse hears 'bout Harriet Tubman."

"Who be dat?"

"She be freein' slaves."

"Where?'

"In a state call'd Merr' Land."

At that instance, Sam came upon them. Amanda knew there would a confrontation between Sam and Dave. She wanted no part of it. Desperately, she wanted to stay in the good graces of Maser Thomas. Being with Dave would not help matters. Both Amanda and Dave stood up when Sam called to them. Amanda saw the defiant look on Dave's face. She touched his arm, but he pulled away.

"Wat are youse two a doin'?"

"Jest talkin'." Amanda answered quickly.

"Dave," Sam smiled, "Maser Thomas sent Miser Andrew back and he wants to see youse."

"Wat?"

Terrified, Amanda covered her mouth. She knew that Miser Andrew was going to whip Dave for not working. For Maser Thomas, Amanda felt that it was never a major problem, but she knew Mister Andrew had to show his authority to keep everyone in line until Maser Thomas returned. She turned away from Dave and looked angrily at Sam. Now she wondered if Sam had reported her delinquency to Miser Andrew. However, Amanda felt that Suckey had reported Dave to Mister Andrew and Sam was just the messenger.

She watched as Dave and Sam left. Shaking her head, she thought about what Dave had said. Sam had interrupted their conversation. Now she didn't know what he thought about Maser Thomas being her father. To her, she had never received any special favors from him. However, it might bother Dearest Sallie that her husband sowed his wild oats with a nigger. Not only that, he had had a child by that nigger and the mother and child were still was on his farm. And yet, she wondered if Dave was lying about that woman, Harriet. She surmised if the story was true, Harriet had already been captured and whipped. Amanda wanted to be a servant in the big house. Listening to the conversation at the dinner table was valuable to her, as the Maser Thomas talked to Miz Temperance as if she wasn't there.

She walked back to her cabin wondering how old she was. Her mother had told her that she was a woman when her menstrual period began and that was about five summers ago. As the blood had run down her legs. Amanda had ran to her mother believing she was dying. Her mother was calm and assured her that it was natural...that it was the cycle of life. This bleeding would come every month and last for a few days. From the ragbag, Martha had showed her how to fix a rag and attach it to her underpants.

When she stepped through the door of her cabin, she smiled. Her mother was in the bed sleeping. She went over and kissed her. Sleep was now the only thing Amanda desired. Without undressing, she slowly went to her pallet and flopped down upon it. As soon as she closed her eyes, she was unconscious.

Chapter 2

A t dawn the bell rang and all the slaves knew it was time to drag themselves off their pallets, splash a little water on their faces and head for the field. Work had to be done. Stekoa Fields was welcoming a true Mistress of the house. That meant everything had to be in readiness when the newlyweds arrived. There would no honeymoon. They were expected at noon. Mr. Andrew and the other wedding party had gotten back just as the sun hid itself. Miz Temperance who was eight-two years old would be arriving with Maser Thomas and his new bride. Deep down inside, Amanda wished that Master Thomas would have sent Miz Temperance instead of Andrew...previously he had, for he knew she could handle the situation. As Amanda crossed the front yard, she saw Andrew, with Dave in tow, giving orders to Sam. She wanted to listen, but she knew that was impossible, just as breakfast was impossible.

With the heat of the day, Amanda realized summer was upon them. It was July 1, 1857 and a new beginning at Stekoa Fields. A permanent mistress was coming and Amanda wondered if the pattern of plight would change. Nervously, she worried about her status. She had never met Miz Sallie, but Cudge could tell her. He had gone to White Sulphur Springs to the wedding. He could tell her all about it. None the less, skipping toward the barn, Amanda hummed a lively tune.

Grabbing a hoe from the barn, she went on to the corn field. Most of the other field hands were already at work. Hoes were digging into the ground as a mournful song rang in the still hot air of the morning. Amanda stopped and listened. Looking across the field, she was amazed as Thomas's slaves worked together. Everyone's hoe seemed to rise and fall at the same time. Not only that, but the song was in rhythm with their work. Under the straw hats to prevent the sun from burning their heads, Amanda could not recognize her fellow chattel property.

"Are you gonna stand der all day?"

Amanda turned around and looked into the eyes of Sam.

"Sorry." Amanda started to explain, but decided to dash to the corn field.

She had never been whipped, but this was a new day. And with the new Mistress coming, it was best to do your work. After joining the others, she sang that mournful song and hoed in rhythm with them. As she worked, she thought of Miz Sallie. She knew she was much younger than Maser Thomas. With all this on her mind, she found this backbreaking work went by quickly. Just as the sun reached its apex in the sky, the horn sounded. It was time for a noon repast. The hoes were put down and the unleavened bread was brought to edge of the field by the small children who carried the repast in baskets.The flavor of the day was spring water, which was in a long trough at edge of the field. Each slave had their own cup. Like all the slaves, Amanda rushed for the basket of bread. She took one piece of bread and hurried to the trough to dip her cup into the lukewarm water.

Sitting down on the ground, she ate the bread and chased the dryness of her mouth by gulping down the water. All of the other slaves did the same. There was no time to waste. The noonday repast seemed to be over before it began. Within fifteen minutes the slaves were back to work.

Now in the heat of the day, the slaves struggled. Their productivity slacked off and the sound of music was no longer heard. The afternoon stretched into an eternity. Amanda tried to think of a happy time, so the drudgery would come to a close. Ironically, the horn sounded around five.

Darkness was still about four hours away. Everyone looked toward the house, but no one moved. Sam took off his hat and wiped the perspiration from his forehead with a handkerchief he pulled from around his neck. He glared at the sun. It glared back.

"Sam," Amanda asked, "Wat's goin' on?"

Before Sam could answer, the horn echoed through the valley.

"I guess it's quittin' time." Sam put his hat back on his head. "I 'pect we's gonna meet the Mistress."

"Yeah," Amanda shouldered her hoe and walk toward the house.

The rest of the slaves followed Amanda. When they came close to the slave quarters, Amanda saw her mother standing in the door frame of her cabin. Mother and daughter looked at each other.

"Wat's be de trouble?" her mother asked.

"We're gonna meet the Mis'ress."

With the others, Amanda continued to the front of the house. Her mother gathered the children and headed there, too. When they had assembled in front of the humble five room home of Maser Thomas, they looked up at the dark hair young beauty. There was the new Mistress standing next to Maser Thomas. Amanda stared at her, as she tried to see if she had any compassion in her face. She saw a slight smile and Amanda took that as a good omen. Mistress and slave eyed each other for a moment. Quickly Amanda dropped her head and stared at the ground.

At that instance, Maser Thomas cleared his throat. Looking up at him, Amanda stared at him in a different light. She studied his face and tried to find any family resemblance between them. However, Master Thomas' voice brought her back to the present. This was not about her, but about the Mistress and the expectations of a slave's life. Would it change with the addition of a permanent Mistress in the house?

"Here at Stekoa Fields, we are a family," Master

Thomas declared. "Therefore I believe it is fitting that I introduce all of you to my bride, my wife."

Thomas paused and put his arm affectionately around Miz Sallie's waist. The newlyweds smiled lovingly at each other before Thomas turned his attention back to his slaves.

"This is Mrs. Sallie Thomas. When I'm away on business, she is the Mistress of the household. All decisions will be hers. She will be sure that your welfare is taken care of."

After hearing this statement, Amanda again stared at Miz Sallie and tried to get her feeling about slaves, especially one that was Master Thomas' child. If Master Thomas said anything else, she did not hear it. It was apparent that Miz Sallie said something to her family. Suddenly there were cheers, as they welcomed Miz Sallie to Stekoa Fields.

Amanda joined her fellow slaves in welcoming and accepting Miz Sallie. She looked over to where Miz Temperance was standing apart from the couple. The stolid expression on her face told Amanda nothing. Smiling, Amanda decided that time would tell. That was all right with Amanda, because she and Miz Temperance had a tolerable relationship. Besides, Amanda would get the inside take from Cudge. Now, it was time to go back to work.

The couple went back into the house, while the slaves returned to their task. Although they cheerfully welcomed Miz Sallie, they begrudgingly went back to the field. Whether there would be productive effort, it would be up to the individual slave. As they grabbed their hoes, they talked among themselves. When they got out of the earshot of the main house, the grumbling became louder.

"Dis is dumb." Dave declared.

"Don't start."

"It is. Stop work jest to be 'troduce to Miz Sallie. Don't even give us a cold drink."

Dave tossed the hoe against a huge stone and the old worn out handle broke and all eyes focused on him. Maser Thomas always tolerated Dave's unruliness, by saying that he was just a child. Without looking back, he headed for the hill. No one moved, as they waited for Sam.

"Alright, let's git back to work." Sam barked. "Maser Thomas wills take care of it."

Begrudgingly, they went back to the field to work until the sunset and darkness covered the horizon.

Amanda was not among them. Unlike Dave who stormed off, she slipped away. She needed to find Cudge and talk to him. Sometimes, she hated Cudge for the freedom he seemed to have. It appeared that some of the slaves at Stekoa Fields had more freedom, than others. She tried to comprehend the situation. Being Thomas' flesh, she could not see treating your own flesh as a piece of property. Tears came to Amanda's eyes as she headed for the barn to put away the hoe. Like Dave, she wanted to toss the hoe and deliberately destroy it. Instead, she sat it down on the hay covered floor and cried.

Cudge found her there. He went over to her and put his arm around her. "Wat de matter?"

"I hate youse." She pulled away from him. "Youse can go anywhere youse wants."

"An' places I ain't too happy with."

'Yeah! Youse jest sayin' dat."

"Nope. "

"Ok, tells me 'bout de weddin'."

"Dat place was huge. Miz Sallie's folks must be pow'r-ful rich. He had more slaves then Maser Thomas has. Youse can find someone ov'r der to jump the broom with."

"I ain't a marryin' nobody."

"Youse will ifen Maser Thomas says so."

"An' leave my mamma. Don't dink so."

"We's ain't got no choice with who we mate."

"Yeah," Amanda pondered the statement. "Youse know that youse git to go ev'rywher'."

"I's just his body servant."

"Did youse see them git marri'd."

"Yeah, I was peekin' thru de window. Couldn't hear much."

"Did she wear white?"

"Yep." Cudge sighed. "She was beautiful."

Fantasizing, Amanda swirled around the stables. "I's gonna be jumpin' de broom in a white dress just like Miz Sallie."

Cudge laughed, "Youse think so."

"It could happen." Amanda reminded Cudge, but she gave no detail on when it was supposed to occur.

Cudge started toward the door. "Gotta go 'fore Maser Thomas comes a lookin' fer me."

"Miz Sallie has his 'tention."

"Yeah, but he might wanna show Miz Sallie around the place. Don't want him angry at me."

Amanda laughed. "Alls youse wanna do is be with Miz Sallie's personal servant dat her daddy gave her as a wedding present. She be mighty light."

"How did youse know dat?"

"Jest do." Amanda stuck out her tongue. "An' her name is Caroline. She's too old fer youse."

Cudge did not response to Amanda. With the wave of his hand, he made his exit.

Now all alone, Amanda allowed her imagination to take over. Although, she was a slave and had informed her mother she did not want any children to be born as a slave, she was still a woman.Her needs were the same as any woman, but she didn't want to be violated as her mother had been. She wanted a man like Dave and his family. Maser Thomas bought the entire nuclear family and promised that they would remain a nuclear family until the children grew up and found a mate. It seemed that Thomas had compassion for his slaves. He may view them as property; but did he also view them as human beings. And yet, Amanda wondered if he thought of her that way.

The sun was slowly disappearing for the day but daylight lingered. That meant that the slaves were still working, while she dreamed. Dreaming was something a slave should never do. Her mother had told her not to weave a

dream too tightly or it would all fall apart. And yet she continued to dream. She imaged herself in a long white flowing
dress with a bouquet of flowers in her hand. A preacher and
her groom waiting for her at the front of a church. It was still
in the back of her mind as Miz Temperance had described
to her so long ago. However, she envisioned a broom as
she and her groom jumped over it to bond their marriage.
Just as she was jumping over the hoe on the barn floor,
Dave came in.

"Wat are youse doin?"

"Nothin'." Amanda assured him.

Dave laughed. "Why ain't youse out in field?"

"I's following your lead."

"Git yerself in trouble with Miz Sallie."

"Maybe."

"Youse think she gonna tolerate us defyin' her."

Amanda shook her head. She did not know the answer to Dave's question. "I don't know 'bout white folks. I's
look at Maser Thomas how he's helps the Indians 'round
here. They call him their chief. Jest don't know. My mamma
came straight fro' Africa. She has a little memory, but most
is lost 'cept some African folk tales her mother tol' her. She
thinks that Maser Thomas has treat'd her fair."

"Youse don't think so."

"Alls I's can say is dat she's still here. He could've
sold her or me."

"Youse dream too much, nigger." Dave shook his
head. "Don't never trust'em."

"I's reck'n youse rite." Amanda cleared her throat.
"Dave, wat a happen'd to youse."

Dave laughed and shook his head. "I's got a good
talkin' to from Maser Andrew. I tink dat he be 'fraid to whip
me 'cause Maser Thomas don't whup his slaves. I's valyou
prope'ty"

Before Amanda could respond, Dave turned and
walked out of the barn. Immediately, she started to follow
him, but she stopped and wondered whether his statement

was the truth. After all, his former master sold Dave and his family to Thomas. Was the white man worthy of their trust? Leaving the barn, she wondered what Dave's punishment had really been. She needed to talk to Dave, but he had disappeared. It couldn't have been with a whip or Dave wouldn't have been able to work. And yet, Amanda felt that Dave was heading for big trouble.

It seemed to Amanda that Master Thomas's marriage was ruining everything. Now she knew that she would be a field hand and never step foot into the main house again. Frustrated, she kicked at the hoe. Maybe jumping the broom would be the best and yet, she thought of the children she would have. They would not be hers, but the Master's. He could sell them without asking her. And yet, she had never observed Master Thomas selling a child from its mother. With Master Thomas gone most of the time, Miz Sallie would in charge and she would do whatever she wanted and justify it after Master Thomas returned. Talking to her mother would not solve anything. Her mother had already told her what she had to do. "Do as youse told" rang in her ear. However Dave's arrival hadn't helped. Now she felt that she could do what she wanted. Just as she stepped out of the barn, Sam came around the corner. She attempted to hide from him, but he saw her.

"Mandy, what do's youse tink youse doin'."

"I'se lookin' fer a hoe?"

"Wells, git it girl an' git back to work. It ain't quittin' time."

Amanda dropped her head and reentered the barn to retrieve a hoe. Sam followed her.

"Girl, has youse seen Dave?"

"No," Amanda lied.

"Look, chile , tat boy's gonna git youse in trouble." Sam patted Amanda on the shoulder and left. She watched him disappear through the open door of the barn. Slowly she picked up the hoe and walked out the door.

Chapter 3

Summer slowly gave way to autumn. Thomas was in Raleigh for the fall session of the General Assembly and Miz Sallie was now in charge. Stekoa Fields was buzzing with activities. The cornfields were waving in the wind with ripe watermelons and pumpkins hidden beneath the green stalks. Harvest time was fast approaching, as the vegetable garden yielded a good crop of beans, squash, cabbage, peppers, greens, and potatoes. All the slaves were busy getting ready for the winter months. No one was idle for there were many things that had to be done.

At Master Thomas' request, Miz Sallie had sent five of the young black bucks to the Love farm in Waynesville. After milking the cows, most of the female slaves were in the fields harvesting the crops. Others were in the kitchen churning milk into butter. This activity went on all year around, because Master Thomas always shipped a load of butter up North. After some of the crops were harvested, they had to furrow the field again to put down turnip seeds to plant winter greens. Amanda was promoted to the kitchen to help Suckey with the task of preserving food for the winter. Leather-britches and dried fruit were hung on strings from the kitchen porch ceiling.

When the cabbages were cut from their beds, Suckey and Amanda had the task of making kraut in crocks. After stringing the green beans, they pickled some of them and put them in jars. Under the guidance of Martha, the little children picked blackberries, huckleberries and elderberries. These berries would be canned as jam or jelly. For medicinal purposes, elderberry wine was brewed. From the apple trees, the early fallen apples were crushed and made into cider, while the apples picked from the tree were sliced and dried in the sun. The sorghum plants were gathered to make molasses.

Besides Stekoa Fields, there were Master Thomas's stores. There was one in Quallatown and another one on Shoal Creek where the road from Waynesville meet Soco Gap. Another store was on Scotts Creek where the road led from Waynesville to Franklin. There was were three more stores, but only Sam knew where they were located. The store on Scotts Creek was in partnership with William Welch and Thomas's father-in-law. The shelves of all these stores had to be stocked. Some of the produce they grew would end up in the two closest stores. The produce that went to Scotts Creek would be bought by the white community. These that were headed to Shoal Creek would be traded or bought by the Cherokees or the white folks in that community. Wagon loads of goods would be transported to the stores. The most important commodity was the butter of about 2,400 pounds, which Thomas annually shipped. Sam always handled the commodities that were taken to and from the stores. Miz Sallie continued to do as Thomas wished. Therefore, she had to trust Sam to do the job.

It was a cool Friday morning and the first tang of wood smoke curled from chimneys in the valley. A chill hung in the air as Amanda rose from her pallet and went over to awaken her mother. However, Martha, although in poor health, was already up. While the young and the able-bodied female slaves continued to work in the fields, Martha took care of their young children who were too young to work in the fields. Amanda marveled at her mother's resilience. After eating porridge left in the pot over the hearth, Amanda went outside to greet the day. With a corncob pipe in her mouth, Martha was seated in a straw bottom chair. A shawl covered her shoulders, as she watched the slave children run and play. She looked around when she heard Amanda come out of the cabin.

Amanda looked at the children playing and tears watered her eyes. Lovingly, she touched Martha on the shoulder. "Youse know. Dis 'minds me of wat youse told me 'bout yo' African village."

Martha sighed, "Dat was long 'go. I 'member de grandmaw watched us children while our folks went to work in de fields."

"Yeah," Amanda said, "but dey was workin fer demself. Der work was der labor. Our labor 'longs to Maser Thomas."

"Don't let Suckey send someone to look fer youse. I's seen youse hangin' with dat Dave boy."

"Yes'sum." Amanda answered. "We's just friends likk Cudge be."

"He's be trouble."

Yes'm." Amanda turned to leave. "I's gotta go."

Last night after overhearing Miz Sallie and Sam talking about going to the Shoal Creek store, she wanted to go. Slowly, she hesitated to go to work in the kitchen with Suckey. She hated going in there. This morning they were going to fix kraut in crocks. Somehow, Amanda had to be excused from that task without being missed. She could not involve her mother in her deception. She hugged her mother and then ran toward the big house. When she got to the front yard, she found Sam and Miz Sallie standing by the supply wagon filled with commodities for Thomas' store on Shoal Creek. Two oxen had been yoked to pull the heavy load. Neither Miz Sallie nor Sam paid any attention to Amanda as she stopped and hid behind an oak tree in the front yard. Eavesdropping, she listened to their conversation.

"Get these supplies to the store at Shoal Creek and tell Mr. James Terrell that Master Thomas needs to have the ginseng shipped to Dr. Isaac Heylin in Philadelphia."

" Yes sum."

"Here, give this to Mr. Terrell?"

Sam took the piece of paper from Miz Sallie and put it in his pocket.

"Be sure," Miz Sallie continued, "that the Indians continue to make those brooms this fall."

"Yes sum. Youse can trust me. Maser Thomas always did."

Miz Sallie sighed, "Okay, I just want everything to go well."

"It will, Miz Sallie, it will."

Miz Sallie turned and went back into the house. Sam watched her and shook his head. Amanda came out from behind the tree and confronted hiim. "Where youse go'n'?"

"Youse know. De annu'l trip to de stor'." Sam stared at her.

" Cans I come long?" She asked.

"Now Mandy, youse knows dat ain't possible. Youse been talkin' to Dave."

"Me an' Suckey finish' d de cannin' and ev' rythin."

"Youse need' d in de field".

"Dere's ' nough workers. Ain't nobody gonna miss me." Amanda pleaded. " I's neber been to one of Maser Thomas's stores. Jest likk to go jest once."

Sam started to tell Amanda that she couldn't go, but he remembered what Yonaguska had taught him. If she had finished her work, she had the right to go. After all, all men were brothers.

"Meet me at de end of de road."

"Okay."

Amanda went to the kitchen and stood just inside the door. Without saying a word, she watched Suckey stirring some cabbages in the pot over the hearth. Feeling her presence, Suckey turned and cocked her eyes at Amanda.

Turning away from Amanda, she went back to her task. "Girl, git to work."

"Suckey, I's a bleedin'."

"Shoo," Suckey shouted, "Out! Youse gonna runt my kraut!"

Before Suckey could say anything else, Amanda left and ran down the road to catch Sam. She caught up with the oxen drawn wagon before it left. Happiness bubbled from Amanda as she sprinted to meet Sam. She and the wagon got there at the same time. With Sam's help, she hopped on and they were on their way.

By noontime, they had arrived at Shoal Creek. Amanda was amazed. She never imagined the extent of Master Thomas' holdings. With all of this, she wondered why he needed slaves. There was more than just one store or shop located here. She punched Sam in the side.

"Does all dis long to Maser Thomas?"

"Yep."

"Wat do all dese shops do?"

"Make diff' rent dings." Sam pointed to one of the shops. "Dat dere is a tannery. He buys animal skins from the Cherokees and he has dem tann'd dere. He also has a tannery at the store in Scotts Creek."

"Wat fer?"

"Make shoes and such." He pointed to another shop. "Dey makes shoes dere an' sell'em."

"Store bought-shoes? Shucks, I's don't wear shoes 'til it be cold."

Sam laughed.

"Can I's go with youse when youse go to Scotts Creek?

"I's 'fraid not. Dat' s an overnight trip. I's haft to board at Miser Love s fer de night."

"Is dat Mis'ress Sallie's father?"

"Nope. Dis here is 'nother Maser Love, but I 'spect dey d be kin."

Looking around, Amanda saw the bustle of activity as the Cherokees and whites moved hurried through this commercial center. Sam guided the wagon to the store and parked around back. He got off the wagon and started to go into the back door, when he remembered Amanda was with him. Turning, he watched as she got off the wagon.

"Girl, youse can't go in de stor."

"I's be alright?"

"Jest stay close."

"Shore."

Amanda watched Sam go into the store. When he disappeared inside, she decided to explore the town. After all it belonged to Master Thomas and she was Maser Thomas's property. Walking through this commercial center, Amanda peeked in all the shops. She stopped at a wagon-making shop and watched the men at work. Before they spied her, she moved on to the next shop.

The ring of the hammer hitting metal on an anvil drew Amanda's attention. Quietly, she walked in and watched a lanky light skin boy shape a piece of metal into a horseshoe. Instantly she knew he was not a Native or white. Although his skin was peachy with the hint of sunburn on his arms, his facial features were those of a slave. Immediately, she knew that he was mulatto. With an air of confidence, she spoke to him.

"Youse belong to Miser Thomas," she said. "I ain't seen you 'round."

The boy stopped and looked at her. "I's been hir'd out. I 's kinda 'long to Miser James Love."

Amanda laughed.

"Wat's so funny?"

"He' s the one who's trainin' slaves to fight a war that ain't here. Maser Thomas marri'd his daughter. "

"It's comin'," the boy said emphatically. "My brothers are 'mong 'em and when it be ov'r, my brothers will be free agin."

"Wat's yer name?" Amanda changed the subject.

"I's William Hudson Casey."

"Dat's a mighty long name fer a slave."

"Yes, but it's mine." William replied angrily. "Wat's yer name?

"Amanda."

"Dat all?"

"Da's nough."

"I guess so." William went back to work.

Amanda stepped closer to William to watch him, but he pushed her away.

"Dis is dangerous. Youse could get hurt."

Obediently, Amanda stepped back and watched William shape the metal into a horse shoe. It fascinated her to see someone mold and shape something useful. It never occurred to her that a slave could master a trade. To her, this was special and she felt that William was intelligent. His milk-coffee skin and his short curly reddish-brown hair made him appealing to her. Not only that, his sweaty bronze upper body was beautiful. All at once, she forgot about not jumping the broom. With William, she wanted to get hitched.

Shortly afterward, Sam returned and found Amanda still at the blacksmith shop. When she hopped on the wagon, Sam sensed an air of happiness around her. Without saying anything to Amanda, Sam addressed the horses and they started on their way home.

"We gonna be late gittin' back."

"I's sorry ifen I made youse late."

"It's 'lright. I sometimes be late. Don't worry."

They rode along in silence as Amanda thought of William. As they approached Stekoa Field, they saw torches in the twilight. Mr. Bumgarner and two other men on horse-back rode out the shadows. They stopped them and stared at the two slaves in the wagon. Amanda felt their stare and she huddled close to Sam. With the sun already settled for the night, there was a chill on the September twilight air. Mr. Baumgartner's slave patrol's presence made the evening air just a little cooler. Both Sam and Amanda kept their eyes down and would not look at them. Not only was the night atmosphere getting cooler, it was also getting thicker as a cloud of mystery now surrounded them. Sitting there, Amanda knew the next move was Baumgartner's. Letting a spit of tobacco juice fly from his mouth that landed on the canvas that lay in the wagon, he made his move.

"What are you doin' out pass sundown?"

"Just got back from Maser Thomas's stor' at Shoal Creek."

"It 'ppears to me like you be running 'way."

"No sir."

Amanda wanted desperately to confirm Sam's story, but she knew that would only make things worse.

"Let me see yer pass," Mr. Bumgarner demanded.

Again Amanda's heart sank. She didn't have a pass. She had begged Sam to take her with him. Now trouble was about to erupt and she wanted to run away. She watched Sam take a piece of paper from his pocket and hand to Mr. Bumgartner. He put the paper up to the torch. Amanda almost cried out. She thought he was going to burn it, but instead he read it. A new fear gripped her, as she glanced up at the other two men. From the torches that they held, she could see the lust in their eyes. Suddenly she began to pray silently. Mr. Bumgarner handed the paper back to Sam.

"So you're Senator Thomas's niggers?"

"Yes sir."

"I don't see this nigger gal's pass."

Quickly Sam made up a story. "She was out picking berries and got lost. I's takin' her home."

"Where's her berries."

"She lost'em back dere a ways."

"I see."

Mr. Bumgarner looked at the other two men. He spat another stream of tobacco juice. "You boys go on and continue yer patrol. I's gonna personally see that Senator Thomas's niggers git home."

The two men left and rode toward Shoal Creek. Mr. Bumgarner gave Sam the orders to continue, which he did. Although they were going home, Amanda wouldn't feel safe until she was once more in her quarters with her mother. When they approached the main house, there was a light in the parlor. The rest of the place was quiet except for the night sounds of the whippoorwills singing a requiem to summer. Sam pulled the wagon to a stop just in front of the main house. Mr. Bumgarner rode his horse beside the wagon and dismounted. After tying his horse to the tethering pole, he walked up to the front and knocked. The trail of oil lamp told Amanda that Miz Sallie or Miz Temperance had left the parlor and made her way to the front door.

"Who is it?" Miz Sallie shouted through the closed door.

"It's me, Charles Bumgarner. I have two of yer niggers. It appears dat they were runnin' away."

Instantly, Miz Sallie opened the door and shined the light in Mr. Bumgarner's face. Behind Miz Sallie was the small dark shadow of Miz Temperance. This made Amanda feel a little better. Miz Temperance stepped out of the shadow as Miz Sallie spotlighted the two figures in the wagon parked in the yard,

"That's just Sam," Miz Temperance remarked.

"Yes," Miz Sallie replied. "I sent him to the store at Shoal Creek."

Amanda was hiding her face from Miz Sallie and Miz Temperance. She was still afraid for she didn't know what Miz Sallie was going to do. After all, she had left Stekoa Fields without permission.

"Who's with you, Sam?"

Miz Temperance knew immediately. "That you, Amanda?"

"Yes ma'am."

A deep frown crossed Miz Sallie's forehead. Amanda huddled even closer to Sam. Immediately Mr. Bumgarner picked up on Dearest Sallie's anger. He looked from Amanda to Sallie.

"So dis little gal left without your permission. Give her to me. I can straighten her out."

"No," Miz Temperance stepped forward. "I gave her permission. She turned and looked at Sallie. "Sallie dearest, I'm sorry I didn't tell you."

"No harm done." Miz Sallie looked over at Mr. Bumgarner. "We can handle this."

"Claimed that she was picking berries and got lost."

"Thanks," Miz Temperance starred at Charles, "I'm sure when Senator Thomas come home and hears about it, he will reward you."

"That gal will be reward 'nough."

"Good night, Mr. Bumgarner."

Mr. Bumgarner tipped his hat, turned, and walked off the porch. Untied his horse, he mounted, smiled at Amanda and rode away. Sam climbed down from the wagon and lent a hand to Amanda. Reluctantly, she climbed down and headed for her cabin. She didn't want to face either Miz Sallie or Miz Temperance. Walking away, she heard Miz Sallie call her name. Nervously, she stepped on the porch and faced both women.

"I's sorry," Amanda stared down at her feet and shuffled them.

"Don't let this happen again." Miz Temperance hissed.

However, Miz Sallie was angry and slapped her across the face. "When Senator Thomas is away, I am in charge. He can't help you if you're already sold down the river when he gets back."

Amanda stared at her in disbelief. Stekoa Fields had always been family. Now Miz Sallie was going to break it up. Tears silently cascaded down Amanda's face. She and her mistress stared at each other through the light from the oil lamp. Miz Temperance turned and walked in the house.

"Do you understand?"

"Yes ma'am."

"Alright," Dearest Sallie challenged. "Now get to bed and get to work in fields in the morning."

"Yes ma'am."

Swiftly Miz Sallie turned away and went into the house. Amanda stood there as the door was slammed in her face. When she turned around to go to her quarters, Sam was already gone. Sadly she went to her quarters. As she stepped through the door, Martha quickly turned from the hearth where she was seated. She ran to Amanda and hugged her.

"Mandy, my baby! Where have youse been?"

"I's sorry I gave youse a scare."

"Sorry! Amanda, youse can't go traipin' off some-where. Youse is a slave. And youse could have got Sam in big troubl'."

"Youse knows where I be?"

"Yes, Sam tol' me."

"Sorry."

"Go to bed girl. An' make shore dat youse git in de fields early. Youse lettin' Dave turn youse into a bad slave."

"No!" Amanda shouted. "Dave has nothin' to do with tis. I jest want'd to see de store."

As Amanda headed for her pallet in the corner of the small one-room cabin, she suddenly remembered some-thing pleasant about the day. Before going to bed, she had to share it with her mother. She caught her mother and danced her around the room. Martha tried to get her to stop, but Amanda continued. Drunk from twirling about the cabin, they ended up exhausted on Martha's bed. Lying there among the covers, Amanda laughed heartily. Martha untan-gled herself from her daughter and the covers. She made an attempt to sit up, but she couldn't.

Breathing hard, she said. "Nigger is youse crazy?"

"Jest happy, Mama. Jest met de man I's gonna jump de broom with."

"I's thought youse didn't want no slave chillen." Martha laughed. "So de love bug got ya 'goin."

Amanda remembered the incident at one of the corn shucking. "I's don't wanna talk 'bout it."

"I ain't." mother replied. "Is another one of those Lufty Indians?"

"No. An' he ain't no slave."

"It's not Sam?"

"He be from Dearest Sallie's father place."

"Gal, youse ain't gonna see him 'gain."

"Might." She snuggly declared.

"Nigger go to bed. Youse hafto be up early. Dey's cutting de brushes 'round de farm."

Amanda sighed heavily and went to her pallet in the corner. Sleep took over and in her sleep, she dreamed of William Hudson Casey, a free man. Some day she was going to marry him.

Chapter 4

The next morning Stekoa Fields was all a buzz about Amanda's behavior. She knew all the gossip would be about her trying to run away and Sam had caught her. Most of the slaves were already up and about. Martha woke up early and found Amanda asleep on her pallet. She was glad she was back. Rumor was that she had left. Suckey had sent Caroline, Miz Sallie personal servant, to ask about her. Martha just said she had gone to the kitchen.

When Martha returned to her quarter, Amanda was still asleep. She knew she had to wake her up before the horn sounded for the field hands to go work. With Amanda's disappearance from the place yesterday, she had to work in the field. Looking down at her sleeping form, she just sadly shook her head. Before Martha could shake her awake, Amanda opened her eyes and her mouth.

"Mama, I met the most handsome guy. He was at Shoal Creek. He says dat he was from Miz Sallie's father, but he ain't no slave."

"Amanda, you tol' me all dis last night."

"I know." Amanda dressed and prepared to go to work in the field.

"Amanda, tat was a seri'us thang youse did."

"I knows. Miz Sallie wasn't happy."

"Wat did she do?"

Just as Amanda began telling her mother about Miz Sallie's reaction, the horn sounded. It was time to go. Amanda grabbed her straw hat and jammed it on her head without putting a head rag to cover her hair. Like a bolt of lightning, she was out the door. The day was going to be a long one. Everyone would be looking at her and whispering about her behavior.

The first person she saw was Sam. She didn't stop, but continued toward the barn. Just as she entered the barn, Sam was right behind her. He grabbed her shoulders and turned her around to face him.

"Youse'll be workin' in the field clearin' de land."

"I knows tat."

"Don't trys to run way."

"Where would I go?" Amanda laughed, "Dis is the only place I know. Wat about you, Sam?"

"Wat do youse mean?"

"Jest as I was a sayin."

"I's been all over dis county. Been in Cherokee land."

"I jest went with youse to Shoal Creek. I don't knows why youse tank I would run way."

"I saw how youse were lookin' at that free nigger."

"He ain't free an' he's ain't no slave like me. Jest borr'w to a white man."

"Youse did like him?"

Amanda didn't answer, but only smiled at him.

They got the tools they needed and left. Sam had to round up the other slaves to work in this unused field to make it ready for next year. Amanda hated clearing land, but today she didn't mind. Working hard would keep the other slaves from talking to her. Most were men. Amanda realized that by the time the work day was over, she would have cuts and bruises from throngs and bushes. Now she wished that she had tied her hair up in a head rag.

Around noon, they stopped for a repast. Amanda headed for water. Instead of drinking the water, she took off her straw hat and poured it over her head. The cool water felt good as it cascaded off of her hair. She knew she would have to wash the tangle mess when the day was over. As a matter of fact, she decided that a dip in the river was in order. Leaning against a tree, she saw Dave. Sweat poured down his shirt and dripped off his chin. With a dark rag from his pocket, he wiped the sweat from his face. He looked up and saw Amanda. Slowly, he walked over to her.

"Wat youse thinkin', yesterday?"

"I guess I wasn't?"

"Youse like it here?"

"It could be worse."

Amanda walked away from him. He followed her.

"Wat you mean?"

"At least youse have your family with youse."

"So's do you."

"Yeah, dat's wat Maser Thomas say."

"Ok," Sam shouted, "Let's git back to work."

Moans and groans came from the group, but they all went back to work. Amanda stayed away from Sam's view and slacked off. The work was backbreaking, but she was not going to complain. She told herself that she could handle it. However, her back ached and her arms were weary. It seemed she could no longer lift them to maneuver the sickle. Each step was slower and slower as she attempted to work. Doggedly, she was determined to finish the work for today. Now it seemed that she was motionless. She stared at the sky and everything seemed to go in circles. The ground greeted her, as the daylight became darkness.

When she finally awoke, she was on the pallet in her quarters. Her mother was wiping her face with a clean white cloth. Her clothing had been removed and she was in a night gown. A blanket covered her. Martha put the cloth down on the floor and picked up a cup. Putting the cup up to Amanda's lip, she raised her head and asked her to drink it. Amanda sipped slowly. Her mother would not allow her to guzzle it all at once.

"Slowly," Martha cautioned, "Just sip."

"I's hafto go back to the field."

"Child, youse jest got too much sun."

At that moment, Miz Temperance, walking with the aid of her fancy cane, came in the cabin. She stood in the doorway. Martha looked up at her. The two women stared at each other. They had walked this journey together. They had worked side by side in the heat of the day. Martha was just a little girl. There was bond between them, but there was culture diversity that kept them apart.

"I just heard, Martha," Miz Temperance came to Amanda's bedside. "I'm so sorry."

"It ain't yer fault'." Martha replied, "Young folks jest don't know der place."

"Let me take her with me." Miz Temperance thought about the separate cottage she sometimes stayed. "She could be my personal servant. She could..."

"It ain't up to me."

"I know. I have to talk this over with Miss Sallie."

"She'll be all right."

"I'll talk to Miss Sallie."

With those words, Miz Temperance turned and walked slowly out the cabin.

Martha went after her with the intention of stopping her, but then, hesitating, she convinced herself that that might be a bad idea. She did not want to split the Thomas household, nor did she want the other slaves to think that Temperance was the mistress of the household when the senator was gone. Putting her shaggy shawl around her shoulders, she headed for the main house. Miz Sallie had been the Mistress at Stekoa Field for three months and war was about to break out between Miz Temperance and Dearest Sallie. She had to put a stop to it. One unruly slave was enough. Before anyone knows it, everyone would be taking sides and a rebellion might erupt on Stekoa Fields.

Amanda spent a week in bed. Rumor had it that Miz Sallie was upset with the unruly slaves and that included Amanda. Miz Sallie brought a doctor in to check her. He reassured Miz Sallie that Amanda was well enough to go back to work. When he left, Amanda got out of bed. She gathered some soap, a towel and clothing,

"Where is youse headin'?" Martha asked.

"I's gonna take a dip in de water. Dat'll 'fresh me."

Martha did not argue with her, instead she went with her daughter. The two walked in silence, for they understood each other. Both were attempting to protect the other. Therefore, Martha told Amanda about the decision. As they walked she told Amanda.

" I's went to de big house to talk to Miz Temperance tat day, Jest as I was 'bout to knock on de door, I heard voices. So I's sit on de stoop and listen'd. I herd Miz Temperance say dat she need to clean up her place an' youse could he'p her."

"I's goin to Miz Temperance's house."

"Yep. Youse needs to git 'way fer a little while."

Amanda was elated. She hugged her mother. In silence and harmony they continued down to the river. With the August sun going down, Amanda knew a quiet exclusive place to disrobe and splash in the river. Bushes and trees hid them from the rest of Stekoa Field. It was her place of solitude, a safe haven to reflect on her life that was squeezed in a box. A box she could not get out. Without any fear of being caught, Amanda undressed and gave her mother her clothing. She jumped in the water, which came up to her waist. The water was sparkling and pure as the last of the sun lit it up. It was peaceful, as she splashed in the water.

Then something or someone moved in the bushes. By the sound of the footsteps, Martha knew it was a man. She turned and put Amanda's clothing on a log and rushed in the bush to waylay the interrupter. She quickly moved through the bushes so that the interrupter would not get near the water. After going about twenty feet, she came face to face with Mr. Bumgarner. Her heart sank. They had been followed. She knew what he wanted and there was nothing she could do about it. Praying, she hoped that he didn't know that Amanda was with her.

"We meet again." Bumgarner spat tobacco juice in the bushes. "Where's that daughter of yours?"

"I don't know."

"I thought I saw her heading this way."

"It was only me."

"Oh, well." He smiled showing his tobacco stained teeth. "Dark meat is dark meat," He grabbed Martha and pulled her farther into the bushes.

Afterward, he rearranged his clothing and walked back up the bank. She waited until she was positive that Mr. Bumgarner was gone. Then Martha straightened her clothing and limped back to the river bank. Amanda was still in the water. She waved to her mother. Neither one spoke because their voices might echo across the mountain. Stepping out of the water, she shook the excess water from her body and dressed. Together, they walked back to their cabin. As they walked, Amanda said quietly to her mother, "Mr. Bumgarner was here."

"Yes."

"He rap'd you."

"He was lookin' for youse. I's jest protectin' youse."

"I knows." Amanda dropped her head down. "Youse can't protect me forever."

Martha put her arm around Amanda and squeezed her tight to her side. "I's can try, baby, I's can try."

Amanda took her mother's hand and the two walked together. The love that they had for each other could only be broken with death.

When Martha and Amanda returned to their quarters, someone was in their cabin. He just went through the door, when they rounded the curve. Both of them stopped. Neither one wanted another encounter with Mr. Bumgarner. Martha had hoped that she had satisfied him and he was on the way home to his family. Slave women were fair game to white men, unless the slave owners forbid it. With Master Thomas gone on business or pleasure, his slaves were at the mercy of other slave owners.

Now he had a wife, who had become the Mistress of the household with his aging mother leering in the background. But Miz Sallie wasn't just any wife; she was the heir to a fortune. As a child she had enjoyed numerous advantages. She was well educated and her father employed a German music master to teach her music. In these rugged mountains of North Carolina, her family was among one of the first settlers and had become the gentility of the area. Now Miz Sallie, their young daughter married a man with wealth and power in the far end of the state. It was a frontier with Cherokees still living in the area. And to make matters worse, her husband was the white chief of the Cherokees. Along with being guardian of the Cherokees, he owned slaves and tried to keep the families together.

Martha told Amanda to wait outside. She didn't want her to encounter Mr. Bumgarner. Slowly, she entered her quarters and was surprise to see Sam standing in the middle of the floor. The two glared at each other.

"Miz Sallie's gonna toss us out this place, so youse can have it."

"No."

"Then wat?"

"She wants to see Amanda."

"So she can sell my baby to that tobacco spitting. . ."

"I 'd really don't knows." Sam assured Martha. "She told me to fetch her."

Martha sighed. "She be rite outside."

Exiting, they found Amanda crouched down behind some bushes,

"Go with Sam, Miz Sallie wanna see youse."

Without any hesitation, Amanda followed Sam. As they walked toward the house in the twilight of the day, Amanda wondered what Miz Sallie wanted. She felt that Dearest Sallie and her mother-in-law were at a crossroad and she was standing right in the middle of it. As they approached the back door, she reminded herself that she was a pawn. She had no choice. Dearest Sallie and Miz Temperance had to make the decision.

"Sam, I's sorry I put youse in the middle this."

"I put myself here by allowin' youse to go wit' me."

Sam knocked on back door. Before he could knock again, the door opened. It was Caroline. For the first time, Amanda looked at her. Her skin was light and she had some features that resemble Miz Sallie. Caroline was one of those mulattos. Everyone could tell that she was a mixed breed, half black and half white. Now Amanda understood. Miz Sallie was fighting that same battle she was, but in reverse roles.

"Miz Sallie is in the parlor." Caroline said. "I's take you dere." She looked over at Sam. "She ass dat you stay here."

Sam sat down, while Caroline led Amanda to the parlor. When they got there, Caroline paused at the door. "Amanda be here at yor request."

Looking over Caroline's shoulder, she saw that Miz Temperance was seated in the room also. Amanda looked over at Miz Temperance, and then she lowered her eyes and stared at the floor.

"Thank you, Caroline." With the wave of her, Miz Sallie said, "You may go."

Caroline curtsied and slowly backed out of the room.

After she disappeared, Miz Sallie looked at Amanda and demanded of her. "Who are you?"

"Amanda."

"You are Amanda."

"Yes ma'am."

"Who am I?"

"You is Miz Sallie Thomas, the Mistress of dis household."

"Then who are you?"

"Slave of Maser Thomas."

"And I am?"

"The Mistress of the household."

"Who makes the decision when the Master is away?"

Amanda hung her head down and stared at the floor. "Youse do."

Miz Sallie pointed to Miz Temperance, who was seated in chair on her right. "Who is that?"

"Miz Temperance Thomas."

"Who is she?"

"Master Thomas's mother."

"Is she the Mistress of the house?"

"No, youse be."

"That again is correct." Miz Sallie smiled. "However, she is eighty- two years old and is much wiser than I am. Therefore, I am going to allow her to take you to her home in Shoal Creek. And while you're there, you will learn how to be a proper house nigger. You will be here ready to leave with Mother Temperance tomorrow when the horn sounds. Do you understand?"

"Yes ma'am."

"Make sure that you have all your personal belongings."

"Yes ma'am."

"You are excused."

Amanda attempted to curtsey and backed out of the room. As soon as she was out of their sight, she ran out the back door. Sam seeing her, he got up and followed. He didn't catch up with her. Shouting her name would only complicate matters. Stopping, he walked the rest of way to her quarters. When he arrived, he knocked on the door. Martha came to the door.

"Martha, is Amanda here?"

"Yes, she be fine. G'night."

"G'night." Sam bowed and went his way.

Martha watched him go, and then she closed the door only allowing the night sounds to creep in. A single candle lit up the room. As Amanda moved around, there were ghostly shadows on the wall. Now Martha studied Amanda as she seemed to flit from one place to another.

"Child, wat's de matter?"

"I's goin' to Shoal Creek with Miz Temperance."

"Wat?" Martha could not believe it.

"Yes." Amanda tossed a blanket on the bed. "She wants Miz Temperance to teach me how to be a house slave."

"Wat's wrong with tat?"

"Nothin'. " Amanda began to pack her personal belongings. "Have you seen Caroline, Miz Sallie's personal servant?"

"Yes, jest fer a moment."

"Look at her." Amanda demanded, "Then look at Miz Sallie. They kinda look alike."

"Now, Amanda," Martha warned, "Don't do this."

"I ain't."

"It be gittin' late."

Chapter 5

The next morning, Amanda was up and ready to go. All her personal belongings were packed and sitting on the floor in front of her. Martha was up also. She decided to walk with her to see her off. Shoal Creek was only about twelve miles away. In no time, she would be back. With sun still half asleep, the horn sounded. Mother and daughter rushed out of their quarters and made a beeline to the main house. When they got to there, they found Miz Temperance was waiting in her buggy with Sam in the driver's seat. A saddled horse was tethered behind the rig.

"Give me your bundle, child." Miz Temperance said as she reached for it and set it in the corner of buggy. "Climb in. We have to be going."

Amanda did as she was told. After she settled in one corner of the buggy, Miz Temperance looked at Martha. "I'll take care of her."

Martha nodded, turned and went back to her quarters. The small caravan left Stekoa Field and headed for Shoal Creek. The ride to Miz Temperance's home was not too far away. It was located in Cherokee country. Coldness filled the air and Miz Temperance shared her blanket with Amanda. The morning was quiet as Mother Nature huddled close to the ground. After a while, the day would burst into activities as the whites, the Cherokees, and the slaves went about their work. Birds began to sing and chirp their songs of gladness as they traveled along the bend of the river.

Amanda wanted to ask Miz Temperance about this trip, but she kept it to herself. She did not think that Miz Temperance could teach her how to be a slave. She knew. There was a long list of do's and don'ts. However, for Amanda there was only one rule and that was to do as you were told.

Looking over at the old woman, Amanda noticed that she was shaking. Lovingly she moved closer to her and wrapped her arm around her. She adjusted the blanket and covered her shoulders more. Huddled together, their combined body heat kept them warm. The cold breeze from the water gave them pause.

"Why couldn't we leave in the middle of day?"

Miz Temperance laughed, "Remember Miz Sallie is the Mistress of the house."

Amanda remembered. She will never forget the slap in the face.

By midmorning they had reached Shoal Creek and were almost at Miz Temperance's home. Amanda looked around at the familiar area and joy came to her soul. Somewhere in this area was Master Thomas's Shoal Creek Store and William Hudson Casey was working for Thomas at his blacksmith shop. Amanda promised that she would help Miz Temperance at her home, but she also promised herself that she would try to find William again.

The buggy pulled up to a modest little log cabin with smoke coming from the rock chimney. There was a small garden spot that needed weeding. It seemed that the corn, pole beans, squash, and potato begged for a little attention. A log fence encircled the cabin.

"We's here." Sam announced and got off the driver's seat. "It looks like Mr. Andrew got the message."

He helped Miz Temperance out of the buggy and walked her to the cabin. Amanda knew that she was not going to receive any royal treatment. Climbing out of the buggy, Amanda stretched and observed her surroundings. She breathed in the fresh air and stared at the smoke that rose from the mountains. It was beautiful. However, it was not the time to daydream, it was time to work. She got Miz

Temperance's luggage out of the floor of the buggy and proceeded to carry them in the cabin.

On entering the cozy comfortable cabin, she saw Andrew. Their eyes met, and then Amanda set the luggage on the floor. Miz Temperance had sat down by the fireplace. Without looking at Amanda, she gave orders for her to place her luggage in the bedroom which was located on the right side of the fireplace. As Amanda obeyed Miz Temperance's orders, she listened to the conversation in living-dining area.

"Andrew," Miz Temperance said, "Thanks for coming up and getting the fire started."

"No problem." He bent and kissed Miz Temperance on the cheek and left.

Sam came into the bedroom where Amanda was putting her mistress's clothes in the wardrobe.

"I's headed back to Stekoa."

"My dings still be in de buggy."

"I took'm out." Sam patted her shoulders. "See ya."

"Yeah. See ya."

Sam was gone. Now she and Miz Temperance were alone.

"Amanda," she called. "How about some coffee."

"Yes ma'am."

Amanda stopped what she was doing and came into the combined living-dining area. A pot of hot coffee was setting on the rack over the fire in the fireplace. She found the cups and placed one on the table. She got a potholder to get the hot coffee pot from the fire. After pouring some coffee in the cup, she handed it to Miz Temperance.

"Dis ought to warm youse up."

Miz Temperance took the steaming cup and sipped the hot coffee.

"You know child that most ladies want cream and sugar with their coffee,"

"Yes ma'am."

Amanda found the cream and sugar and offered it to Miz Temperance. She curtseyed and asked, "Anythin' Ise can help youse with?"

Miz Temperance laughed. "A napkin, please?"

Scurrying around the unfamiliar surroundings, Amanda was able to find a cloth napkin and present it to Miz Temperance. She stood at attention just a few feet away from Miz Temperance. Patiently she waited for her to give her more instruction. The next move was Miz Temperance and Amanda stood her ground. Miz Temperance handed the half full cup of coffee to Amanda.

"This coffee is terrible. I hope you can make a better cup. Your mother use to make the best coffee."

"Yes ma'am." Amanda took the cup and set it on the table.

"Child," Miz Temperance announced. "I'm tired."

"I's help youse to bed."

"No," Miz Temperance laughed. "Get my knitting. That will help me stay awake."

"Yesum."

Amanda got her knitting and gave it to her.

Without warning the day was quietly disappearing, therefore Amanda had to get busy and get everything in order. She went outside and walked to the small garden. With a hoe in hand, she began to separate the weeds from the roots of the planted crops. After she finished, she went back inside and inventoried the supply in the house. The cabinet and root cellar were well stocked. The only thing she had to do was to clean the house and attend to Miz Temperance's needs. With Miz Temperance still knitting, Amanda began cleaning the house.

After cleaning the house, she fixed Miz Temperance a midday meal. And then she went up to clean the loft. As she stood there, she remembered that sometimes she had spent weekends with Miz Temperance. On Sundays, she had gone to church with her. And yet, she had to sit in the back, while Miz Temperance sat up front. That was years ago. Miz Temperance was no longer the Mistress of the household. Dearest Sallie was. Looking out the window she could look down and see the surrounding area. Hence she decided this was where she would sleep. It was private and comfortable. However, after supper, Miz Temperance told her that she would sleep at the foot of her bed. Amanda was crushed, but she would do as she was told.

Bedtime came and Amanda held Mz Temperance by the arm, as they went into the bedroom. Her mistress sat down in a chair. Quickly Amanda took the pitcher which was set inside the ceramic wash bowl and filled it with water hot from the kettle hanging over the fire of hearth, adding a little cold water from the pump in the kitchen. On returning to the bedroom, she poured some into the wash bowl. Next she helped the older lady remove her clothing.

While Miz Temperance was washing up, Amanda turned down the bed coverings. Before going to bed, Miz Temperance knelt down at the side of the bed and prayed. When she was ready, Amanda helped her into bed and gently covered her up. Then she fixed a pallet at the foot of Miz Temperance's bed and lay down for the night. As she lay there wide awake, she thought of William Hudson Casey, who was somewhere down the road. She slipped off into her dream world, where the face of William appeared.

Chapter 6

Being a personal servant of Miz Temperance was sometimes repulsive. Every morning, she had to take the bedchamber to the branch that ran along the back of house. After tossing the waste in the branch, she cleaned the pot. During the day, they could use the outhouse, but it was a far piece for the aging Miz Temperance. Therefore, Amanda made sure that any time during the day; the bedchamber was immaculately clean and available to her mistress.

Breakfast was served to her in bed as Amanda brought the tray of fried potatoes, fried eggs, country ham, grits and a cup of coffee to her mistress. As her lady ate, Amanda sat at the table and gobbled down her breakfast. She knew eating at the table with her mistress was forbidden for a slave. Since it was only her and Miz Temperance, she felt no harm was done. When she was with Mez Temperance she had found a taste of freedom.

On fifth day at Shoal Creek, Amanda decided to venture out to find Thomas's Store. She surmised it couldn't be far away. On the ride to the store with Sam, she was too excited to remember which way they went. Studying the comings and goings of the white settlers and Cherokees, she felt she needed to go farther on down the road. After serving Miz Temperance her breakfast, Amanda emptied and cleaned the bedchamber and brought it back in the house. When she returned from cleaning the bedchamber, she removed the breakfast tray from Miz Temperance bedroom and washed the breakfast dishes. Going back into the bedroom, she assisted Miz Temperance in dressing herself.

"Wat's youse gonna do 'day?"

"I thought I would get some more knitting done. With Christmas coming soon, Christmas gifts are in order."

"Yes ma'am."

"What are you going to do?"

"Mosey on down road."

"What are you looking for?"

"Maser Thomas's Store."

"What do you need girl?"

"Well, I's figure you might need some thread."

Miz Temperance took a folded sheet of paper out of her pocket. "Here." She handed the paper to Amanda, who took it and put in the straw basket she was carrying. "Just give it to the clerk. He'll fill my order."

"Yes ma'am."

"Now don't play around. I want you back here before noon." Miz Temperance picked up her knitting needle. "The clerk is Mr. Terrell. You understand, Mr. Terrell."

"Yes ma'am."

Amanda got her shaggy shawl and threw it over her shoulders. Before Miz Temperance could say another word, she was out the door. Skipping along, Amanda felt free, but she knew it was a false feeling. She was just free to go to Thomas's Store to fetch some things for her mistress. However, she hoped that William was still at the blacksmith shop. She could talk to him about his life. Barefooted Amanda thought of her personal appearance. Her dress and head rag were clean, but faded. Young and in love, Amanda felt she was presentable.

Swinging the basket as she skipped happily down the road, she reminisced about their first encounter. She tried to recall what she was wearing. She didn't have any idea she was going to meet William Hudson Casey. She was barefooted and dressed to work in the kitchen. Therefore, she had her apron on and a head rag on her head so that her hair would not get in the food they were going to prepare.

With the apron gone, Amanda felt free,

"I's free," she whispered to the birds that chirped in the trees and the birds' chirping seemed to echo that feeling. As she continued on down the road and the birds seemed to follow with their chirping that sounded like that they were singing "Free, free!"

Just as she rounded a curve, she saw Mister Andrew walking toward her and she surmised that the store wasn't too far away. She stopped. Nervously, she waited for him to approach her. She kicked red clay clots with her bare feet and stared at the ground. Without looking up, she knew Mister Andrew was directly in front of her. Patiently, she waited for him to speak.

Mister Andrew cupped her chin in his hand and the two looked at each other eye to eye. Amanda was frightened.

"What's the matter, nigger?" Mister Andrew smiled sheepishly. "Are you running away again?"

"No, Miser" Amanda managed to say. "I's goin' to de store for Miz Temperance."

"Go." He laughed.

"Yes'um."

Amanda quickly scooted by him and continued to the store. She didn't look back to see if Andrew continued on to see Miz Temperance. When she saw the store, she broke into a run. Just as she got in range of the store, she stopped. The place was busy with Lufty Indians and settlers. Now Amanda had no one to protect her. Deep down, she knew the Luftys wouldn't bother her. They were Master Thomas's people. He was their chief and Thomas had allowed them to go to some of Luftys' ceremonies.

Looking around, she spied the blacksmith shop. Listening, she could hear the anvil being struck. Someone was working and Amanda prayed that it would be William. When she got there to the opened doors of the shop, she saw the muscular arms of the blacksmith. It was William. She straightened up her clothing and wet her lips. She looked in her basket to see if the list was still there. It was. There-fore, Amanda made the decision to run across to the store and give the list to Mr. Terrell. She would pick it up later.

Retracing her steps, she went to Thomas's Store. As she approached the counter, there were two Lufty men in front of her. They were negotiating with Mr. Terrell. Amanda hung back. She started to walk around the store, but Mr. Terrell's booming voice stopped her.

"Hey, what do you want?"

"Miz Temperance wants these things," Amanda took the list out of the basket and walked over to Mr. Terrell. The two Luftys glanced at her, and then walked out the door.

"Who are you?"

"Amanda,"

"Ok," Mr. Terrell took the list from her. "Mr. Andrew said that you might be by sometimes."

Mr. Terrell studied the list, and then he proceeded to get the items from the shelves. Amanda had to wait. She had hoped that he would take the list and she could go visit William. He seemed to take his time and talked as he did.

"How's Mrs. Temperance? I haven't seen her in a while."

"She be fine."

"You like your new Mistress?"

"Yes sir."

"Is Mr. Thomas's mother at home?"

"Yes sur."

Amanda set the basket on the counter and waited for Mr. Terrell to return with the items that Miz Temperance needed.

"She's knitting." Mr. Terrell laughed. "Christmas is on the way."

He picked two skeins of knitting yarn and carried them to counter with the rest of the items Miz Temperance needed. Humming a Christmas tune, Mr. Terrell added the items on the cash register, and then he put the total in a ledger. He closed it and put it back behind the counter. After arranging the items in the basket, he handed it to Amanda. As she turned to go out the door, Mr. Bumgarner stepped through the door.

"Morning," Mr. Terrell greeted him.

"Mornin'," Mr. Bumgarner replied.

"Is your slave patrol keeping tabs on them niggers."

Amanda didn't wait to hear the answer. Swiftly, she left the store and hurried to the blacksmith shop. She hoped Mr. Terrell's conversation would make him forget about her. Deep down, she knew that was not to be. She had a dilemma on her hands. Desperately, she wanted to see William and talk to him for a little while. Perhaps if she stood in the shadows of the shop, he wouldn't see her. Therefore, she looked back to see whether Mr. Bumgarner was peeking out the store window, but only the displays stared back at her.

When she walked into the blacksmith shop, she found William hard at work. The sound of the hammer hitting the anvil was music to Amanda's ears. She stood there and waited until the hammer stopped.

"William Hudson Casey," she announced.

He looked up and smiled.

"'Member me?"

"Ifen it ain't Amanda. Wat's youse doin' way out here? Mr. Thomas's place is fur piece up the road."

"Come to see youse."

He laughed. "I's know dat Mr. Thomas ain't lettin' youse come dis far."

Amanda laughed also and proceeded to tell him her story.

"How did youse know I was still down here?"

"Let me tell ya the rest of the story, Dearest Sallie sent me down here to learn how to a personal maid to Miz Temperance,"

"Who's dat?"

"Dat's Master's mama."

"Oh, I see."

59

"When dey sent me down here, I knowed I'd see ya."
He laughed again.

"Why youse laugh at me?"

"Youse is funny."

Amanda smiled at him. She just hoped that that laughter was one that said, "I like you." As she stood in the shadows, she saw Mr. Bumgarner head toward the Tannery. That meant, he was going away from Miz Temperance. Sighing, she knew that she had to get back to the cabin. She had delayed her return long enough.

"I's hafto go William or Miz Temperance ain't gonna be too happy with me."

"Sure," he flashed that smile again. "Will I see youse 'round?"

"P'haps!" She was totally surprised at his question. Maybe he was interest in her. And yet, she didn't know when they could get together. There was no way that she would jeopardize his loyalty to Master Thomas. They were not free with Mr. Bumgarner and his night patrol, the end results would be a beating.

"We's meet 'gain." Amanda promised.

With her loaded basket across her arm, she ran to the door as William called out to her.

"Call me Bill."

Without stopping to acknowledge that she heard him, she continued to run. Instead of running down the road, she went through the wooded area. It had been a long time since she been at Miz Temperance's place, but she knew a shortcut. In no time, she was at the cabin door. A little out of breath, she composed herself before going inside.

"You're late," Temperance continued to knit.

"I's sorry." Amanda put down the basket. "I guess I stay'd too long a lookin'."

"Did you see Mr. Andrew?"

"Yes ma'am."

"He said you seemed a little nervous."

Amanda didn't answer. She couldn't tell her she was

afraid of Mister Andrew. Not only Mister Andrew, she was cautious about all white men. Their eyes told her they were evil and there was nothing she could do about it. She had to just stay away or she felt she would fall victim to them. She recollected that her mother related to her she thought they were going to devour them. And yet their Master did take their dignity away from them. They were property, just as the hog that ran wild in the hills.

At that moment, there was a loud knock on the door. Amanda froze. She looked over at Miz Temperance.

"Answer the door, child."

Amanda went toward the door. Through the window, she saw the burly figure of Mr. Charles Bumgarner.

"It's Mr. Bumgarner."

"Let him in." Miz Temperance scolded her. "Don't keep him waiting!"

She opened the door and Mr. Bumgarner burst in the room without being invited. Amanda backed away. It seemed Mr. Bumgarner was ready to pounce on her like a wild animal. He stopped when he saw Mrs. Thomas.

A sheepish smile played about his mouth. He removed his hat and bowed to her. "Mrs. Thomas, I didn't know youse was here."

"What can I do for you?"

"I saw this nigger down at the store. I thought she was running away again."

"No, Mr. Bumgarner. She is here with me."

Like a little boy caught with his hand in the cookie jar, Mr. Bumgarner stood there with his hat held tight with both hands. "I's sorry. I was just looking out fer yer welfare."

"Thank you, Mr. Bumgarner." Mrs. Thomas continued to ply the stitches as she knitted. "Good day."

"Good day, Mrs. Thomas." He bowed to her, looked over at Amanda, turned and left.

"I'll fix youse something to eat."

Without waiting for Miz Temperance to rely, she left the room.

"I'm not hungry." Miz Temperance called, "Come in here and talk to me."

Slowly Amanda came back into the room.

"Child, I was there when you were born. I watched you grow up. Something is troubling you. What is it?"

"Slavery?"

"Child, that the way it is. Remember the Bible says that your people are descendants of Ham. You were born to be a slave and serve us. You see Ham looked on his father while he was without clothes. So God punished him."

Amanda didn't say anything. She couldn't read, therefore she took Miz Temperance's word.

"Understand, Amanda?"

Amanda hung her head down.

"You see, you are childlike. We have to protect you. That's why Senator Thomas doesn't send you away when you are unruly. Someday, you will learn."

Stupefied, Amanda just stared at Miz Temperance. And then she shook her head and walked outside. The fresh air cleared her head. As she looked down the road, she saw Mr. Bumgarner. With his buckboard full of supply, he seemed to be headed home. Amanda knew she better get back inside before he saw her. It was getting night time and she had to secure hers and Miz Temperance's safety.

A short time after supper, there was a knock on the door. Miz Temperance sat by the hearth and continued her knitting. Amanda and Miz Temperance looked at each other.

"Child, see who it is?"

"Yes sum."

Amanda looked out the window and saw two shadowy figures in the moonlight.

"Dey look likk Luftys"

"Let'em in."

Amanda opened the door and came face to face with two Lufty young men. As they came through the door, Miz Temperance realized that one of them was wounded. Immediately, she recognized them. Amanda closed the door.

"Little Crow," Miz Temperance asked the wounded Lufty. "What happen?"

"He fell on a stick and injured his foot." His companion said.

Amanda moved from the door and got rags from the rag bag and some salve to doctor the wound. Miz Temperance cleaned the wound out and bandaged it up. She tried to get the two to stay for the night, but they thanked her and disappeared into the darkness.

Within a week, Amanda and Miz Temperance returned to Stekoa Field. Although she was home, she was not comfortable. In her heart she knew she had betrayed Master Thomas when she persuaded Sam to ride with him to Shoal Creek. Now she had to behave herself until Thomas came home.

Chapter 7

The New Year was fast approaching and Stekoa Fields resembled a deserted farm. Winter had set in and most of the slaves were idle. Amanda was glad the impervious plowing and harvesting was over. It was the time of year to commemorate the birth of Christ. With Master Thomas home from the General Assembly in Raleigh, Amanda sensed a touch of security. She hoped that Miz Sallie would forget to tell Master of her behavior.

Two days after Thomas was home, she was called to the main house. Immediately, she knew that she was in trouble. Sam came to fetch her. And the look on his face told her that Thomas was not pleased. As they made their way to the main house, she didn't question Sam about it. She evaded the situation by asking him about the news that he had overheard from the Master's dinner table.

Trying to be upbeat, she asked. "Wat's goin' on in de white man's world?"

"Wat do youse mean?"

"Sam, don't act dumb."

"Amanda! Youse bet worry 'bout yerself."

"I knows, but I jest wanna know."

"Youse 'member dat slave dat was a tryin' to sue Missouri fer his freedom?"

"I's too little to 'emember."

"Well, yo mother does. It seems dat he loss."

"Dis is bad fer us."

"Yeah. Master Thomas call'd it de Dred Scot Decision. It seem'd dat de courts done kept him in slavery."

"Sam, it ain't bad for youse. Youse is Master Thomas's fav'rite. I's knows dat youse have 'ccount at his store in Shoal Creek and youse can buy anythin' youse want,"

Laughing, Sam asked, "Girl how do youse knows so much?"

"Jest do."

By that time, they were at the main house. Amanda started to go in the back door, but Sam directed her to the kitchen. She didn't want to go into the kitchen and be scolded in front of Suckey. Usually, he would come down to the quarters and talk to Martha about her behavior. Now that Thomas was married, he sent for her. Going into the kitchen, the aroma of country ham being cooked filled the air. Looking around, she found that Suckey was nowhere in sight. She and Thomas were alone.

"Youse send fer me, Maser."

Amanda saw the frown that was etched across his forehead. "What's this I hear about you trying to run away?"

"I wasn't, Maser," she tried to assure him. "I only want'd to see yo' store."

"I see," Thomas held his chin in his hand and reflected on Amanda's remarks. "Mistress Sallie and Suckey seem to believe that you were running away."

"No sir."

Looking at Thomas, Amanda knew that Suckey was always trying to get her into trouble. Now that Suckey had Miz Sallie on her side, she wondered what Suckey had told Miz Sallie about her. Everyone on Stekoa Fields knew that Suckey was jealous of Martha. Now she knew that William Holland Thomas was her father, she understood. It seemed that Suckey and her children were part of a bargain Master had made. In other words, Suckey's children were not born on Stekoa Fields.

"Now look, Mandy," said Thomas, as he put his hands on her shoulders. "Mistress Sallie wants to sell you to Charles Bumgarner and I told her that I would sell no slave to him."

A chill went through Amanda, as Master Thomas continued to verbally chastise her for her behavior.

And then, Thomas' voice became soft and gentle. "It's the Christmas season. Here is my gift to you. I'll never sell you, nor will I permit Mistress Sallie to do so. However, you must obey her."

"Yes'sum."

She wanted to hug him, but she was no longer a child. They stared at each other and then Amanda lowered her eyes. He affectionately patted her on her head and left. She stood there stunned, but the silence was broken by the heavy footsteps of Suckey as she entered the kitchen.

"I's guess youse got yo' upcomin'."

"Yeah," Amanda replied without looking at Suckey.

Slowly she walked out into the cold morning air. It was refreshing to know where she stood at Stekoa Fields. Skipping, she went back to her quarters. She would never tell anyone about the conversation with Master, but she also knew she had to be good. Her inner soul told her that she was just a mere nigger slave. Anything could happen. Master Thomas could die and Miz Sallie could sell her.

Chapter 8

On December 25, while most of the country was celebrating Christmas, the folks in the mountains of Western North Carolina were just about to prepare to celebrate the true Christmas. Although President Franklin Pierce had celebrated the event at the White House in 1852 on December 25, Stekoa Fields would observe Christmas on January 6.

With New Year's Eve and Christmas just a few days away, Amanda watched the preparation from a distance. And yet, she knew that she would be involved in getting the house in order. The house would be cleaned. It was always a ritual with Miz Temperance that Stekoa Fields get a face lift before the New Year. It was the coldest month and Miz Temperance had the slaves cleaning house.

Just at the crack of dawn, the horn alerted all the slaves that they were wanted at the main house. Without hesitation, all the slaves assembled in front of the house in a matter of a few minutes. The new slaves wondered what the assembly was all about. Even Martha stood with them. Some anticipated it was Christmas time and the Master was going to give them a gift. However, neither the Master, nor the Mistress was on the porch to greet them. Being slaves, they depended on the Master to remind them of a holiday. For a slave, one day was the same as the day before unless the master told them differently.

"Wat's the point of a standin' here in this cold?" Dave asked.

"Wait an' see," Martha answered.

"Oh, shut up ole woman. Youse don't knows de time of day."

"Dat my mother," Amanda reminded him.

"Don't care." Dave shouted. "I's goin' back to . . ."

At that moment Sam came around the house.

"Ev'rybody knows dat de place needs a good cleanin' 'fore Christmas. All youse womenfolk go 'round de back and git yo' instructions from Caroline. Now youse boys will be afixin' up the outside."

Sam's voice trailed off as Amanda and the other female slaves went to the back of the house. Caroline ordered Martha and Suckey to clean the silverware and the crystal chandelier in the dining room. Amanda felt good, because Martha's legs were bothering her. By doing the silverware and the chandelier, Martha could sit down to get the task done. She just hoped Sam had already taken the chandelier down, so Suckey wouldn't demand that Martha do it. For the chandelier had to be taken apart piece by piece before being carefully washed in vinegar-water. However, Amanda couldn't dwell on that, because Caroline was barking out other orders.

"Mandy, youse an' Flossie take dose rugs out fer the chillen to beat be dust out,"

Amanda and Flossie, another young single female slave, rolled up the rug from the parlor and took it outside. They hung the rug on the clothesline for the children to beat the dust out with sticks. Returning to the house, they removed the rugs from the other rooms to be dusted outside. Amanda remembered the days that she dusted the rugs. Now she was given the task of scrubbing the bare hardwood floors. Down on her knees with Flossie, Amanda took an oaken bucket filled with hot soapy water and rags to clean the floor. As she scrubbed the floor, she wished she had the task of turning the mattresses and putting new goose feathers in the pillows. However, Caroline had saved that task for herself and Suckey's little daughter, Colette. It didn't matter who did what as long as each task was done efficiently.

Hence to make the task seem light and make the day go faster, the slaves sang:

On the sixth day of January his birthday shall be.
When the star and mountains shall shout with glee
As Joseph was a-walking thus did the angels sing?
And Mary's son at midnight was born to be king.

When the female slaves were busy cleaning the house, Amanda knew the male slaves were outside beautifying the place for the twelve days of Christmas and the New Year for the spring. Of course, the barn had to be cleaned out and most of the tools had to be repaired. For breaking a tool was a form of slave rebellion. She laughed to herself because knew Dave had his share of rebelling. After repairing the tools, they had to be put away until it was planting time again. As she was thinking of those tasks that were being performed outside, she knew the blacksmith had to repair Miz Sallie carriage and reshod the horses. Usually Master Thomas hired Mr. Bumgarner to do the job, but the two men had bickered about how unruly slaves should be punished. As Amanda worked, she hoped Master Thomas had hired out Bill to do the blacksmithing. With this thought and the continued singing among the slaves, Amanda found the task tolerable.

By the end of the day, Amanda was exhausted. As the twilight moved across the sky, she slowly made her way to her cabin. There was no more singing in the air, as the silhouette of bent bodies trudged ever so slowly to their hard lumpy pallets. Amanda entered her cabin to the mixture of the savory smell of turnips with wild greens and the unsavory smell of mustard plaster. Slowly she went to the hearth and sank down in the chair. Her supper was hanging in the pot over the hearth. She knew her mother was home because of the stench of the mustard plaster. Tears formed in her eyes for she knew that the ulcers on Martha's legs were opened and the mustard plaster was put on to try to heal them. Sighing, she knew the task of cleaning Miz Sallie's house was not complete. Tomorrow morning at the crack of dawn, she would have to go back. Going to the bed, she looked down at her mother who seemed to sleep undisturbed and untroubled. She bent down, kissed her and arranged the cover about her shoulders. As she turned to back to get her supper, the door to the cabin creaked open. Sharply, she turned around and found Bill standing in the doorway.

"Wat are youse doin'?"

"I's hir'd to shoe Maser Thomas' hoss."

"Don't just stan' dere, come on in."

Bill came into cabin and closed the door. Amanda could tell that he was surveying the room. She followed his eyes, and she saw that he was glancing at the sleeping form in the bed.

"Dat's my mother."

"Yeah," Bill answered quietly.

"Youse wants some to eat?" Before Bill could answer, Amanda continued on hurriedly. "It's just turnip and greens. My Mama cook'd it."

Bill laughed. "Shore."

"Sit down." Amanda offered him the chair by the hearth.

After he sat down Amanda hurried about to fix him something to eat. The cabin was quiet except for the noise she made as she dished out the food. She handed him the cracked plate, which was filled with cooked turnip greens. After finding some cold corn pone on the table, she gave it to him. Lovingly, she stood over him as he ate. Although she had worked from sunup to sundown, she was elated to be able to serve Bill his last meal of the evening. Smiling, she wished she could do that all the time.

Her mother's even soft snoring seemed to circle the room. To Amanda, it suggested that she needed sleep. Morning would come before she knew it, and it would back to work. She stifled a yawn, as she took the empty plate from Bill and sat it on the table. As she turned to join Bill at the hearth, she found that he was right behind her. Almost falling, Bill caught her in his arms. They stared at each other.

"Youse look tir'd." He kissed her on the forehead.

"I is." Amanda sighed. "But I's glad to see youse."

Silence engulfed the room. Amanda didn't want Bill to leave. However, she couldn't let him stay there. It would not be fair to her mother.

"Youse got a place to sleep?"

"Yeah," Bill answered, "In the barn."

Amanda untangled herself from him. "Is there any other hired hands sleeping in the barn?"

He went to her and smiled. "Nope, just me."

Taking her in his arms, they kissed. After the passionate kiss, he started toward the door, and then he turned and stretched out his hand to her. "Youse wanna join me."

Noiseless and quickly, she joined him at the door. Hand in hand, they left the cabin to find privacy in the barn among horses and carriages.

Although Amanda was tired, the night air awakened her. Not only that, she had Bill walking by her side. Everything seemed to be beautiful and in step with nature. Her heart pounded as they strolled to the barn. Stekoa Fields was quiet. It seemed everyone was sleeping. When they got to the barn, someone else was occupying it.

"Sh," Bill said in whisper. "I'll git them out."

Amanda caught his arm. "No, they have a right to some privacy."

"But I was told that was my sleeping quarters." Bill assured her. "Youse stand in the shadow."

Amanda shook her head and stood in the shadow of the barn. Making a lot of noise, Bill went into the barn. The next thing Amanda saw two shadowy figures running in two separate directions. One went toward the main house, the other one went toward the slave quarters. Bill came back out and invited Amanda into his private stall for the night.

The next morning, Amanda awoke to find Bill by her

side. She rolled over and found herself on straw. And then she remembered where she was and snuggled close to him. His grayish-green eyes popped open and held her closer. And yet Amanda knew that they had better get up, the night of their romantic interlude was over.

"I's hafto go."

"I know." He kissed her, and then sat up.

Amanda got up and attempted to get the hay off her clothing and out of her hair. Slowly Bill got to his feet and assisted her in getting it off. A quick kiss and Amanda dashed out of the barn to her cabin. When she opened the door, Martha was already up.

"Girl, where has youse been?"

"In de barn with Bill."

"Maser Thomas ain't gonna like that." She shook her head sadly. "He's gonna want you to mate with an older man."

"Mama!" She cried, "I don't wanna an older man."

"Child, sometimes you don't have say."

Amanda didn't say anything. Being a slave you never had a choice. One just does what the Master tells you.

It was the crack of dawn, and Master Thomas needed their labor. From dawn to dusk, they were at the beck and call of their mistress and master. The days were never theirs, only the nights. Sighing Amanda went over to the hearth and looked in the cooking pot. There was some porridge in it. Getting two cracked bowls, she served their breakfast in silence. Mother and daughter had nothing to say to each other. Between them, they knew the score.

So they went back to the main house to finish preparation for the holidays. Flossie and Amanda had cleaned the floor in parlor and now they had to arrange everything back in its place. And the most important was the Christmas Bush. As Flossie and Amanda were putting furniture back, Flossie grabbed the Christmas Bush.

"Dis old plant needs to be thrown out," Flossie was ready to toss it in the yard.

"No," Amanda stopped her.

"Master Thomas can git 'other one."

"Flossie," Amanda scolded her. "Youse is new here. Dat's de Christmas Bush."

"I's herd of a Christmas Tree, but not bush dat stay in yer de 'hole year."

"Well, let me tell youse. Dat dere branch is fer Christ's birth. De thorns are for his cru'ifivion an' death. Dem dere paper roses are fer His resir'ection an' life."

"Who thought of dat."

"Dat's one of Miz Temperance's things. I guess." Amanda shrugged her shoulders. "'lease she tole me dat when I was little."

"White folks haft some pow'rful strange ways."

"Yeh," Amanda sighed.

Flossie took the Christmas Bush inside and placed it in the parlor. "Not only do dey haft a Christmas Bush, dey haft a Christmas tree."

With parlor being the last floor to clean and the furniture replaced, Flossie and Amanda were assigned to another task to get ready for the holidays. Amanda couldn't remember the task. All she could think about was Bill. Although she was tired, she stopped by the barn on the way to her quarters. Disappointed, Bill was not there. Hurriedly she went to her cabin, hoping he was there. When she got there, Master Thomas was standing in yard. The look on his face told that something was wrong.

"Is my mama alright?"

"She's fine." He said and guided her into the house. "Let's go in."

They went inside and he closed the door. Her mother wasn't home.

"Mandy, rumor has it dat that you want to jump the broom with Mr. Love's blacksmith."

"Youse mean Bill."

"Yes, but. . ."

"With yo 'mission?"

"Can't do it."

Without thinking Amanda questioned him. "Why not?" As soon as she spoke, she realized that she was out of line. Turning away from Master Thomas, she spied the clothes from the big house, which needed to be ironed. She went to the hearth and retrieved the flat irons and placed them hot coals in the hearth. She cleared the table top and put a white clean cloth on it. She had to face him when he spoke.

"Look, we're family. I have to take care of my people. I know that boy is not for you. He's ain't dry behind the ears."

Turning away from him, Amanda continued to prepare for the task at hand. She couldn't look at him. Family, she thought.

"So if you want to jump the broom, I believe that Power and Alfred are more seasoned. Besides you will be living together. Mr. Love's people live on other side of the mountain. You couldn't see him every week, only weeks at a time."

Anger tingled Amanda's skin. She could not believe that Master Thomas was treating her like an animal.

"You understand what I'm saying. You haven't slept with that boy have you?"

"No sir." Amanda lied.

"Remember that we are family and a family stays together.' He patted her on the head like a dog. "Just tell me which one you want."

Without another word, he was gone.

Hurt and humiliated, Amanda went to her pallet and threw herself across it. Tears poured from her eyes, as she cried silently. As she lay there, she realized that indeed she was only a piece of property. It didn't matter that he was her father. Nothing mattered any more. She was a valuable piece of property that had the potential of producing other pieces of property for Master Thomas to hire out or to sell. And William Hudson Casey was not to be her mate.

At that moment, Bill strolled through the door. "I just saw Mr. Thomas come out of here."

Amanda leaped off the pallet and ran into his arms. He held her tight against his chest. She felt safe there, but she knew it was only a temporary haven. For a slave, the only safety was perhaps death.

"Did he hurt you?"

"No," Amanda managed to say, "He didn't touch me."

"Why de tears?"

"Youse goin' back to Mr. Love."

"Yeah," Bill pulled a little pouch out. "I just got paid. But it ain't enough to buy my freedom back."

"Wat do mean?'

"My mother is a free person, but she contract'd us to Mr. Love."

Contract'd?" Amanda stepped over to her mother's bed and retrieved one of Master Thomas's shirts. She stretched out on the table and went to test the iron. "So youse have to give Mr. Love parts of yo' money."

"Something' like dat."

"Sounds like slavery to me."

"Yeah. Mr. Love be here. I's gotta go back with him."

He kissed her and then he was gone.

Bill was gone and she didn't have the heart to tell him the truth. Eventually, he would find some sweet young nigger at White Sulphur Springs. Stekoa Fields was too far for him to visit her. Master Thomas had someone else in mind for her to mate.

If I was white, Amanda thought, I could choose my own mate. Master Thomas is my father and my master. You're just a nigger slave. No more or no less. I am like Caroline. I am a mulatto, but I got most of my mother's genes. Therefore, I am a black nigger slave.

After Bill left with Mr. Love, Amanda felt all alone. New Year's Eve was approaching and the love of her life was gone. She would not be able to share the traditional New Year's meal with him. All day long, she went about her work with a heavy heart. Deep down in her heart she knew that Master Thomas had told Mr. Love that Bill was not to come to Stekoa Fields. Now there was reason why Bill wouldn't be here. Like Caroline's man, Bill would find someone else.

With the house being clean from top to bottom, Amanda had nothing much to do. Only the house slaves were needed by the mistress. Therefore Amanda remained around her quarters and helped her mother, whose legs were bothering her again. With mustard plaster, she applied the mixture on her ulcerated legs. Helping to clean the main house had taken its toll on Martha. This did not help Amanda's emotional state. And yet, she knew she had to remain calm. She didn't want to do anything that would cause the New Year to be a disaster.

"Child," Martha said, "Youse been mighty quite 'day."

"Jest worri'd 'bout youse."

"Jest gittin' old."

"Too old to be a workin' like youse did."

"Did he love youse?"

"Who, child?"

"Master Thomas?"

"Child, I's don't know." She sighed, " I's jest know dat he kind and gentle."

"And did youse love him?"

"Shore, I did."

"Why don't you sit back and lax." Amanda reminded her mother, "Youse done 'nough fer him."

"I tri'd. Maser Thomas brung me from a long ways to dese mountains. I's 'member being on de back of buckboard with my feet a draggin' de ground."

"How old was youse, mama?"

"Don't knows, but I's little thing."

"Little? How little?"

"Alls I knows is dat I walk, talk, an' work in de fields."

"Yeah," Amanda replied sarcastically. "Dat all dey want us fer."

"Back ten, Maser Thomas would work in de field with me. Even his mammy would come an' work."

"Yeah."

"Maser Thomas, he be a good man. I's 'member dat one time, he sat up all nite with dis poor sick nigger. She be a little thing."

"He be good man." Amanda said sarcastically.

"Girl, I's don't likk yer tone. He done rat by me.".

At that moment, there was a knock on the door. Amanda hoped that it was Bill. However, on opening the door, she found Cudge was standing there. Looking at him, Amanda found that he had grown taller. They greeted each other with a hug.

"Cudge," she said gaily, "Maser Thomas doesn't need yo' services?"

"Not rat now." Cudge replied. "How's yo mammy?"

"She's fine. She's restin' rat now."

"Dat's good 'cause Maser needs youse at the big house.'

Amanda groaned. "Now wat?"

"Youse know dat Maser and Miz Sallie is gonna haft a New Year's Eve party."

"I's a field hand. How does I know?"

"Is youse mad at me?"

"Nope." She took Cudge by the hand. C'mon, let's go."

As they walked to the big house, Amanda questioned Cudge about his stay in Raleigh.

"Mandy, dere were tall buildin'. The roads be pav'd. People be everywhere. Youse know I saw few black folks. Some of dem were free folks."

"Youse talk to'em."

"Some young folks."

"Wat's dey a sayin'?"

"Talkin' 'bout 'bolitionist."

"Wat's dat?"

"Folks whose a tryin' to git our freedom."

"Dat good."

They had reached the big house and all conversation

stopped. Cudge went into back door where Miz Temperance greeted her. That meant that Miz Temperance was going to spend the holidays with her son. However, she was not called to the big house to greet Miz Temperance, but Miz Sallie wanted her to help serve at the party.

"How are you doing?" Miz Temperance asked.

"Fine."

"I told, Sallie that you would be great to help serve the party,

"Yes'um."

Miz Temperance handed her a black dress with a white opened collar and white apron to go over the dress. Included was also a white dainty cap to wear on her head to hide the nappy bushy hair.

"This is your uniform. You have to be nice and be on your toes tonight. Remember what I taught you."

"Yes"um." Amanda took the clothes from Miz Temperance.

"You can go to Suckey's quarters to change."

"Yes"um."

Like a zombie, Amanda went to Suckey's quarters and changed clothes. She folded her clothes and put them on the bed. Going in the kitchen, she found Suckey busy making preparation for the party.

"How's it goin'?"

"Well, if it isn't Mandy. I hadn't seen you in a while."

"I put my other clothes on your bed."

"Youse changed in my quarters."

"I was tole to do so."

"Okay." She shook her head sadly. "We have no privacy."

"Nope, Miz Suckey," Amanda laughed, "We's just niggers."

Amanda started toward the kitchen door, but she stopped and turned to Suckey, who was busy fixing deviled eggs.

"Wat's they gonna serve?

" 'ors d'euve."

"Wat's dat?"

"Dey call it finger food."

"Deviled eggs?"

"Yep," Suckey laughed. "I's makin' small sandwiches an' fixin' cavare."

"Wat's dat?

"Miz Sallie said it be fish eggs."

"Fish eggs!"

"I 'pose all de eatible food are gonna be on trays."

"Youse got it."

Amanda left the kitchen and returned to the main house to get approval from Miz Temperance or Miz Sallie. As she came through the hall, she saw Miz Temperance in the parlor. Silently she walked in quietly and curtseyed to her.

"Miz Temperance," she announced, "I come to show ifen I 's look 'lright."

Miz Temperance, who was knitting, stopped and looked up at Amanda. "You look fine."

Amanda curtseyed again. "Thank you, Miz Temperance."

She tried to make a quick exist, but Miz Temperance called her back. Amanda hesitated. She didn't wish to talk to her. Miz Temperance is the master and she was the slave. There was nothing they needed to talk over. The years spent with Miz Temperance, Amanda felt they had bonded. For Amanda, she was grandmother, who kept her while Master Thomas and her mother worked in the field. And yet, she never had the nerve to call her grandma.

"Amanda." Miz Temperance said, "Why are you sad? Something is bothering you. You can tell me."

"I guess I's didn't git wat I wanted for Christmas."

With those words, Amanda turned and ran out of the room. She didn't stop until she was outside in the back yard. She folded her arms on the big oak and allowed her head to rest on her arms. Tears streamed down her face. Silently she cried, but she knew that she had to get ready to serve the party. Slowly she moved away from the tree and wiped her tears on the clean white apron.

Noises in the front warned Amanda that some guest had arrived. She went to the kitchen to inform Suckey. When she entered the kitchen, she found that Caroline was already there. She and Suckey were arranging the food on the trays. Amanda looked on.

Caroline glanced over at Amanda. A smile crossed her face, then a deep frown. Amanda knew that Caroline was going to say something very important to her.

"Look, Amanda," she said, "Don't goof up. This is Miz Sallie coming out party. Maser Thomas wants to show her off."

"Yeah," Suckey echoed. "Ain't no beauty like her and Maser married her. She's high society."

Amanda stood there and shook her head. She knew this event was something new for the folks in the valley. The fifty-year-old man wanted to show his neighbors, his twenty-five-year-old wife.

"Well," Amanda picked up a tray of food. "Ifen we's don't serve, they will starve." She looked over her shoulder, "Youse best pick a tray and come on."

When they got to the house and into the huge parlor, it was full of neighbors and relatives. Amanda tuned them out as she served them food and drink. At midnight, the guest at the big house celebrated the coming of a new year. At stroke of nine from the clock on the mantle pieced, some-one began to sing "Auld Lang Syne."

Chapter 9

I t was now 1858 another New Year of slavery for Amanda. Bells rang and gunshots filled the air. There were all kinds whooping and hollering that seemed to echo off the Smoky Mountains. However, down in the slave quarters, there was silence. After the party was over, Amanda went back to her cabin. Sleep called her and she answered the call when her head hit the pallet. And, yet at the crack of dawn when the bell rang, she crawled off the pallet and made her way back to the main house. Quietly she entered the house from the back door. She lit a kerosene lamp and walked to the parlor. It had to be cleaned up before the family awoke. As she stepped into the parlor, she shone the lamp around the room. She stopped where the Christmas Bush was standing. It was still intact. She had mixed feeling about that bush. As a slave, she knew she didn't need any more bad luck.

Placing the lamp on the mantle, she began cleaning up the room. Caroline came to help. By the time the master and mistress got up everything was back in place. Carolina and Amanda had even put up the greenery with the anticipation that Christmas which was only five days away.

Everything seemed peaceful, as each slave avoided the other. They knew that after Christmas, it was back to work. Besides, it was New Year's Day and all kind of superstitions filled the air. Not only did the slaves observe those traditions and superstitions, the white folks did also. Amanda was tempted to upset the ox cart, but she felt bad luck would make it worse for the slaves. Therefore, when she was ordered to go to the kitchen, she didn't hesitate. Suckey was there and it was either obey or quarrel with her. She obeyed to keep the peace.

"Suckey," Amanda sighed. "I ain't gonna argue with youse. I 'member was Miz Temperance says 'bout New Year's Day."

"An' wat was dat?"

"Youse shouldn't quarrel on New Year's Day or youse be quarrelin' all year long."

"I guess youse rat. Wat youse come here fer?"

"Miz Sallie wanna know ifen youse a fixin' the New Year's Day feast."

" 'Course. We's gonna haft field peas with ham hocks, turnip greens and heapin' of sweet taters. Dis here meal is shore to bring good luck an' wealth to all."

"Shore." Amanda said sarcastically. "Fer de master an' his family."

"Now Amanda!"

"Yeah, I's know. None of us slaves need any bad luck."

Leaving the kitchen, Amanda reported the news to Miz Sallie. Everyone on Stekoa Fields could eat the traditional New Year's Day feast. This was one of the days that master and slave partook of the same meal. The slave dinner would be set up outside with an old barn door as a tabletop with four barrels for the legs. From the main house's ragbag an old tablecloth was tosses over the old barn door. Suckey cooked the meal for the Thomas's, while each female slave in quarters pitched in and cooked their meal. It was like a potluck supper, but it had all ingredients to make the slaves' life good for 1858.

It was at this gathering that Power and Alfred became part of Thomas's slave family. Right away Flossie spotted them as they came for dinner. Amanda saw them, too. As the two walked to potluck supper of wild greens, ham, sweet taters, and other delicious dishes, Flossie sized them up.

"Amanda...look...fresh meat."

"Yeah, I see."

"Nobody wants crazy Dave and his brothers are too young."

"Dey're all yer."

"Come on, Mandy. Mature men."

"Is dat wat Maser promised youse?'

'No!" Flossie answered angrily. "Wat are youse talkin' 'bout?"

"Good God," Amanda started to walk away, but Flossie grabbed her arm. "Here dey come."

"Wat did youse make dat on the table." Power said as he looked deep into Amanda's eyes.

"Nothin'." She said, "I ain't no cook 'round here."

"And you?" He turned his attention to Flossie.

"I fixed the greens."

"I bet dey are delicious."

"Com'n," Flossie insisted, "Git youse a plate an' pile it up."

Amanda watched as Power flirted with Flossie. She glanced over where Alfred was standing and knew that Alfred wanted Flossie. The two were going to fight over Flossie. She knew that Master would perhaps have the last say. What did it matter, for she had no interest in them? She got a plate of food and took it to her mother. Remaining at the cabin she listened to the merriment. Everyone on Stekoa Fields was happy except Amanda. Her world was falling apart.

Her mother had joined the celebration. Alone in the cabin, Amanda thought about Bill...William Hudson Casey. He consumed her every minute. Dreaming about him always left her exhausted, but happy. No boy had ever made her feel this way, not even Charley, the handsome Lufty Cherokee, who was her partner when they shucked corn two or three summers ago.

Tears came. Amanda wanted them to stop then from falling, but her emotions would not let her. Silently, she cried. Going over to the bed, she laid across it. Hoping sleep would consume her so that she could dream about Bill. For it would only be in her dreams that she would or could see him.

Then a knuckle knocked on her door.

"Go away."

"Mandy," a male voice called her name. "Mandy, it's me, Power."

She started to tell him to go away, but she changed her mind. Slowly she got up and wiped the tears from her face. When she opened the door, Power walked right in and closed the door behind him.

"I talk'd to yer mama. Are you 'lright?"

"I's be fine."

"It be a new year." He took both of her hands in his. "Let's cel'brak'?"

He tried to get her to dance the jig with him. At first Amanda resisted, and then she gave in and danced with him. For it was a new year and there should be no quarrels.

Two days later, as Amanda made her way to the big house, she saw Sam and Cudge. They were headed toward the woods. Sam had an axe slung over his right shoulder. Right away, Amanda knew that Master Thomas had sent them to fetch a Christmas tree. Also out and about were Power and Alfred. They were making their way towards the woods also. The two slaves were purchased from Mr. Abraham Wiggins of Macon County. The slaves had been bought on an installment plan. When Mr. Wiggins died, the two slaves were still legally be a part of his estate. After a lengthy court battle, Master Thomas had to pay Wiggins' heirs the remaining charge. The two slaves were bought to work at Shoal Creek with Mr. James Terrell as their boss. It was rumored that Master Thomas had bought them to Stekoa Fields to meet some young female niggers. Amanda knew she was one of unattached female niggers.

However, Amanda had no desire to become acquainted with either one of them. When she saw them, she

VICTORIA A. CASEY MCDONALD

tried to walk by without speaking to them. She increased her speed as she walked, but Power came up beside her. He fell in step with her and walked with her, as Alfred trailed slightly behind.

" G' mornin, Amanda."

"G'mornin, Power."

"Tanks fer lettin' me share New Years with youse."

"Shore. I jest want'd the new year to start off rat." She laughed, "Mama 'lways tol' ifen a man comes to yer door first, you hav' good luck de 'hole year. Tanks fer cheerin' me up."

She started to move away, but he stopped and caught her arm. She stopped also.

"Dis here is Alfred."

Amanda looked from Power to Alfred. "Goods to meet youse."

"We's gonna spend Christmas here."

'Yeah," Alfred agreed. "We's gonna go git the Yule log."

"Git the biggest hickory stump youse can find." Amanda moved away from Power.

"We's plans to." Power assured her.

Alfred shook his head in agreement.

"Youse make shore dat youse soak it real goods in de riv'r, so's dat it will burn fere'er."

"Shore," Power agreed. "The long'r it burns, de mor' time fer ev'ybody to just rest."

"Yeah."

Laughter spilled from Alfred's mouth. "Youse mean in som'one arms."

They didn't wait for Amanda's reply. She watched as they headed for the woods.

She felt that everyone on Stekoa Field knew that Bill was sent back to the Loves' farm.

Of course, she wished she could spend some time with Bill, but Master Thomas had already spoiled that. Now Power and Alfred tried to flirt with her, but she pretended that it didn't happen. At this point, she didn't want a mate if she couldn't have Bill. And yet she had permitted Power to enter her mama's house. They had only danced and talked, but Amanda knew he wanted more. She hated herself for giving in to superstitions.

She continued on to the main house. After helping with the New Year's party, she was now working as a house servant. As she went about her chores, she saw the house was a constant reminder of Bill. She didn't want to see Master Thomas or Miz Sallie. It seemed they just wanted her to work as house servant so that they could keep an eye on her. However, she tolerated the situation because she could talk to Miz Temperance.

Around noon, Sam and Cudge returned with a huge balsam fir. Although, Christmas was three days away; Miz Sallie wanted to put the tree up now. Usually at Stekoa Fields, the tree didn't go up until Christmas Eve. Amanda shook her head as she realized that Miz Temperance was no longer in charge; Miz Sallie was. All morning, she had been rearranging the furniture in the parlor to accommodate the Christmas tree. Miz Sallie had decided to put it the corner near the hearth. From the parlor window, the tree could be seen. Any passerby would be able to see the beautiful tree. The slave children strung popcorn for decoration, while Amanda and Flossie made ribbons to adorn the tree.

Excitement was in the air, as the slave children anticipated the coming of another feast and holiday. Since Master Thomas and Miz Sallie didn't have children, the slave children hoped they would favor them with a Christmas gift. Each child was eying the crate of oranges that had arrived at Stekoa Fields. For the last few years, the pungent smell of an orange being peeled signaled the Christmas season for the slave children. An orange was a rarity in the mountains of Western North Carolina and only appeared in Thomas' store at Christmas. This luxury awaited the slave children, but Amanda had no taste for it, as she had already received her gift and she didn't want another one.

After working in the big house all day, Amanda went to the cabin. Upon opening the door, she found Power sitting at the table with her mother. Their conversation stopped when Amanda entered. She looked from her mother to Power.

"Wat's youse doin' here?"

"Just came to talk with yo' mama."

"I's tir'd. I's gotta git up in de mornin' an' slave fer Miz Sallie."

"I's a goin'." Power got up and head toward the door. "Ple'sure Martha."

After Power left, Amanda stood there and just stared at her mother. She couldn't believe that Power had the nerve to come to her cabin.

Anger rose in her throat as she choked out. "I dare'im."

"He just came to visit, chile."

"Yeah," Amanda sighed. "Why ain't he slavin' like I's be doin' 'stead of sittin' 'round like he's owns de place."

Turning away from her mother, Amanda went to her pallet and tossed her body across it. In a matter of minutes sleep claimed her body. As she lay there, she dreamed of Bill. She saw him running across the field to greet her. Both of their arms were out stretched. Just as they were about to embrace, she woke up in a cold sweat. Sitting up, she realized she was on her pallet. Bill was not there.

Chapter 10

It was now Christmas Eve and Amanda was assigned to the big house. Caroline got a three-day pass to spend Christmas at White Sulphur Springs. Hence Amanda would take Caroline's place while she was gone. Amanda worried about Caroline, because Bill had told her that her man was with another woman. Before she left Amanda wanted to tell her, but felt that would be too cruel. At any rate, with Caroline was gone, Amanda became Miz Sallie personal servant and Flossie helped Suckey prepare the food and clean the house.

Everything seemed to going well, but deep down, Amanda was troubled. With a stolid look on her face, she served the Thomas's. She was on her best behavior and yet, she couldn't help being angry at Master Thomas. He was mating her with Power, and she didn't want him. Besides that she had to see Mr. James Love again. He would remind her of Bill, the love of her life. As she moped about the house, she tried to keep her anger from showing; but Miz Temperance knew her too well.

"What's troubling you, girl?" She asked.

"Nuthin'."

"For the last few days, you haven't been yourself."

"I's fine."

"Remember the Christ child, who gave his life for us." She patted Amanda's hand. "My son is treating you well, since I moved."

"Yes sum."

"How is your mother?"

"She's fine."

"You know Mandy; I just left so Miss Sallie could be the only Mistress at Stekoa Fields. You understand?"

Amanda just shook her head.

It being Christmas season, she didn't want to dampen Miz Temperance's spirit. Instead, she went about her chores, helping her Master prepare for Christmas. She didn't know how Miz Sallie would observe Christmas with the slaves, but remembered what Miz Temperance did.

In the past, all the slaves were invited to the big house. They would gather around the front porch to put the last of the roses on the Christmas Bush. Each slave's family placed a rose on the Bush. Miz Temperance invited her family, the Colvards of Cherokee County. They would gather in the parlor and just before the clock on the fireboard struck midnight; Master Thomas would light the Yule log. As the log hissed and burned, Miz Temperance would have each person toss a sprig of holly into the fire to rid the house of evil spirits. Then she would tell the story of Christ's birth. Although she was a slave, Amanda and her mother shared this moment with Master Thomas and his mother, Miz Temperance.

This year, Amanda decided that she wasn't going to attend the celebration. She would have her own celebration in her cabin. After all, her slave cabin needed to be cleansed and all the evil spirits taken away. So while most of the slaves were at the house helping them get rid of evils spirits, she would get her own Yule log and put it on her hearth. From the big house, she had stolen some sprigs of holly. Before she left the big house, she found Sam. He was inside the barn. Humming a Christmas tune, he was carving a toy for Cudge. Sam looked up when she came in.

Wat can I's do for youse?"

"I's need a Yule log."

"Master Thomas 'lready got one.

"Dis fer me."

"I see."

"Youse wanna great big one. I knows youse wanna take all de evil spirits out of yo' mama's house."

"Cans youse help?"

"I 'pect I's can. Gotta go git fire wood for the kitchen. its kinda gittin' low."

"Youse shore youse won't forgit."

"Nope."

She hugged his neck and kissed him on the cheek. "Thanks, Sam."

"I's drop it off at the cabin sometimes 'morrow."

Amanda left the barn and went on to her quarters. When she got there, she told her mother that Miz Temperance asked about her and requested that she come tomorrow.

The next day, when Amanda came home, she found her mother was gone. Walking in the cabin, she also found Sam had gotten the Yule log. It was damp and just big enough for the small hearth. Lying on the bed, she saw some sprigs of holly. At her request, Martha had cleaned up the place. The dirt floor had been swept. The bed covers were pulled up and the table was cleared. Amanda lit the candle that was on the table and sat down by the fireplace. She chanted quietly allowing the evil spirits to go away. Afterward, she took the Yule log and placed it on the fire in the hearth. Immediately sparks flew as the wet log attempted to burn. As the Yule log smoked, Amanda realized that she was going to smoke up the place. Then all the evil spirits will stay. Running to the door, she opened it and there stood Power.

"Wat in the world are youse doin'?"

"Gittin' rid of evil spirits like youse."

He laughed, "Yo' mama tole me to come."

"Wat fer?"

"Said dat youse be awaitin'."

"Waitin' fer wat?"

"Look," He held her by the shoulders. "Maser said dat

youse is mind."

"No, Power. Jest cause I was kind 'nuff to let youse spend some time with me New Year's day...I ain't yours."

"Maser say so."

"I's ain't no piece of meat fer youse to chew on."

As they talked the Yule log continued to hiss and let off a lot of smoke. Both, Amanda and Power started coughing. Before Amanda could stop him, Power took a rag off the hearth and jerked the Yule log out of the fire and ran to the door. Just as he got to the door, he let it fly. All the while that Power was attempting to eliminate the house of smoke; she was beating him on the back.

"No! No!" she cried. "No!" She fell to the floor and sobbed. "Youse ruin'd ev"ything."

Power stood over her.

"Git out," she shouted, "Git out."

Leaving the door opened, Power quietly left. The ritual of the Yule log was ruined. To Amanda that meant a bad omen. Things were not going to be all right for the rest of the year. Power had ruined it.

When Power returned with a slightly damp Yule log in his arm, Mandy was asleep in the bed. Still holding the Yule log, he looked at her sleeping form. He wanted her, but she wanted nothing to do with him. He went over to the hearth and carefully placed the Yule log on the dying embers. A trail of fine white smoke went up the chimney as the fire tried to consume the log. Living in these parts, he knew the ritual. From his pocket, he took some holly sprigs and flung them one at a time into the fire. He tossed three. One was for Martha, the other for Amanda and the last one was for him. He wanted to join this household.

Mandy still didn't stir. Power returned to her bed and thought of the cold barn, which he had to sleep for the night. In this cabin, beside Amanda would be cozy. When morning came and she saw the Yule log burning, she would be happy. Removing his shoes and his shirt, he slid quietly into the bed and wrapped his arms around her. She stirred in her sleep and there was a smile etched on her face. In her sleep, she whispered Bill and snuggled up against Power's body.

When morning came, Power untangled himself from Amanda and left. She was still in her dream world, when the bell from the big house rang in her ears. Getting up, she felt almost refreshed. In her dreams, Bill had made love to her. Looking around, he was gone. Going over to the hearth, she found a Yule log burning and the remains of holly branches. Hence, Bill had been there and placed the log in the fire or was it Power. Anger engulfed her body.

"Damn it." she said as she stared in the flames at the Yule log.

Superstitions got the best of her thoughts. If Power completed the ritual, he would be hers before the year was gone. It wasn't fair. She tried to rebuke the ritual, but she didn't know how. Everything was falling apart. In her dreams, it was Bill, not Power who had made love with her last night. She had to believe that. Bill was somewhere on Stekoa Fields. She had to find him.

When Amanda wasn't working, she searched for Bill, but she never found him. She didn't ask anyone about him. Deep down, she knew it was Power, not Bill, who had shared her bed last night. All during the week of Christmas, Amanda avoided Power. She didn't want to know the truth and yet the smile on his face and the wink of his eyes told Amanda that it was he, not Bill, who violated her body. She was vexed. With Christmas over, Power and Alfred returned to Shoal Creek and Amanda was glad they were gone. And she was saddened that Miz Temperance returned to her home on Shoal Creek.

Chapter 11

Shortly afterward, Senator Thomas returned to Raleigh and Cudge went with him. Sam was in charge of all the slaves, but he had to have Miz Sallie's Approval. The Yule log had since gone out and the slaves at Stekoa Fields were busy getting ready for spring planting. Seeds had to be ordered and field cleared from the late planting season. Everyone was doing their share of the work. Amanda was promoted to be the personal maid of Miz Sallie, because Caroline remained at White Sulphur Springs to be with her man. Although Amanda didn't like the idea, there was nothing she could do about it. However, she could keep up with the "white" news. From the crack of dawn to the twilight of the evening, Amanda spent her time in the big house. When the last light of day was lost, she made her way to the slave quarters to nurse her mother

Flossie remained in the kitchen with Suckey. Like Amanda, Flossie returned to the slave quarters at night. As they walked along, they noticed the sky was clear. The stars seemed to dance about in the heavens. A shooting star shot across the sky as the cold February weather engulfed them.

"Dat was beau'ful," Flossie remarked.

"Dat shootin' star," Amanda laughed.

"Did youse make a wish?"

"Dere's no need," Amanda looked in the sky in search of it. "Only de white man gits his wishes.

"I's made a wish."

"Wat?"

"Ifen I tell ya, it won't come true."

They were near Amanda quarters. She broke off from the trail, waved to Flossie and made her way to see about her mother. As she walked through this short cut of unfamiliar territory, she thought about Power. She hoped that he wasn't waiting for her. Sighing, she wished she had made a wish and perhaps Power would be out of her life forever. Perhaps, she should've wished for Bill to return to Stekoa Field. Sadly, her tears cascaded down chin bone on to the ground. No sound came from her lips, but she heard the cry of a coyote and she knew it was love howl. Wiping the tears from her eyes, she said to night sky, "Hopes he finds the love of his life."

t had been almost three months since Amanda had experience her menstrual cycle. She felt her abdomen and she knew she was with child, but she didn't know whether it was Bill's or Power's. And yet it didn't matter, the child belonged to Maser Thomas, another piece of valuable property. She thought about Power and his wishes to be free. Maybe they could escape and find their way to Harriet's Underground Railroad. Eavesdropping on dinner conversations, she knew Harriet had come into the Deep South and led some of her people to freedom. The train went up and perhaps that meant north. Power would help some.

Just thinking about this, she began to hum a merry tone as she skipped toward her mother's quarters. As she hurried along the dark foreign trail, she stumbled over some rocks. As she fell, she hit the hard winter frosty ground. Landing with a powerful thump on her stomach, the sound echoed in her ears. Slowly, she got to her knees and tried to force herself to stand. However her legs refused to cooperate with her mind. Sinking back to ground, she sobbed.

A few minutes later, Dave, who was prowling around in dark, heard her sobbing and came to her aid. Kneeling beside her, he lifted her up in sitting position and held her in his arms. He allowed her to cry until there was only a whimper coming from her lips. The starry sky gave Dave some light, as he brushed the dried tears from her face.

"Mandy, are you hurt?"

"No."

"Is youse shore?"

"Yes. I's jest angry with mysel'." She insisted, "Jest help me up, so's I's can git home."

"Ok."

Amanda put her arm around Dave's neck and he helped her to her feet. Testing her legs as she put all her weight on Dave, she realized nothing was broken. Never the less, she leaned on Dave's shoulder as they made their way to her quarters. Without knocking, Dave opened the door and guided her into the house. Darkness engulfed the room, except the aura of light from the hearth that attempted to keep the coldness out. He maneuvered her to the chair nearest the heat. From the light of the fire, Amanda discovered there was blood dripping down her legs. Panic took over, but Amanda kept it to herself.

"Dave, wake up my mother." She insisted. "She'l hel' me."

"'Light rite." He went over to the bed and gently aroused Martha out of her sleep. "Martha, Amanda needs youse."

Instantly Martha was awake. Sitting up, she looked around the room. Seeing Amanda slumped in the chair, she got out of bed and hurriedly went to her.

"Youse bleedin'!" She turned to Dave. "Dids you hurt my baby?"

"No!" Dave declared. "I's foun' her."

"Help me lay her down on her pallet."

Without hesitating, he carefully picked up Amanda and carried her to the pallet in the far corner of the room, while Martha gathered her healing portions and clean rags. She carried the medication to the table and lit a candle.

"I'll take care of dis, Dave. Youse go git some wood".

Without questioning her, Dave went outside. Martha cleaned up Amanda who laid there staring into space. It was quiet. After she treated for her wounds, Martha tossed the bloody rags into hearth. Just as she finished, Dave returned with an arm load of twigs and tossed them on the smoking rags.

"Martha, she be 'lright?"

"Fine, jest hep me git her in bed."

Dave picked up Amanda and laid her on the bed.

"Go now...'fore dat damn patty wagon git you. Youse can come back 'morrow."

Without answering Dave left. Martha cleaned up the blood and the room. Because of the night, she secured the lock on the door so no creature, animal or human could get in. Amanda had left a blood trail and coyotes might track it to their quarters. For the remainder of the night Martha lounged in chair, but she didn't get any sleep.

Morning came and Martha confronted Amanda about her accident. Amanda told her what happened and assured her mother that Dave had nothing to do with it. She was grateful that he came along when he did.

"Amanda, are youse going to work at de big house?"

"Yeah, why not?"

"Youse knows dat youse was with child?"

Amanda dropped her head. "Knowed, but I didn't wanna tell youse."

"Who be de father?"

"Power, I spect."

"Dis is our secret."

"What 'bout Dave?"

"Dat don't know anythin' 'bout babies." Martha patted her on the shoulder. 'I's gonna bury de fetus."

"I ain't with child any more?"

"Wen youse fell de child was born, but wasn't ol 'nough to live." Martha sighed, "But youse has to go to work."

Amanda was weak, but she went to work.

Chapter 12

When the last of February rolled around, Miz Sallie finally got a letter from the Senator. Amanda handed it to her as she sat in the parlor. Amanda always lingered near when the mail arrived. She listened to see if Miz Sallie was going make some kind of comment. This morning as she read the letter, Amanda saw excitement in her eyes.

"It's coming!" She said merrily. "Mandy, it's coming!"

Amanda thought Sallie was talking about the rumor of a war between the North and the South.

"Wat's comin'?"

"My piano."

Puzzled, she looked at Sallie. She wasn't quite sure what she was raving about. Amanda figured it was some kind of expensive property. It seemed to her white folks collected property to do with as they pleased. This was something that Miz Sallie would play with, then probably toss it aside when she was tired of it.

Miz Sallie rang the tiny bell on the table and Sam came quickly into the room.

"Yes sum." Sam bowed to Miz Sallie.

"I just received a letter from the Senator."

"Yes sum."

"My Christmas present is in Atlanta."

Now, Amanda knew that it was some type of property.

"Dat's nice," Sam assured her.

"It's my piano."

"Yes sum. When will it arrive?"

"You got to send someone from the store after it."

"Youse wanna me to go down Shoal Creek and tell Mr. Terrell?"

"Yes," Miz Sallie demanded as she waved her hands at them. "Now, both of you go. I'd like to read Senator's letter in private."

"Yes sum."

Amanda left the room.

"Miz Sallie," Sam bowed again, "I needs a pass to go to Shoal Creek."

"I'll get you one. Now go."

Sam left the room to find Amanda just outside the door. When they were out of earshot of Miz Sallie, Amanda demanded, "Wat's a piano?"

"It's a music instrument."

"Like a fiddle."

"It's bigger. Folks say dat it has keys of ivory."

"Ivory?"

"Yeah. Youse know dat the tusk of an eleph'nt."

"Don't know wat youse talkin' 'bout?"

"Nigger, an eleph'nt is an animal in Africa."

"Oh!"

"Ax yo mammy. She be know."

"Shore."

Amanda went about her chores in the big house, while Sam left to make arrangement to get the piano to Stekoa Field. Every day Miz Sallie would ask about the piano. Amanda didn't know how far Atlanta was, nor did she know anything about a piano. However, Miz Sallie would educate her before it arrived.

"Mandy," she asked on the third morning. "Did my piano come?"

"I's don't think so, Miz Sallie."

"It a beauty. There is one at White Sulphur Spring in the music room. I learn to play the piano as a little girl. All my sisters learned to play. My father thought it was socially right that we learn to play the piano."

"It's bigger than the drums the Luftys play?"

"It most surely is bigger. And the music you play on it is beautiful! It's not just boom, boom, boom, like those drums. It's music, classical music!"

Amanda listened and learned. However, for Miz Sallie, the waiting was torture.

"There's sheet music that has notes. You play by notes, Mandy. You use all of your fingers when you play the piano."

"All yo' fingers?"

"Not all at once, Mandy."

Amanda watched as Miz Sallie pretended to play the piano. As she did, she hummed a tune, which sounded beautiful. She looked up at Mandy. "You see, each finger has certain keys to hit to make music."

As Miz Sallie described the piano to Amanda, she began to visualize it. When she went back to her quarters, she played the piano on the table.

"Playin' de piano."

"Miz Sallie got youse wantin' to play de piano?"

"It seems dat way."

Chapter 13

A couple of weeks went by before the piano arrived. Nigger Dick, wagoneer slave of Master Thomas who worked at Shoal Creek store, came to Stekoa Fields. On the wagon pulled by two oxen was a large crate. Power and Alfred held the crate as they stood on each side of it. They appeared to be guarding the tied down crate. Being wintertime, most of the slaves were idle. It was late when the wagon with the heavy load slowly came up the driveway, the slave children following close behind. Something new was arriving and the slaves wanted a glance at it before it went into the big house. Amanda was straightening up the house for the night when she heard and saw all the excitement from the parlor window.

"Miz Sallie," she shouted. "I 'lieve yo piano has arriv'd."

Miz Sallie rushed into the room and looked out the window. "I believe it has. Sam!" she called.

Sam hurriedly made his way to the parlor. "Wat is it, Miz Sallie?"

"My piano has arrived. All the way from Atlanta!"

"It's shore has."

Sam just stood and watched.

"Go help'em!" Miz Sallie seemed beside herself with happiness.

Sam left the parlor and went out the front door with Mandy following him. She too was anxious to see the piano, but she tried to hide her excitement. Amanda tried to tell herself it was just another piece of property that Sallie could play and toy with. By the time she got outside, Alfred and Power already had the crate opened. The gang of slave children gathered around the wagon, as Nigger Dick was trying to push them away.

"Youse kids gotta git 'way. Scoot."

Amanda came down the steps, so fast, she almost tripped. Quickly Power grabbed her left arm to prevent her from falling. His grip was powerful, as he looked into her eyes. A toothless grin lit up his face. For a split second their eyes locked, and then Amanda turned and jerked away. Immediately, he let go, but he continued to stare at her. She felt his eyes staring at her.

"Stand back," she ordered and the slave children obeyed.

While she kept the children back, Power and Alfred with the help of Nigger Dick and Sam unloaded the piano. It was a square four-legged Chickering piano with a swivel stool. As the four slaves carried the piano, Amanda heard Sallie calling her. She left the children in the capable hands of her mother and dashed into the house. She ran around the house and entered from the back door. Running down the long hall, she was in the parlor beside her mistress in a matter of seconds.

"Yes sum."

"Open that door and let them in,"

"Yes sum." Amanda sighed.

Rushing to the front door, she held it open as the four slaves carried the piano into hall. After they got the piano in the hall, Amanda closed the front door on the curious onlookers. The four put the piano down in the hall. Perspiration ran down their black faces. From around Power's waist, he pulled a large kerchief and mopped the sweat from his shiny coffee face. He winked at Amanda. She turned away from him and looked at the piano. She couldn't leave because she knew that Sallie would need her assistance. She moved to the farthest corner of the room and watched as the men rolled the piano into the space Miz Sallie pointed to. In a few minutes, the piano was setup and ready to play. Miz Sallie opened the keyboard and lovingly ran her fingers across the ivory. She looked around for the stool, but it wasn't there.

"This piano didn't come with a stool?"

"Yes sum," Power answered. "It be still on the wagon."

"Mandy," Miz Sallie ordered. "Go get it."

"Yes sum."

Amanda quickly left to get the stool, Power followed her. Quicker than Amanda, he bounded down the steps and leaped into the wagon to retrieve the stool. She stood by the wagon as Power with the stool in his hand, leaped off the wagon and stood just inched away from Amanda. He smiled down at her. She grabbed for the stool, Power put the stool out of her reach.

"Who are youse?"

"I's a slave just like youse."

"Youse belong to Senator Thomas, too. Youse is the one dat Alfred and me talk'd to when we were a goin' after dat Yule log. I's met yo' mama. Didn't git dat cabin cleanse of evil spirit?."

A twinkle danced in his eyes and Mandy knew he was the one who replaced the Yule log and slept with her.

"I's here ain't I?" Amanda reached again for the stool. "Let me haft it. Dearest Sallie ain't gonna be too happy."

Power laughed and handed her the stool. She snatched it from his grip and ran into the house.

Miz Sallie had seen the whole scene. When Amanda got inside and put the stool in front of the piano, Miz Sallie sat down at the piano. As she adjusted the stool, she scolded Amanda.

"I saw you out there flirting with him."

"No," Amanda said, "He be a flirtin' wit' me."

"Sure." Miz Sallie tickled the ivory. "That sounds great."

"Yes sum."

Miz Sallie smiled devilishly at Amanda. "Go ahead, talk to him."

Amanda couldn't disobey Dearest Sallie. She looked at Dearest Sallie, who had gone back to playing the piano.

"Nature calls," Dearest Sallie sang. "Nature calls again. When the winter is cold, nature calls."

Amanda was rooted to the spot, as Dearest Sallie turned and smiled at her. "Go. And on your way out, tell Sam to come here."

"Yes sum."

She left and gave Sam the message.

Chapter 14

Since it was late, Nigger Dick parked the wagon and oxen in the barn. They weren't going to risk being caught by Mr. Bumgarner's Patrol. This was the message that Sam converted to them from Miz Sallie. She also had Martha to stay with her that night.

All this scheming was done without Amanda's knowledge. That night, as she entered her cabin, she found Power seated at the table. Looking around the room, she saw her mother was nowhere to be found. Panic gripped Amanda's heart. Rushing into the room, she fell on her knees at Power's feet.

"Oh,no!" she cried, "Not mama!"

Power took her hands in his and pulled her onto his lap. "Yo' mammy's fine."

"Wat are youse doin' here?" She attempted to untangle herself from his arms.

"Just wanna talk to youse."

She tried to slap him, but he held her hands too tightly. Looking into his hazel lazy eyes, she knew that Dearest Sallie had sent him. There was nothing she could do. He was too strong for her. His tall dark frame was strong and muscular as he held her on his lap. There was that silly grin, which spread across his face.

"Youse like me, Mandy," He continued to grin.

"Let me go." Again, she tried to get away.

"Suckey says dat youse is available."

"Not to you."

"Youse think youse better dan anybody 'lse."

"I's a slave just likk youse."

"An' we's just likk de dogs an' the other animals on dis place."

"No," Amanda protested. "I's a person. I's likk to choose who I be with."

"Likk youse did when youse tossed me out."

"I knew'd dat it was youse. You replac'd my Yule log, ten came to my bed whiles I was asleep."

"Maybe?" He kissed her on the forehead. "My wife was sol' from me 'fore Master Thomas bough' me. He says ifen I jump de broom with anyone on Stekoa Fields, we won't be separated."

Amanda felt sorry for him, but she didn't willingly accept his sexual advances, although she had unknowingly already given in to him.

Chapter 15

The next morning the three slaves of Thomas's went back to Shoal Creek. Amanda lay on the bed in a fetal position. She felt that Miz Sallie had violated her by allowing Power to come in and have his own way with her. Indeed, she felt like an animal. With Bill, it had been beautiful, but this was rape. Lying there she wondered if Master Thomas had force himself on her mother.

Slowly, she got up and went outside. The day was cold and dreary. Looking up in the sky, Amanda saw the snow cloud. Before the day was over, it would snow. She surmised that the world itself was not happy with the way peope treated each other.In need of being cleansed, Amanda realized that the river was too cold to submerse her body. Therefore, she would get water from the rain barrel and bring it back inside. The top layer of the water was frozen. With the bucket, she broke the thin sheet of ice and got a bucketful.

Time was short and Amanda had to hurry. Shortly, she would be needed at the main house. Pouring the icy cold water in the huge wash pot hanging over the hearth, she hoped it would heat quickly. Her mother always said that a watched pot never boils; therefore, she prayed that water would get lukewarm. She went outside and got more wood to fuel the dying flames. As she waited, the small cabin seemed to close in on her. The walls appeared to be moving in, and then moving out. She realized that her imagination was playing tricks with her.

Since there was a little water in the pot, the process of heating the icy water did not take long. After all, the pot held heat. In a short time, the water was lukewarm. Amanda took the dipper and poured some in the old chipped basin that her mother had retrieved from the big house. Effectively and quickly, Amanda washed and dried herself, and then she dressed. She felt a little better, but her inner soul was torn apart. Although she was stolidity, she had to appear happy.

With her shabby shawl tucked about her shoulders and chest, Amanda emerged from the cabin with all hope dashed. Just as she stepped out the door, Flossie came running to her. Happiness bounced off of Flossie's feet and Amanda didn't want to know why. And yet, she knew Flossie would tell her.

"He came!"

"Who?" Amanda laughed, "The Bogey Man?"

"Dat's not funny." Flossie skipped along in front of Amanda, and then she stopped and faced her. "Youse knows dat Miz Sallie sent him to me."

"Alfred?"

"Yes."

"Wat did youse do," Amanda said sarcastically, "Roll in the hay all night."

"Shore did."

"Are youse gonna jump de broom with'im?"

"Ifen dat wat Missy wants."

The two walked in silence. Amanda had no more to say. When they got to the big house, Flossie went to the kitchen to inform Suckey of the night's event. Mandy watched her go, and then walked in the back door of the big house. She lit an oil lamp that was setting on a side table. She went upstairs to the Master bedroom, she found her mother sleeping on a pallet at the foot of the master bed. Miz Sallie was still asleep. Mandy thought she might be up playing that piano. She looked at her peaceful sleeping form and wondered what she was dreaming about. Was it the love of her life Willie or Willie's gift, the piano? Shaking her head, Mandy knew that Miz Sallie was dreaming about both of them.

Amanda opened the curtains in the Master bedroom, so the morning light could awake her Mistress. With the lamp she went back downstairs and checked to see that all the room were neat and in order. As she was going the walk through, her mother came downstairs. The two faced each other. Martha looked away from her daughter and started for the back door. Mandy followed her.

When the door closed behind them, Mandy verbally attacked her mother. "How could youse do dis to me? Allowing Power to rape me, when youse wouldn't allow Mr. Bumgarner to do so. Is dat de way Master Thomas did youse? Come into yo' room an' violate youse."

"Please, Mandy, I had nothin' to do with it."

Ashamed and hurt, Amanda dropped her head. "Go Mama. I's know we be slaves. We be owned by Maser Thomas and his wife. Go back to the slave quarter 'til dey need yo' help 'gain."

She turned her back on her mother and headed for the kitchen. She moved slowly because she couldn't face them. Suckey and Flossie were recapping last night love encounter, which was orchestrated by Miz Sallie. Mandy tried to approach this as business. It was personal and she didn't want to listen to their bubbling voices of happiness. Just how long will it last. Suckey had children, but their father wasn't around. Master Thomas didn't want to break up a family, but he forgot the father. His only father figure was Yonaguska chief of Luftys and the chief adopted him.

As she went into the kitchen, she found, Flossie and Suckey talking as they fixed breakfast for Miz Sallie. She stopped and listened to them. Then she picked up a tray that was already fixed.

"Is dis for Miz Sallie?

They stopped and looked at Mandy.

"Yeah." Suckey answered.

"I's take it to her." Mandy took the tray and started out the door, as Suckey called after her.

"Is Miz Sallie gonna play dat piano all day today?"

"Did youse herd it all night, while Nigger Dick was bedding youse down?"

"I herd dat Power was sent to your place."

"Who tole youse dat?"

"A littl' birdy."

"Yeah, I jest bet."

"Come on Mandy," Flossie assured her, "It be fun. We ain't gonna see them again."

"Wat ifen youse git with child?"

"I'll be took care of. Just likk Suckey's children."

"We's slaves. They can sell yo' child."

"Senator Thomas doesn't do dat."

"Wat 'bout Miz Sallie? She might."

The two looked at each other. They had not thought of Miz Sallie. Amanda left them to think about it, while she returned to the household to give Miz Sallie her breakfast in bed. When she got to the bedroom, she knocked on the door. There was no answer. After knocking three more times, she slowly opened the door. Sallie wasn't in the room. Her bed clothing was on the unmade bed. The wardrobe was opened, which indicated that Miz Sallie was dressed and somewhere downstairs. Then Amanda heard the piano. Someone was softly playing it.

Mandy shook her head and retraced her steps downstairs and then followed the sound of the music. Miz Sallie was seated at the piano. Mandy watched her hands as they glided over the black and white keys. It seemed like magic to Amanda. If only she could play beautiful music. The fiddle and the drums could not compare with the piano.

When Miz Sallie finished the piece, Amanda announced, "Here's yo' breakfast."

Miz Sallie looked up at Amanda. "Mandy, isn't that beautiful."

"Yes sum."

"I could teach you to play."

"I's don't know." Mandy laughed, "Dere too many black and white keys."

"It's not that bad." Miz Sallie showed Mandy the scale as her fingers moved from end of the piano to the other. "C, D, E, F, G, A, B, and again C, D, E, F, G, A, B. Over and over they are the same notes. It's just that the pitch gets higher or lower."

After she finished the diatonic scale, she turned to Mandy. "Did you hear the different sounds?"

"Yes sum."

Miz Sallie moved from the piano stool and picked up her tray of food. "It's cold."

She shoved the tray toward Mandy. "Go get me some more breakfast. This is cold."

Amanda took the tray and left. She went to the kitchen and fixed another tray of food for Miz Sallie. Suckey wasn't pleased, but Mandy explained that Miz Sallie was too busy playing the piano.

"We herd it." Suckey said. "Is she gonna play dat thing all day long."

"I's think it's sounds beautiful."

"I'd rather listen to Sam play is fiddle."

"Yeah." Amanda agreed.

"Here's Miz Sallie's tray. I hope she shuts dat thing up."

"Yeah," Amanda took the tray and left.

She heard the music once more and followed it. Placing the tray on the dining room table, she reminded Miz Sallie that her breakfast was hot and ready for her. Without waiting for Miz Sallie to reply, Amanda went upstairs to begin her work. She went to the Master bedroom and tossed the dirty linen off the bed. Taking the bundle of linen in her arms, she took them downstairs and placed them in the ante room off the back entrance.

As she went back upstairs, she noticed that Miz Sallie was eating her breakfast. Amanda sighed and continued her chores in the Master bedroom. From under the bed, she took the covered bed chamber and set it outside the bedroom door. From a chest at the foot of the bed, she selected clean linen for the bed. Humming softly, she made the bed, which included putting the bed spread and arranging the pillows on the bed.

Before she forgot, she retrieved the bedchamber from the hall and took it outside. Disregarding the coldness, she dumped the body waste into the outdoor toilet and cleaned the pot with rain water from the barrel. After cleaning it, she returned it to the bedroom and placed it under the bed. Going over to the vanity set, she cleaned the porcelain wash bowl. She tossed the remaining water out of the decorative porcelain pitcher that matched the wash bowl out the window. After putting the vanity set back in place, she swept the room and shook the dust off of the small rugs by shaking them out the window.

Before she left, she surveyed her work, then swept the upstairs hall and made a quick check of the other bedrooms. As she glanced at them, she promised herself that she would clean those rooms of spider webs that were hidden in corners.

From downstairs, she could hear Miz Sallie once again playing the piano. Amanda was sure she was lonely out in the wilderness without her siblings. The piano became her companion. At least, she could sing along with the music she played. Sometimes it was music that Sallie called classical, that had no words. When that occurred, Mandy make up words to fit the occasion and this was one of them.

Bill, my love is a smithy
Who hammers all day
Bill, my love is smithy
But he has been sent away!

Mandy made up many songs buried in her brain. And

each time she sang one of the songs as she worked, there was always a different twist. However, the song about Bill was always the same. It was a mournful song that Mandy hummed as she worked. This made the day go faster. When Miz Sallie wasn't playing the piano, Mandy hummed. Some days, Miz Sallie demanded that Mandy rest awhile and listen to her play. Other days, she attempted to teach her the diatonic scale. Side by side at the piano, Miz Sallie allowed her to tickle the ivory.

"Come on, Mandy." Miz Sallie positioned Mandy's fingers, on the piano keys. "It's easy.

"Mandy tried it again and again. Therefore, when the members of the household went to church, Mandy would sneak in the house and play the diatonic scale. Over and over, she attempted the scales until one Sunday morning, it all came together. As she played the diatonic scale, she recited the letters aloud. "C, D, E, F, G, A, B."

Suddenly she stopped. Again she played the scale and repeated each letter. It made her happy, for she realized those notes were letters...letters that white folks learn to read. Closing the piano and putting the piano stool back in place, Amanda ran out of the house. She hurried to her quarters. Sliding through the front door, she shouted to her mother.

"Mama!" she called.

"Calm down" Martha reminded her. "Don't shout."

"Listen, did youse know dat de musical on a pinan was the same letters white folks use in writin'?"

"Girl, has youse been on dat pinan 'gain?

"Yes. I learn'd the note scale."

"Somebody gonna tell Dearest Sallie."

On their dirt floor Amanda made letters. Martha watched as Amanda formed them. She really didn't understand, but she thought the alphabet started with C. However, Martha cautioned her not to tell anyone for slaves were forbidden to learn how to write.

"Yes sum."

Chapter 16

The winter months passed, but Amanda never saw Bill again. It seemed that Mr. Love kept him at White Sulphur Springs. However, Power came on the weekends to see her, just as Alfred courted Flossie. Senator Thomas was still in Raleigh and Miz Sallie played the piano. It appeared she was happy with her toy. She taught Amanda the scales and attempted to teach her the notes on pieces of music, but Amanda couldn't get all those shapes in her head. This is what made Amanda happy, not the courtship forced upon her. She longed for Bill. However in March, Miz Sallie announced there was going to be some slaves' marriage. Right way, Mandy knew she was one of them. Sadly, she listened to what Miz Sallie told her. As usual, Miz Sallie had Mandy sittingt beside her at the piano.

"This is a love song," Miz Sallie announced, as she played. "You've been seeing Power." Amanda knew she was catch between a rock and a hard place. No matter was she did or said, it would get back to Miz Sallie. She was the slave and Miz Sallie was the Mistress.

"Power said he loved you and wanted to marry you."

Amanda froze. She couldn't answer. She just listened as Miz Sallie told her what was to happen.

That evening as she sat in her cabin with her mother, Flossie came dashing through the door. She grabbed Amanda up and danced her around the floor. She knew that Miz Sallie had told her the news. All the folks in the slave quarters were buzzing about the news.

"Youse herd de news."

"I's herd."

"We's gonna jump de broom Friday night unter de stars."

Martha looked surprisingly at Amanda. "Youse too."

"Wat do youse think?"

"I guess youse are."

Flossie stopped and looked at Amanda. "Ain't youse happy?"

"Yeah." Amanda answered.

"Let's go over to the big house and look in the rag-bag."

"Okay." Flossie hugged Amanda. "But times awastin'."

Flossie dashed out the door into the night. Amanda looked at her mother. Neither one of them said a thing. Each had their own thoughts. Just in few days, Amanda would be in loveless marriage and there was nothing she could do about it. She could run away, but where would she go. Hiding among the Luftys was a good idea. After all Senator Thomas was their chief and her owner. She had no choice. Marrying Power was final.

Flossie and Amanda rummaged through the ragbag and found two discarded dresses which needed a few alterations and repairs. Both girls went to the seamstress and asked her to fix them. They tried on the dresses at the seamstress cabin in the slave quarters. The seamstress assured them the dresses would ready by Friday night.

At sundown on Friday, Power and Alfred arrived from Shoal Creek. With them was Mr. Terrell, who would perform the ceremony. Dick, the wagoneer, left to haul a load of supplies for the Senator. Suckey was upset. In front of the main house, the slaves gathered. From the ragbag, Amanda wore a faded blue and white checkered dress, while Flossie wore a washed-out brown one. Power and Alfred wore their usual clothing, except they had acquired an old suit jacket from Mr. Terrell.

Sam played the fiddle as the piano music flowed out the big house. It seemed so romantic as each couple stood before Mr. Terrell. Two older slaves held a broom out in front of the two couples. Power held Amanda hand tightly. He looked at her and smiled his toothless grin. Amanda couldn't smile, only tears smarted her eyes. Listening to the classical music being played on the piano, Amanda thought of Bill. More tears came down.

The music stopped and Mr. Terrell opened a book. Neither of the couples knew what kind of book it was. It didn't matter, they would jump the broom.

Mr. Terrell said, "Do you two couple want to be man and wife?

They all said yes.

"I announce you man and wife." He raised the book in the air and shouted, "Jump the broom!"

Flossie and Alfred quickly jumped over the broom and the slaves shouted and whistled. Then, Power forced the hestitant Amanda to jump over the broom. Claps and shouts echoed through the valley. Another nigger had gotten married at the Thomas place.

They celebrated with apple cider provided by Dearest Sallie. Alfred and Power had passes for the weekend. Mr. Terrell would return and take them back Sunday afternoon. Now Mr. Terrell had to get back to Shoal Creek. Saturday was always a busy day at the store.

Two empty cabins had been cleaned out by Alfred and Power. Now the two couples ran a gauntlet as the slaves stood on each side. Flowers and weeds were tossed at the couples as they ran through it. Laughter and happiness filled the air. It was a gala for all the slaves at Stekoa Fields...except Mandy.

Finally the two couples found their respective cabin. When they got to the door of their cabin, Power picked up Amanda and carried her inside. Someone had lit the candle, which set on the table with two old chairs setting around it. Power carried her to table's edge and sat down in one of the chairs. With the weight of both their bodies, the chair's legs gave away and they went crashing to the floor. Power landed on the floor with Amanda still on his lap. He held her tight and laughed. Amanda thought it was funny and she laughed and cried at the same time. Gently, Power tried to wipe her tears, but they continued. Now she was laughing out of control. Crying and laughing, Amanda couldn't make herself stop. Power held her as she sobbed and giggled. Now she couldn't catch her breath. She was breathing heavy. He attempted to shake her, but she still laughed and cried, gasping for breath as she did. Without another thought, Power slapped her across the face. As quickly as she started, she stopped and whimpered like a defeated animal.

In all truths, she was defeated. She laid her head on his chest. Slavery had defeated her. Slavery had degraded her. It didn't matter for she had been turned into a mere piece of property.

"Is I yer' now?" She looked up at Power. "Wat kinda of tricks do youse wanna me to perform?"

Power kissed her forehead. "Amanda, I love youse."

"We can't love Mr. Power. We can't. We's just someone's property."

Chapter 17

Their life began together and yet apart. Amanda understood his need for another woman after his former Master had sold his wife. She still loved Bill and sometimes pretended Power was Bill, but never mentioned his name. The best thing about their jumping the broom was that Power worked at Shoal Creek at the store. He could only come on the last weekend of the month. Amanda counted the days down by marking the days with a stick at the corner of the hearth. When she was small, she learned to count for her mother taught her. On the day before he was to come, she prayed that Mr. Terrell would want to keep him. When that happened, she was ecstatic. During the winter months, she would miss his warm body next to hers. And yet, she continued to think about Bill.

It was April in the hills of Western North Carolina when the creation of life began again. The sights, the sounds, and the smells of springs were creeping over the land. On Stekoa Fields, the slaves were in the fields as they planted corn in the furrowed soil. Getting their feet and hands in the soil, the slaves began to help Master Thomas make another profit off their labor. Singing filled the air as they sang to make the work go faster and the time seem short. As Amanda left her cabin, she smelled the fresh-turned earth and pungent odor of wild onions. Looking up in the sky, she saw the rain clouds gathering to cleanse the earth and help the crops grow. A robin was chattering and whistling in the dawn, as the crows cawed from the edge of the cornfield.

Everything seemed to be in bloom except Amanda. After jumping the broom with Power her life was miserable. Power's weekend would be next week. She didn't wish to see him. And yet, the rebirth of Mother Nature infected her gloomy mood. As she went into the big house, Sam met her at the door.

"Don't disturb Miz Sallie."

"Wat's wrong with her?"

"She's in the family way."

"Wat?"

"She's gonna have a baby."

"Who told you?"

"I's seem it often 'nough." Sam put his right hand on her shoulder. "Now look, I want youse to git her some them unleavened biscuits and milk. I's goin' to git Doc Welch."

"Yeah."

"Don't be angry 'cause youse not in de family way."

"Yeah."

"Look and don't tell Miz Sallie."

"Don't she know?"

"Don't 'ppear dat she does. Let Doc Welch tell her, not us."

Amanda did as Sam told her. She went to the kitchen to get the biscuit and milk. When she got there, Suckey and Flossie were huddled together. It appeared to Amanda that they were talking about Miz Sallie's condition. She wondered why they should be so happy about Miz Sallie being in a family way. To Amanda, it was only another white person to eventually tell them what to do.

"I came to git milk an' biscuits for Miz Sallie."

"She's jest now gittin' up."

"It seems so. Sam done sent fer de doctor."

"De doctor!"

"Dat's wat I said."

"Lord," Suckey said. "I sure hope it ain't somethin' catchin'."

With that statement, Suckey made Amanda realize

they didn't know about Miz Sallie's delicate condition. Their happiness was something else. Now she needed to know what was going on between Flossie and Suckey. She knew that Flossie had jumped the broom the same time she did. He was scheduled to come up to see Flossie the same time as Power. Perhaps he had slipped over to see her last night and she was telling Suckey about it. Being married to another slave who didn't live with you was hard. And yet, it wasn't worth being caught after dark without a pass by paddy rollers. They would take the slave to whipping post and flog him fifty or more time.

Amanda inquired, "Wat's up?"

Flossie tightened her dress across her stomach. "Don't youse see, I's gonna have a baby."

Amanda almost dropped the tray. She couldn't believe her ears or her eyes. This was the second slave girl with child on Stekoa Fields. Master Thomas's real property value was going up. Amanda stood there and shook her head. Suckey came over and hugged her.

"Youse didn't 'low Power in yo'pants," Suckey said.. "Time will tell."

Amanda needed to get out of there. She didn't want their pity and quite frankly, she didn't deserve it. Quickly, she filled the tray with a saucer of biscuits and a glass of milk. She glanced at them for moment, and then left the two alone to pity her.

When she got to the Master bedroom, she put the tray down and automatically began straightening and fluffing up Sallie's pillow. Looking at her, Amanda saw she was pale, but that was natural for this time of the year.

"Here's yo' food."

Amanda turned to leave.

"Don't go," Miz Sallie cried. "Stay with me until Dr. Welch gets here."

Around noon, Dr. T. K. Welch's buggy came up the driveway. Sam was driving the buggy, as the doctor relaxed in the passenger's seat. As soon as the doctor got of the buggy, Sam stepped down and tied the reins to the hitching post in front of the house. Amanda watched as the doctor walked up the steps and quickly opened the front door for him.

"She's rat upstairs in de fron' bedroom."

She took the doctor's coat and hat, hanging them on the coat tree. Dr. Welch grunted as he went upstairs. Quietly, Amanda followed him, entering the room just behind him.

"Doc's here, Miz Sallie,"

Dr. Welch put his bag on the chair and processed to Miz Sallie's bed.

"I'm glad you came, Dr. Welch. I was feeling nauseated this morning."

"How do you feel now?"

"Fine, I suspect," Miz Sallie smiled, "I guess I just panicked 'cause the Senator isn't here."

Amanda knew was her cue to leave. She went around the bed and got the covered bed chamber from under the bed. Leaving the room, Amanda went to empty the chamber and do her other chores that Flossie hadn't gotten. Sam met her as she was coming down the hall.

"How is she?"

"Doc Welch is with her. She looks fine to me. She jest had mornin; sickness."

"Yes, youse right, Mandy," Sam laughed nervously. "I's jest wanna take care of Master Thomas's mistress while he's gone. I guess I's best go tell Miz Temperance."

"Shore."

Amanda continued. She left Sam standing. Going outside, she emptied the bedchamber in the outside toilet. After cleaning it, she took it back to the bedroom. By the time she returned to Sallie's bedroom, Dr. Welch was gone. Miz Sallie was still in bed and Amanda noticed that there was a glow about her. It seemed that Sam had been right.

"I'm going to have a baby," Miz Sallie announced. "I've got to write Willie and tell him."

"Dat's great," Amanda tried to sound excited.

Miz Sallie sighed. "I know you want a child, too."

"Yes sum."

Amanda thought, "Now Flossie and the other slave's baby will be your baby's servant. They'll grow up together, but will never live together as equals."

"Wat did Dr. Welch tell youse?"

"Oh, I can get up and move about. After all, I'm only having a baby."

Youse right."

"The doctor said that I could get up. I think I will."

"Okay," Amanda walked toward the door. "I's clean up the house."

"Wait?"

Amanda stopped.

"Let's practice the piano."

"Now Miz Sallie, youse knows I can't."

"Of course you can." Sallie got out of bed and headed toward her wardrobe. "I'll get dress and you go down and straighten up a little bit."

"Yes ma'am."

Amanda went downstairs and straightened up the parlor. Looking at the dining room, she saw much to do. Going on into the back room where the ragbag and other cleaning materials were stored, Amanda found what she needed, and worked until the room was spotless. When she finished, she came to Miz Sallie, who was in the parlor at the piano. Looking at the grandfather clock in the corner, she realized it was pass noon.

"Miz Sallie, you need to eat. Remember, you're eating for two people."

"Alright."

"I's sees wat I can get from the kitchen."

Miz Sallie went back to playing the piano, while Amanda went to the kitchen for food. On entering the kitchen, Flossie and Suckey rushed to her side. She knew they wanted to know about Miz Sallie.

"Wat's wrong with Miz Sallie?" Flossie asked.

"The same thing wrong with youse."

"She's 'pectin'."

"Yeah." Amanda continued, "Can anyone of you fix Miz Sallie some lunch?"

"Sure."

They hurried around fixing some food for Miz Sallie. After placing it on a tray, Amanda carried it to her. She set the tray on the sideboard in the dining room, and then she got the proper silverware and set the table. She transferred the plate with the food on it, and the glass of buttermilk to the table. Surveying it, Amanda realized she had forgotten to place a napkin on table. Getting a cloth napkin from the sideboard, she placed it beside the plate.

Amanda went into the parlor and curtseyed to Miz Sallie, "Lunch is served, Mad'm."

"Bring it in here."

"It's 'ready on the dining room table."

"All right."

Miz Sallie went into the dining room to eat.

Amanda waited to make sure everything was as Miz Sallie wanted, and then she went upstairs to clean the Master bedroom. The linen on the bed had to be changed, the bedspread shook out and the floor swept. The vanity pitcher had to be filled. As usual, she gathered the rugs in the room, and went to the verenda to shake them out.

Knowing that Miz Temperance was coming, she made sure the other bedroom was clean and followed the same ritual...but this time, she dusted for spiders and other insects, not only in Miz Temperance's room, but in the hallway, also. She changed the bed and made sure the bed chamber was under the bed.

After awhile, she assumed that Miz Sallie had finished with her meal, and went back downstairs. She found her lady in the parlor. Then, as Miz Sallie played the piano, Amanda watched.

The two spent a lot of afternoons at the piano. The instrument fascinated Amanda. Sometimes Miz Sallie would let Amanda play the scale and Miz Sallie would scold her if she didn't place her hands right.

Chapter 18

The next day with all her luggage, Miz Temperance arrived on Stekoa Fields. She was going to be a grandmother. With Master Thomas gone, she would take care of Miz Sallie. It was afternoon when Sam pulled the carriage into the yard. From the house they could hear the piano playing. Sam helped Miz Temperance out of the carriage and escorted her to the door. Without knocking, Miz Temperance walked in. She paused before going into the parlor. As she walked in, Miz Sallie looked around. The two women smiled at each other, and then Miz Sallie got up and rushed into her arms.

"Mother," she cried. "What brings you here?"

"Sam came and fetched me."

"You know I'm going to have a baby."

"Yes!" Miz Temperance replied. "I came to help."

"That's great," Sallie said, "But I'm going home."

"Home," Miz Temperance asked, "You mean White Sulphur Springs?"

"Yes, I want to be near my family. Willie won't be here until December."

"I understand."

Amanda knew Miz Temperance was hurt. Now Miz Temperance had to make a decision. She just got here and Dearest Sallie was talking about leaving.

"Mother," Miz Sallie held Miz Temperance's wrinkled hands. "I want you to stay here and take care of the house and manage the slaves."

"Of course, I'll be glad to do that."

124

Amanda moved in the shadows. As the two women talked, Sam carried Miz Temperance's lounge upstairs. When Sam went upstairs, Amanda left the parlor to allow the two women their privacy. She went out the back door and waited for Sam. When he emerged from around the house, Amanda stopped him.

"Miz Sallie is going to stay with her folks in White Sulphur Springs."

"I know." Sam reflected. "She's not going rat now."

"Miz Temperance will be in charge."

"Someone has to be."

"I see trouble."

"With who?"

"Dave."

"He jest 'lieve he be free."

"I's like to 'lieve that too."

With those words, Amanda walked off.

Miz Sallie didn't leave until the next morning. When Amanda arrived, she was still in the bed. Miz Temperance was up and about. She had gone to the kitchen to obtain her own breakfast. Therefore, Amanda went to Miz Sallie's bedroom to see if she could help her get ready to go. It seemed that Miz Sallie and Amanda had bonded; now she was leaving to go home to White Sulphur Springs to have her first child. As she walked upstairs to the master bedroom, she remained herself that she was a nigger slave. Miz Sallie had been lonely for companionship and she just happened to be available.

When Mandy went upstairs, she found Sallie staring at a photograph of her husband, whom she affectionately called Willie. There were tears in her eyes, but Mandy could understand her sadness. Master Thomas was way down in Raleigh and she was stuck here in the mountains. She wanted to cry with her because the love of her life was somewhere at Sulphur Springs. The two women had something in common, but their social world was at opposite ends of the spectrum. Hence, Mandy decided that she would not overstep the boundary and keep their relationship as the status quo.

"Let's me hep youse pack." Mandy said, "I's git yo trunk from the attic."

"Get Sam to do that," Miz Sallie continued to stare at the photo. "God, I wish he was here."

"Yes ma'am."

Mandy turned and started out of the room, but Miz Sallie's voice stopped her. The voice of her mistress told Mandy that she needed someone to talk with and this nigger slave was available.

"Yes ma'am." Mandy repeated herself.

"You know when Willie starting courting me, he thought my friends would tease me about dating an older man. So he kept his visits a secret."

"Yes ma'am."

"You know he watched me grow up. Everyone thought Willie was going to be a bachelor all his life. I guess he was waiting for me. Deep down, I suppose I was in love with him all my life. With my father being his business partner, he would come to the house. I would peek around the curtain and watch him as he talked business with my father."

"Yes ma'am."

"You know Willie is shy."

Amanda didn't answer, she was thinking about the difference in Mr. Willie and Miz Sallie ages. Perhaps she could understand Master Thomas's wish for her to have a more mature man in her life, but that wasn't what she wanted. Sallie continued to talk, but Mandy was no longer listening. Whatever, she said it went in one ear and out the other.

Miz Sallie laughed and that got Amanda's attention.

"Most of his friends figured he would never get married, but I got him, the love of my life. You know he asked me would I love him when he got old and grey. I will love him forever. But you see, I hate him being so far away. He's always championing someone else's cause. That's the reason he became a Senator and he is a very religious man. He wants me to teach the Lufty women my Christian virtues."

"Yes ma'am." Mandy cleared her throat. "Miz Sallie, don't youse think that you need to get to packing? The morning' will be gone 'fore youse know it."

"Oh, yes" Miz Sallie said, "Yes, I must get packing. Pops will be worried if I don't arrive before dusk. I sent Sam over yesterday to tell him I'm coming."

Miz Sallie put the photo on the bed. Getting up, she began preparations for the journey home. She tested the water in the pitcher and handed to Mandy.

That water is too cold," she demanded, "Go fetch some hot warm water."

"Yes ma'am." She took the pitcher from Miz Sallie and raced downstairs to get some warm water.

On her way down at the foot of the landing, she met Caroline with a pitcher of water. The two looked at each other.

"I's take this on to the kitchen."

"No," Caroline held the pitcher up. "Let's put the water from this pitcher in her pitcher or she'll be angry.

Not wanting to upset the Mistress of the house, Amanda allowed Caroline to pour the warm water in the pitcher she held. Afterward, Amanda handed the full pitcher to Caroline and Caroline gave the empty pitcher to Amanda.

I need to clean," Amanda smiled, "Youse take care of Dearest Sallie."

"Will do."

Amanda watched Caroline go up to Dearest Sallie, and then she started to clean the house. She decided to start in the parlor. The first thing that caught her eye was the piano. She would miss Miz Sallie playing. Before the day was over Miz Sallie and her music would be gone. Lovingly, she touched the keys. There would silent in the big house until she returned with her baby.

As she cleaned, Miz Temperance came into the room.

She sat down and picked up her needle point she had been knitting. Amanda didn't speak, but continued to clean. Footsteps came down the hall and Amanda anticipated that Sam was in the home. Entering the parlor, Sam stood there.

'Is Miz Sallie ready?"

"She's getting ready right now." Miz Temperance answered. "Why don't you fetch her some breakfast? You know she has to eat for two people."

"Shore."

Sam left and got breakfast for Dearest Sallie. All the people slave and free continued to do their work. Just before eleven, Sam, Caroline, and Dearest Sallie were on their way to White Sulphur Springs.

Chapter 19

With Miz Sallie gone, Miz Temperance took charge. She officially appointed Sam as the driver. He was to report to her of any insubordination among the other slaves. Now Sam could not do as he pleased, but do Miz Temperance's bidding. Amanda wondered if Sam had the mentality to do the job. When Miz Sallie was presented, Sam allowed Dave to do as he wished without any reprisals. Sam always waited until Maser Thomas returned from Raleigh and reported the incidents to him. Now it was different. Amanda heard Miz Temperance tell Sam that punishment was to be given to any slave who disobeyed.

It was the beginning of the season for planting. There was no time for laziness. Everyone had to work. Amanda wondered how Sam was going to handle the situation with Dave. She wanted to talk to Dave, but she knew it would only result in an argument. And yet Amanda felt she had to make the attempt to have some kind of order at Stekoa Fields while both Master Thomas and Dearest Sallie were absence.

However, confronting Dave would be a difficult task for she knew he wouldn't understand. Therefore, she decided to mind her own business. After all, she was now a house slave since Caroline went back with Miz Sallie. Now Miz Temperance had appointed Amanda to be her personal slave.

Planting season went fine. The growing season approached and the field hands work became more demanding. Every day they had to weed the garden to keep the unwanted plants from choking the vegetables. Amanda listened as Sam reported the day's activities to Miz Temperance. All was going well, until July. The sun beat down from heaven and the work went slower. Sam reported that Dave was rebelling causing the other slaves to follow his lead.

"Miz Temperance, youse gonna hafto do somethin'."

"Sam," she pointed her finger at him. "I gave you the job."

"Yes'um."

With his hat in his hand and eyes staring at the porch floor, he backed away, then quickly turned and walked away. Miz Temperance sighed and stared out into the scenery before her. Amanda, who standing behind wanted to run after Sam. She couldn't. And yet, she realized she had to do something. Desperately, she had to talk to Dave. At that moment, she decided she would appeal to him for the sake of the other slaves. Therefore, after Miz Temperance bedded down for the night, she left the big house to find Dave. She went to river and found him seated on the bank. As she approached, she heard a tiny splash of water. The moonlight above gave her light and direction. Quietly, she sat beside him. He looked over at her.

"I's ain't seen you out in the field."

"I's in de house a helpin' Miz Temperance."

"Oh, I's forgot. Youse her grandchild."

"Tat may be true, but I's still a slave."

"Yeah." He skipped another rock through the water. "Youse gotta easy job."

"Howes wou'd you likk to empty bed pans...scrub floors...run fro' the house to de kitchen 'bout three or fore times a day."

"Bett'r tan in de hot sun."

"At leas' youse git some sunlig't."

"More tan I's wanna."

"Youse knows tat Sam 'port'd youse to Miz Temperance."

"Wat she gonna do?"

"It be up to Sam. Dave, youse gotta. . ."

"Be wat?" Dave stood up and pointed his finger at her. "I's 'pose to be free."

Quickly Amanda rose and covered his mouth with her hands. She tried to talk to him, but he pushed her away and she fell into the water. As she splashed into the water, Sam came through the bushes and weeds. Amanda went under and immediately surfaced.

"Wat de hell are youse doin'?"

Sam's fist caught Dave right across the mouth and he went down. In anger, Sam went after him and began to pound him in the face with his fist. Amanda scrambled out of the water and attempted to stop Sam's furious attack on Dave. Dripping wet she pounded him on the back with her fist.

"STOP IT." Her voice seemed to echo through the hills.

Sam pushed her away. Without saying a word, he got up, looked at her with hate in his eyes and walked away.

Now Dave and Amanda were alone. Standing there, she remembered Sam's words. Trouble indeed was headed her way. She needed to get out of those wet clothes and go back to the big house. Going over to Dave, who was slowly getting into a sitting position, she saw his swollen face.

"Dave, I's sorry." She hugged him. "Let's me help youse."

He untangled himself from her and went to the water. With both hands cupped in the water, he brought his hands up and wiped his face. Amanda stood and watched him. Slowly, he turned to her.

"Go away."

The two stared at each. Amanda turned and walked away. She went to her mother's quarters. Quietly, she slipped into the shanty and stripped off the wet clothes and found something to wear. Taking the wet garments, she tossed them on bush behind the shanty. As she walked back to the big house, she hoped Miz Temperance would not notice the difference when morning came. When she returned to the house, Amanda crept through the backdoor, tiptoed noiseless to Miz Temperance bedroom and lay on her pallet at the bottom of her bed. A troubled sleep awaited her.

The morning brought a brand new day. She didn't know what to expect from Sam or Dave. Miz Temperance had told him to handle it. Somehow, Amanda had gotten herself right in the middle. All day long, she waited for Sam to report to Miz Temperance. She stayed close to the big house because she didn't want hear the rumor. Dave's face would tell it all, but that was partly her fault. When Sam came to report to Miz Temperance, Amanda listened from behind closed door.

"Everythin' is fine." Sam reported. "We just had a miss un'erstandin."

"Fine," Miz Temperance replied. "That's fine. Let it stay that way."

"Yes'um."

Peeking out the door, Amanda saw Sam walk away.

All sorts of rumors ran through Stekoa Field. Amanda didn't responded to any of them. She knew what had occurred. It was between Sam and Dave. Some said that Sam had taken a whip to Dave. Others declared that Sam and Dave had a fist fight.

Miz Temperance didn't seem to care as long as the work was done. Therefore when harvest time came, each slave did their job to preserve food for the long winter months and provide product for Master Thomas's stores.

Chapter 20

On December 16, 1858, Master Thomas and Miz Sallie had their first child. It was a boy and they named him William Holland Thomas, Jr. Everyone at Stekoa Fields got the news from Sam who had gone to Waynesville on an errand for Miz Temperance and he had stopped by White Sulphur Springs before coming back to Stekoa Fields. Amanda was still working in the big house. She didn't know whether she would continue there when Miz Sallie came back with her baby. Caroline would probably return.

Time had arrived for Stekoa Fields to be clean for the holiday. Christmas was still being celebrated on January 6, although some places in North Carolina were celebrating it on December 25. Miz Temperance had brought her Christmas Bush from her home and set it in the parlor. With Little Master Will not yet a month old, Amanda anticipated that Miz Sallie would spend Christmas at White Sulphur Springs. It appeared that Miz Temperance would be the only white person on the place, but then, Miz Temperance decided to send for Mr. Andrew Patton, Amanda listened as she talked to Sam about the prospect of finding him.

"Sam," Miz Temperance feeble voice addressed him. "I know Mistress Sallie will be staying at White Sulphur Springs until spring. I want you to go to Shoal Creek and get Andrew."

"Yes sum."

"Tell him that I want him to spend the holidays with me here. You can explain it to him."

Amanda now realized the idle hands of the slaves would be no more. Most of the slaves had taken advantage of the absence of Mr. Willie and Miz Sallie. Since it was wintertime, no real harm was done. Sam was building the winter fires for Miz Temperance and had sent a couple of young male slaves into the woods for more fuel, Therefore, Amanda didn't understand why Miz Temperance needed Mr. Andrew. However, as she thought about it, Amanda realized that Miz Temperance needed company that was her own kind. Mr. Andrew was her kind.

Later that day as she was going to her cabin, she wondered if Mr. Terrell would allow Power and Alfred to herd the hogs to the market in Waynesville. Although Power was her man, she still didn't love him, but she respected his desires to be a man.

As she slowly walked to her mother's cabin, a light snow began to fall. She hoped it would leave a white blanket by morning, and then by the time Mr. Andrew arrived, the weather wouldn't allow them to work outside. But she would have to trudge through the snow to the big house. If the snow continued, Amanda knew Miz Temperance would send for her before the night was over. When she entered the drafty cabin, she found Flossie was there with her baby who had been born two months previously.

"It's beginnin'' to snow out dere."

"Yeah, I's knows." Martha answered. "Dat why I's toll' Flossie an' her young'un they can stay here."

"I's thought youse were gonna stay at the big house?" Flossie looked up at Amanda.

"I is. Jest thought I's see wat my mama was doin' an' she be 'lright."

"I's fine."

Amanda went over to Flossie who was nursing the baby. She smiled down at the chubby infant.

"He be cute."

"Danks." Flossie looked up at Amanda. "When is youse an' Pow'r gonna have a youn'un."

Amanda wanted to laugh, but she just smiled.

"Youse is pregn'nt."

"Is youse?" Martha went over to Amanda.

"No!" She laughed in attempt to hide her anger. It was an anger that was directed at slavery. Before she gave Martha or Flossie time to question her anger, she continued to talk. "Look, I gotta git back to de big house."

Without looking back, she walked out the door. Outside the snow continued to fall and coldness crept in her bones. She looked up at the heavens, and then she folded her arms against her chest. With her head bent, she hurried to reach the safety of the big house for she knew now that her mother was all right. She went around to the back of the house and quietly entered. Going into the parlor, she found Miz Temperance seated in the rocking chair. Seated on the floor beside her was Colette. Colette's shiny gray eyes glanced up at Amanda. A smile crossed her face and Amanda returned the smile. Miz Temperance was asleep and in her lap was unfinished knit baby bootie that was still attached to the ball of blue yarn.

"Mama tol' me to stay," Colette shyly remarked. "I's can go home ifen youse wanna."

"No, honey," Amanda reassured her. "Youse go on up an' sleep on de pallet in Miz Temperance's room. I's git her to bed."

"Yes sum." Colette got up and did as she was told.

Amanda tenderly shook Miz Temperance from her nap. As she attempted to awaken Miz Temperance, she thought that this elegant old lady was her grandmother. She wanted to hug her and tell that she loved her. Growing up around her, Amanda knew she had taught her many things. Her own traditions she had instilled in Amanda's inner being.

"Yes, yes," she opened her eyes and quickly looked around the room. "What is it? What is it?"

"Grand..." Amanda stopped. "Miz Temperance," she took the knitting from her and set it on the table beside the rocker. "It's jest me, Mandy. It's time to go to bed."

"Sam get back."

"Nope," Amanda reassured her. "He's be back 'morrow."

"I sure hope he can find Andy."

"He will." She helped her to her feet. "Rat now, it be bedtime."

Miz Temperance allowed Amanda to guide her to her bedroom. Amanda helped her undress and put on her flannel nightgown. After tucking her in bed, Amanda joined Colette on the pallet at the foot of the bed.

When morning came, Amanda saw that there was a blanket of snow on the ground. Before leaving the big house, she made sure the fires in the fireplaces were burning. She also had shaken Colette awake and instructed her of her duties for the day. As Amanda trudged through the snow to the kitchen, she saw the curl of smoke coming from the chimney. The smoke seemed to catch the morning air and disappear among the snow clouds. All was quiet. The scene appeared to be a picture from Miz Sallie's picture viewer. She stood there for a moment, and then she continued on to the kitchen. Now the only sound was the crushing snow beneath her feet. All Amanda had on besides her dress was an old shawl she held tightly about her shoulders and wool rags tied on her feet. Adorning her head was a head rag, which kept the snow off of her head as well as hid her matted, tangled, kinky hair.

Hurrying into the kitchen, she found Suckey scurrying about the room. It appeared to Amanda that most of the bustling around was to keep warm. She stopped when Amanda entered and folded her arms across her chest.

"Well," Suckey said, "It fin'lly snow'd."

"It 'ppears so."

"Did youse come by de house?"

"Stay'd dere."

"Where be Colette?"

"Gittin' Miz Temperance ready for de day."

Suckey sighed.

"Looks likk ev'rythin' gonna be at a stan'still."

"Yep."

"Herd dat Miz Temperance done sen' fer Mr. Andy."

"Yep. Sam wen' af'er'im yissday."

"I's glad it snow'd."

Amanda understood. Even if Sam and Mr. Andy returned, there would be no work for all the slaves. Shortly some of the male slaves would be shoveling snow from the path from the big house to the kitchen. The front porch had to be clean off and the trail to the toilet had to be shoveled. Other slaves would be feeding the livestock, but the beginning preparation for the spring crops would have to wait. The jersey cow had to be milked and the cream taken off the top to make butter. Someone might have to go to the cold cellar for provisions for the kitchen.

I didn't matter whether Mr. Andy was here or not, the everyday operation of Stekoa Field had to be done. Amanda felt that Miz Temperance didn't need Mr. Andy. All the slaves were willing to work for the old woman. After all, she was Master Thomas's mother. Then suddenly Amanda understood why Temperance felt that she needed him. She had to remind herself that a white man on the place would make Miz Temperance feel better. Although Nat Turner's rebellion occurred sometime ago, Amanda felt that Miz Temperance didn't want that to happen while the Master and Mistress were absent.

Around noon, Sam made it to Stekoa Fields with Mr. Andy. Sam drove the wagon up to the front porch to allow Mr. Andy to climb down. Without knocking, he came into the house and went into the parlor where Miz Temperance was in her comfortable rocker. He went over to her and kissed her.

"How are you?" He asked.

"Lord, Andy!" She seemed surprised. "It's good to see you."

"You did send for me?"

She perked up and began knitting. "Of course. With

Willie and Sallie both away, I want you to run the place."
   "Be glad to."

Chapter 21

It was a lazy day, when Mr. Andy took over. The cold crept through the cracks of the slaves' cabins. Any kind of heat was welcome. When darkness fell upon the place, everyone headed for the warmth of their dwelling place. The first thing they did was to put wood on the small fire banked during the day. No one allowed their earthen hearth to smolder and die. All winter long smoke curled from the earthen chimneys of the drafty cabins. Slave children gathered broken branches and twigs from the woods. They supplied their families and other slave families with fuel for their hearth. Sometimes it was hard to find branches and twigs from the forest floor when it was covered with snow. Other times, these children had to give up the branches and twigs that they found to furnish heat for the Master's house.

The wintry snow still covered the ground and kept the slaves inside their cabin most of the time. Their yearly supply of flour was getting low. If the snow continued, the slave families would go hungry. Filling their stomach with snow was better than nothing. Some put traps out to catch any small wild animal that ventured to eat the bait.

Mr. Andy felt it was necessary for the slaves to remain in their cabins. Each night he would go down to the slave quarters with the pretense of checking their welfare. Unbeknown to Miz Temperance, Mr. Andy enjoyed going down to the slave quarters. Living among Luftys and black slaves, he was taught from Master Willie, his adopted father that it was socially acceptable to fraternize with the slaves. However, Amanda knew how Mr. Andy did his fraternization. She was just glad she was a house slave.

The New Years and Christmas came and went. The holidays were now over and 1859 burst in without Willie or Sallie at Stekoa Field. Miz Temperance was content to sit by the fireplace in the parlor. Usually just after supper, she quietly read her worn Bible, or knitted something for the natural grandson she had yet to see. Therefore, she never missed Mr. Andy's presence. Just before she went to bed, he would bid her good night and slip into the darkness.

Amanda made it her business that Colette went home to Suckey before the veil of darkness came upon the place. She didn't want the responsibility of something happening to Suckey's daughter. Colette wasn't needed to fan the flies and mosquitoes from Miz Temperance as she and Mr. Andy ate their supper. After all, deep winter had sent the insects into hibernation.

It was the middle of February and the snow had not gone away. As a matter of fact more snow moved in. Stekoa Fields seemed so isolated and the fields still needed to be made ready for planting season. With snow on the ground, it was impossible for them to get the ground ready. Mr. Andy had the slaves continually clean the snow off of the front porch and the driveway. Amanda knew this was so he could make his way to the slave quarters. As Amanda bedded down on the pallet in Miz Temperance's room, she felt save, but she worried about her mother and Flossie. Each night, she listened to the light snoring of Temperance; while she kept her ears atoned to the sounds of Mr. Andy's footsteps as he crept back into the big house. When she heard the door of his bedroom close, she sighed with relief and allowed sleep to overtake her tired body.

However, on this particular night, Mr. Andy didn't retreat to his bedroom, but quietly opened the door to Miz Temperance's bedroom. Over the light snoring of Temperance, Amanda heard the door as he slightly opened it. Immediately Amanda pretended she was asleep and perhaps he would go away. She felt he wouldn't take the chance of awaking Miz Temperance. To try to convince him of her deep slumber, she too allowed some snoring sounds to emit from her mouth. All was still, but the snoring of the two women.

"Mandy," Mr. Andy whispered in the darkness.

Chill went through Amanda's body. All the time, she had been worried about her mother and Flossie's safety. Now she felt that her own safety was endangered. No one was around to stop him. The only thing that she hoped would deter him would be her forged sleep. She snored just a little louder, as Mr. Andy tiptoed into the bedroom. Amanda knew all was lost, because Miz Temperance was a deep sleeper. Shaking her lightly on the shoulder, he attempted to awaken Amanda. She still forged sleep, but Mr. Andy was not to be deterred. Roughly, he shook shoulders and pulled the thin worn blanket off of her.

Bending down to her right ear, he whispered. "Mandy, I need you."

Now her body shook from his words as well as from the cold winter air that penetrated her body. A slight cry escaped her mouth, as he jerked her up in sitting position.

"Mandy," he whispered angrily, "I need your help. I'm dying here."

Without allowing Amanda to speak or protest, he dragged her to her feet and led her out of Miz Temperance' room to his bedroom. There was nothing she could do. Mr. Andy could do what he pleased with her as long as he didn't physically destroy her.

The next morning Amanda felt dirty. Andy had used her body without asking her. He showed her no respect. Somehow, she needed to tell Power. Power deserved to know. But as of now, it would be her secret. She would tell no one. And yet, she couldn't look or be near Andy. If he came into the room where she was, she left. The only thing that kept her sanity was that she kept Colette safe.

"Are you all right," Miz Temperance asked Amanda.

"I's fine,"

"This winter has us all down in the dump."

"Yes ma'am."

I can git Sam to go over to Shoal Creek and get Mr. Terrell to let Power spend some time with you this weekend."

"No," Amanda begged. "No."

"All right, I'll leave it alone."

However, when the weekend rolled around, Power was at Stekoa Fields. As Amanda was leaving the big house to check on her mother, Sam had just returned from Shoal Creek and Power was with him. He saw her first and ran across the yard. When he caught up with her, he put his arms around her waist. Immediately she jerked away. She balled her hands and began beating him on the chest.

He caught her fisted hands and held them. "It be me, Power."

"Power, wat are you doin' here?"

"I got a pass fer de weekend."

"Please go back." Amanda cried.

"Amanda, Is' love you."

"I's know, but I's don't love you. I's 'spect you, I will ne'er love youse."

"Why youse wants me to come?"

Amanda just shook head. She had other things to do. "We's talk later, I promise."

She kissed him and walked away without looking back. As she was walking to kitchen, Mr. Andy fell into steps beside her.

"Your man's waiting on you," He smiled sheepishly.

"I know."

"He's at your wedding cabin."

Amanda didn't answer, but continued toward the kitchen. She was at the point of tears. Now she understood Mr. Andy's reasoning to have Power come. Ashamed, she didn't want to face Power again. Giving herself to Power was what Mr. Andy wanted. If she became pregnant, Power could be the father or Mr. Andy could be the father. Everyone would believe it was Power's child.

Suddenly, she turned around and headed to their wedding cabin. With the shabby shawl held tightly around her, she opened the cabin door. Power was standing by the hearth warming his hands.

"C'mon in." he grinned. "Close de door, youse lettin' all de cold in."

Amanda closed the door and walked over to him. They stood face to face. Tears formed in Amanda's eyes. He took her in his arm and they kissed. Amanda was the first to break away. She sat on the bed and he came and sat beside her.

Wat's goin' on?"

Wat ifen I tol' I was rap'd."

"By's 'other slave, I's kill'im."

"No!"

"Den, who?"

" A white man."

"Name."

"I's can't give youse dat."

"Why?"

"Remember, youse said dat we's likk dogs. Bitches don't hav' no choice wen 'other dog rides her."

"I's so sorry, I said dat." He took her in his arm and held her tight. "I's sorry."

"Ifen you can live with dat, I can live with dat. Dere is no dig'ity in a slave marriage. When we married, I wanna to marry someone else. We lov'd each other, I was tol' no. I 's given 'self to him, but he wasn't season'd 'nough."

"And I's be?"

'YES!" Amanda looked him in eyes.

"Where's do we go fro' here?"

"Ifen you wanna me I's yer. I'll neber deny you my body. It is yer."

Power got up from the bed. "An' yo' soul?"

"I's workin' on dat."

Amanda rose and went to him. Now they stood only inches apart. Amanda stared at Power. She wanted to be in love with him, not just love him to take away the hurt and shame in her heart. The guilt was hers and she wondered why she told him. Tenderly, he embraced her. When his arms surrounded her body, she almost froze. It was only a slave marriage, but Amanda felt she should be loyal to her partner no matter if she loved another. Therefore she welcomed his embrace. For Power and Amanda, this was a new beginning.

When the weekend was over, Power and Amanda had consummated their jumping the broom. It matter not how far away from each they would be. Each would be loyal to each other.   Power returned to Shoal Creek to slave and Amanda returned to the big house. Even the winter weather was breaking, as the snow seemed to hide away in the red clay soil. The wintry sun shone on the white dirty snow, slowly dissolving it into the ground. As the ground welcomed the watery snow, the activities on Stekoa Fields were put in high gear. It was time to work.

Chapter 22

Within a week's time Master Willie and Mistress Sallie returned home. With them was their three month old son Little Will. Seeing the couple and their child, Amanda realized she didn't want a slave child. She did not care whether the father was Power or Mr. Andy. Hence she decided to go to her mama to make sure she did not have a child, especially from the sexual encounter of that harried weekend.

After finishing her chores at big house, Amanda went to her mama's cabin. She didn't have to stay with Miz Temperance because Caroline returned with Sallie and Little Will.

As she left the big house under the shadow of darkness, she was accosted by Mr. Andy and dragged in the woods. She thought he had left for Shoal Creek and she would not have to see him again. She made no attempt to cry out for she knew it was useless.

As she lay on the cold hard ground where Mr. Andy had left her, she knew what she had to do. Slowly she got up and straightened her clothes the best she could. Tears stung her eyes, but she angrily brushed them away. Dragging herself out of the woods, she went to her mama. Her mama could concoct up some herbs so that she could abort. Master Willie wasn't going to make a profit off her body.

When she got to her mother's cabin, Flossie was there. On entering the cabin, Amanda wanted to turn around and run. Looking into the eyes of Martha and Flossie, she knew they knew something was wrong. Martha came over to her and put her arms around her. Flossie's eyes seemed to bulge out of their sockets.

"Wat happen'd to youse?"

"Andy!" Flossie stated emphatically.

"How did youse know?" Amanda asked.

"He's been down 'round de quarters."

"Mama," Amanda cried, "Youse mean dat he's been here?"

Both Flossie and Martha nodded their heads.

Amanda moved away from her mother. Sadly she just shook her head in disbelief. It didn't make sense. While Master Willie was away, his adopted son seemed to be trying to make Master Willie a profit off the female slaves.

"No," Amanda shrieked. "I's ain't havin' no slave child."

"It could be Power's," Flossie warned her.

"No!"

"Ain't nothin' we's can do 'bout it."

"I's can."

She looked over at her mama.

Martha went over to the hearth and sat by the fire. As her mother stared into the flames, Amanda felt she wasn't agreeing with her decision. Silence filled the room, as three women glanced at each other. Flossie looked from Martha to Amanda, and then she left mother and daughter to work out this dilemma

"Mama," Amanda begged with affection. "I's need yo' he'p."

Martha just shook her head. "Why?"

"It ain't rat."

"Is dis rat?"

Martha lowered her head and stared again into the dancing flames of the hearth.

"Wat ifen I's got rid of youse?"

"Wat do youse mean?"

"Jest wat I's say."

"Youse were rap'd?"

"I's guess youse can say dat. Come to my bed an'

said dat I was his. I had to do as I was tol'. He wasn't gonna hurt me. And he's ke'p comin' back."

"How am I know, mama? I's want Power's child, not Mr. Andy's." Amanda went over to her and put her hand on shoulder. "I's only knows dat ifen I's has a child, I don't want dis one."

"So's youse want me to make shore dat dere be no child."

"Yeah."

"'Iright," Martha reassured her.

Chapter 23

The sweltering months of summer were just beyond the horizon. Once again, Miz Sallie and Flossie were expecting with their second child. Besides Flossie, three other female slaves' mother-to-be was trying to cope with the heat. Although these slaves were with child, they still had to work. Flossie and the other three were field hands and they had to weed and hoe. All Miz Sallie had to do was to sat around and wait for the blessed event. For the slave women, Amanda felt it was a curse and was elated she wasn't one of them. Secretly, she wondered if Andy was the father of slaves' babies including Flossie's expected child. With Caroline as Miz Sallie's personal servant, Amanda did most of the housework. She found herself running to and fro between the kitchen and the main house. If Suckey weren't giving her orders, then she would get orders from Caroline who declared the orders were from Dearest Sallie.

And yet, Amanda didn't mind because she could hear all the gossip. At the summer break of the General Assembly in Raleigh, Senator Thomas hurried home to talk about the new political party. It seemed the creation of the Republican Party was to elect a president who was against slavery. Just from the conversation between the Senator and Andy, it seemed their first presidential candidate was defeated in the 1856 presidential election. Now Mr. Love tossed his hat into the political arena. With Willie backing him, he was running for the state's House of Representatives. They had just returned from a rally in Sylva.

Caroline was taking care of Little Will whom Willie nicknamed "Junaluska," while Amanda served dinner to the happy couple and his in-law family and listened to their conversation. She noticed that Sallie and her sister Mariah were talking about the blessed event, while Master and Mr. Love were discussing politics with Sallie's nineteen-year-old brother Matthew trying to become part of the conversation. Standing at the sideboard, Amanda eavesdropped on the two men's conversation, while Colette fanned flies off the food.

"Yes," Master Willie said. "I've heard a lot of rumors about this Abraham Lincoln."

"Yeah," Mr. Love answered. "He's sure made a name for himself when he took on the Little Giant last year for U. S. Senate race in Illinois."

"He lost." Willie tried to reassure Mr. Love.

"That's true, but he sure made a name for himself."

"Not in the southern states."

"I heard that he's a Southerner." Matthew finally joined in on the conversation.

"Son. . ." Master Willie started to answer, but Miz Sallie interrupted him.

"Papa," she insisted, "You two need to stop talking about politics. You can do that on the campaign trail. I've heard enough today at the rally. You should think about your family...the other child we're expecting."

Miz Sallie turned to Amanda. "Go get the dessert."

"Yes ma'am."

With Colette's help, Amanda collected the dirty dishes before leaving the room. As they were leaving, she heard Miz Sallie whisper to Master Willie that they shouldn't talk politics in front of the servants. Amanda continued to the kitchen without waiting to hear his answer, while Colette returned to the dining room to keep the flies and mosquitoes off the Loves and the Thomas's. When she returned to the dining room with the dessert, she found the conversation had turned to their farms and how the crops were trying to survive the sweltering heat. Mr. Love was still talking about the campaign, while Sallie kept changing the subject. She knew before the night was over, both men would complain about how lazy most of the slaves were.

After dinner, the men folks went into Willie's office, while the womenfolk settled in the parlor. Amanda remained with the sisters and hung in the shadows of the room, as the two siblings entertained themselves. Miz Sallie sat down at the piano and began playing Stephen Foster's "Willie, We Missed You," while Miz Mariah picked up the needlepoint she had been working. Colette remained at Miz Sallie's side, fanning her. Perhaps she could go. It was getting late and Amanda wanted to get back to her cabin. Just yesterday, she had gotten word that Power coming home tonight. Although she didn't want to see him, she knew that he was coming to see if she was pregnant. Lord help her, she had Martha to help her abort the baby. She just couldn't have a child born in slavery. Besides, the child might have been Mr. Andy's instead of Power's. What would Power do?

"Amanda," Miz Sallie commanded.

Amanda heard Miz Sallie, she didn't answer right away. Her mind was on Power. When she repeated her herself, she immediately came to her side.

"Yes ma'am."

"Go get me a glass of water."

"Yes ma'am." Amanda started out the door, but Miz Mariah stopped her.

"Girl, is there any wine around here?"

"I's don't knows."

"She doesn't know. Mariah, she's just a slave." She turned to Amanda and said, "Tell Sam to get some wine."

"Yes ma'am,"

"Elderberry," she said.

"Yes ma'am."

Amanda left and headed toward the kitchen. First she went into the pantry to see if she could find the wine. After looking around a while, she decided that she should go into the kitchen and ask Sam like Miz Sallie said. After all, Sam knows where everything and everybody was on Stekoa Field. She knew that he would probably be in the kitchen. It seemed that he spent a lot of time there to make sure that Suckey managed the kitchen correctly. On more than one occasion, she had seen Sam quibble with Suckey about the management of the kitchen. Although Suckey cooked all the delicious meals for the Thomas's, she was not permitted to eat any of the meals. A slave family was given its monthly rations of cornmeal and fatback. Thinking about it, she started toward the kitchen. Stepping outside, someone grabbed her arm and pulled her around the old oak. She knew instantly who it was.

"Power, wat on earth are youse doin' here?"

"I's send youse word dat I would be here."

"Youse's gonna hafto wait."

"Wat's youse doin'?"

"Miz Sallie and Master Thomas has compan'." She moved away from him. "I hafto do wat I's tol'."

Power sighed, "All right. But ain't Miz Sallie got her own person'l slave?"

Before she could answer him, he disappeared into the darkness. Amanda looked around, and then she continued on to the kitchen. When she entered, she found Suckey and Sam huddled together with an air of excitement about them as well as a frightened frantic atmosphere.

"Sam," Amanda said. "I come to fetch wine for Miz Sallie and Miz Mariah."

Sam confronted Amanda. The look on his face made Amanda back away. "Amanda, do youse knows who's here?"

"Yeah, Power. Why?"

"He be here without a pass."

Amanda's heart raced like a locomotive flying down the railroad. "Oh, my God!"

Power was her partner; she didn't want the paddy rollers to pick him up. Perhaps he made to the cabin or he's hiding in the woods. This was all her fault, that Power was out there somewhere with danger all around him. For Amanda knew that the paddy rollers had intensified their vigilance on slaves' movement at night. And yet, her immediate concern was to serve wine to Miz Sallie and Miz Mariah.

"Sam. I still need to git dat wine fer Miz Sallie an' her guest."

"Okay," Sam padded her on the shoulder. "Wat kind?"

"Elderberry.."

Sam left to get the wine. Amanda stood there stunned. She and Suckey just stared at each other. Silence. In a few minutes Sam returned with the wine. He got two goblets, uncorked the wine bottle, and poured the wine into the goblets. Then placed each item on a silver tray and handed it to Amanda. Nervously, she took the tray. She looked from Sam to Suckey for some kind of support, but either seemed to give any.

When she got back to the house, she found that Sallie wasn't happy and Colette had been dismissed. Miz Mariah was still seated at the piano and their brother, Matthew had joined then. He was standing by the piano as Miz Mariah picked out a tune, but everything stopped when Amanda arrived.

"You took your time."

"Yes ma'am." Amanda agreed. "Youse know dat Sam 'lways takes his time."

"Just set the tray down and go get Master Matthew a goblet."

"Yes ma'am."

Amanda did as she was told. Going into the dining room, she took a goblet from the sideboard and brought it back to the parlor. She placed it on the tray and poured some wine into it. After handing each of them a goblet of wine, Amanda hung once more in the shadows. Desperately, she wanted to go. She needed to know the where about of Power.

Miz Sallie cocked her eyes over at Amanda. "Go."

Quickly Amanda left. She ran to her cabin with the expectation of seeing Power safe and sound inside. However, when she entered, the cabin was empty. Panic took over. Dashing out of the cabin, she sprinted back to the big house. Instead of stopping there, she ran on to the kitchen, which greeted her with darkness. Scampering to the back of the kitchen, she noticed a candle glowing through the back room window where Suckey slept. Like a wild woman, she pounded on the door until Suckey opened it.

"Amanda! Suckey said as she held the candle up to Amanda's face. "Wat's de matt'r?:

"Can't find Power."

"It be gittin' late. He probabl' on de way back to Shoal Creek."

"Dose paddy rollers be out dere?"

"Girl, it be best dat youse go back to yer' cabin. Youse ain't got no business prowlin' 'round."

Suckey closed the door, leaving Amanda standing in the dark.

Amanda made an attempt to find Sam, but he was nowhere to be found. Defeated and dejected, she went back to her cabin and crawled into bed. Her mother wasn't there to comfort her because she now lived in the single women's quarters. This cabin now was occupied by Amanda and Power. Miz Sallie wanted it that way. Tears formed in Amanda's eyes and she cried herself to sleep. However, that deep sleep was suddenly disturbed when there were loud shouts and thundering horses' hooves, echoing through the slave quarters. She sat straight up in the bed. Panic-stricken, she froze. And yet, she heard the voices, angry male voices, vibrating in her ears and all though Stekoa Field.

She knew Power had been caught.

Chapter 24

The next morning, Amanda rose listening to the bell rang. It was time to go to the big house. Usually, she stayed there and slept on the pallet in the Master's bedroom, but now Willie was home. As she greeted the rising sun, Amanda felt that everything was all right. Nothing seemed out of the ordinary. It just seemed like another day at Stekoa Field. At least, she hoped everything was on the up and up.

When she got to the big house, she began her day's work by setting the table for breakfast. Then she went to the kitchen to see how long before breakfast could be served. As always when Mr. Love visited, he was up and about before Willie. Amanda found him leaning against the oak just outside the back door. With him was the sunrise. He looked around when Amanda approached.

"It's a beautiful morning," He announced.

"Yes sum."

Amanda inched away from him, knowing she shouldn't; although Mr. Love was not her master, he was a white man.

"Mistress Sallie tells me that you take care of her while Caroline takes care of the baby."

"Yes sum."

"Take real good care of her."

"Yes sum."

"Go along now." He waved his hand. "I can smell that country smoked ham and potatoes."

"Yes sum."

Amanda went on to the kitchen. The aroma of this country breakfast filled the air as she came through the door. Suckey was taking a pan of biscuits from the earthen oven. Looking around, she saw the dishes of steaming potatoes and scrambled eggs were waiting to be transported to the dining room sideboard. Without greeting Suckey, Amanda put the two serving dishes on a tray and left. When she returned, she took the sliced country smoked ham and other breakfast items to the big house. Either Suckey or Amanda spoke to each other as they worked. When the last of the food was transported to the big house, Amanda remained there to serve Master Thomas and his guests.

This morning at the breakfast table, there were only Master Thomas, Mr. Love and his son Matthew. Amanda liked being present when Master Thomas and his gentlemen friends were alone. Without the womenfolk, the men talked about politics and economics. She had to put on her stolid face so that they wouldn't be aware that she understood what they were saying. After serving each plate, she stood by the sideboard and listened.

"Pops," Matthew said. "You think that the Republican Party will win the next election. They came mighty close the last time."

"I doubt it," Mr. Love reassured his son. "The Democratic Party is fairly strong. Senator Douglas of Illinois would be a good candidate for the next election."

"Don't you think that the South will most likely want Vice President Breckinridge? After all, he's from Kentucky."

"But, Pops, Douglas believes that the people of a territory have the right to prohibit slavery before the territory becomes a state."

"That doesn't set well with some folks around here." Master Thomas commented. "That's why I would pick Breckinridge."

Before anyone could answer, Mariah seemed to float in the room with Colette at her heels. She went around and kissed her father on the forehead, while Colette took her place at the sideboard, All the gentlemen rose and Cudge, who was standing by Amanda quickly pulled a chair from the table so Miz Mariah could be seated. She took the seat and Cudge gently pushed it back up to the table. Without Miz Mariah saying a word, Amanda poured milk in the glass on her right.

"Wat cans I's git yo, Miz Mariah?"

"Some of that county ham, eggs and grits with some of that redeye gravy on my grits."

"Yes sum."

Amanda did as she was told.

"It's mighty quiet around here, this morning. I heard the bell ringing and I couldn't get back to sleep."

"Most of the slaves are in the field."

"What was all that noise about late last night?"

"Oh," Master Thomas sighed. "It was just the slave patrol."

"They catch anybody?"

Amanda almost dropped the pitcher of milk, while she waited for Master Thomas' answer. She prayed that Power was safe. Perhaps, he did make it back to Shoal Creek. Putting the pitcher back on the sideboard, she again resumed her position and listened to the rest of the breakfast conversation.

"Nope," Master Thomas answered. "Charles takes his job real serious."

"He should." Mr. Love concurred. "Someone has to keep the niggers in their place."

There was not going to be an argument about that. Master Matthew and Miz Mariah looked at each other, but Amanda couldn't figure out their reasoning. Basically, it wasn't her business. That was a matter between the Loves. The moment was gone as Master Willie started talking about his favorite subject, the Western North Carolina Railroad. He had gotten into politics because he felt that North Carolina needed some internal improvements. He was the chairman of the Committee on Internal Improvements and one of the additives was that the state needed a railroad system across the state.

"The Western North Carolina Railroad is slowly coming about." Mr. Love commented.

"It seems like it's going to be a lifetime."

"I understand that Chum and Patton are advertising for slaves to work on the railroad. I saw some flyers in Asheville a while back."

'We're going to have to do something."

"What about the Blue Ridge Railroad project?"

"Don't know where that's going." Master Thomas sighed hopelessly. "There's no chance. South Carolina legislature didn't appropriate any more funds for the project. I've been pretty optimistic about it, but it sure seems like the future for that interstate line is in deep trouble."

"That's all you think about." Mariah rose from the table and went over to Matthew. She took him by the hand and attempted to pull him from the chair. Reluctantly, he got up and followed her.

"Matt and I are going to explore this place."

"Be careful," Master Thomas called. "Cudge, you go with them."

"Yes sir, Master."

Cudge left.

Breakfast was over. Amanda cleaned up the dining area. Afterward, she took a breakfast tray up to Miz Sallie, who was still in bed. All morning, she hadn't seen Flossie. Amanda hoped that everything was all right. Being pregnant was no excuse for not working.

Around noon, Master Thomas sent Sam to Shoal Creek. Amanda wanted to talk to him before he left, but never got a chance. She had other things to do. Lunch had to be served to Master Willie and his guests. It was Friday and Mr. Love had to get back to campaigning. With the weekend coming up, he felt that there would be a lot of gatherings where he could speak. After lunch the Loves were leaving for White Sulphur Springs.

Part of the morning, Amanda helped Miz Mariah pack her valise and assisted Master Matthew with his baggage. She wondered why the Loves didn't have personal servants to assist them. Everyone knew that Mr. Love was the biggest slave owner in Haywood County. Mr. Love had his body servant, Josiah, but he never associated with Master Thomas' slaves. She wanted to ask him about Bill, but she never had the nerve. For if she was seen with one of Mr. Love's slaves, someone would report to Power. Life was misery enough without making Power jealous. Perhaps that was why he sneaked up here. News traveled fast in this mountainous region. With Mr. Love campaigning for the state legislature, everyone in Jackson County knew that he was coming, and Amanda thought that might be why Power came to check up on her.

Then it suddenly occurred to Amanda. Suckey had been very abrupt with her when she inquired about Power. A smile came across her face. No one on the place ever saw Josiah. Amanda always felt that he and Sam hung together. After all they were both personal slaves to their masters. When Sam went to Shoal Creek, Josiah didn't go with him and he wasn't seen around the farm. After attending his master, Josiah seemed to disappear. There was only one place that he could be, he and Suckey were together. That was why Suckey had closed the door in her face. Josiah was in her room. With everything ready for the Loves departure, Amanda crept out the back door. Hiding behind the old oak, she spied on Suckey. She hoped that Josiah would go to her before he left for White Sulphur Springs. It seemed like an eternity as she waited for him to say his good-byes to Suckey. During that time, she prayed that she wasn't needed. Just as she was about to abandon all hope of seeing the two of them together, Josiah and Suckey came out of Suckey's room. They kissed. When Suckey disappeared back into the kitchen, Amanda walked toward Josiah. She had no intention of asking him about Bill, but her heart took over. Josiah was a big man with long legs. Amanda had to run to catch before he got to the front of the house.

"Josiah," she called.

He turned and stopped.

She ran to him. "I's. . ."

"I knows who youse be."

"Look, I just wanna ass youse 'bout. . ." She turned and walked away.

"Wait," he called. "You wanna know about William Hudson Casey."

"Yes!"

"He be in the hands of Master Love."

"He be a slave."

"Don't know. His mammy is free."

"Free?"

"Yep. It seem'd dat his mammy sold'em to Master fer a lot of years of serve. Master done loan'im out to somebody way in Asheville."

"I see."

"Child, I has to go." He patted her on the head. "Youse love'm, don't youse."

'Yes," Amanda whispered.

Josiah walked away and his long stride got him to porch in time. On the other hand, Amanda had to run to get to the back of house to get in. She ran into the house to find Miz Sallie pleading with her father.

"Pops," she begged. "Can't you stay over until Sunday?"

"I'm afraid not." Mr. Love looked over at Miz Mariah. "But Mariah can stay if she wishes."

"How about it?" Sallie pleaded.

"Sure."

Perhaps with Miz Mariah around, Amanda might have some free time. Lunch was served without any problems. Miz Sallie found everything to her satisfaction. Amanda was happy, but she still wasn't free until Mr. Love and his son left. Then she had to clean the remainder of the house. She wanted to know what had happened to Power. There was no one she could talk to for that information. She and Suckey weren't speaking to each other. Amanda felt someone on the place must know something. Flossie, whom she hadn't seen all morning, could perhaps shed some light on the commotion that occurred last night.

At the twilight of the evening, Amanda finally left the big house. She was drained both physically and emotionally. As she started toward Flossie's cabin, she saw Sam returning from Shoal Creek. Sam had left in a wagon, but he returned riding a horse. The quick gait of the horse told Amanda that something was amiss. Stopping in her tracks, she hurriedly retraced her steps back to the big house. Before she got to the house, Sam had dismounted, tethered the horse to the hitching post in the front of the house and sprinted toward the back door. Amanda broke into a run and tried to catch him before he entered the house. She was too late. By the time she got to the back door, Sam was already inside. Nervously, she remained there. Something was wrong and she had a feeling that it had to with Power. She crept around the house and crouched beneath Mater Thomas' office window. Perhaps, she could eavesdrop on their conversation.

"What?" Amanda recognized Master's voice

"He be in stocks at Shoal Creek."

Master Willie stormed. "He's not the law. Look, I want you to go Webster and get Sheriff Davies."

"Not t'night."

"Yes."

"I don't dink so."

"Sam!"

"No, Master Thomas. It be dark out dere. Ain't no nigger in his rat mind gonna be out wonderin' 'round out dere. Not with wat dey did to Power."

Amanda fell to her knees and tears silently fell from her eyes. She crawled away from the window and tried to stand up, but but her body wouldn't cooperate. Therefore, she crawled back to her cabin. Desperately, she wanted to know what happened to Power, but mentally she didn't want to know. Somehow, she managed to get to the cabin and crawl in the door.

"Chile," Martha came to her daughter's rescue. Instead of pulling Amanda to her feet, she knelt beside her. "Chile, wat's de matt'r? I herd rumors 'bout Power. I jest came o'er to see."

Amanda laid her head on Martha's right shoulder. In great sobs, she cried uncontrollable, Martha allowed her to cry as she wrapped her arms around her daughter. At that moment, there was a knock on the door.

"Martha," Sam's voice drifted through the door.

"C'mon in" Martha shouted.

Sam came into the cabin and found the two women hugged up on the floor. Martha looked up at Sam.

"Wat's de trouble, Sam?"

"Wat's wrong with Mandy?"

Martha shook her head.

"She knows, doesn't she?"

"Knows wat?"

"Power was caught last night without a pass. De paddy rollers got'im jest as he got to Shoal Creek."

"Oh, my God!" Martha hugged Mandy tighter. "He be dead?"

"No, he's been beaten badly and dey put'im in the stock in the middle of the street."

Amanda whined like a little child. Her world had been shattered and she felt it was her fault.

Chapter 25

The next morning Amanda was up before the work bell chimed. She dressed and went to the big house. There was an oil lamp shining in the window of Master Willie's office. She saw two silhouettes in the room. One was seated behind the desk and the other one was standing with a slight bend. The two had to be Master Thomas and Sam. She knew he was sending Sam to fetch Sheriff Davies. Outside, a horse was tethered at the hitching post in front of the house. Willie was sending Sam into Webster to report the public whipping of Power. Amanda hoped Sheriff Davies would punish Mr. Bumgarner. From the shadows, she watched the two men walk out of the house. For the first time, she saw Sam used the front door. A servant always used the back door, especially if he was a slave. After Sam untethered the horse and mounted it, Willie gave him instructions.

"You know where the jail is in Webster?"

"Yes sir."

Willie handed Sam a leather bag with a strap on it. Sam put it over his head and let rest on his left shoulder.

"I want you to take that to Sheriff Davies."

"Yes sir."

"Here is your pass in case someone asks you. And remember, Sam, go over the mountain. That's a short cut."

"Yes sir."

Sam reached down and took the pass. He put it in his pocket and he was off. Willie stood and watched him until he was out of sight, then he slowly walked back into house. At that moment the bell told the slaves, it was time to get to work. Amanda had stood there and watched, too. Master Thomas was powerful; therefore Amanda believed that he could fix it. Sighing heavily, she went around the house to enter from the back door. Just as she got to the back door, the horn sounded for the slaves to dress and head for the field. Going inside she began to work. Mariah was there and Amanda hoped that Sallie and Mariah would entertain themselves. She was not in the mood to be at their beck and call. She needed to be nearby when Sheriff Davies came.

As she went out the door to go to the kitchen, she saw Mr. Bumgarner on the premises. She knew Master Thomas and Bumgarner were going to get into a heated discussion and she wanted to be there. However, duty called. She got breakfast from the kitchen and placed it on the sideboard. Colette was already to do her duty when there was a knock on the front door. Amanda went to answer it. As she opened the door, she stood face to face with Mr. Bumgarner.

"Tell, your master that I 'm here and I need to talk to him." Mr. Bumgarner said as he stepped into the foyer of the house.

"Yes sir."

Amanda went to Master Willie's office and rapped on the door.

"Who is it?"

"It's me, Master."

"Come in."

Amanda opened the door and announced, "Sir, Mr. Bumgarner wishes to see youse."

"Let him in."

Amanda returned to Mr. Bumgarner and escorted him to Willie's office. When Amanda opened the door, Willie waved Mr. Bumgarner to enter. He went in and Amanda closed the door behind him. She lingered at the door, until she heard footsteps on the stairs. Quickly moving away from the office, Amanda positioned herself at the sideboard. Miz Mariah came down for breakfast. Sallie was not with her. Lately, because of morning sickness, she had been skipping breakfast.

Colette served Miz Mariah her breakfast, while Amanda went up to see about Dearest Sallie and Little Willie. When she got to the nursery, Dearest Sallie was breast feeding Little Willie. Amanda could tell that Dearest Sallie was tired. Pregnant with another child and she was still breast feeding.

"Youse need to wean Little Willie."

"He needs the milk."

"Yes sum."

"I'm sorry about Power."

"It ain't yo' fault."

"It's my business. Power is a value piece of property to my husband."

Amanda became angry, but she could not say anything. She turned her back on Miz Sallie with the pretense of looking out the window. As she turned back around to speak, Caroline came in the door.

"Miz Sallie," Caroline said softly. "I have Little Willie's bath ready."

Sallie had finished feeding and burping him. She handed the child to Caroline. She got up and headed for her room, then turned back to Amanda. "You need to clean the Master bedroom. The linen needs to be changed."

"Yes sum."

"And make sure that Mariah's sleeping quarter is clean. She will need clean linen also."

"Yes sum."

Caroline was bathing Little Will, while Amanda would spend most of the morning cleaning the upstairs. As she left the nursery, she headed for the master bedroom, when she heard angry voices downstairs. She stopped and listened.

"Damn, Charles, you had not right to whip him that

way and leave him there."

"Senator, I had every right. Your niggers act like that they can do anything they want to. They hafto be punished or they'll run all over you."

"So you gonna destroy my property. That's money. And you're gonna pay for it."

"You can come and get'im. I believe your niggers got the point."

Mr. Bumgarner headed out the front door. As he left, he reminded the Senator.

"You caused the Luftys to remain in this area. When Jackson ordered their removal, they all should've gone."

The door slammed and Mr. Bumgarner was gone.

Looking down from the landing, Amanda saw Master Thomas, who was red in the face. Quickly she moved away from his view and started her morning routine.

In the nursery, she heard Little Will's laughter, as her own heart cried out in angry. She could do nothing. Sadly, she began to hum "Steal Away" while she worked. Cleaning up behind her owners and their folks, Amanda hoped that Power was back at Stekoa Field and she would take care of him. Humming and praying, Amanda knew the owners thought she was happy.

Chapter 26

That afternoon some time before the sun went down, Alfred brought Power to Stekoa. The buckboard from the store was used to transport him. The buckboard didn't stop at the big house, but proceeded to the slave quarters. As it rumbled through the driveway, slave children followed it. Quickly the news spread that Power was home.

For Amanda, it was bitter sweet for she could not go to him. Duty called. She had to serve supper to the master's family. There was no time off for personal matters, although Power needed her. As she was setting the table for the last repast of the day, Miz Sallie reminded her that there would be another guest. Without questioning her, she set another plate. When she passed in the hall, she noted that Master Thomas' office door was closed.

Dinner was ready and the fourth person entered the room just ahead of Willie. To Amanda's surprise, it was Sheriff Davies with his goatee and long slim face. The badge he adorned on his vest told the story. They sat down to eat. Colette stood by and fanned the flies away. Amanda served them from the sideboard. As they ate, there was an eerie silence. Conversation was almost none, as they tiptoed around the important issues of the day.

Miz Sallie and Miz Mariah finished first. Miz Mariah left before her sister and spoke to the guest.

"It was nice meeting you, Sheriff Davies,"

The sheriff stood up and bowed slightly. "The pleasant was mine."

Miz Sallie went around to Master Willie and kissed him on the cheek.

"Don't stay here all night and talk politics."

"We won't." Master Willie laughed.

The ladies left and the two men were alone.

"Coffee, Sheriff?"

"Yeah, I believe I will."

"Amanda?"

"Yes sir."

From the sideboard, she retrieved two cups and saucers and placed them on the table. Then she got coffee and poured into each cup.

"Is dat all, sir?"

"Yes. I want you to clear the table and take the dishes to Suckey. Go home."

"Yes sir."

Amanda almost fainted. Steadying herself, she removed all the plates and silverware from the table. It took her three loads to get them to the kitchen. On her second trip back she heard Sheriff Davies' voice.

"Senator, I'm gonna serve Mr. Bumgarner these papers, but he's gonna win in court."

"He ruined my property."

"The nigger was running away,"

"No, he was going home."

Amanda made some noise and the two men hushed.

Gathering the last dishes from the sideboard, Amanda had heard enough. She would not try to spy on the two men; the judgment was already handed down. With a heavy heart, Amanda went to her cabin. When she got there, she noted a candle burning and the cabin appeared to be empty. Panicky she ran inside and found her mother nursing Power. He lay on the pallet on the floor. He seemed to be asleep. Going closer, she saw the whip marks on his back. She was appalled. Desperately she wanted to hug him...to take him in her arms and comfort him. Standing there, she imagined him locked in the stock, beaten; not only a visible one, but an inner one. She hoped that didn't destroy his soul.

Her mama sat at the table where the candle was. Sleep was trying to claim her, as Amanda stepped over to her and touched her on the shoulder. She turned and looked up at her daughter.

"I's glad youse here."

"I's couldn't git 'way."

"Youse is here, now. He's been callin' fer youse."

"Go home. I's take care of'im".

Martha gave Amanda some salve she had mixed in a bowl. "When he wake up, put this on his wounds."

"Yes ma'am."

Martha left the couple alone. Amanda contemplated about solving this problem. Power was a man, but treated like an animal. She felt responsible for part of his problem, most of all she blamed the Antebellum society. Everything they do is orchestrated by the master. Even they could choose the man you marry. Power needed to get away from this area, not as a runaway. Then it came to her, Master Thomas could hire him to work on his precious railroad. She would talk to Power about it.

Chapter 27

Sunday came and with it, the circuit-riding preacher. He had finally gotten around to this end of Jackson County. And in these parts, there were a lot of folks to covert to the Christian faith. Besides the white inhabitants, there were the Luftys and the slaves who had to be saved. So when the bell rang on Sunday morning to arouse the slaves from their restful sleep, most of them couldn't understand. On Stekoa Fields, Sunday was always a day of rest, except for those who worked in the big house or when the crops were threatened to be ruined by Mother Nature. The crops were maturing and it wasn't time to be harvested. And yet, the slaves reluctantly made their way to assemble in the front yard of the big house. Everyone was present, except Dave, who constantly ignored the bell.

Perhaps they were free. This notion ran through Amanda's mind as she trudged through the morning dew. Now she could take life in her own hand. As a free person, she could make her own choice. She didn't have to live with Power. And yet, after the beating he took from Mr. Bumgarner and his paddy rollers, she felt she had an obligation to him. It was apparent he loved her.

However, her bubbles burst when she listened to what some of the others were talking about among themselves as they headed for the big house. Some suspected that Dearest Sallie had had her second child and Master was going to announce the blessed event. Others, who were older including her mother, felt that they were going to be preached to by the circuit-riding preacher.

When they gathered in the front yard, Sam was waiting for them. Master Thomas was nowhere in sight. An atmosphere of gloom took over the crowd. It seemed when Sam was in charge; it meant some kind of work detail. A lot of grumbles and mumbles went through the gathering; Sam simply raised his hand and quieted them.

"Master Thomas tol' me to tell youse dat Rev. Asbury will be here sometimes dis afternoon to save yer souls."

"Dank yo Jesus," shouted a male slave. "It seems likk months of Sundays since we's been preach'd to."

"Youse rat," Martha agreed. "Jesus wanna know ifen heben is still my home."

"Hallelujah! Praise de Lord!"

"Dank God! Now we's gotta go home an' doll oursel'es up fer de preacher." Martha squeezed Amanda's arm.

"He's ain't nuthin' but a white man," Amanda countered.

"Girl," Martha tried to reassure her. "He be a man of de cloth."

Amanda didn't answer as the jubilant feeling spread throughout the gathering. God had not forgotten them. As they dispersed, Amanda walked with her mother back to her mother's cabin. Since Power was brought to Stekoa, Martha was living in the single women's cabin. Amanda tried to go see her as much as possible, but it was difficult. With her duties at the big house and nursing Power back to health, she had little time to see her. Arm in arm, mother and daughter walked back to the quarters.

"Mama," Amanda remarked. "Do youse 'member dat we use to go to church with Miz Temperance?"

"Yeah, we's had to set in de back."

"Dat was long 'go."

"Yeah," Martha sighed. "An' aft'r dat we slaves snuck off to de woods to worship. But dose paddy rollers stopp'd dat."

At the mention of the paddy rollers, Amanda became angry. She would never forget the degree of beating Power took at the hands of the paddy rollers. The opened wounds on his back from the many slashes of the whip were deep and many. His back reminded her of the crisscross lines she had made in the dirt as a child. And yet, as a child, she could take her feet and erase those lines. For Power, those lines would be permanent. Scarred.

Amanda squeezed her mother's arm. "It ain't right."

Martha patted her daughter's arm.

"Dose paddy rollers had no right."

"Master Thomas said dat dey did."

Mama," tears pooled up in Amanda's eyes. "He jest wanna to see me."

"Child, ev'n de law couldn't do anythin' 'bout it. Master Thomas tri'd. He tol' me dat Power should've been out without a pass. Dat's de law. Stock'em ans beat'em. It don't matter ifen its Master Thomas' property or someone else. We's just gotta learn."

"Youse b'lieve dat."

Martha didn't answer.

"It jest ain't fair."

By this time, they were at the cabin. Martha and Amanda looked at each other. The silence between them was deafening. Other slaves walked by them. There was jubilance among them, but for Martha and Amanda the joy had slipped away. Turning away from her daughter, Martha walked toward Flossie's cabin. Amanda watched her for a little while, and then she went inside.

Upon entering the cabin, she found Power sitting on the side of the bed. Beads of sweat covered his body and Amanda knew he had struggled to get up. Hurriedly, she went over to him and gently helped him back in bed. Without much protest, he allowed her to do it. She laid him on his stomach and his scarred opened wounds stared back at her. She needed to dress those wounds and put some more of Martha's mixture on it.

"Where's youse been?"

"At the big house."

Power groaned. Amanda knew he was in pain. Gently, she took the herbs Martha mixed and applied it on the wounds. Amanda knew it hurt. Over and over in her mind, she wanted to ask him why he left that night. Deep down, she knew the answer, but she didn't want to hear it from Power's lip. After she finished putting the salve on, she covered the wounds with a clean rag so insects wouldn't lay their eggs.

Sighing heavily, she sat down on the bed and watched Power as his shoulders rose and fell. Amanda knew he was sleeping. Now she could prepare herself for church. Service wouldn't be until the sun reached its apex in the sky, then start down again. Therefore all the slaves were dolling themselves up to attend.

The first thing Amanda did, as did the entire slave women, was to remove her head rag. When the head rag came off, it released nappy matted hair that no comb could go through it. She knew she had to wet her hair to make it more manageable. Looking around the room, she noticed tthe oaken bucket was empty. That meant she had to go and get some water. Not only that, she had to go to the barn and borrow the sheep steel brush to comb the tangles out of her hair.

Untangling her hair alone would be a long and tedious job. Hence, she decided she would seek her mother's help. Together, they used to comb and style each other's hair when Miz Temperance was the mistress of the place. Digging into the scrape and trying to rid it of dandruff, dirt and lice was no fun; but it had to be done. Amanda dreaded this, but she had to look her best at the church meeting. She knew now...it didn't matter to her that preacher was white.

Just as she was leaving, Martha was coming up the trail. Looking at her, Amanda noted that she had her head rag off and her hair mirrored hers.

"I knowed dat youse couldn't stay 'way from Power

dat long. So's I's thou't I's come to youse."

"Git yer hair comb'd an' styl'd fer church."

"Yeah!"

"I was jest gonna go o'er to the barn an' git dat steel brush."

"I's got it."

Amanda and Martha were all set to tackle their kinky matted nappy hair. Amanda took the oaken bucket and went outside to fill it with rainwater from the huge barrel. It was believed that rainwater would cleanse the hair. Mother and daughter went outside to shampoo each other hair. After their hair washing, they used the small iron used to press clothes to smooth out their hair. With a hot knife, they wrapped their strands of hair around it and pressed the hair with the small clothing iron. They continued this method until they had curls all over their head. This took two hours. In and out of the house as they heated the iron and knife on the hearth. They fixed each other's hair.

Finally when they entered the cabin for last time, Power was awake, but he was still in bed. Turning toward the creaking of the door, he saw Amanda and Martha. Surprisingly he looked at them. A frown crossed his forehead. He had never seen Martha or Amanda all dolled up. He couldn't believe his eyes.

"Glory be," he managed through his pain. "Dis must be heben."

"Jest 'nother day of rest." Martha assured him.

"Youse is fer real."

"In de flesh," Amanda smiled at him.

"Why?" Power struggled to get up. "I's gonna die?"

Amanda went to him and gently helped him resume his prone position. "No! No!"

"Amanda is rat. We's jest dressin' up fer the preacher."

"A preacher?"

"Yep."

"A white preacher?"

"A man of the cloth, Power."

"Do it matt'r?" Martha stated. "Jest dink of when youse git to heben. Ev'rythin' will be diffi'rent."

"Woman," Power stormed. "Youse is crazy. Dere ain't no heben, Lt's only hell, likk it is down here."

"Youse don't know. De Bible. . ."

"Don't gimme any of dat Bible stuff."

"Dat's blasphemy."

"Woman git out of here. Dis here is my cabin."

Although Amanda and Martha knew that Power couldn't force Martha out, it was time to go. They stared at each other. Without another word, Martha left. Disgusted, Amanda leaned against the door. Arguing the point was useless. She realized that with Power's condition, there was no reasoning with him. After fixing him something to eat, she found herself nodding in the chair.

Chapter 28

The bell chimed and Amanda jumped up. At first, she thought it was the next morning. Then, she realized it was time to hear the preacher. Sam told everyone that all slaves were required to attend the service. There was no way she could get out of the gathering, but she did persuade Sam that Power was not in any shape to go. They were told the preacher was going to take a count based on the number Sam gave him. And when they got back, they had informed Dave, who refused to go.

Wearily, Amanda got up and straightened her clothes. She looked over at Power, as he slept. Just as she was tiptoeing out of the cabin, Dave walked in.

"Power ain't goin', I ain't goin'."

"Do me a favor."

"Ifen youse ain't goin', stay with Power."

"No prob'em."

"Danks."

She tiptoed out the cabin, closed the creaking door and prayed Dave would stay.

Martha met her outside and they went to the clearing together. When they got there a few older slaves were already seated on the logs. Rev. Asbury was present and he stood by the makeshift pulpit. The preacher counted the slaves as they arrived. This meant that everyone was expected to attend and those who didn't would probably be flogged. Thinking about it, Amanda felt Master Thomas had arranged for the preacher to come to remind them they were

slaves. It was apparent that Willie didn't want what happened to Power to befall any other of his valuable property.

Anger seized Amanda and the reverence of the situation was gone. Even the rays of the sun, bursting through
the trees and the sweet chirping of the birds, could not shake
the rage tearing at her heart. To her Rev. Asbury was a devil
in a preacher's suit.

Now Rev. Asbury had finished counting and it was evident that someone was missing. Silence filled the air, as
they waited for Asbury to spout the Gospel. He had a worn
black Bible and a badly torn brown hymnal. He picked up
the hymnal and flipped through it to select a hymn. He
chose "We're Bound for the Promise Land" and began
'passing out' the hymn. In other words, he read the first two
lines, and then the slaves would sing. Then he would read
the next two lines afterward the slaves sang. On and on
Rev. Asbury 'passes out' lines while the slaves sang. He
even gave the hymn its pitch and the slaves followed along.

"On Jordan's stormy banks I stand
And cast a wishful eye
To Canaan's fair and happy land
Where my possession lie.""

They sang several hymns before Rev. Asbury got to
his sermon. He had built the slaves' spirit high. When he
spoke, he wanted to have their full attention and singing
brought them close together. As usual Rev. Asbury ex-
pounded with text that dealt with Blacks being slaves and
their obedience and servitude to their master.

"For the good book says to be obedient to your master
for the good of your soul." He shouted to the slaves.

Looking at Asbury's audience, Amanda felt they were
disappointed. All eyes seemed to focus on her. Deep down,
she and Power were the target out this religious gathering.
This was Thomas's way of keeping his slaves in line. After
the service, Amanda left with a bitter taste in her mouth. She
knew that Rev. Asbury had been allowed to preach to them

because of what Power had done. Either mother or daughter talked about the sermon. When they arrived at the single women's quarters, they hugged, and then Amanda went to the big house to serve supper to Sallie and Mariah. She was thankful that cleaning up after the two didn't take long.

When she got to their cabin, Dave had already left. She wondered if he really stayed with Power. However, she knew her mother had come over and made sure he was comfortable. At this moment all she wanted to do now was sleep. Looking around, she found that someone had brought Power something to eat and changed the cloth that covered his wounds. She slipped into the bed beside him.

Chapter 29

The next morning, Amanda was up and ready to go before the horn sounded. She needed to run over to the single women cabin to see her mother. Just as she was about to go out the door, her mother entered.

"Mama, I be jest thinkin' 'bout youse."

"I be a thinkin' 'bout who was gonna take care of Power while youse is at the big house."

"Danks fer comin'."

"How be he?"

"He be restless." Amanda remarked, "He needs to git out of here."

"He'll be a goin' back to Shoal Creek soon."

"No, I mean out of dis 'hole system."

"Youse is not thinkin' a tellin' him to run away?"

"No! Lord God, no!"

"Den wat?"

"De ot'er day I herd Master Thomas say dat his railroad want'd slave to hep lay de tracks."

"An' youse wants me to ass him?"

At that moment the horn sounded and Amanda had to go. She couldn't wait for Martha's answer, but she knew she would mull over it. Hurrying to get to the big house, she ran into Dave who was heading the same way. He fell in step with Amanda and began a conversation.

"Amanda, youse hafto tell Miz Sallie why I wasn't at dat preaching."

She laughed. "Why weren't youse at de service?"

"Now, Mandy, youse knows."

"I's tell Miz Sallie dat you were a tendin' my man."

"I was."

"Youse weren't dere wen I got home."

"Yo' mammy came an' tol' me to leave."

"Wat are youse up dis mornin'?" Amanda demanded, "The fields be back dat a way."

"Been call to come by Master Thomas."

"Good luck to you."

They entered the house from the back door. Amanda continued on in and made her way to the bedroom upstairs. She didn't see where Dave went. As usual, she spent the morning serving breakfast, emptying bed chambers, changing bed linen, and washing clothes. Caroline was taking care of Little Will, while Miz Sallie and her sister went to Shoal Creek. The Senator spent his time closeted in his office.

Around mid- morning, Master Thomas summoned Amanda to his office. Stopping was she was doing, she presented herself to his office. She knocked on the door and announced herself.

"Mandy come in."

She opened the door and walked in. "Yes sir."

"Rev. Asbury said that all you niggers didn't get to the gathering."

"Well, Master, youse know dat Power couldn't go."

"I'm aware of that." He looked up at her.

"Dave didn't go 'cause I ass'd him to take care of Power fer me."

"I see." Master Willie sighed, "It appears to me that Dave needed to attend the gathering more then you."

"Yes sir."

Willie waved her out the door. "That's all."

Amanda hesitated, and then she turned and started out the door.

"You need to talk to me."

"No sir," Amanda left.

After she left, she wondered if she should have mentioned about allowing Power to work on the railroad. However, she didn't have time to dwell on the situation. Duty called. Perhaps her mother would mention it to him. Mandy believed her mother had a good relationship with Master. Whether it was a personal or solid friendship, Amanda didn't know. As she worked, she recalled what her mother had said about Power's beating. The law was the law.

With Miz Sallie gone, there was only Willie for lunch. However, he told Amanda, he didn't really want anything. Amanda was happy about it as she continued to clean the house from top to bottom. She watched from the bedroom window, as Willie strolled across the lawn and headed toward the slave quarters.

After cleaning the Master bedroom, she went into the nursery where Little Will was sleeping and Caroline was seated in the rocker half asleep. When Mandy came into the room, she jumped up and went to Little Willie's crib.

"He be fine, Caroline."

Caroline sighed, "Dis git to me."

"Youse don't likk babies."

"I's lov'em. I's been with chile three times an' lost all three."

"I's sorry to hear dat."

"Then I goes to White Sulphur Springs an' my man got hisself 'nother woman. It's jest ain't right. Miz Sallie is ready to have 'nother one. I ain't got nothing." Tears formed in Caroline's eyes and silently dropped.

Mandy was stunned. "Cans I's ass youse a question?"

"Wat kinda question?"

"'Bout yo father."

"Didn't know my mammy. She died wen I was born. But I's look at Miz Sallie and her sisters. I look lik'em."

"Youse think dat Mr. Love be yo pappy?"

"I shore do."

"My pappy is Master Thomas and he wouldn't let me

jump de broom with de man I love."

"Youse love William Hudson Casey."

"How do you know?"

"He talked 'bout youse when I's at Sulphur Springs"

"He wanna know ifen youse were with child."

"Oh, no!"

The two now shared a secret. Mandy felt sorry for Caroline because she never knew her mother. Amanda thought of what she did to prevent pregnancy, while Caroline had three miscarriages. She hugged Caroline and allowed her to cry on her shoulder. Then Little Will woke up crying. Caroline went to him, while Mandy proceeded to clean the room. As she cleaned the room, she sang the song she composed about Bill.

> *Bill, my love is a smithy*
> *Who hammers all day*
> *Bill, my love is smithy*
> *But he has been sent away!*

All afternoon as Amanda finished her duties that song rang in her head. She got involved with the song; she completely forgot that she was at the big house. As she seemed to float into the parlor, she stopped when she saw that Miz Sallie and Mariah had returned. Ironically, Sallie was playing a tune at the piano.

"What were you singing?" Miz Sallie asked.

"Nuthin'," Amanda said. "Jest somethin' I made up."

"Let's hear it." Miz Mariah demanded. "let's hear it."

Amanda looked from Miz Mariah to Dearest Sallie and back again. She realized she could not tell them that it wasn't their business. After all, she was just a nigger slave and Dearest Sallie's husband owned her. Her body was theirs, but not her soul. Without any more fanfare, Amanda sang the song "Bill, my Love is Smithy", and then she dashed out of the room to make a beeline to the pantry. However, she was stopped by Master Thomas.

"Amanda, I need to see you"

"Yes sir." She wiped the tears from her face and walked into his office.

"Let me tell you what I'm going to do for you and Power." He looked at her, but she had no response. "The railroad needs a lot of good men to build the tracks. I'm hiring out Power to do slave labor. Maybe this will teach him a lesson."

"Yes sir."

Amanda left the office. She wanted to shout for joy, but she restrained herself. A slave wasn't supposed to shout and holler in the Master's house. However, she could sing. Then she remembered her encounter with Dearest Sallie and her sister...and knew she shouldn't sing anymore. Happiness was on the inside, but she wiped her face of all emotion and begrudgingly went about her duties.

Chapter 30

Being the white chief of the Lufty Indians, Master Thomas had to make sure they remained in Western North Carolina. To do that Master Willie would go to the different ceremonies. He wanted Miz Sallie to involve herself in the Lufty women virtues. Therefore, he decided she should visit the reservation and get to know the womenfolk. Since Mariah was visiting, she could go with her. It was August and the Green Corn Ceremony was going to be performed. He felt the ceremony would be great and allow Miz Sallie to observe the culture of the Native Americans.

The morning of the adventure into the Native American culture would be fun, especially for Miz Mariah. Miz Sallie was a little apprehensive about the entire outing. She demanded Little Will wouldn't go with them. Flossie would take care of him. Amanda and Caroline would accompany the two ladies. Sam would drive the carriage and Cudge would go along for the ride. Amanda and Caroline sat on one end of the carriage and Miz Sallie and Miz Mariah sat on the other end which had a top to keep the sun out. For Amanda, this would take her mind off of Power. It was a chance for her to see some of her Lufty friends whom she hadn't seen in years. She only hoped they would remember her.

As the carriage left the Stekoa Fields, Miz Mariah was talkative.

"What's the Indians like?" she asked.

"Haven't you seen an Indian?" Miz Sallie asked instead of answering her question. "Ask Amanda, she lived around here."

"Well, Amanda" Miz Mariah demanded, "What are they like?"

"They are darker than you and lighter than me."

"Dat ain't wat she a talkin 'bout." Cudge reminded Amanda.

"Why don't youse tell her?"

"Ok, I's will."

"Let'em find out themselves," Sam remarked. "I 'lieve dat all folks needs to judge fer themselves."

As they drove down the road to Shoal Creek, their carriage was stopped by Mr. Bumgarner. Since the top covered Miz Mariah and Miz Sallie, he had other ideas.

"What are you doing out here?"

"I's takin' Miz Sallie and Miz Mariah to Shoal Creek?"

Mr. Bumgarner laughed. "Those two niggers don't look like'em."

Miz Sallie looked out from the shade. "Mr. Bumgarner, I'm right here. It would be helpful if you would leave my people alone."

Bumgarner tipped his hat. "I's sorry, Miz Sallie, I didn't see you."

"I believe my driver told you what he was doing."

"Just didn't see ma'am." He smiled showing his tobacco covered teeth."You know I'm just trying to keep the niggers in line."

"Thank you, Mr. Bumgarner." She answered. "But we must be on our way. Sam, we have to be going. "

"Yes sum."

Sam snapped the whip at the pair of horses and rode on down the road, leaving Mr. Bumgarner behind. Amanda sighed, as did Caroline. Mariah laughed.

"It's not funny." Miz Sallie reprimanded Mariah. "That man is dangerous."

Around noon, with their personal slaves, Miz Sallie and Miz Mariah arrived at Shoal Creek. Sam parked the carriage in front of Thomas' Store. Sam went inside and bought cigarettes and crackers, which he put on his account. Miz Mariah and Miz Sallie, with the help of Cudge, stepped down out of the carriage and also went inside. Cudge followed them. Amanda and Caroline remained in the carriage. Amanda looked around and her eyes stopped at the blacksmith shop. It was operating, but she knew that Bill was not there.

"Caroline," Amanda pointed to the blacksmith shop, "Dat were I met'im."

"Who?"

"Bill."

"You mean William Hudson Casey."

"Dat's his name."

They laughed as Cudge came back to the carriage with crackers in his hand.

"Wat are youse laughin' 'bout?"

"Nuthin'." Amanda got out stretching her legs. "Why don't youse go ov'r dere an' see who the blacksmith be."

Cudge chimed, "It ain't Bill."

At that moment the rest of their party came out of the store. They got back in the carriage and went to the Wolftown community where the Green Corn Ceremony was being celebrated. As they got closer to Wolftown, they all now felt uneasy about intruding on the Luftys sacred ceremony. But Master Thomas had assured them that they would be welcomed. As they entered Wolftown, they saw a huge field of corn. In the middle of the cornfield was a lookout tower, where an individual was stationed. Right away, a horn blew as they approached. Miz Mariah and Miz Sallie became frightened, but Amanda tried to calm them.

"Dey're not gonna to hurt youse." Sam tried to reassure them.

However, this did not calm the fear of the two, because echoing in the air was a war whoop. Looking up the road, there were about a dozen Luftys running toward them.

"Sallie!" Miz Mariah shouted, "make him turn around."

They surrounded the carriage. Sam stopped and jumped off the seat of the carriage.

"Where are you going?"

"James Crowe," Sam said, "This is Master Thomas's wife Miz Sallie and her sister Miz Mariah.

"Chief Thomas?"

"Yes sum."

"Welcome." He bowed, "to the Green Corn Ceremony. We perform it when the new corn is ripe enough to eat. We do not eat the new corn until the ceremony is finished. We have sent runners out to tell all the towns of nation about where and when we will celebrate. It is seven moons after the full moon, therefore, we will celebrate. Everything is in readiness."

"Thank you." Miz Sallie said.

They all got out of the carriage and walked into Wolftown.

Crowe continued to talk and explained the ceremony. "We gather seven ears of corn from each town. And from different fields. Since you are Chief Thomas's wife, I will explain this sacred ceremony to you. For days we have been preparing for this day."

As he talked about the preparation for the Green Corn Ceremony, Amanda was looking for a friend, Mary Tuskha. As she recalled she lived in Wolftown with her grandparents and other extended family members. Mary had a little brother, who used to chase her. Walking with the others, she tried to remember his name, but it didn't come to her. Years of separation and culture had faded away memories that perhaps would be buried forever.

"Mandy," a voice from her past called to her.

She stopped. Caroline stopped, too.

"Did youse hear my name called?"

Caroline nodded her head.

"Mandy?"

She turned around and came face to face with a grown slightly obese woman. Amanda didn't look at her obesity, but stared at her face. Amanda looked into those blue-blue eyes she remembered...her eyes had sparkled, even when she was angry. This was her friend.

Amanda ran to her and hugged her. "Mary," she cried, "Mary Tuskha."

Hugging Amanda, Mary mumbled, "It is you, Mandy."

"Yes, it be me."

Tears rimmed both girls' eyes. They stood there and just stared at each other. The years had matured them because of the culture in which they lived. An existence that was dominated by men had made them. By the age of twelve, both were ripe to be given to a man.

"It's been a lon' time." Amanda held on to her hands and stared at her.

"Yes, a long time." Mary agreed. "The last I saw you we was at a shuckin' at Stekoa Field. Do you still live there?"

"Yes," Amanda dropped her head. "I was forc'd to jump de broom with a man I don't really love, but I's 'spect him."

"Jump de broom," Mary smiled. "What is that?"

"Dey call it a slave's marriage."

"Does this not give you your freedom?"

"No, I's still a slave an' a behold'n to a slave. And we both are behold'n to Master Thomas."

"Chief Thomas?"

"Yes."

"Amanda," Caroline said nervously, "We's hafto go."

"Yes, I know. Miz Mariah will be callin' fer me."

Mary and Amanda hugged each and promised that they would talk again before the Green Corn Ceremony was over.

Caroline and Amanda moved through the crowd until they found Miz Sallie and Mariah. The two were seated on the ground on Lufty blankets. Their personal servants sat on the ground behind them. Neither one of the women turned around to scold them. Their attention was on the ceremony. However, Sam gave them a dirty look.

"We have fasted for six moons. We must put out the sacred fire and light it again."

They watched as the sacred fire was extinguished and then rekindled. As the sacred fire burned, the shaman held up a deer tongue and spoke in Cherokee. Then he put the tongue into the sacred fire. Taking kernels of corn from the seven ears of corn that had been gathered from the seven clans were thrown on the fire. A powder made from tobacco was sprinkled on the fire, which made the fire shoot up to the heavens. After the sacrificial offering, the shaman offered a prayer dedicating the corn to the Great Spirit in the sky.

Food had already been prepared from the new corn. They bought it to the people and fed them. There was Indian cornbread, bean bread, corn on the cob, and other Native American corn dishes. The Luftys, the slaves, and the slave owners ate together. It didn't matter your station in life, they celebrated the Green Corn Ceremony together.

Before they left to go back to Stekoa Fields, Amanda was able to talk to Mary again. It seemed that Mary was beholden to an older man, who already had two wives. She had three children, whom she adored. Amanda thought of how she had a destroyed life. She hugged Mary for she knew she had accepted her fate, while Amanda was still trying to deny hers.

"Keep the fate." She told Mary.

"When many moons have passed and the moon has come full circle two more times, there will be the Atohuna, the Reconciliation Ceremony, which is a bonding of friendship. You and I need to do that."

"Yes," Mandy agreed.

You know 'bout the New Moon Ceremony."

"I kinda 'member it."

"It"s when we believe that the world was created. Sort of like the whites celebrating a new year."

"I's tries to come."

Chapter 31

Now September's gentle winds whispered in the oak trees, and their green acorns clung on for life. Around Stekoa Fields, the blue-black fox grapes fell from their vines, which reminded all the slave that summer was fading away. It was time to get ready for the autumn leaves to fall and for the winter months to once again bring a hush over the farm. Harvest time was here and all the slaves were busy. Physically Power had healed, but the scars on his back and in his mind remained. Amanda saw the distant look in his eyes. She knew he was patiently waiting for an opportunity to escape. Mr. Terrell didn't want him at Shoal Creek. Now he was relegated to Stekoa Fields until Master Thomas could arrange for him to work on the Western North Carolina Railroad. As for now he was just a field hand.

Work songs filled the air to ease the laborious job they performed. Amanda listened to those mournful songs and knew Power was perhaps begrudgingly lifting his voice to that chorus. She remembered she use to sing those songs. Now she was a house slave and she didn't have to sing those mournful songs so often. And yet, her heart was heavy. Miz Temperance had gone back to her little house on Shoal Creek and Amanda missed her.

When Amanda and Miz Temperance were alone, she would tell Amanda all about her life before coming to Western North Carolina. She had told Amanda she was a distant cousin of the Calverts, who were the Proprietors of Maryland. Even her husband, Master Thomas's father was a cousin of President Zachary Taylor. So with Master Thomas marrying into the Love family of Haywood County, this allowed him to continue to maintain his social status. To Amanda, it was a fairy tale.

With Master Thomas' continuous slave population growth, his social status elevated. Flossie and Alfred had a baby boy and were now expecting another one. Several slave women were in a family way. It seemed all the fertile women slaves were pregnant, except Amanda and Caroline. Although Amanda had not wanted a child born into slavery, she now wished she could become pregnant. Perhaps if she were with child, Power would feel better about his manhood. Now Power was a shell of a man. Together, Mandy and Power were a miserable couple. At this point, she didn't care about any economic value Master Thomas would place on her child; she desperately wanted a baby.

For a while with Dearest Sallie and Master Thomas expecting their second child, Amanda was needed at the big house. She didn't see Power much. It seemed as if he was still in Shoal Creek. However, two months past, Dearest Sallie had lost her child. Little Will was only about seven months old, when Sallie had the miscarriage. Being weak, she couldn't provide enough milk for Little Will. One of the slave mothers had to be the mammy to him and he would be beast fed by one of new expectant slave mothers. Like a cow, Flossie was chosen to do the job. It was thought that Flossie needed to wean her son because she was expecting another child. At first Flossie was ecstatic and bragged about in the quarters.

"I's Little Will's wet nurse."

"That's great." Amanda answered. "But wat of yo own chile?"

"Wat 'bout'im?"

"He needs milk."

"I's gotta wean'im."

"So has Little Will?"

"But Dearest Sallie can't do it."

"I knows." Amanda shook her head and walked away.

Now standing in the big house and reflecting on all these things, Mandy listened to the mournful songs from the fields. Flossie was in the nursery, while Dearest Sallie and Miz Mariah were out riding around, with Caroline and Sam. Sam was driving the carriage, while Caroline took care of the ladies personal needs. Amanda thought all was quiet in the house, until she realized that some of the mournful singing was coming from within. Going to the nursery, she found Flossie breast feeding Little Will and a mournful tune escaped Flossie's lips. She stopped and listened carefully. Perhaps she wasn't hearing correctly. She watched Flossie seated in the rocker and feeding the baby. Her eyes were closed and Amanda saw tears escape from her closed eyelids. This couldn't be the Flossie she saw a few weeks ago. Where did her happiness go?

"Wat's de matt'r?" Mandy interrupted Flossie's singing.

"Nothin'."

"Youse seem so unhappy."

"No," Flossie fought back tears. "Not really."

"Where's yer li'l one?"

"He's fine," Flossie tried to smile. "I's gonna have 'nother one."

"Yeah." Amanda said sadly.

"How's Power?" Flossie quickly changed the subject'

"Fine."

"Give'm a baby."

Amanda wanted to curse Flossie. And before she could stop herself, she produced another lie. "I is."

"Youse means you gonna have a baby?" Flossie's eyes watered with tears of happiness.

Now both women were almost in tears. Amanda looked away from Flossie for she knew her own tears were not tears of happiness. Quickly, she left the nursery and went about finishing her work. When she reached the parlor, she found the two sisters had returned. They were laughing and talking, while Carolina stood in the shadows. Amanda shook her head. She could understand why Dearest Sallie wasn't taking care of Little Will. The miscarriage was a tragedy, but at least she had Little Will and Willie. Amanda felt she had nothing.

From the nursery, Amanda heard Little Will crying. Dearest Sallie quickly got up and left the parlor. Caroline followed her; Mariah remained and sat at the piano. She began playing the ballad "Jackson County Gal." Amanda was always leery of Miz Mariah. There was something about her she didn't trust. She and her brother Matthew always seemed to have some kind of scheme. Hurriedly Amanda attempted to leave the room, but Miz Mariah stopped tickling the ivory and called to her.

Amanda stopped, she didn't turn around. "Yes sum."

"You are Amanda?"

"Yes sum."

"Your mother is Martha?"

"Yes sum."

"Take me to her."

Amanda wondered what Miz Mariah wanted with her mother, but she knew she couldn't question her motive.

"Master Matthew and I tried to find her when we were here with our father."

"She be sick."

Miz Mariah was already up and headed toward the door. From the rocker, she retrieved her shawl. She put it around her shoulders and walked pass Amanda. It was evident to Amanda that Martha's sickness wasn't going to deter Miz Mariah from seeing her.

Angered and frustrated, Amanda led Mariah down to the quarters. As they walked, Amanda tried to figure out what Mariah wanted. It was too late for her mother, who was known as a conjuring woman among the slave population, to save Dearest Sallie's baby. However, her knowledge of herbs and roots, which she learned from the Luftys, had prevented her from becoming pregnant. Now she wished that she hadn't done it. Her pregnancy would make Power happy, although the child could have been Mr. Andy's or even Bill's.

When they approached the single women's cabin, they saw small slave toddlers in the yard. Martha was attending the children. While the toddlers were playing, two slave infants were lying on a blanket. The infants were asleep as the September sun graced their bodies. Sitting in an old rocker, Martha had another infant in her arm. She was feeding the infant from a bottle. There were no other people around, but Amanda could hear their mournful singing from the fields.

"Dere she be," Amanda pointed Martha out to Miz Mariah.

"Is she inside?"

"No, dat's her, Miz Mariah." Amanda answered. "She takes care of the chillen dat are too young to work while their mammies work."

"She doesn't work?"

"She be too old to work in the fields. Master Thomas lets her take care of de chillens."

"What's wrong with her?"

"She be ol' an' her legs are botherin' her."

"I see." Mariah pulled the shawl tightly around her body. "How is her mind...all right?"

"I 'spect so."

It was strange that Amanda and Miz Mariah stood just in front of Martha and talked about her as if she wasn't human. Although Martha saw them, she didn't acknowledge them. Martha and Amanda didn't greet each other, because they knew their place. Mariah was in charge and the next move was hers. A smile came across Miz Mariah's face, as she approached Martha. She looked down at the child Martha was feeding and then she glanced at Amanda.

"Take that pick-a-nanny," Miz Mariah ordered.

"Yes sum."

Amanda and Martha stared at each other. Hesitantly,

193

Amanda took the infant from her mother and cradled the baby in her arms, as she continued to feed the child. Looking in the infant's face, Amanda knew this was one of Mr. Andy's babies.

"Auntie Martha," Miz Mariah affectionately called Martha. "Can I talk to you?"

Martha got up and walked over to Miz Mariah. However, as she walked pass Amanda, her eyes questioned Amanda. Amanda shook her head to tell her that she had no clue. Together, Miz Mariah and Martha walked away from her. She stood there and watched them go. Dejectedly, she sat in the old rocker and attended to the children. She couldn't imagine what she wanted from her mother. What knowledge could Martha give a white woman? Then laughter rose up in her throat, as she thought about her mother's ability to cure and to abort babies. Could Miz Mariah be expecting a baby and she wanted to get rid of it? Perhaps she was ill? As a child, she could recall that her mother took sties' off her eyes by mumbling some kind of mysterious words as she flashed her hand across the infected eye. Then she blew on the eye. The next day, the sty was gone. Amanda surmised that Master Thomas told the Loves of her mother's conjuring.

Looking into the sky, Mandy could tell that it was getting near suppertime. She had to get back to the big house or she would be punished. With Master Thomas away, Amanda tried not to make any problems for herself. Sometimes Dearest Sallie's temperament wasn't the best. And yet, Amanda hoped she was having a good time with her son.

After being fed, the baby went to sleep. Amanda didn't lay the infant on the blanket with the other babies. Tenderly she held the baby to her bosom. She thought of Mary and her situation. It wasn't the best, but she loved and adored her three children. She had nobody to love. With tears cascading down her face, Amanda carefully laid him on the blanket with the other three infants. Staring at the others she wondered if Andy, too, had sired them. Looking around at the toddlers romp and play, she tried to speculate to whom each toddler belonged. Nervously, she played that game. However, it matter not who the father was, a child deserved to live. She wiped the tears from her eyes and waited for Martha and Mariah to return. Just as soon as they returned, she was heading toward the big house.

It seemed like they were gone forever. Finally they appeared. Miz Mariah seemed to be glowing with happiness, but Martha's face was stoic. In Miz Mariah's hand was clutched a small leather pouch as she attempted to hide it with her shawl. Amanda pretended she didn't see it. Miz Mariah didn't stop, but she continued on up to the big house with Amanda following her. Looking over her right shoulder, she saw her mother put her pipe in her mouth and sat down in the rocker. To Amanda, her shoulders seemed to slump down.

When she got to the big house, she went directly to the kitchen. Suckey had finished putting the final touch on supper. She looked around, when Amanda came through the door.

"See dat youse made it."

"Yeah, I's 'lawys do."

Amanda went about her work. She took platters of food to the dining room and placed them on the sideboard. Quickly she sat the table before Dearest Sallie and Mariah entered the room. After they were seated and after Miz Mariah offered grace, Amanda served the two ladies. Flies still came into the house to pester the ladies as they ate. Hence Colette fanned the pests away from their food, while Amanda stood by the sideboard to eavesdrop on their conversation. Perhaps, Miz Mariah would reveal the contents of the pouch. Cocking her eyes at Mariah, Amanda felt she wanted to tell Miz Sallie the secret. And yet, Miz Sallie rattled on and on about Little Will.

"So Little Will is growing?"

"I say."

"That's good," Miz Mariah said. "I just wished I had someone to share my life."

"You'll find someone."

"Most all my friends are married. Miz Mariah took a small pouch from her bosom. "Look!"

"What's that?"

"It's a love portion."

"What?"

"A love portion."

"Where did you get it?"

Miz Mariah smiled.

Amanda knew, but it wasn't her place to tell Sallie. Laughing to herself, she realized that was why Master Matthew and Miz Mariah wanted to find her mother. She wanted to tell Mariah that her father could arrange a marriage for her. After all, he does it for his slaves. She forgot that slaves were property and Miz Mariah was Mr. Love's daughter. However, Mandy will never forget the Green Corn Ceremony. Color or social status didn't matter. Looking over at Miz Mariah, she realized it didn't matter when you're trying to find a mate.

Chapter 32

As Power and Amanda walked in the moonlight on a Sunday night, she thought of her friend Mary Tuskha. Another full moon had come and gone and she wondered if the New Moon Ceremony had begun. She would like to go and mend the broken friendship between Mary and herself.

Painfully, she recalled the incident that had torn them apart. They were always trying to get the attention of Lufty boys who they thought were cute. Corn shucking at the Thomas' was fun. When the Luftys came, she rushed to a brave's side and asked him to be her partner. His dark jet black hair hung down to his shoulders and the copper coloring of his skin made Amanda want to touch him. Everything was perfect, even his teeth. Charley was his name.

All the girls wanted to shuck corn with Charley. This was not only the Lufty girls, but the slave girls as well. And that year, Amanda asked him and he accepted her invitation.

The night was alight with the big bonfire. Everyone had partnered as the shucks from the corn flew in all direction. From the corner of her eyes, Mandy saw Mary. She was shucking corn with one of the slave boys. Mandy could tell she was unhappy. Amanda really didn't care, she had Charley. She knew it would only last for the night and Charley would go back home. Mary could have him after the night's festival was over.

Just to make Mary jealous, Amanda scooted real close to Charley as they shucked corn together. Their hands touched often and Charley just smiled at her. Of course Mandy returned the smile. IT WAS MAGIC.

Then Sam got his fiddle and began to play a merry tune. As Sam played and danced the jig, it seemed that everyone got up. Charley dragged her to her feet and they pranced around the ground like two proud peacocks. Amanda looked over at Mary, who was not dancing. Whoops and hollers exploded through the air as the merriment continued.

Finally Mary and her partner jumped to their feet and started dancing the jig. With corn all over the place, the dancers found themselves getting closer and closer to the big bonfire. Somehow, Charley slipped on the grass or an ear of corn, something. At any rate, Charley fell into the bonfire. Charley screamed and Amanda stood there horrified. She couldn't move. Charley's clothes were on fire, as everyone just watched.

At last Sam turned around and saw Charley go headlong in the fire. His beautiful long hair was also aflame. Sam pulled him out of the fire and smothered the flames with his body. Charley was alive, but he was never the same. His scarred face frightened most kids and his baldhead on top made him look old.

Amanda remembered Mary's words as she shouted "You did that on purpose."

"No." Amanda cried. "No. He tripp'd. I tri'd to grab'em."

"Just 'cause youse black, youse wanted him black."

Amanda told this story to Power as they walked. She had never spoken about it until now. Her childhood friend Mary never came around to play anymore.

"She blam'd me."

"An' now she wanna forgive youse?"

"Yes."

"Let her."

"Power, youse don't understan'. I hafto be dere at the New Moon Ceremony. Dearest Sallie ain't gonna let me go."

"Ifen it on a weekend, youse mite can go."

"I's guess so."

"I's 'lieve dat she said it was gonna be on the third full moon."

Power smiled at her. "It's a full, let's not waste it."

The next morning when Mandy went to the big house, she was unusually happy. There seem to be a bounce in her walk as she moved from the big house to the kitchen to serve breakfast for the household. Colette handled the breakfast duties, while Amanda went upstairs to clean up the bedrooms. After cleaning the upstairs, she tackled the parlor. As she was putting the room back in order, Miz Sallie came in. She sat at the piano and tickled the ivory. Amanda felt she was in a good mood and this would be a good time to ask her about obtaining a weekend pass. However, Amanda was wrong; Dearest Sallie gave Amanda a tongue slicing.

"Mandy," Miz Sallie answered. "You have to realize they are not your kind. The Senator only takes care of them because Chief Yonaguska adopted him. You see, Chief Yonaguska thought he was an orphan because his father was dead. So when Yonaguska died, he became chief. He was so grateful that he bought land for them and made sure they didn't have to leave this area.

"You're not going up there to get some notions in your head like Sam has. He thinks he is a brother to the Senator. He's just a nigger slave. Everyone must stay with their own kind. Do you understand?"

Amanda kept her eyes staring at the floor. "Yes sum."

By the time Amanda started to slave quarters, she was emotionally whipped. Power couldn't cheer her up. It seemed to Amanda her world was falling apart. The friendship with Mary was important to her and now it was gone. Didn't Dearest Sallie know the Luftys were her husband's people? It hadn't been long since Dearest Sallie had attended the Green Corn Ceremony. It seemed that the two communities had bonded. Now Amanda couldn't go visit a friend for a weekend.

Chapter 33

November was hog killing time at Stekoa Fields; it was overshadowed by news that John Brown had raided Harper's Ferry. Amanda couldn't comprehend the complex picture. But she knew it had to do with freeing slaves. John Brown, along with his army, was caught and tried for treason. All this meant to Amanda was that someone was fighting for her freedom, but they lost. Looking around the place, Amanda realized they could storm the big house and kill all the white folks. And this must've been going through Miz Sallie's mind, when the male slaves didn't help slaughter the hogs. They were relegated to salting the meat. Master Thomas had a herd of wild hogs that roamed the woods around the place. He would have them herded to market over Soco Gap to Waynesville. Before herding them to Waynesville, he had three cut from the bunch to be slaughtered.Two of them would be slaughtered for his smokehouse, while the third one was for his mother.

The female slaves, under the watchful eyes of Sam and Miz Temperance, cut and ground the lean meat into sausage. After they ground the sausage, they cooked it and canned it in jars. Since this required a lot of womenfolk, Suckey was found in and around the kitchen bustling and ordering several female slaves. They made liver mush and souse meat from the ears and the feet. For his reward, Master Thomas had some hog feet pickled for Sam. He knew that was Sam's favorite thing.

To get the rest of the herd to Waynesville, Alfred and

200

Power were usually assigned to round them up and herd them to the Waynesville market. Sam was assigned to go to Shoal Creek and get Alfred. Before he left for Shoal Creek, he came to Power and Amanda's cabin. When he entered, Amanda knew that Sam had come to talk to Power about helping build the Western North Carolina Railroad.

"Power," Sam said, "I convinced Miz Sallie to trust you to help round up those wild hogs in the mountains."

Amanda spoke before she thought. "I thought Master Willie was gonna git'm a job helping build the railroad."

"Master Willie ain't a lettin' anyone off de place. Why?" Power asked.

"Too much is goin' in de world rat now."

"It ain't rat, Sam. Master promis'd me."

"Nuthin' dat I can do.'

"Okay," Power said. "I's your man."

Sam left. Amanda looked over at Power. She knew he was up to something.

"Mandy, I ain't coming back. With John Brown an' his army being caught, dere ain't gonna be no freedom."

"Where will youse go?"

"Freedom."

"Master Thomas 'llowin' youse to herd de hogs. He still trusts youse."

"Tell me why I should stay?"

Silently Amanda stood there. She could tell him she was expecting a child, but she couldn't lie to him. And yet, she wondered if Flossie had already spread the rumor around the quarters. Working at the big house, Amanda avoided the other slaves. After a long day at the big house, she came to this cabin and tried to keep Power happy. Now as they stood face to face in their slave cabin, Amanda realized the effort had failed. Both of them searched each other face for some sign of commitment, but she turned away and stepped over to the hearth. Tears smarted her eyes as she stared down at the dancing flames. She felt Power's hands as he placed them on her arm. She turned and faced him.

"Mandy, I heard some rumors. I's been waitin' fer youse to tell me."

"Wat?"

"Are youse with chile?"

Amanda lowered her eyes and shook her head.

"Flossie said. . ."

"Power," Tears rolled down Amanda's cheeks. "Youse don't understan'."

"Andy?"

"He. . ."

"Damnit" Power exploded. "He was a braggin' 'bout it at Shoal Creek 'fore this."

"I want to be with child, but I's want it to be yers."

"And youse not."

"No."

Power sighed, "Okay, Mandy. I's be back. Dat Lincoln will free us."

"Who's he?"

"He is gonna be powerful. Whites folks 'round here shake in deir boots when his name is said."

Amanda had heard Master Thomas and Mr. Love talk about this Lincoln. But with Mr. Love winning the election earlier this month, Amanda resolved there was enough Southern whites to stop him. She just looked at Power and shook her head. Standing there, she watched him pace the floor like a caged bear. Tears of pain slowly cascaded down her cheeks. She couldn't stand to her man, who was looked upon as a boy by the white man, tied up into a knot and locking his emotions deep down inside of him. It was only when he was behind closed doors with his love ones that he could show how he really felt. Amanda threw her arms around his neck. She embraced him with all her being. As she clung to him, she felt his hard muscular body melt. He returned her embrace and together, they stood in each other arms and sobbed.

The next morning at the crack of dawn, someone knocked on the door. They stared at the door. It was like a death sentence, as the knock persisted. They quickly got out of bed. Lovingly, they looked at each other. Traces of half-dried tears were etched on their faces. Close to Power, she attempted to remove the evidence from his face. He kissed her hands and walked out the door.

Amanda walked outside behind Power. She watched as he and Alfred headed for the woods.

With her bundled-up baby in her arms and another one in the oven, Flossie watched also. It was bad enough that their men had to leave, but their departure was not of their own making. Sighing heavily, Amanda realized that even though they weren't paid for their labor, they did have food, shelter, and clothing,

Flossie spied Amanda and approached her. At that point, Amanda didn't want to talk to anyone, especially Flossie. Flossie and Alfred had a child, but for Power and her, it was different.

"Mornin'," Flossie said. "It's beautiful."

"Yeah," Amanda replied.

Alfred said dat dey wouldn't hafto be gone dat long."

Yeah."

"By Christmas time, dey'll be back."

t was still morning at Stekoa Field and the two of them had to get to work, Flossie had to breast freed Little Will and Amanda had to clean. Amanda grunted at Flossie and started for the big house, while Flossie hurried to the single women's cabin to take her child to Martha.

Today, the last of the three hogs was being slaughtered. Amanda saw Master Thomas' neighbors gather again in the front yard to do the job, while the male slaves were sent to clear the fields and bushes around the place. Miz Sallie was still frightened by the news of John Brown's raid and she didn't want slaves with weapons near the big house.

After they killed the hog and had gotten all the meat, the intestines and the heads were left for the slaves. From the first two hogs some of the slaves had gotten their intestines, which they called chitterlings. Today Amanda would get her portion of chitterlings, but she would have to clean them by the moonlight; knowing she wouldn't have a chance to fix them for Power.

Two days later, Alfred brought Power's body down the mountain. He carried his friend in his arms. Blood, fresh and dried, covered Power's lifeless body. Martha ran to the big house to tell Amanda. The sun had just climbed high in the heavens and flakes of snow danced in the air, when all of Stekoa Field heard the mourns of Amanda as she dropped to her knees beside Power's body. She took him in her arms and showered his corpse with tears. Suddenly everything stopped at Stekoa, as they gathered around Amanda.

Through blinding tears, she looked up at Alfred. "How? Wat happen'd?"

"These wild boars, they kilt'im. Dey jest came a charging' at him and he jest froze. He jest froze."

Sam came to Amanda's rescue. He bodily lifted Amanda away from the dead body of her mate. Amanda stood petrified with her mother's arm around her. She didn't move until Sam and Alfred took the body away. Slowly the slaves went back to work. It was not a holiday. The news of Power's death reached all at Stekoa Field. In a daze, Amanda went back to work. Maybe if she returned to work, she wouldn't have to think about it.

The next day, after the day had begun and Amanda had finished serving breakfast at the big house, she was given permission to bury Power. She, her mother and Sam went to the little plot Master Thomas has set aside for his slaves to be buried. The ceremony was short and sweet.

Amanda put flowers on his grave and constructed a makeshift wooden cross which she placed at the head of his grave. A medium flat-shaped stone was placed at the foot of the grave. She stood there and thought of the times they spent together. It wasn't all good and it wasn't all bad.

Chapter 34

A t the tender age of eighteen, Amanda became a widow. And yet she never considered herself properly married. It was just "jumping the broom" because that was what Master Thomas wanted. Sadness filled her heart for she had come to respect Power and to understand his need to become a father. It wasn't to donate Master Thomas another piece of property, but he wanted to prove himself a man. Now he was dead.

Maturity comes with trials and tribulations and Amanda felt she had been through a lot. And through it all, she still loved Bill. It didn't matter whether Master Thomas would force another sex partner on her.

Hope dashed when the news finally reached the slave quarters about the fate of John Brown. Shock waves went through the slave quarters, as they realized that Brown and his army were defeated. Not only were they captured, John Brown was hung. Amanda had hoped Brown was coming to free them.

Now everything was like a whisper in the wind. Even the year slipped away and 1860 came in without incident, but somehow, it brought with it a sense of anticipation. The New Year's Day meal of field peas, winter greens and ham hocks brought them no luck. Master Thomas and Miz Sallie were still in charge and the reins seemed to be tightening. With Miz Temperance no longer the Mistress of the Stekoa Fields, the holiday changed. Christmas was celebrated before the New Years. She couldn't understand how anyone could change Christ's birthday. Even the Christmas Bush was no longer part of the Christmas celebration.

Shortly after the New Year, her mother died quietly in her sleep. Flossie found her when she went to take her son Daniel to the single women cabin. She touched her body and it was cold. She screamed and ran out the door.

"Amanda! Amanda!"

On her way to the big house, Amanda heard Flossie calling her. She knew something was wrong. She stopped and ran toward Flossie. As the two met, Flossie fell into Amanda's arms. Daniel was far behind; as his little chubby legs tried to keep up. Seeing him, Amanda was elated that he was alright.

"Flossie," she asked, "Wat is it?"

Your mother," she cried, "She be dead."

Amanda broke loose from Flossie and ran to the single women's cabin. When she rushed in, she saw her mother lying peaceful on the pallet. Her eyes were closed and just seemed to be sleeping. As Amanda knelt by her mother, she saw a smile on her face.

Taking her mother's cold hand, she kissed it. "I love you, mama, I love you."

She heard Flossie come and she felt her presence standing over her. Amanda also knew that Flossie was crying, as was her little boy.

"Mama," he cried, "Wat be 'rong wit Granny?"

"She be asleep." Flossie picked up Daniel. "She be ready to go to heben."

Amanda looked up at Flossie. "Take Danny with youse. And tell Dearest Sallie dat mama is dead. I's stayin' with her."

Flossie squeezed Amanda shoulder and left.

All alone, Amanda still had no tears for her mother. She had done the best she could. A victim of her circumstances, Martha had lived a good life. As a slave she wasn't beaten, but was taken advantage of by the system. Before she came to these mountains, she had lost her true identity.

Sometimes she would remember her little village in West Africa. Amanda could cry for the past she allowed to slip away. Master and Mistress had a past and knew from where they came. Amanda had nothing. She had just the memories of her mother in the field as she slaved away her life. All she did, Martha did it for the Master.

Taking the shabby blanket, Amanda covered her mother's face. She waited for someone to tell her what to do. She was not going to leave her mother's side. The household could feed themselves. She knew Dearest Sallie would put Flossie in her position. At that moment Sam came. He went to the pallet and started to uncover the corpse.

Amanda pulled his hands away. "She's dead."

"Dearest Sallie needs you at the house."

"No, I will not leave mama,"

Sam and Amanda stared at each other.

"No," Amanda repeated emphatically, "No. This is my mother. When I bury her, then I's might come back."

"Amanda, I understand yer grief. "Morrow be church day. I herd Dearest Sallie say so. We can bury her with an arousing goodbye.

"Okay, Sam." Anger took control of her. "Youse tell Dearest Sallie dat I's serv'em lunch."

"We can't leave her here."

"Take her to my place."

Sam was not going to argue with Amanda. However, he didn't know how Dearest Sallie would take it. He carried the body to Mandy's cabin and left to report to the Mistress. Amanda washed her mother's body and put her on one of her ragbag dresses. With a sheep brush, she combed her hair. Miz Temperance came over as Mandy was putting on the finishing touches.

Quietly she came in and stood behind her. Mandy was so busy she didn't know anyone was in the room. And then she felt Miz Temperance's presence. The vibes filling the air were not hostile. Turning, she came face to face with

Temperance, who had a sad smile on her lips. Mandy had forgotten that Miz Temperance hadn't gone back to Shoal Creek.

"Child, I'm so sorry. You have my deepest sympathy."

"Thank you, Miz Temperance."

"Tomorrow will be a good day to bury her." Miz Temperance suggested. "Seeing how it is Sunday."

"Yes ma'am."

"That clearing you folks have your gathering for Sunday will do for the funereal services."

Mandy half-listened as Miz Temperance arranged Martha's funeral. She wondered what Miz Sallie had to say. However, she did not have time to dwell on that, as Miz Temperance continued.

"Child your mother deserves a proper burial. I'm going to ask Rev. Asbury to conduct the services."

Mandy wanted to protest, but she knew Miz Temperance had persuaded Dearest Sallie to allow her to try to make sense of all of this. This had to be a compromise between Dearest Sallie and Miz Temperance; therefore,, Mandy decided to accept it. Before she left, Temperance gave Mandy a bottle of vinegar.

"Put this on your mother so she won't smell up the house." Miz Temperance cautioned her. "Don't pour it all over her...you know, dab it on."

"Thank youse, Miz Temperance. Please tell Dearest Sallie dat I's be there to serve lunch."

Amanda spent the rest of the day at the big house. She cleaned the upstairs. Master was home; therefore, she was expecting him to give her his condolence. Avoiding most of the household, she did her job. As she did her job, she thought of the many times Martha walked through and cleaned this house.

After finishing her evening chores, Amanda headed out the back door, when Dearest Sallie stopped her.

"Mandy," she said, "You have my condolence. We are sorry for our loss."

"Thanks."

"I understand that you plan to have service and burial tomorrow."

"Yes ma'am."

"Senator Thomas asked me to tell you the plans are fine."

"Thanks."

Dearest Sallie touched her tenderly on the shoulder. "I know how you feel. I lost my mother when I was twelve."

Amanda could see that her concern was genuine.

"Thanks."

"And don't come in tomorrow."

"Yes ma'am."

When Amanda got back to her quarters, she found that a coffin had been constructed and her mother was lying peaceful in it. Flossie and Alfred were there, along with Cudge. On entering the cabin, Cudge ran to her and hugged her.

"I'm sorry." Cudge cried.

"It's alright. Mama be in a better place. She be free now."

"Most of de folks came by."

"It's late," Alfred announced. "We's need to git some sleep."

"Yes," Amanda agreed. "Thanks fer ev'rything."

When everyone left, Amanda was alone. She went over to the coffin and looked down at her mother. "Youse be at peace now, Mama."

Chapter 35

The next day was a blur to Amanda. It seemed that all the people on Stekoa Field were there. All morning, people came in and out. Even some of Luftys came to pay their respect to Martha, the slave of their Chief Wil-Usdi. Among them was Mary Tuskha. The two women embraced. Before Mary could say anything, Amanda spoke. She did not speak about her mother, but about the relationship she wanted to mend with Mary,

"Thank youse fer comin'. I's sorry dat I couldn't come to the New Moon Ceremony."

"That's not 'mportant."

"To me it was." Tears came to Amanda's eyes. "I's cry not fer my mama's death, but de death of our friendship. Fer I's know dat mama is at peace."

"An' our friendship is not dead." Mary declared. "I try to understand your position in your world. In my world, you are my sister."

"Thanks." Amanda sniffed. "And youse be my sister."

After the sun had reached its apex in the wintry sky and started to make it's descend for the day, Rev. Asbury made his appearance. Sam, Alfred, and Dave were among the six pallbearers who transported Martha's closed coffin to the burial site in the wood. With Mary and Flossie by her side, Amanda followed the coffin. All the other slaves were already at the gathering. Flakes of snow slowly came down from the heavens as the funeral procession marched up the hill. Not only were there flecks of snow in the air, but the mournful voices of the slaves reached up to meet them in the heavens as they sang *"Steal Away."*

When they got to the burial site, Amanda was surprised to see Master Thomas standing there in front of the mass of slaves and a few Luftys. She wondered if he was going to speak. Standing between Mary and Flossie, Amanda tried to listen to the graveside ceremony. She remembered nothing. Finally it was over as Dave and Sam took shovels and covered the coffin, which had been lowered into the ground with ropes. Amanda stood there until the last shovelful of dirt was delivered on her mother's grave. With the wild flowers she had gathered, she placed them on the freshly covered dirt. The flecks of snow stopped. The heavens had stopped weeping for it had welcomed Martha home. Mournfully, the slaves sang *"Steal Away"* once more. With that song ringing in her ears, Amanda walked away.

Chapter 36

Now Amanda was all alone. Within a space of three months, she had lost the two people who loved her. And yet, she had found a true friend in Mary Tuskha. On Sundays when it was sort of downtime for the slaves, Mary would come over to Stekoa Fields. The two would talk about their childhood and how they lost contact with each other. Although they lived about four miles apart, they had never visited each other since they were twelve. Childish things were over and Mary had become a woman. No more corn shucking at Stekoa. It was time for her to find a mate.

"I was no longer permit'd to come here."

"And I couldn't go see youse,"

"I understand. Your slavery is forever. In our culture, youse can become part of the community."

"I see."

"Why does Chief Wil-Usdi hold you as a slave, not let you become part of his family."

"He says dat we are family."

Mary just shook her head. She didn't understand the ways of the white man. "How did youse git here? I have seen blacks among my people, but they act like they are free. Did the white man steal you from my people?"

"My mother came from far 'way. A place call'd Africa."

"Africa?"

"A place that youse must cross water to git here."

"And what do you know 'bout that land?"

"Nuthin'."

"That is sad." Then as if she had solved the problem, Mary jumped up and danced around. She took Amanda by the hands and the two danced in circles. Around and around they went until they were dizzy and fell to the ground. Both of them laughed.

"Look," Mary stated. "I will tell you my story and it can be your story. And I will adopt you into my tribe, the Lufty Cherokees."

Amanda just shook her head. "This be foolish."

"No, it is right. Amanda, do you realize that was what we fought 'bout years ago?"

"I thought it be ov'r a boy?"

"No, it was over your lack of a past."

Amanda laughed. "Ok, I will a'cept yer past."

Hence every time Mary and Amanda met, Mary would tell her of her people's past. Amanda listened and learned about the Lufty Cherokee. In the meanwhile, the farm was growing in chattel property. Flossie and the other slave women had their babies. Little Will and Danny played together. Flossie was happy that her son was Little Will's companion.

Chapter 37

It was 1860 and a new president was going to be elected in November and the Southerners were worried. As Amanda served the Thomas's, there was always talk about Abraham Lincoln and that the newly formed Republican Party was anti-slavery. It seemed that Lincoln was against slavery and was going to free them if he was elected. In May the Republican Party met in Chicago to elect their party's candidate. The top man was Lincoln and on the third ballot, he was elected. This news sent panic in the South. Neighbors were coming over, questioning Thomas about the coming election. Thomas reassured them that Breckinridge would save the South and be elected the next president of the United States.

The next time that Mary visited Amanda told her all about it.

"They want to keep us slaves."

"What do you mean?"

"I's really don't know. All's I know a man named Lincoln wanna free us."

"How?"

"Wen he 'come president."

"That will be great! Then youse can come to see me."

"Yes!"

It was Sunday and Miz Sallie had Rev. Asbury come to Stekoa Fields to preach to the niggers. Amanda had overheard her talking to him. She didn't like the way they were acting. Dave was really becoming unruly and she couldn't get the house slaves to tell her anything. There was a hush-hush she didn't like. Therefore, she wanted Rev. Asbury to preach again that they were born to serve the white man.

All the slaves were to attend and Rev. Asbury had to make a count. At that time, Thomas had fifty-four slaves. Amanda knew Dave wasn't going to attend, but she convinced Mary to attend the gathering. She only hoped that he would just count the slaves without getting names. As they arrived, Rev. Asbury, he counted them without looking at them. Because Mary had attended the gathering, he counted fifty-four.

After singing hymns, Rev. Asbury preached about how the slaves were born to serve. Quietly the slaves listened to Rev Asbury. Amanda knew he was nervous about the gathering. Here he was alone with fifty-four niggers and he was afraid they might attack him. The slaves held their peace. Afterward, the slaves went quietly back to their quarters.

"What was that?" Mary asked.

"Our sermon for the month."

"OK."

"The Bible tell'em dat we be servant to them fer life."

"Mandy, I got to go."

"Youse be safe."

"Don't worry, I got someone waiting fer me just outside."

The next morning Amanda went to serve Miz Sallie and her family. After breakfast, she was called to the parlor where Miz Sallie was seated at the piano. She was softly playing a tune that Amanda recognized as the tune she sang "Bill, My Love is a Smithy." Right away, Amanda felt that Dearest Sallie was up to something and whatever it was, she wanted no part of it. And yet, she was a slave and she had to do as she was told.

"Miz Sallie, did youse call me?"

"Yes," she replied as she continued to play that tune. "You know this tune?"

"I's 'fraid not."

"That's the tune I was playing when you sing about Bill. Who is this Bill?"

"Jest someone I made up."

"Mandy," she demanded. "You know him."

"Yes ma'am," Amanda dropped her head down. "He's at yer father's place."

"I'll talk to Senator Thomas about it. I know you have lost Power and your mother. I just want to do something nice for you."

"Yes sum."

Mandy and Miz Sallie stared at each other. Although it was unwritten rule that Mandy not look Miz Sallie in the eye, but she did. She needed to know whether Miz Sallie was sincere or she wanted something from her. Dearest Sallie's sweet smile was always deceptive; therefore Mandy looked her straight in the eyes. Neither of the two blinked. Realizing she was slave, she turned her gaze away. Without saying another word, Mandy left.

Always listening to their table conversation, Mandy obtained information about the Democratic Convention. It was unquestionable that the North and South were having trouble deciding on a candidate for President of the United States. It seemed that the South wanted Breckinridge and the North wanted Douglas. The whole thing was confusing to Mandy, but she figured that the Democrats were split. Sitting alone in her quarters, she attempted to understand the meaning to it all. It appeared that the South was running scared if Lincoln would become President. And if he was against slavery, he could free her.

Chapter 38

I n the middle of June, Miz Mariah came to Stekoa Fields. It was rumored that Dearest Sallie was once more pregnant. This time Miz Mariah was going to make sure that all would go well. Traveling with Miz Mariah were two personal servants. One of them was Rozette, her personal maid and the other one was her personal driver. Amanda saw them as the carriage pulled up and stopped at the front door of the big house. She had just finished putting the laundry on the line and was taking the basket back into the pantry. Realizing that it was Miz Mariah, Amanda surmised the rumor was true. She stopped and watched the driver jump down from the carriage, dropping the basket as he turned her way. Without consciously knowing what she was doing, she started across the yard toward the carriage. Abruptly, she stopped and just stared. Her eyes were playing tricks on her.

"It's about time you got here," Miz Sallie bounded down the front steps.

"The carriage broke down and William had to fix it,"

"I see that you have your personal maid."

"Yes, I thought that Pops wasn't going to let me have one until I got married."

"Come on, let's go into the house. Rozette can handle your valise and your boy can put the carriage away."

The two women went into the house. As soon as Amanda heard the door shut, she ran to the coach house where the driver had gone. By the time she got there, he had unhitched the horses from the carriage and was rubbing one of them down. She stood in the doorway and watched him. Her heart sang with happiness. With Power gone, she was alone and available, she wondered if he had jumped the broom with another slave girl.

"William Hudson Casey!" she whispered. "Wat are youse doin' here?"

He turned and glanced at her, then he went back to his work. "Master Love sent me. I's not de main blacksmith. Rat now I's Miz Mariah's driver."

"I's sees?"

"I's herd dat youse jump'd de broom with Power." He turned to face her.

"Didn't wanna. Dearest Sallie's doin's."

"Ain't wat I herd."

"Bill." She threw her arms around his neck. "I luv youse."

"Where be Power?" he said as he pulled away from her.

"He be dead."

"Dead?"

"Yeah." Amanda processed to tell Bill the details.

"I's sorry." He took her in his arms. "And I herd dat youse lost yer mother."

"Yes."

As he comforted her on her losses, he shattered her world. "Look, Mandy." He cleared his throat. "I's got some-one else."

Amanda tore herself from him. She was stunned. Turning, she ran back to the big house. Going into the pantry, she crouched in a corner and cried softly. Dearest Sallie brought Bill back into my life for nothing. She thought with Bill back, she believed everything would be all right. But Bill didn't want her and Dearest Sallie knew it. He had some-one else. Those words ring in her head, but there was an-other bell that called her to serve. Instantly, she knew that Miz Sallie was summoning her, but she refused to move.

"Amanda!" Dearest Sallie's voice boomed in her ears.

Slowly, she got to her feet and wiped the tears from her face. Immediately, she knew the voice echoed from the nursery. On entering, she found the two sisters. Miz Mariah had Little Will on her lap, who seemed to be happy as Mariah bounced him on her knees. Danny stood by and laughed.

"Yes sum, Dearest Sallie," Amanda said sarcastically. "Did youse call?"

"When is lunch going to be served?"

"We's been a waitin' on Miz Mariah."

"She's here."

"Then I's go see."

Amanda dashed out of the room and ran to the kitchen. When she got there, she found that Suckey had it ready. All she had to do was take it to the dining room to serve it. At the kitchen table, Rozette was eating. The two young female slaves glared at each other. As they measured each other up, Amanda knew they both wanted Bill's heart. Once she thought she had his heart, now she didn't know. His stinging remarks felt like a sledgehammer had slammed into her heart. Did she dare try? Looking over at Rozette who dressed in castoffs of Miz Mariah, Amanda knew she was going to fight for Bill.

She took the lunch tray to the dining room and sat the food on the sideboard. The dining room table was already set. Colette had done her job and all Amanda had to do was to turn over the silverware and the goblets. After that, she ring the dinner bell. In a few minutes, Miz Sallie and Miz Mariah entered the dining room and sat down. With her fans, Colette was at her station and Mandy served then lunch.

As she served them lunch, she was thinking of ways to win Bill's heart. Anxiously, she wondered where and what Rozette was doing. She felt she had the advantage because she was older and more mature than Rozette. Rozette's appearance was more sophisticated than hers;

therefore she decided she needed to change that.

After finishing her lunch duties for Dearest Sallie, Mandy went to the pantry where the ragbag was kept. Perhaps she could find one of her Mistress' castoffs that weren't too raggedy. Frantically, she tossed rags out of the barrel. At the very bottom, she found a dress that hadn't been torn for rags or personal hygiene use. Amanda took the dress out and tossed it aside. Then she hurriedly pitched the other castoffs and rags back in the barrel. Picking up the dress, she rolled it up and put it under her right arm. Before dashing out of the pantry, she peeked out to see if the coast was clear.

Without looking right or left, she sprinted to the slave quarters. All the slaves were working in the fields. As she headed for the single woman cabin, she realized her mother was dead. She stopped in her tracks. She had to fix up the dress herself. There was no way would she tell anyone about the dress. Going on to her quarters, she put the dress away.

Duty called. She ran back to the big house, but as she passed the coach house, she paused to see if Bill was around. He was nowhere to be found, but the carriage was still there. To Amanda that meant he was still on the place and Rozette was too. She only hoped Miz Mariah needed her service.

It was getting late and Mandy had to get the clothes off the line. Hurriedly, she got the laundry wicket basket out of the pantry room and dashed outside to remove the clothing from the line. Tomorrow, she would have to iron them and that would take up most of the morning. As she was taking the clothes down, she felt she had no time for Bill. It would be fruitless for her to fix the dress. Bill had told her how he felt.

"Here, let's me he'p youse."

She turned and saw Bill with the basket.

"Ifen youse wanna."

"Look, I's sorry for wat I said. I talked to Uncle Sam.

He tol' me ev'rythin'."

"And?"   "Mandy, I said dat I's sorry. An' I don't have a 'pecial girl."

As she continued to remove the clothes from the line, Amanda didn't say anything. Both were silent, as Bill followed her with the basket. Then Amanda broke the silence as she hummed a tune.

"Wat's youse humming?"

"Just a song I made up. Youse wanna heard it?"

"Sure."

She began singing....

"Bill, my love is a smithy.
Who hammers all day.
Bill, my love is smithy.
But he has been sent away!"

"I's back now. Youse gonna add 'other verse."

"I guess I could. Let's me see."

Amanda sang as she made it up.

"Bill, my love is a smithy.
Who has come back to me.
Bill, my love is a smithy.
I'll never let him free."

Amanda took the basket of clothes and went into the back door of the house. As she stepped into the house, she met Rozette, who was leaving. The two glared at each other. Each believed that Bill was theirs.

Chapter 39

Since Miz Sallie was with child again, Miz Mariah was going to spend the summer with her. June slipped quietly by and the North Carolina General Assembly recessed for the holiday. That meant Master Thomas would come home. Just listening to Miz Sallie and Miz Mariah's conversation, Amanda knew all the Love clan was going to spend the Fourth of July in Jackson County. Their uncle, Dr. John C. Love and his family lived in the Webster area of Jackson County, as did their younger uncle Dillard. When Master Thomas came home, it was apparent that Mr. Love was coming with him. Not only was Mr. Love arriving at Stekoa Fields, but Matthew would be coming with him. It seemed that the remaining siblings of Dearest Sallie were already in Webster.

Amanda wondered if she could stand having all the Loves around. She thought that, perhaps, she would remain at Stekoa Fields, while they went to celebrate their independence. After all, she had nothing to celebrate.

Master Thomas arrived at Stekoa Fields on the morning of the 29th of June. With him was Master Matthew. Immediately Miz Mariah and Master Matthew had their heads together. Now that Miz Mariah knew Martha had died, Amanda wondered what did the two had in mind. And yet, Amanda had other worries. Bill was still there spending most of his time driving Miz Mariah and Miz Sallie around with Rozette and Caroline along to assist the two women. She had to remain behind and clean the house. All the while

Bill and Rozette were gone, Amanda fretted about what the two of them were doing while Miz Sallie and Miz Mariah were visiting friends. Amanda even became a bit jealous of Caroline, although the two were friends.

However, when Bill returned from chauffeuring the Southern ladies around, he would seek her affection. He was always asking her to sing his song. After she finished with her work at the big house, she'd sneak out to meet him. Usually, they met in the coach house where Bill had a tiny room. Those stolen moments were short, because she had to return to the big house.

When Master Thomas came home, Amanda decided she would approach Master Thomas about her relationship with Bill. She knew the last time, he had denied her. Since she had been sharing a cabin with Power, perhaps he would allow her to share it with Bill. After all, she was a woman now and needed a man in her life. However, Amanda felt she could never be alone with Master Willie without Dearest Sallie. She had to do something. Her only ally was Miz Temperance, who had come for a short visit while her son was home.

After lunch when all were quiet, Amanda found Miz Temperance in the pantry. She seemed to be hunting for something, when Amanda interrupted her.

"Miz Temperance," she said timidly."Can I's talk to youse?"

"Sure," she turned to face her. "But you have to find something for me. Young folks just don't know how to organize a pantry."

"Yes ma'am."

"Find me some candles." She said. "They are usually right here. I need to set them on the table tonight. You know today is Miz Sallie and Master Willie's wedding anniversary."

"Yes ma'am."

Amanda found the candles and gave them to Miz Temperance. "I've talked to Suckey. She is going to cook a special dinner for just the two of them."

"Yes sum."

" Now, girl, what is it?"

"Will youse talk to Master Thomas fer me?"

"It's about that boy?" She shook her head. "Well, ain't it?"

"Yes sum."

"You still want to be with that young whippersnapper?"

"Yes sum."

"Girl, your mammy's dead. You are asking me for advice." She chuckled. "He's your kind, isn't he?"

"Yes sum."

"Just as long as you stick to your kind," Miz Temperance said sadly. "Don't go mess around with those Indians. You hear?"

"Yes sum."

Amanda and Miz Temperance left the pantry. Miz Temperance went toward the parlor and Amanda went outside. The fresh air cleared her head, as she tried to make any sense out of what Temperance had told her. Stick to your kind, she had told her. Therefore, that meant Bill could share her quarters.

The rest of the afternoon, Amanda was elated. She went about her work with a smile. Going upstairs, she headed toward the nursery because she heard the cry of Little Will. As she entered the nursery, she found Flossie trying to get Little Will to go to take a nap. At this time of day, it was naptime for Little Will. Danny and Flossie's other little one was already asleep, but Little Will was fighting it.

"I's see Little Will is up to his old tricks."

"I's 'fraid so."

Flossie was cradling the two-year-old in her arms, trying to rock him to sleep. Since Miz Mariah arrived, Flossie had become Little Will's nanny. She stayed in the big house and attended to Little Will's every need. This arrangement didn't bother Flossie because Alfred was at Shoal Creek store and her children were permitted to stay with her.

Amanda patted Flossie on the shoulder. "Good luck!"

She turned to leave, but Flossie said, "I see Bill is back. Dat blue-eyed Rozette, is who I's be worried 'bout."

"He be mine."

"He be a man."

Flossie always had a way of making Amanda angry. Hence she made her exist before Flossie could add to her story.

To try to forget Flossie's remarks, Amanda buried herself in work. The place was immaculately clean for Amanda scrubbed every corner of every room. By suppertime, Amanda still had some pinned up anger and energy. She served supper and cleaned the dishes. For the first time in serving Dearest Sallie and her family, she didn't listen to the table conversation.

However, she did notice that Dearest Sallie and Master Willie were not at the supper table. She had forgotten that today was their third wedding anniversary and Miz Temperance had planned a special dinner for them. Before she got out the back door, Miz Temperance informed her that she would be serving that special dinner. Hence she had to stick around until the event occurred. The couple had gone to Shoal Creek and was expected back around eight. It was about six-forty. On Miz Temperance's order, she was forbidden to leave the big house area.

She went outside and leaned against the old tall oak and waited for Cudge to pass. He was the only slave she could trust. As she waited for Cudge, she remembered she hadn't seen him all day. Being Master Thomas' body servant, he must have gone with the couple to Shoal Creek. Maybe, Bill would come and see why she hadn't finished the day's work. Just as she saw him coming toward the big house, Miz Temperance called her from the house.

Dashing into the house, she replied," Yes sum."

After getting her instructions, Amanda went back outside and made a beeline to the kitchen. Bill called her, but she continued toward the kitchen. When she entered, Suckey was talking to Sam. They stopped and turned their attention to her.

"Wat do Miz Temperance want?"

"Is de food ready?"

"Of course?"

"It smells good. Wat it be?"

"Roast duck."

"Well, let's me tell Miz Temperance."

She hurriedly left the kitchen and crashed into Bill. He caught her before she fell. "Hey, why ain't youse home?"

"I's a still a slaving. It be Dearest Sallie and Master Willie's wedding ann'vesary and Miz Temperance planned a cozy dinner for'em."

"Jesus!" He threw up his hands and walked away.

She couldn't go after Bill. She returned to the big house and reported to Miz Temperance. In a few minutes, the couple arrived. Amanda set the table for two with their finest silverware and dishes. Everything was perfect. The goblets were placed on the table and Amanda poured wine into both of them.

She heard Miz Temperance wish them happy third anniversary, as they walked arm in arm into the dining room. Amanda smiled and they were seated by Sam. Amanda served them and stood by the sideboard as they ate.

Around nine-thirty, she headed straight for the coach house. On entering Bill's tiny room, she found he wasn't there. Her anger boiled. She stormed out of the coach house and went to her quarters in the slave row. On entering the dimly lit cabin, she found Bill waiting on her. She said to herself, as she undressed, 'He's my kind.'

Chapter 40

The next morning when she arrived at the big house to perform her duties, she discovered the Thomas' and Loves were going to Webster to celebrate the Fourth of July. Flossie was going to take care of Little Will and Danny was going with them. However, her little one had to remain behind. Amanda knew that Rozette would be going for she was Miz Mariah's personal servant. It seemed all the house servants were going except her. Desperately, she wanted to go and would do practically anything to be a member of the party.

Just as she finished serving breakfast, Amanda was summoned to the Master bedroom. Nervously she went. The first thought that came to her mind was that Dearest Sallie was upset about Bill spending the night in her cabin. Perhaps they needed Bill and they couldn't find him. She didn't want Bill to get in trouble because of her jealousy.

"Yes sum," Amanda said when she got to the room. "Youse calls fer me?"

"Yes. I need you to come along on this trip. We'll be spending the night at Webster Hotel. I need your help since Mother will be going."

"Yes ma'am!" A smile broke across Amanda's face.

"Now run along and put on your best dress. You're a house servant. Please look like one. Just remember all the things Mother taught you."

"Yes sum."

Amanda started out the door, when Dearest Sallie

called her back to the room.

"Yes sum."

"I have an old dress that I was about to toss in the rag-bag. I'm sure you can wear it."

Dearest Sallie went to her wardrobe and came back with a calico blue slightly faded dress. Amanda took the dress from Sallie and examined it in the morning light of the window. The dress seemed perfect, except for a small tear in the fold of the dress. Amanda surmised no one could see it. Laughing to herself, Amanda knew that Dearest Sallie was only taking her because her sister had a personal servant. The dress was to make sure that Amanda was dressed just as well as Rozette. Amanda was grateful for Miz Sallie's envious nature.

"Hurry, now," Dearest Sallie urged. "We'll be leaving soon."

"Yes sum."

Amanda left with the dress tucked under her arm. Running down the back stairs, she ran into Caroline.

"Where's youse goin' in such a hurry?"

"I's hafto change. I's goin' to Webster."

"Dat's great," Caroline smiled. "I guess youse an' Rozette can fight o'er Bill."

Racing to her quarters, she was elated. When she shot through the door like a bullet, she found that Bill was still there.

"Came back fer mor'."

"I's love to," Amanda laughed. "Youse best be haulin' your black ass ov'r to de big house. Don't youse know dat they be goin' to Webster fer some kinda celebration."

"I knows." He tried to take her in his arms, but Amanda pushed him away. "I's find someone else."

He laughed and hurried out the door. For a split second, Amanda stood there, and then she discarded the dress she had on. In a few minutes, she emerged from the cabin in the faded blue calico dress. Being summer, Amanda went barefoot. She loved feeling the dirt between her toes.

However, she noticed that Rozette wore shoes. As she made her way back to the big house, she wondered if she needed a pair. The freedom of her feet told her she didn't need them. Besides, Bill liked her being barefooted. He said that being barefooted showed freedom.

Chapter 41

The entourage left for Webster just before noon. Sam was driving the oxen drawn buckboard that had a canvas cover. In the back with all the household's valises were Amanda, Rozette, Caroline, Flossie, Danny and Cudge. In the two-seated carriage that faced each were Miz Sallie with Little Will and Miz Mariah, who occupied the back seat. Mr. Love and Miz Temperance were seated in the front seat, which faced the ladies. Bill was driving the carriage, while Master Thomas and Master Matthew were riding alongside on prize stallions. They were hoping to arrive at Webster Hotel before supper was served. Amanda didn't care when they arrived. She had never been to Webster or any other town. She wanted to know what it felt like to be in a town and to see all the hustle and bustle Bill had told her about.

When they arrived at Webster Hotel, it was still daylight. The town was buzzing with excitement as they prepared for the celebration of the Fourth of July. Everything seemed to be draped in red, white and blue. A platform was setup on the lawn of the courthouse. Children were running to and fro. Amanda knew, however, they would be called for suppertime and soon it would be bedtime. Bill stopped the carriage in front of the hotel, but Sam continued to guide the buckboard around to the back. Now Amanda wondered where she would be sleeping tonight. Sam parked the buckboard in front of the hotel stable. He got down and collected the valises and carried them to the back stairs of the hotel.

Cudge helped his father. Bill came around with the carriage. Immediately, he unhitched the horses and found a stall for them,

Amanda and the other female slaves jumped off the wagon and waited for them to be called by their Mistresses. Flossie and Danny went to the back entrance. She knew Miz Sallie wanted her son to play with Little Will. Although Flossie had an infant daughter, they were left behind in another slave mother's care. Amanda knew she was Temperance's personal servant and her service would be required immediately. Hence, she left the others and started toward the back stairs. At that moment, Sam came around the corner of the hotel. Amanda stopped because she knew Sam was going to give them their orders. All the slaves who had arrived from Stekoa Field gathered around Sam.

"Eatin' an' sleepin' 'rangement is likk dis. Nows ev'ybody will eat in de kitchen." Sam surveyed the slaves in front of him. "Amanda, youse sleep on a pallet in Miz Temperance's room. Rozette, youse sleep on a pallet in Miz Mariah's room. Caroline. Youse sleep on a pallet in Miz Sallie's room."

He looked over at Bill. "Us men folk is gonna sleep in the coach house."

Amanda was ecstatic. Being Miz Temperance's personal servant would be a breeze. She could sneak down to see Bill, when Miz Temperance turned in early. She glanced over at Rozette. She smiled at her and walked away. Being the personal servant of Miz Mariah was a demanding job and Amanda surmised that Rozette would not have time to sneak away to see Bill.

Caroline and Rozette followed Amanda into the hotel. They entered through the back door, which led directly to the kitchen. When they entered the kitchen, Amanda saw other blacks eating. Sam was leading the way. They didn't get a chance to talk to the other blacks. Right now, they had to know where they were going to sleep. They went up the back stairs without going through the white dining room.

One by one Sam showed the personal servants to their Mistress' rooms. He opened the door and ushered them inside with instructions they were to remain until their Mistress arrived from supper.

After the door closed to Miz Temperance's room, Amanda looked around. The bed was high off the ground with four posters. The high headboard had an elegant design on it. There was a ceramic basin and pitcher set sitting on a stand with clean towels on the towel rack. Everything in the room was more elegant than the furniture at the big house at Stekoa Field. Looking under the bed, she saw the bedchamber, which had the same design as the pitcher and basin.

Miz Temperance's valise was on a chest at the foot of the bed. Amanda took the valise and opened it. She took Miz Temperance's clothes out of the carpetbag and put them away. In the cedar wardrobe, she hung up Miz Temperance's dress and placed her floppy straw hat on the top shelf. In the dresser, she placed her underwear. Like an efficient personal servant, she arranged Miz Temperance's flannel nightgown on the bed and put her robe across the arm of the chair. Now everything was ready for her when she came in to go to bed.

Amanda went to the window and looked down at the street of Webster. It was still daylight as the long summer day tried to cheat the darkness. Patiently, she would wait for the darkness because she would be able to begin her social activity. She knew that Miz Temperance would not stay up until the midnight hours. Sleep would overtake her long before the clock struck nine. While Miz Temperance was still at supper, Amanda retraced her steps. She went down the back stairs and started for the coach house. Just as she got outside, Caroline stopped her.

"Where are you headin'?"

"Jest getting' some fresh air."

Caroline laughed.

"An' wat's so funny?"

"Youse were jest headin' fer de coach house."

"Maybe?"

"He ain't there."

Amanda turned and went back to the hotel. She ran to Miz Temperance room. When she got there, Miz Temperance was seated in the room's only chair. She stopped short and stared at the old woman. "Youse finish'd supper,"

"Wasn't that hungry."

"Youse a fixn' to go to bed?"

"Yeah," Miz Temperance grunted. "I need some water."

"Yes sum,"

Amanda picked up the water pitcher and went downstairs to fetch some water. She had to go outside to the water pump, which was located at the back of the hotel. As she approached the water pump, she saw Bill coming from the coach house. It seemed that they saw each other at the same time, as they threw up their hands to each other. Amanda stopped as Bill ran across the back yard to greet her.

"Wat's youse up to?" He took the pitcher from her.

"Jest getting' water fer Miz Temperance," Amanda replied as they continued toward the pump.

"She be ready to turn in?"

"'Pears to be."

They were now at the pump. Bill handed the pitcher to Amanda. She put the pitcher at the mouth of the pump and Bill pumped the water, as they continued to talk.

"Dis is de real world," Bill explained,

"It shore has a lot of white folks."

"Yeah, it do."

"On Stekoa Fields, dere's a lot of Indians and black folks."

Bill laughed as he stopped pumping and took the pitcher from her. Together, they headed back to the hotel. Silence came between them as Amanda walked kicking the dirt with her bare feet. When they got to the back stair case,

Bill handed Amanda the pitcher.

"I's see youse later," Bill said squeezing her hand. "'Night?"

"Yeah." Bill smiled. "Meet me at the coach house."

"As soon as Miz Temperance is a snorin'. Real good!"

Bill laughed and kissed her on the cheek.

Amanda watched him go, and then she hurried on to the back stairs of the hotel. When she got the second floor where the household of the Loves and Thomas's were lodging for the night, she met Master Thomas. She attempted to just walk on by without speaking, but he stopped her.

"Where have you been?"

"Getting' water fer Miz Temperance."

"It best that you stay in the hotel. The law ain't too happy with so many niggers in town."

"Yes sum."

She went on by him and hurried to Miz Temperance's room.

Chapter 42

The next morning Amanda was awakened by the explosion of firecrackers, followed by the sound of a rooster crowing. She jumped up and looked around. At first the surroundings were unfamiliar as she tried to remember where she was. It wasn't Stekoa Fields. Then her memories flooded back. It was the Fourth of July for the white folks and she was in the town of Webster. The Thomas's and the Loves had journeyed here to celebrate the Fourth with Miz Sallie's uncles and their families. She realized she was in Miz Temperance's hotel room.

Sitting on the pallet she slept on in Miz Temperance's room, Amanda thought about the time she spent with Bill last night. Hugging her knees, she remembered finally sneaking out of the room and meeting Bill at the coach house. It had seemed Miz Temperance would never fall asleep, but around ten o'clock, an even rhythmic snoring emitted from her mouth and Amanda left. Under the moonlight, Bill and Amanda felt free as the preparation of the Fourth of July continued around them.

Just at that moment in reminiscing of that evening with Bill, Amanda was abruptly dragged back to the present. Miz Temperance grunted and turned over in her sleep. Amanda jumped to her feet again and came to her aid. The morning sun slowly came creeping in the hotel window. To keep Miz Temperance from awaking, she attempted to close the curtain.

This only woke the old lady. She sat up and panned

the room. "Who's there?"

"It's me, Amanda."

"Come here, child."

Amanda went to her bedside. "Yes sum."

"Help me out of this damn high bed."

"Yes sum."

Amanda quickly went to Miz Temperance and helped her out of bed. Her frail, but strong body under the flannel nightgown was easy to handle. Within a few seconds, Miz Temperance was out of the bed. Standing on the cool hardwood floor, she leaned against the bed and slightly pushed Amanda aside.

"Get the bedcamber.."

"Yes sum."

Amanda reached under the bed and drug out the empty bed chamber. She took off the lid and set it where Miz Temperance could use it. Turning away, Amanda went to the window and looked down at the activities below. She saw wagonloads of white families already pulling into town for the celebration.

"Girl, where were you last night?" Miz Temperance said.

"Rat here."

"I called for you, but you never answered."

"I's went to empty an' wash out yer slop jar." Amanda replied nervously. "I's hope it weren't anythin' 'portant."

Miz Temperance grunted, "No, I just wanted to talk, that's all."

A sigh of relief escaped Amanda's lips. She was thankful she had taken the bed chamber with her when she went to see Bill. Now Miz Temperance would not be suspicious of her whereabouts if she had found her missing. Now her alibi worked, or at least she thought it had.

"You went to see that boy. Didn't you?"

"No ma'am," Amanda lied. "Just went to empty the slop jar. I guess I got lost in the dark tryin' to find my way back."

"Sure," Miz Temperance went to the chair and sat down. "Now take that slop jar out of here and get me some clean water in that pitcher so I can clean up a bit."

"Yes sum."

"And don't go near that coach house."

"Yes sum."

After putting the lid on the bed chamber, she went to the washstand and got the pitcher, which was half full of water. Going over to the bed chamber and removing its lid, she poured the reminder of the water in it. Closing the lid again, she carried both the pitcher and bedchamber out of the room. She hurried down the back stairs. As she was going out the door, she almost ran into a mulatto middle-aged woman. Quickly, she stepped aside and allowed the woman to pass. Amanda watched her as she went into the kitchen. And then she remembered that Miz Temperance wanted her to hurry. She found the outhouse and dumped the waste from the bed chamber into it.

Going to the pump, she was pleasantly surprised to find Bill there. Goose bumps covered her body, although it was a warm morning. She stopped and just stared at him. Dancing like fireflies in the night, her mind clicked off and on. In the back of her mind, she reminded herself of her duties to Miz Temperance. She just needed to rinse the bed chamber out and get fresh water for the pitcher. Steadying herself, she walked over to the pump.

Bill looked up as she approached and a smile played about his mouth. "Youse be up early."

"Miz Temperance sent me to git som' water."

He moved away from the front of the pump. "I's he'p youse."

"Danks," Amanda managed to say. "I's gotta hurry."

"Shore," Bill pumped the water into the pitcher.

Afterward, the two stared at each other, but the silence was broken by a male voice.

"What are ya'll doing back here?"

Water slouched out of the pitcher, as Amanda turned

toward the voice. A white man stood there with a badge pinned to his vest. She knew that it was High Sheriff Duge Davis. She had seen him at Stekoa Fields after Power had been beaten by the paddy rollers.

"Jest gittin' water for my Mistress." Amanda lowered her eyes.

"Move along," Sheriff Davis ordered.

"Yes sum."

Amanda started for the hotel, when she heard High Sheriff talking to Bill.

"To who do you belong?"

"I's 'long to Master James Love of White Sulfur Springs."

Now Amanda was out of earshot of their voices, as she hurried to Miz Temperance. As she passed through the kitchen, she saw the mulatto cook busy at work. She wanted to talk to her, but there wasn't time. When she got to Miz Temperance's room, she knocked on the door.

"Come on in Amanda." Miz Temperance's voice flowed through the door.

Amanda entered and put the pitcher on the wash-stand and the bed chamber under the bed. Afterward, she poured the crystal clear pump water in the basin and placed a face towel on the stand. Slowly Miz Temperance went to the washstand to freshen up for the day. While she was washing up, Amanda laid out her clothes. Within an hour or so Miz Temperance was ready to face the day. She sat down to rest her bones for a minute.

The two women stared at each other. Mistress and slave girl, they had been together all of Amanda's life...though the good times and the bad times. Amanda felt Miz Temperance was more than just her former mistress. They understood each other, although a veil sometimes masked Amanda's true feelings. In the presence of Miz Temperance, Amanda strived to maintain a happy-go-lucky disposition. Slowly Miz Temperance got out of the chair. Quickly, Amanda went to her side to assist her. She held her arm as Miz Temperance retrieved her cane from the right arm of the chair.

"You're so much like your mother."

"Danks."

"You just trust us white folks a little bit. The sparkle in your eyes tells me that you're happy about something."

Amanda didn't answer.

Miz Temperance laughed. "Just like your mother."

"Yes sum." Amanda mumbled.

They were in the hall now. Amanda reached back and closed the door. Miz Temperance steadied herself with her cane. Together, the two headed downstairs to the dining room.

On the way, Miz Temperance was very talkative. Amanda had heard all this before; yet she pretended to be listening to the old lady's ramblings. Concentrating on getting Miz Temperance safely to the dining room, Amanda continued to respond with the classic answer.

"Yes sum." Amanda answered when Miz Temperance paused to get her response.

"So you do want that young whippersnapper?"

"Wat?"

Amanda realized that Miz Temperance was no longer talking about how she had raised Master Thomas alone. The old lady had turned her attention to Amanda's affair. And yet, Amanda knew she didn't really control her destiny. Her life was in the hands of Master Thomas and Miz Sallie. This was one of the times that the veil came between them. Silence surrounded them as they approached the bottom step. The other members of the Thomas and Love families were already in the dining room.

"I saw the way you looked at him."

"Wat?'

"Child!" Miz Temperance just shook her head. "I know you're after him," She laughed. "You're afraid that Mariah's mulatto slave gal is gonna get him." She made no attempt for Amanda to reply. "I'll talk to Master Thomas on your behalf."

Chapter 43

Amanda didn't respond. She deposited Miz Temperance at the dining room table and proceeded to the kitchen area. After all the other slaves had breakfast, Amanda lingered in the kitchen. She wanted desperately to talk to the mulatto cook. The two women glanced at each other, but their eyes never met. It seemed a long time before everyone was gone, leaving Amanda and the cook alone.

"Youse belong to Mr. Webster?"

"Who?" The cook laughed.

"Mr. Webster. He do own dis hotel?"

"Webster Hotel is just a name. Mr. Luck owns this here hotel."

"Oh!" Amanda corrected herself. "So youse 'long to Mr. Luck?"

"I don't b'long to anyone. I be free,"

"Free?'

"Yeah. My name is Annie Grimes."

Amanda hesitated to respond. In her mind, she thought of Bill and realized that Annie also had a last name. She didn't. She was just a slave and slaves don't have last names. They were just the property of the owner.

"Wat's yer name child?'

" Amanda." She just stared at Annie. She couldn't believe that she was free. "How'd get free?"

"Born that way."

Amanda didn't have a chance to ask Annie any more questions. As always, Cudge came to get her. Hence, she told Annie goodbye with the hope that it wasn't truly a good-bye. Later on, she hoped to talk to her again. But right now, she had to go with Cudge.

Stepping outside, Amanda noticed it seemed like the white world had invaded her territory. This was the first time in her life the whites outnumbered the blacks. Living on Stekoa Fields, there was always more blacks than whites. Sometimes when Master Thomas' Indian friends came, the Luftys outnumbered them all. Now Amanda understood why they weren't free. The whites were everywhere. People had come from miles around to celebrate the Fourth. On foot, some had trudged from their mountain homes to join in the celebration. Others drove in by sled, buggy or wagon. The young and the old were there. It seemed the town had or-ganized this get-together. Amanda had seen handbills nailed to trees advertising the events that were going to take place. As she recalled, there was going to be an ox race, a sack race and a barrel race. Of course, the Fourth of July in these parts would not be complete without a greased pig chase.

As she made her way to the front of the hotel, she found the street was lined with white folks. On the hotel porch, she spied the Senator and his family along with other guests. It seemed the dirt road in front of the hotel was turned into a race track. Looking up the street, she saw they were going to have an ox race. There were about a dozen or so young fellows seated on their ox. Among the contestants was Cudge. He was representing Stekoa Fields. He and a slave of Thad Bryson's were the only blacks in the race. There was excitement in the air. In charge of getting the race started was High Sheriff Duge Davis.

Sheriff Davis had a white handkerchief in his hand. When he dropped it, there was a mad dash for the finish line. In all the confusion, some of the riders lost their seat on the top of their oxen as they attempted to ride the wild beast. Some of the oxen leaped, kicked and bucked as the young riders tried to switch them. Cudge managed to stay aboard his Master's ox, but two other fellows were ahead of him. The crowd was cheering on their favorite. So naturally, Amanda shouted for Cudge to win the race. When the winner crossed the finish line, it wasn't Cudge or the Bryson slave. A white fellow won the race. Cudge came in third.

After the ox race, there was a barrel race. This race was strictly for the white folks. About a dozen barrels with both ends opened were placed on a course about forty yards apart that ran through town. The object of the barrel race was to carry three eggs through the barrels without breaking them. Amanda laughed as the young white males tried to maneuver the course without breaking the eggs.

By the time the barrel race was over, it was getting near lunchtime for the white folks. Picnic baskets appeared as families searched for a good spot around a hugh area cleared out for folks to picnic. A low platform sat at one end of the area. As the families ate their lunch, the local politicians spoke to the crowd from that platform. This seemed to be a good time to state their position if they were running for office.

In November, there was going to be a Presidential Election and the Democratic Party found themselves split into the Southern platform and the Northern platform. Thomas was running for re-election for a North Carolina Senatorial seat. He would be making a speech along with other local politicians. It was important that the Democratic Party win the presidential race for the newly formed Republican Party had nominated Abraham Lincoln. And yet, with a split party and Stephen Douglas running an independent campaign, the South needed all the votes they could muster for their candidate John C. Breckinridge.

Listening to the speeches, Amanda tried to figure out where the issues on slavery stood. To her, it was apparent the white man had everything under control. Just seeing all the white people, she realized once again how the slaves were outnumbered.

As the afternoon events began, she sneaked away

from the crowd and went into the kitchen of the Webster Hotel. She was hoping to find Annie still at work. When she entered the kitchen, she found her preparing the evening meal for hotel guests. Annie was humming a Negro spiritual. For a moment, Amanda stood and watched her before she turned around.

"Oh!" Annie said. "It's youse."

"Yeah." Amanda answered timidly. "I's jest wanna ax youse somethin'."

"Look, girl. |I's free. I's been free alls my life."

"Youse ain't got no Maser.?"

"Nope."

"Is youse marri'd?"

"Yeah."

"Youse got a family likk de white folks?"

"Look, youse can be free."

"I's can't. Got no place to go."

"Times be changin'. Herd dat Lincoln's gonna free de slaves."

"He ain't president yet."

"He's gonna be."

"Dey'll kill'im 'fore dat."

"Girl, I gotta git back to work."

Annie went back to work. Amanda knew she wasn't going to talk any more. As quietly as she came in, she left. Although Annie was free, Amanda felt she was not completely free.

Wandering around Webster was not good for a slave. With all the white folks, a slave could end up in jail until his master claimed him. Although Amanda didn't know it, Sheriff Davis was well aware of all the slaves who came to town with their masters. As she made her way back to the courthouse where all the politicking was going on, the High Sheriff stopped her.

He caught her by the arm and jerked her around. "What are you doin' wanderin' 'round here? Where's your mistress?"

"She be o'er yonder." Amanda said nervously. "I's just went to r'lieve myself."

"You 'long to Mrs. Sallie Thomas?"

"Yes sum."

The sheriff gave her a shove toward the courthouse. "Git where you 'long."

"Yes sum."

Without looking back, Amanda hurried through the crowd. Just as she got close to the Thomas's and Loves'spot in the pinic area, someone grabbed her from behind. It was Charles Bumgarner. Her heart raced. She hated Mr. Bumganer. She wanted to run, but she didn't want to make a scene. Miz Sallie would be upset with her and she didn't want to cause any trouble. Like a good obedient slave, she didn't look at Mr. Bumgarner, but she stared at the ground.

"What are you doin' wanderin' 'round here by yourself?" He shook her violently. "You tryin' to run away 'gain?"

"No, Mr. Bumgarner," Amanda plead. "I's had to go r'lieve myself. I's goin' back to Miz Temperance."

Mr. Bumgarner laughed. "I's saw you talkin' to that free nigger."

Tears began to silently drip from her eyes. She had been caught and Mr. Bumgarner was going to whip her like he did Power. However, fate intervened as two of Mr. Bumgarner's buddies came running up to him.

"C'mon Charles."

"Yeah," said the one. "The greased pig chase is 'bout to begin."

"Stay here, gal." Bumgarner told Amanda. "I gotta win me some money."

Chapter 44

Mr. Bumgarner and his buddies quickly weaved their way through the crowd. It seemed just about every man and boy in the county had entered that race. Amanda stood there and watched as the throng of males readied themselves to try to capture the greased pig. The sheriff started the chase by shooting off his pistol. Suddenly there was a mad scramble to catch the allusive greased pig.

` She watched Mr. Bumgarner and his buddies join the wild chase. Now she didn't know what to do. Mr. Bumgarner had told her to stay there, but Sheriff Davis had instructed her to get with her mistress. As she was trying to make up her mind, someone tapped her on the shoulder. Frightened, she turned to see Bill's smiling face.

"I's didn't mean to scare youse."

"I's glad to see youse."

"C'mon, I's wanna show youse som'thin'."

"I's gotta git back."

Bill took her by the arm and led her through the crowd. She thought that he was taking her to Miz Temperance, who was seated on the hotel porch. However, Bill guided her pass the hotel and away from the pinic area to a vacant lot, which was no longer empty. In a circle there were a crowd of older mountain men who voices were loudly cheering. Money was held high in the air, as each man challenged another. Because of the excitement, Amanda and Bill were able to squeeze through the crowd. Amanda wanted to leave, but Bill held her arm tightly.

As they emerged from the crowd, Amanda saw large crude roped off square. Standing in the far corner was the darkest and biggest Negro slave she had ever seen. He wore raggedy trousers that came to his knees. His barrel chest was bare and sweaty. On the ground was another slave, who was out cold. A white man dressed in fancy suit was collecting money from the irate crowd.

"Don't y'all have a champion around here?" The man in the fancy suit declared. "All they have to do is stay three rounds with my champ."

It was evident that the locals wanted to win back their money. To Amanda and Bill's surprise, among that throng of crowd was Master Matthew Love. He grabbed Bill by the arm and started to leave. However, an overalls clad man grabbed Bill...and Matthew was no match to the crowd of mountaineers.

"Git that nigger outta de ring." The mountaineer pushed Bill toward the ring.

"No!" Matthew protested. "He ain't a boxer."

The mountaineer pushed Matthew down. "You be in on this with dat fancy pants."

Amanda could not say anything to protest. She stood there mortified, as the mountaineer announced. "Here's my nigger champ'n."

He took the unconscious slave out of the ring and tossed him aside like he was a rag doll. One of the men pointed to Amanda and told her to take care of him. Amanda obeyed. Hurriedly, she found some water and dashed the entire bucket on the unconscious slave. Quickly he revived and looked at Amanda.

"Youse tryin' to drown me?"

"Jest savin' yer life." She helped him into a sitting position.

He was badly beaten, but he would survive. She left his side and went to see about Bill's fate. When she returned to ring, she found that Master Matthew was on his feet. It was evident he could do nothing for Bill. They had stripped Bill to the waist and his shirt was trampled beneath their feet. In the ring the fancy dressed white man gave Bill instructions. All around her, men were betting. Most men were betting against Bill. She even saw Matthew get in the act. Anger took over, but Amanda held her peace. Silently, she prayed that Bill would be all right. Looking at the giant black man, Amanda knew Bill couldn't win. And yet, he had to win or the man who had declared him his champion would be angry.

"Alright, gentl'men," Fancy Pants announced, "Your local champion hafto stay in the ring for three rounds with Sambo."

A bell rang and the fight was on. Loud shouts and cheers erupted, as Bill quickness enabled him to avoid Sambo's powerful punches. Just as the first round came to a close, Sambo was able to tag Bill with a glancing blow on the chin. Bill's knees buckled, but the bell saved him. The mountaineer, who declared Bill as his champion, came to his aid. Realizing this was fun and games to these men, she dared not interfere. She watched as the mountaineer gave Bill some water from a pail, then dumped the remaining over his head.

The bell rang for the second round. Amanda had found Bill's shirt and was hiding herself with it. Once in a while, she peeked out as the crowd roared with approval. Bill was still on his feet, but Amanda could tell that Sambo was relentlessly chasing him all over the ring. Small and quick, Bill became elusive, as Sambo swung wildly. Angrily, Sambo lunged toward Bill and missed. Bill countered quickly with a hard solid right to the mid-section. With his left, he landed a punch on Sambo's right jaw. Sambo staggered back and Bill went in for the kill. At that instant, the bell rang to end the second round.

Angry shouts erupted from the crowd. Bill, "The local champion" was about to knockout Sambo. Silently tears cascaded down Amanda's cheeks, as the bell for the third round sounded. She saw the anger and frustration in Sambo's eyes. If he landed a solid punch on Bill's lean body, he would knock him out. Bill was tired as Sambo angrily slashed out at him. Some punches landed, but they were just glancing blows. However, the bigger man was now backing Bill into a corner. If he got him in the corner, Sambo could pummel him with body punches. Sambo threw a punch, Bill was able to duck and escape the corner. Chasing him, Sambo was able to cut him off and land a crushing blow to the jaw. Bill's head rocked back and Sambo charged in. Instinctively, Bill put his hands up to protect face, but Sambo pummeled the body. Bill tried to remain on his feet, but Sambo continued to hammer.

Amanda didn't know that she spoke aloud. "Bill," she screamed. "Fall, fall down! He's gonna kill youse."

At that moment the bell rang. Looking over where the bell was, she realized that Matthew had hit the bell to end the round. Fancy Pants couldn't say anything, because the mountaineers would have mobbed him. When Bill staggered across the ring, the mountaineer lifted him up on his shoulder and declared him the winner. The crowd roared. Amanda watched. She couldn't move. The mountaineer took Bill to Amanda. He fell into her arms as the mountaineer went to collect his winnings. Before he left, he came back over to Bill and Amanda.

He placed some money into Amanda's hand. "Give dis to him. He earned it."

Amanda held the money tight in her fist. "Danks."

The mountaineer was gone, before Amanda could say anything else. A chilly silence filled the air as the crowd quickly dispersed. Even Fancy Pants and Sambo loaded up their wagon and disappeared. All left, but Amanda and Bill. She sat on the ground and held his pummeled body on her lap. Like rocking a baby, she hugged Bill close to her beast. Someone tapped her on the shoulder. Looking up, she stared at Matthew. Amanda wanted to curse him, but she knew that he had stopped the fight.

"Hand me the money." Master Matthew demanded. "Clean him up as best you can."

Chapter 45

Reluctantly she gave him the money and did as she was told. She didn't know how much money the man had given her, but it felt like a lot. However, she surmised it wasn't enough to buy her freedom. And yet, she knew Bill was trying to buy his freedom back from Mr. Love. That small amount might have helped. It was gone and there was nothing she could do about it.

Slowly she got up and helped Bill to his feet. Moans and groans came from his lips. He had stayed three rounds, but at a cost. His battered body was heavy against her, but she had to get him back to the hotel.

"Bill," she whispered. "We hafto to get back. Jest hold on to me."

He put his arm around her shoulder and tried not to put all his weight on her. Although his legs were weary and weak, he managed to move one in front of the other. When Bill and Amanda got back to the hotel, Master Thomas and Mr. Love were waiting for them at the coach house. It was quiet evident that Matthew had hatched up a lie to tell them. There was nothing either one of them could do. After all, it was a white man's word against theirs. To add to the tragedy, the tale was told by Mr. Love's son. Amanda realized that Master Matthew was covering his tracks, because Bill was a value piece of property. Therefore, it had to be someone else fault and he had put the blame on Amanda for his father damaged goods.

"Where have you two been?" Mr. Love asked Bill.

"We thought dat we go see a boxin' match." Bill replied. "I hope youse didn't mind."

"Look at you," Mr. Love barked. You look like you were one being punched."

"Well, sir," Bill kicked dirt. "I guess I was."

"What?" Mr. Love was irate. "If I sold you now, you wouldn't be worth much. Where's the men who staged this fight?"

"Dey be gone."

Master Matthew was standing in the shadow. Mr. Love turned and addressed his son. "Go get the sheriff."

Matthew mumbled, "Yes sir."

As Master Matthew went after the sheriff, Master Thomas questioned Amanda.

"Is that what happened?"

"Yes sir. We were jest gonna watch, but they made Bill fight."

"James, why don't you let your brother look at Bill?"

Mr. Love walked off and went to hotel to fetch his brother Dr. John Love.

"And you, Amanda." Thomas scolded her. "You were purposed to be my mother personal servant. And you're out gallivanting with him."

"I's sorry."

"Sorry don't get it." Thomas shook head from side to side. "You're like children. You always need someone to clean up your mess. Now I'm going to give you another assignment. You are to take care of Bill as well as caring care of my mother."

"Yes sir."

"Now go see if my mother needs your service."

"Yes sum."

As Amanda left to go upstairs to Miz Temperance, Dr. Love and Sheriff Davis arrived. She didn't look back. Her only hope was that Bill would not be in trouble. It seemed every step she took, the reality of the world was dark and meaningless. Desperately she wanted to be alone, but she knew Miz Temperance would not allow her. Seeing it was suppertime, Amanda decided to go to kitchen and get a bit to eat before going upstairs. When she entered, she found the Thomas' and Loves' slave eating.

"Where haft youse been?" Cudge asked her.

"'Round."

"We were worried when you didn't show up to hep Miz Temperance?" Rozette interjected.

Caroline said, "I's glad youse safe."

"Danks, Caroline."

Sam stood up. Everyone knew that instructions were going to be given to them. " After sundown all slaves are to stay off the street. Any slave caught will spend the night in jail. Each slave caught, Senator Thomas will have to pay one hundred dollars for their release. And if you get caught, you will be punished when we get back to Stekoa Fields."

Amanda listened. And yet, Master Thomas wanted her to float from the hotel to coach house. It seemed he wanted her caught.

"We's be leaving early 'morrow. So youse need to get some sleep. Amanda, do youse know where Bill be?"

"He proba'ly be in de coach house."

All eyes turned to Amanda. It was apparent they wanted to know more. However she told them nothing, as she continued to eat. After she finished, she headed for the back stairs to go up to Miz Temperance's room. Peeking around the corner, she saw Mr. Love and Master Thomas conversing with Sheriff Davis. She couldn't hear what they were saying, so she went on upstairs. When she got to Miz Temperance's room door, she knocked.

"Who is it?"

"It be me, Mandy."

" C'mon in."

Slowly Amanda opened the door and stepped inside the room. Miz Temperance was seated in the chair. In her lap lay a book. It was apparent she had been reading and had fallen asleep.

"Is youse ready to go to bed?"

"I could use some sleep. It's been a long day." Miz Temperance yawned. "But it was a good day."

"Yes ma'am."

"All the decorations were great. Webster really knows how to celebrate our independence day."

"Wat's dat?"

"That's when we won our freedom from Britain."

"Oh!"

Slowly, Miz Temperance rose from the chair and placed the black book on the dresser. Amanda moved to lay her nightgown out on the chair. And then she took the bedspread off of the bed and folded in up, lying on the chest at the foot of her bed. She pulled back the top sheet and fluffed the pillows. All was ready for Miz Temperance to hop in bed. Amanda helped her get undressed and folded her clothes so they would be ready to pack in the morning. While Miz Temperance was brushing her teeth with stems from the black gum tree, Amanda closed the curtains so the light wouldn't come in. Then she checked the bed chamber and the water in the pitcher. By keeping busy, Amanda hoped that Miz Temperance wouldn't question about her whereabouts during the day.

Amanda faked a yawn as Miz Temperance took down her hair, which was halfway down her back. She watched as she put a night cap on her head. Before she went to bed, she knelt beside the bed and prayed. When she finally climbed into bed, Amanda went to the window and stared down at the courtyard. She knew she would have to face Dearest Sallie before this was all over. Thinking of the incident that took place, she came to the realization that she hated white men. They lied to get what they wanted. Or sometimes, they just took what they wanted without asking. Standing there, she thought about the mountaineer who gave her the money that Master Matthew stole. He knew he could get away with it.

Sighing, she said to herself, "Independence day...it ain't free."

Chapter 46

When Miz Temperance head hit the pillow, sleep came. Amanda stayed a few minutes, and then she quietly left the room. She crept down the back stairs and raced to the coach house. Safely inside, she leaned against the wall to catch her breath.

"Amanda, is that you?"

"Yes." She walked over to Bill and sat down beside his bruised body. Tenderly she touched his thigh and he flinched. "Sorry," she whispered.

"I feel likk I's been run o'er by a train."

"Do's youse need any thin'?"

"Wat did Doc say?"

"Bruised ribs." he said. "Dey feel likk dey be broke,"

Quietly she sat there and listened to him breathe. It was hollow and shallow. She wanted to hold him, but she knew his whole being was sore. Sometimes during the night Amanda fell asleep and was awaken by Bill, who was moaning and groaning in his sleep. It seemed that light from heaven was shining through the cracks in the wall and adorned Bill's face. As she recalled, they were to get an early start. Hence she woke Bill and then she went to the hotel to help Miz Temperance get ready. Running across the courtyard, she saw it was going to a great day. The sun was shining and the birds were chirping. Amanda began to hum a merry tune. Without knocking she entered Miz Temperance's hotel room. On entering, she found Miz Temperance was still asleep. Instead of waking her, Amanda prepared everything, so when she got up she could begin to get ready for the trip home. With a beautiful morning outside, she opened the curtains and when she did, Miz Temperance opened her eyes.

" G'mornin," Amanda said. "It be a beautiful morning.

"Good Morning to you," Miz Temperance shared Amanda's happiness.

"Everythin' be ready fer you." she said. "I's be back shortly."

Amanda left and went back to the coach house to see about Bill. When she got there, he was sitting up. Looking at him, she felt a little better. Dr. Love had examined him and concluded nothing was broken, just bruising. She helped him to his feet and they walked out together to the kitchen for breakfast. After dropping Bill off, she returned to Temperance's hotel room to pack her valise. On entering, she found Miz Temperance was dressed and ready to go. Together they went to dining room where Miz Temperance could eat breakfast.

Returning to the hotel room she packed Miz Temperance's personal belongings. She carried the valise downstairs and put it on the back platform. Peeking into the kitchen, she checked on Bill. She didn't see him. Going to the coach house, she found him gathering his belongings and putting them in a knapsack. Slowly, he looked up and saw Amanda. A half grin graced his face. As he walked toward the buckboard setting in the back of the hotel, he saw Sam coming out of hotel with more luggages.

Together, Sam and Bill loaded the buckboard while Cudge brought the rest of the luggage to them. While the luggage was being loaded, the two-seated carriage was brought around to the front of the hotel for the ladies. All three personal servants were there to help them climb into the carriage. When they finished their duties, they went back to buckboard. By that time the luggage was packed in the canvas covered buckboard and Amanda and her fellow slaves got on board. Cudge and Bill left and took their position on the carriage, and although Bill had bruised ribs, he drove with Cudge beside him. Coming up the rear was Master Matthew and the Senator on their horses. In matter of few minutes, Webster was lost behind them as they traveled back to Stekoa Fields.

The next morning Bill remained at Stokoa Field to mend and heal, when Mr. Love left for White Sulfu Springs. Cudge accompanied Senator Thomas to the General Assembly. Being four months pregnant Dearest Sallie had to run the place. Hence Miz Mariah stayed with her sister as did her personal servant, Rozette. Miz Temperance was not to let her daughter-in-law go it alone, so she stayed. Master Matthew wanted to remain on Stekoa Fields, but his father needed him at home. When Amanda found out who was staying and who was leaving, she was satisfied. Without telling them at the big house, she moved Bill into her cabin. If Dearest Sallie found out, she said nothing to Amanda.

With Sam acting as the overseer, Sallie knew the jobs would get done as August rose on the horizon. The hot sizzling sun seemed to beam down as the summer months rolled on. Harvest was the order of day, as the slaves worked in the field. The corn and pole beans were picked. But Miz Sallie decided there would be no shucking party. Potatoes had to be dug and the cabbage cut from their stems. The fruits on Stekoa Fields were in need of being picked, also. Then the kitchen crew could can, dry, and pickle to put up food for the winter.

Everyone was busy, even the children. They had the job of picking up the apples laying on the ground. The children also went into the woods and picked up a variety of nuts. Some children brought in wood and kindling for the winter.

Besides her duties at the big house, Amanda nursed Bill back to health. It seemed that everyone blamed her for his misfortune. Matthew twisted the story and there was nothing Amanda could do about. She had never told Bill that the mountaineer had paid him for his gallant challenge, because Master Matthew had taken it. Maybe, he did know it and that was why she was happy that Master Matthew went home. When the evening came most slaves were dragging their feet and Amanda was one of them. Cleaning the house had become burdensome. With Dearest Sallie expecting sometimes in December, Miz Mariah inspected her work daily. If she wasn't satisfied, Amanda had to do it over. With Bill mending, she couldn't stay at the big house. Therefore, she went to her quarters. She made sure that Bill had food and drink.

It seemed that her world was closing in on her. At least, Bill was in her care. Every morning when she woke, Bill would be by her side. She would cook some dough bread and leave it for him. Coming back to her quarters, he was there. Most of the time, he would be sleep. She washed him and put some of her mother's salve on his bruises. Sometimes she would sing to him. This was a duty of love.

It was the middle of August and Bill was healing. The bruises were gone and the swelling had gone down around his eyes. He once again looked like Bill and Amanda was happy. The only concern she had was that Mr. Love would come and take him away. Therefore, if any one asked about him, she lied. For in her mind, this was a match and she needed him. Any night now they would be able to resume their affair.

The kitchen staff was busy making jam and jelly. They canned pole beans and dried some. Miz Mariah came to her and told her that she would have to help with the canning. That meant more time at the big house. She noticed that Caroline and Rozette had very little to do. They were Miz Sallie and Miz Mariah's personal servants. Amanda was angry, but she had no one to talk with.

Tired and exhausted, Amanda decided that she needed to go to her quarters. She told Suckey, she wasn't feeling well and she should not be around food. Surprisingly, Suckey agreed.

"Go," Suckey said,"Youse been workin' too hard."

"I jest need some rest. I shore don't wanna Dearest Sallie to get wat ever I have."

"We can handle it."

"Danks."

Amanda slowly dragged herself to her quarters. Her head ached along with every bone in her body. As she approached her cabin, she saw a candle was lit. Usually, Bill never lit a candle. It was always dark when she came. Her steps were no longer dragging, there was a skip in her gait. Her tired body almost ran as she got to her door. As she opened the door, she was taken back with what she saw. Rozette was lying on the bed with Bill. It seemed they were kissing.

"Wat in hell is youse doin'?"

"Jest keepin'm warm."

"Git out of my house."

"He's mine." Rozette argued.

"Amanda," Bill spoke for the first time. "I let her kiss me."

Amanda stood there.

"Rozette, ifen youse don't leave. . ."

She walked by Amanda. "He'll tell ya."

After Rozette left, Amanda went over to the bed and sat down. Tears ran down her face. "Why?"

"I's sorry."

"Wat did I do?"

"I guess I ain't a one-woman man."

"Do youse love me?"

Amanda touched his bare chest. He pulled her down to him and kissed her. Amanda tried to pull away from him, but he held her to him. She didn't know what to think. All she knew was she loved him and she couldn't control her emotion when he was around.

Morning brought only sadness for Amanda. Deep down, she knew she was going to have to let him go. She wished her mother was here to give her some advice. The institution of slavery made them animals and there was no sense of right or wrong. It was whatever the Master said. Crying was not going to help. Going to Webster showed her another lifestyle. She had met a free black person, but she also realized that Annie wasn't completely free. Amanda detected Annie's feelings, although she tried to hide them.

Sitting there in the chair by the hearth, which was in need of more fire wood, Amanda waited for the bell to ring. Like the rising of the sun, the bell told her when to go to the big house. Usually, she went before it rang so that she could get ahead start with her work. Today, she decided to allow the bell to ring before she moved.

All was quiet outside. Listening carefully, Amanda tuned her ears to Mother Nature. Somewhere in the woods, a coyote howled and another one seemed to return its call. Laughing, she thought of herself and Bill. He called and like an animal in heat, she went to him. Now he was charming someone else.

Bill stirred in his sleep and turned over. He stretched his arm out to feel the soft body of Amanda. Only the lumpy mattress was there to greet him. Looking toward the hearth, he saw Amanda, who seemed to be staring into the dying fire.

"Come back to bed," he said as he patted the empty spot. "It be warm'r in here."

Amanda turned her head and looked at him from over left shoulder. "Why don't youse git yer black ass out of my bed an' go git some wood to put on dis fire."

He laughed. "Youse be a little hot dis mornin'."

"Not fer youse."

"Last night, youse were."

"It be a new day, William Hudson Casey."

Amanda got up and went outside. Down in the valley, the August morning air was cool. Standing just outside the door, she stretched and held her arms up to the heavens, leaving them there for a few seconds. Breathing in the fresh mountain air, she promised herself she would not pursue

Bill's love. Going to the side of the cabin, she picked up an arm load of wood and it brought inside. She dropped the load beside the hearth. Picking up a couple of sticks of wood, she laid them on the dying embers, which sparks danced off the wood. With a stick, she poked at the fire.

Coming up behind her, Bill hugged around her waist and held her tightly to him. She made no move to stop him, as he turned her around to face him. They stared at each other as he attempted to kiss her. She turned her face away and the kiss was planted on her neck. With that opportunity, his teeth bit into her neck, but she pushed him away.

"No, Bill," she declared. "It be o'er."

"Amanda!"

"Go on back to Rozette." She looked him dead in the eyes. "I nurs'd youse back to health. Mr. Love will wants youse back to defend his home. Youse can't stay here."

"Youse puttin' me out."

"Ten I will leave an' live in the single women's cabin."

Amanda walked out the door in the morning light. Since the bell never rang, Amanda knew it was Sunday. It would be an easy day for everyone. Perhaps Mary would come over and they could share their feelings. She went to the big house, but it appeared that everyone except Little Will was sleeping in. Going to the nursery, she found Flossie dressing him for the day. Danny was seated on the floor playing with a top. Amanda went over to him and picked him up. Not wanting to be picked up, he started to cry. She sat him down so he could resume playng with the top.

"I's fig're youse be still in bed tossing around with Bill."

"Nope."

"Where is he?" she asked. "Is he gone?"

"Don't know." Amanda laughed to keep from crying. "I's left'im in the cabin."

Amanda kissed Danny and left before Flossie asked any more questions. Coming down the back stairs, she saw Rozette just before she cut the corner to go to the kitchen. She decided to follow her. At this point Amanda didn't care who was in the kitchen, she was going to tell Rozette what she thought of her. However, when she turned the corner, Rozette hadn't gotten to the kitchen. Amanda called her name, she stopped and looked around. She waited until Amanda approached her and the two stood face to face.

"Wat 's youse want?"

"Just to tell youse wat's I think of youse." Amanda pointed her finger in Rozette's face. "Youse are an animal. Youse goes into someone else's den an' rob."

"He 'vited me in."

"Youse can keep'im."

With those words, Amanda turned and walked away.

Entering the house by the back door, Amanda returned to the upstairs and found her way to Miz Temperance's room. She was still in bed, not asleep. Sitting there with the black book opened with her gray hair flowing down across her shoulder, Temperance looked up from her reading.

"What are you doing here?"

"It be breakfast time." Amanda said."Do youse wanna be served in bed."

"I haven't had that offer in a long time." She smiled. "Pamper me today."

"Yes ma'am."

Amanda left and retraced her steps to the kitchen. When she entered, Rozette was still there. She completely ignored her and addressed Suckey.

"This morning, Miz Temperance is having breakfast in bed. Will yous pleas' fix a tray so dat I migh' take it to her?"

Suckey laughed. "Are youse shore youse ain't gonna tak' to Bill?"

Holding back her anger, Amanda gritted her teeth. "Wen hell freeze o'er."

Silence filled the room. Flossie looked at Rozette, then glanced at Amanda. Without engaging into any more conversation, Suckey fixed a breakfast tray for Miz Temperance. She handed it to Amanda, who bowed when she received it and left them to their own vices.When she got to Miz Temperance's bedroom, she observed that Miz Temperance was still reading from the little black book. After putting a cross knitted bookmark in the book, Miz Temperance laid it on the bedside table. Amanda put the tray on the vanity. She stepped over to the bed and straightened her Mistress's pillows. While arranging the pillows, she glanced at the black book. Just by the texture of the book and the bold lettering, she knew it was a Bible. When she was little, she remembered Miz Temperance carrying it to church. She didn't ask her about it. It was the Bible's history that made her a slave. Going to the vanity, she took the tray with legs and placed it across her lap. She took the cloth napkin and put it around her neck and then she headed toward the exit.

"Have a Great breakfast!" she smiled. "Call me wen youse be finish."

"Wait!"

"Yes sum."

"How is that boy?"

"He be fine. As a matt'r of fact I jest left him at my quarters. I's movin' to the single women cabin."

"He doesn't need you there."

"No'um." She turned to go. "I's hafto git to cleanin'."

Chapter 47

It was Sunday and the Thomas household went to church, leaving Miz Temperance in charge. Amanda decided she would take a chance and get a pass from her to go to Shoal Creek. It would be good time to see Mary again. She surmised that the New Moon Ceremony was coming up. This year, she was determined to be there. As soon as carriage drove out of the driveway, Amanda made a beeline to the big house. She didn't have to worry about Sam, because he had driven Dearest Sallie and her crew to church. Going in the back door, she knew where Miz Temperance would be. It was her favorite place to spy on the activities of the farm. As a child Amanda had sat with her and listened to her talk about her life. Hence, Amanda stepped into the parlor where Miz Temperance sat in her rocker near the window.

"I saw you coming," she said. "What's on your mind?"

"I's a wonderin' ifen youse could write me a pass to go to Shoal Creek"

"What?"

"A pass to Shoal Creek."

"What's down there?".

"A friend."

Miz Temperance sighed. "Girl, you're just gonna get in trouble."

"Please." Amanda promised. "I's won't git in trou'le."

"Trouble just follows you, child."

"I's wanna renew my friendship with Mary."

Miz Temperance laughed. "I recall that name."

"'Member when Charley fell in de bonfire an' got badly burnt."

"I sure do. That was terrible."

"She blam'd me."

"Why don't you wait until they get back from church and Sam and I can go with you."

"That'll be too late."

"No it won't." Miz Temperance thought a minute. "Child, we need a man along. You can't walk off by yourself."

"Yes sum."

Amanda knew that Temperance was right. Not only would she safer with a man, there would a white woman with them. She left the big house and went back to slave quarters. Since she was not going to live in the cabin she shared with mother, she had to get some personal things out. As she approached, she prayed that Bill wouldn't be there. Knocking on the door before she entered was the safe thing to do. She knocked three times, but no one answered. Easing the door open, Amanda peeked in the room, it was empty. Quickly, she went in to gather her things. She took her extra dress and her shawl that were hanging on the wall. Looking around, she packed her dishes in among the dress and shawl and laid them on the blanket on the bed. She got the merger food supply and placed them with the other items. Swiftly she tied them in the blanket and started out the door. She stopped dead in her tracks. Bill was coming in the door.

Either one of them stepped aside; they just stared at each other.

"I's jest came to git my things."

"'So, I's see."

Bill pushed his way in, making Amanda back up. She almost dropped her bundle. He slammed the door and angrily took the bundle from her and tossed it on the bed. As the bundle hit the bed there was a sound of breaking dishes.

"Damn youse." She screamed at him. "Youse broke my things."

"Mandy," he tried to reassure her. "It weren't nothin', but castoffs from the big house."

"Youse dog!"

Before Bill knew what had happened, Amanda dove into him and knocked him down. Sitting astride of his stomach, she hammered away with her both fists. Bill was totally surprised as her fists rained down blows on him in the chest and face before he was able to protect himself with his arms. After being hit several times, he managed to grab her wrists and hold off her vicious attack.

"Amanda," he tried to calm her. "I's sorry. I's sorry."

Tears covered Amanda face and a sicken sob came from her throat. "Youse broke my things...my mother's things."

Bill was mortified. "I's sorry."

Amanda was still straddling him. He took her head and pressed it to his chest. Tenderly, he stroked her hair as sobs came from Amanda. He rolled her over until he was atop of her. Her legs were still around his body and he took advantage of her.

Afterward, Bill left her there on the floor. Sitting there, she was angry with herself. Slowly she got up and straightened up. She went to bed and got her bundle and walked out the door.

"Animal," she said, "I's an animal."

She took her things to the single women cabin and put them on her bed. Being Sunday, everyone was out and about the farm. There was nothing important to do. The woods became some slave's couples' haven, while other found refuge in their own quarters. Alone, Amanda changed clothes and headed for the big house. The carriage was back, which meant that Dearest Sallie and Miz Mariah had returned from church. Dinner was being served by Caroline while Rozette fanned the flies. Sam was probably in the kitchen, eating.

Amanda entered the back door of the big house and hid in the pantry. She listened as the ladies of the house talked about the church service. It seemed when they made a point about the sermon, their would forks hit their plates. Then she heard Miz Temperance's voice. She tiptoed closer to the dining room.

"I'm getting Sam to take me over to Shoal Creek."

"Mother," Dearest Sallie asked. "You're not going alone."

"I thought I would take Amanda with me."

"That's fine." She replied. "But I'll be needing Sam in the morning."

"Let Sam take a horse with him and he can ride back this evening." Mariah injected.

"Okay, Mother," Dearest Sallie said.

"I will." Miz Temperance replied. "Caroline, please get Sam from the kitchen and tell him to meet me out front at the carriage."

"Yes ma'am."

When Caroline headed for the back door and Miz Temperance excused herself from the table, Amanda scooted out of the pantry and went out the back door. She ran halfway to the slave quarters, and then she started walking back. As she was walking back, Caroline saw her.

"Amanda" she called, "Miz Temperance 'quire yer presence out front."

"Danks, Caroline."

Amanda went to the front of the house, while, Caroline went to the kitchen for Sam. When she got to the carriage, Miz Temperance was on the porch.

"Yer carriages 'wait you."

Miz Temperance came down the steps and Amanda helped her into the carriage. Just as she did, Sam came around the house. He saw Amanda and Miz Temperance in the carriage.

"Sam," Miz Temperance commanded, "Saddle a horse and tie it to the back of carriage. Amanda and I will spend the night at Shoal Creek. You can come on home with the horse."

"Yes ma'am."

Sam went to the barn and saddled one of horses. On his return, he hitched it to the back of the carriage and then hopped into the driver's seat. They were off to Shoal Creek.

Chapter 48

When they arrived at Shoal Creek, they went to Miz Temperance's house. Sam made sure they were settled before he left to get back to Stekoa Field. He unhitched the horses from the carriage and put them in the barn. The horses were put in a stall in the barn and Amanda rubbed them down and fed them. She and Miz Temperance looked around the house to see what had to be done. Together, they worked to clean up the place. Since they got to Shoal Creek late, Temperance persuaded Amanda they would visit Mary the next day. They cleaned out the pantry and rearranged it. Amanda put clean linen on the bed. The fireplace had to be lit, so Amanda went outside to find some kindling to start the fire. The long fireplace matches were hanging near the fireplace. Bring dry leaves from outside, she lit the fire. Before dark, she carried in enough wood for the night. In no time, it was nice and cozy.

While Miz Temperance sat by the fireplace and read the Bible, Amanda cooked supper. She found some corn meal and sour milk and made sour dough corn bread. In the cellar, there were some dried pole beans and some ham.

Just as she finished preparing their evening meal, a knock came at the door. Amanda went to the door and opened it. To her surprise, Mary was standing there.

"Mary!" Amanda said, "C'mon in. How did you know I was here?"

"Sam told me. I was at Stekoa Field today."

Mary walked in and looked around the place. "This is nice. Is this your place?"

"No, it belongs to Miz Temperance."

Amanda introduced Mary to Miz Temperance.

"So you are Mary Tushka." Temperance said. "Do you live in these parts?"

"Yes," Mary replied. "I's a Lufty Indian. Your son is our chief."

"Would you like to have supper with us?"

Mary looked over at Amanda. Amanda shook her head in an affirmative way.

"Does my friend, Amanda get to sit at the table with us?"

"Of course," Temperance assured her.

As Amanda set the table for three, she realized it had been a long time since she had sat down and eaten with Miz Temperance.

In the backwoods of Western North Carolina an Indian, a white person and black slave sat down together and supped.

Darkness had fallen by the time Amanda and Mary stopped talking. Hence Miz Temperance insisted that Mary spend the night at her little cabin. The two slept in the loft, while Temperance slept in the bedroom. When morning came, Mary still didn't go home. Amanda wondered if everything was all right. She tried to remember what she said about her marriage. If Mary was in trouble with her people, Amanda didn't want them to think Miz Temperance had anything to do with it.

By mid-morning, some Luftys came by. It looked like a hunting party. Mary went out and talked to them. Looking out the window, Amanda tried to get a feel of the situation. The stoic look on their faces told her nothing. She trusted Mary. If they were going to harm them, they would have already done so. Finally they left and Mary came back into the cabin.

"Wat's the trouble?"

"A bear attacked my people last night."

"Is it comin' dis way?"

"No, but they go to tell Dearest Sallie."

Miz Temperance was sitting by the fire. "Did you say that they are going by Stekoa Field?"

"Yes."

"Can you catch them and tell Dearest Sallie that I'm staying here for a while?"

Without answering her, Mary ran out the door and shouted to them. Amanda went outside to see if they were still in sight. One of the Luftys sprinted to Mary, who gave him the message to relay to Stekoa Field.

At noon Miz Temperance sent Mary and Amanda to the store. As they walked down the dusty road, Amanda was apprehensive about going. When they approached the store, she glanced over at the blacksmith shop as the sound of a smithy striking an anvil reached her ears. She knew it wasn't Bill. He was probably at Stekoa Field licking his wounds.

The two young ladies were acting like little girls and Amanda realized that was what most white people thought of them. At this moment Amanda didn't care. She and Mary were friends. Here was someone who was not connected to her everyday life. She was someone who could give her a new perspective on the outside world. Amanda felt she needed to broaden her views. Being a slave only narrowed her version. And yet Amanda yearned to read, so she could discern things for herself.

"Hey, Mary." Amanda asked, "Can youse read?"

"Not 'Nglish," Mary declared.

"Wat cans youse read?"

"De Cherokee language."

"Youse means that the Cherokee language be writ'n down."

"Yeah."

"Is dere any books written in dat language?"

"Shore. De Bible is.

"Mary Tuskha, youse is a lyin'."

"It be the truth." Mary continued proudly. "We's even have a newspaper."

"Teach me to read it."

"I's don't know. It's kinda sacred to our people."

Amanda sighed. "Ok."

By this time they were at Thomas's store. They went inside and Amanda handed the list of items to Mr. Terrell.

He took the paper and looked at it. "Is Miz Temperance planning to stay awhile?"

"Yes sum." Amanda answered.

Mr. Terrell retrieved the items from the store's shelves and put them in the basket Amanda set on the counter. He turned and reached for the ledger and quickly turned back to Amanda.

"Are you Power's nigger?"

"He be dead."

"I'm sorry to hear that. I thought he simply ran off."

"He be dead."

"Sorry to hear that."

"Yes sum."

He turned back around and got the ledger. For a few minutes he wrote in the ledger, and then he turned back to them. "Tell, Miz Temperance I charged her for these items."

"Yes sum."

Amanda picked up the basket and left the store with Mary trailing behind her. She was walking so fast that Mary had to run to catch her.

"Wait up," Mary said. "What 's the troubl'?"

"Nothin'."

"Somethin's wrong."

"How's can he make Miz Temperance pay for this? De store belongs to her son."

"Dat de white man's way."

"It ain't rat?"

The remaining distance to the house, the young ladies were silent. Each had their own thoughts. Amanda plodding down the road likes an old plow horse, while Mary sauntered just a step behind. When they got to Miz Temperance's house, they put the items in root cellar, which was inside the house hidden under a Cherokee rug in the living area.

"Did you get everything?"

"I suppose," Amanda handed her to list. "Here be yer list. I's can't read."

Miz Temperance took the list and called off the items on the paper. As she did. Amanda gave her an affirmative answer. While, she confirming the list, she gave Mary a sinister look. Everything had been purchased.

After supper, Mary and Amanda sat on the steps of Miz Temperance house. There was chill in the air as the Autumn weather cooled the evening. Mary had a stick tracing Cherokee syllabus in the dirt. Amanda watched her as she drew letters Amanda had never seen before.

"Wat's that?"

"Cherokee alphabet."

"Ne'er seen any letters likk dat."

"Dey differ'nt. It's the Cherokee syllabus. Sequoyah created it."

"Who?"

"He was Cherokee, who made up symbols from the Cherokee language so we can write things down."

"Can youse teach me?" Amanda cried. "Hey them look kind of like the music scales Miz Sallie was a teaching me."

"They are alphabets. One be Cherokee an' de other is the white folks."

"Can youse teach me?" Amanda repeated.

"I's can try."

"I wanna know what the Lord say 'bout color'd folks."

"Wat you talkin' 'bout?"

"All white folks say dat the Lord punished us for somethin' that happen'd long time ago."

"Wat was dat punishment?"

"To serve de white folks."

"I's don't know."

Mary continued making symbols in the sand as Amanda watched. And then she ran off the porch and found herself a fallen tree branch and broke off one of its limb. Standing in front of Mary, she tried to copy the symbols. And yet, as she copied them, she didn't know their meaning. For this evening Amanda was satisfied she was able to make the symbols. Maybe tomorrow, Mary would tell her what each symbol meant.

For the rest of August, when the evening hours came, after supper, Mary and Amanda sat outside on the steps. With their sticks, they drew symbols in the dirt. Mary would tell Amanda what each symbol meant. And yet, somehow Amanda forgot them the next day. The trouble was it needed to be written down and Amanda had no paper on which to do that.

"I jest can't 'member dose crazy lookin' symbols."

"I's hard to do."

Chapter 49

Besides learning the Cherokee Syllabus, during that month Amanda was able to go with Mary to the Green Corn Ceremony. With September coming in on the horizon, Mary told Amanda about another ceremony before the New Moon Ceremony. Held in late September, it was the Ripe Corn Ceremony celebrating the maturing of the corn crop. It was held outdoors under the stars. The celebration lasted for four days and on the last day there was a feast. Amanda watched as the men carried a green bough in their right hand and danced. The women were not allowed to be in the square where the men danced.

Miz Temperance was content to sit by the fire and knit. Christmas wasn't too far away, therefore she had started making gifts. Each time the girls went out they were escorted by Mary's male relatives. Hence Temperance was not too worried. She had been in this neck of the woods for a long time and Lufty Cherokees had never bothered her. Besides, William Holland Thomas was their chief.

On their return from the Ripe Corn Ceremony, Miz Temperance was surprised when Amanda told her there were two more ceremonies. All the ceremonies were sacred to the Luftys as they thanked the Great Spirit in the sky for allowing the corn to grow and mature. But this last two were very important to Amanda and Mary.

Miz Temperance told them Sam had come and was returning in the morning to take them home. Mary and Amanda were hurt. It seemed each time they were close to mending their friendship, something happened. This time they were going to take matters in their own hands. Miz Temperance could go home, but Amanda was staying.

During the night while Miz Temperance was sleeping, Amanda and Mary made plans. When the dawn crept upon them, with Mary leading the way, they walked to Mary's village, which was the Birdtown people.

Amanda never thought of punishment, it was a time of bonding with Mary in eternal friendship.

Chapter 50

The next day, Sam rode into Birdtown community. Amanda had known he would find her. However, she was determined she wasn't going back with him. And if he couldn't convince Dearest Sallie she wasn't a runaway, everything would work out fine. So Amanda and Sam sat down on the ground in front of Mary's family long house to discuss the situation.

"Miz Sallie is upset."

"Sam," she pleads. "I need dis time with Mary."

"I know."

"She is my sister, just as Yonaguska was your brother, not your slave master."

"I knew that had to be the reason, but Miz Sallie ain't gonna accept that as an excuse fer youse running away,"

"I ain't runnin' away."

"Mandy, ifen Mr. Bumgarner hears 'bout dis, you's dead meat."

"Tell'em I's sick an' can't travel rat now."

"Alright. I'll come back when I's git word dat youse ready to come home."

Sam mounted his horse and rode away. Amanda watched him go with the hope in her heart that they believed Sam's story.

When the new moon appeared in October, the Luftys celebrated their new year. This was the time of year the Great Spirit in the sky created the world. Each family brought some crops from their field to share. Mary's family brought pumpkins and corn to the ceremony. The Ceremonial dancers led the people to the water to be dipped in for purification seven times. As Amanda was dipped into the water seven times, she felt she was going to be sick. After being dried off, the holy man in the village predicted Amanda's health for the coming year by using the Ulvsuti Crystal,

"In my crystal of the future, I see you jumping a broom with good health and happiness."

"With who?"

"The crystal does not know, only you."

"Bill," she whispered. She knew he chased all the female slaves. If he marries her, those days would be over.

The day after the Great New Moon Ceremony, Amanda had a sore throat and a nasty cold. The shaman of the village gave her some medicine to get rid of her sore throat. If Sam came, she would truly be sick, but Sam didn't arrive. At Amanda request, Mary sent a party out to see if there was news about her. When they returned, there was no news. That made Amanda feel a little better. Perhaps Sam had convinced them she was sick.

Ten days later, the Reconciliation Ceremony got underway. It dealt with relationships between two people. Although Amanda and Mary had rekindled their childhood relationship, this ceremony would bond it for life. It symbolized for them the uniting with the Creator and the purification of body and mind. At the end of the ceremony the sacred fire was rekindled. Amanda watched as the holy man lit the fire that rekindled the sacred fire. Chills ran up and down her spine for she knew she and Mary would have universal love for each for life.

The next day, Amanda journeyed back to slavery. As she and Mary departed from each other in the flesh, Mary handed her pouch.

"Take this," she said. "You may need it when youse get there."

Without questioning her, Amanda took the pouch and

slung it over her right shoulder. And then, they embraced.

Mary said, "This is not goodbye, but I'll see you soon,"

Amanda's salutation was the same. She said, "Next time, I'll see youse af'er while."

Escorted to Stekoa Fields, she had no fear about the future. She knew Mary was her loyal friend forever. Arriving at Stekoa, she told the Lufty escorts to go home. They bade Amanda, not a farewell, but told her they would see her.

Walking proudly up the driveway, she was felt like a new person. She looked at the big house and knew those within would try to keep her body captured, but her soul was free. With determination, she walked to the cabin that she had shared with her mother, Power and Bill. She knew Bill would be asleep with some nigger woman by his side. He was hers, not that other nigger woman. The holy man had said it and she believed it as she touched the pouch at her right side.

However, when she opened the door, she found Bill alone. The old worn blanket was tightly wrapped around him. From her perspective, she knew he was chilling. Rushing into the room, she took the pouch from her shoulder and tossed it on the table. And then went over to him, and she pressed her warm body against his chill one. Preparation beaded off his forehead. Although he was chilling, his body was burning up. He was dying and there was no one to help him.

She closed her mind to that thought and decided she would help him. With an empty bucket, she went outside, got some cold water from the rain barrel and brought it back inside. She tore a strip of cloth from her secondhand petit coat and dipped in the cold water. Wringing some of the water out of it, she put the cold wet rag on his forehead.

Chapter 51

Looking around the room, she found there was nothing for him to eat. The fire in the hearth was just tiny embers. Mandy realized if she had not returned, all would be lost. Racing outside, she got a hand full of fire wood. On reentering the cabin, she put part of the wood on the dying embers. Sparks flew and the fire came alive as smoke raced up the chimney. She took the limp warm rag off of his forehead and dipped it in the cold rain water, wrung it out and applied it to his forehead. He was still burning up as the cold wet rag became lukewarm. She looked at the bucket of water and knew what she had to do. However, that would not be enough water. The river, the mighty Tuckaseegee would work. If the Oconaluftee could purify her, then the Tuckaseegee could do it for Bill. And yet, how was she going to get him to the river. He was just too heavy for her to carry.

The door opened and Sam walked in. They looked at each. And then they both looked at the bed where Bill lay.

"I see youse 'turned." Sam smiled. " Dearest Sallie thought you came down with something because of Bill's illness."

"Wat be 'rung with him."

"Don't know."

"Y'all haven't call fer a doctor."

"Doc Welch was called, but he didn't know."

"Sam, I can't let him die. I was purified in the waters of the Oconaluftee. I figured on purifying Bill in the Tuckaseegee and ev'ythin'll be alright."

"Mandy, dat be crazy."

"No."

"Nigger, wake up. De boy's no good."

"I love'm,"

Spying the pouch on the table, Sam picked it up.

"Put dat down," She yelled.

"It looks likk somethin' from the holy man."

"It be from de holy man."

Sam took the pouch and handed it to Amanda, who took it from him. "Youse needs to take and open it. Wat's e'er in it, give it to Bill."

Reluctantly, Mandy took the pouch and opened it. In it she found small jar with something in it. She showed it to Sam and he seemed to recognize it as a medication for high fever that the shaman used for him in the past.

"Wat is it?" Amanda asked.

'It'be used to rid a fever."

Sam took the bottle and found any empty cup. He poured a small portion of the mixture into the cup and then filled the cup half-way full of water. After stirring it up, he hand the cup to Amanda and then went to the bedside. Sitting down, he lifted Bill's head and asked for the cup with an outstretched hand. Amanda gave it to him and watched as he gently poured it down Bill's throat. Nervously, she watched as it seemed that Bill was gagging and coughing as the medication went down.

"Youse killin' him."

"He be fine."

Bill's body jerked as the medicine entered his insides. Coughing continued to come from deep within. And then without warning, Bill raised his head, turned his face to the floor and vomited. Sam was lucky he was able to move quickly. Bill tried to sit up, but he couldn't. He just laid his head back down on lumpy pillow and sighed heavily. Amanda came to his side and just looked down at him. She wanted to touch him, but was afraid that Sam had killed him.

"Bill," she called softly. "Bill, I's luvs youse."

His eyes flickered open and stared at Amanda. She sat on the side of the bed and held his head to her breast. The fever was gone. She couldn't believe it. Questioningly, she looked to Sam for an answer, but he didn't have one.

"The holy man knew."

" Knew, wat?"

"Someone had put spell on him."

"A spell?"

Immediately, Amanda thought of Rozette. She wanted to claw her eyes out. She had to confront her, but not in the big house. The two needed to meet alone. The first thing she had to do was spread the news Bill was well.

"Sam, please don't tell'em dat I's home. Jest tell'em dat Bill is on the mend."

Sam left. Amanda waited and watched.

Within the hour, Rozette entered the cabin and went over to the sleeping form of Bill. Amanda had hidden behind the door as she came in.

"Well, well, well," Amanda said softly. "I knewd it was youse."

Quickie, she turned and faced Amanda. "I 's sees youse back,"

"I' is."

"Don't know wat happen'd to Bill. He jest seem'd to git sicker an' sicker while youse were away."

"With yer help."

Amanda stepped over to her and looked her dead in the eye. As she looked at Rozette, Amanda could see the fear in her eyes. Just a few inches away from each other Amanda spoke.

"You ever try dat 'gain," she spat. "I'll put a spell on youse won't ever recover from."

"Honest," Rozette backing away. "It weren't me,"

"Get out and don't tell anyone dat I's here."

"I won't."

Rozette left.

Amanda went to Bill and lay beside his sleeping form.

Chapter 52

After supper when everyone was settling in for the night, Amanda walked over to the big house. She entered the back door and went into the pantry. As she walked in Caroline was putting something away,

"Caroline."

"Amanda!" She replied, "Where in de hell have youse been?"

"In Birdtown."

"I heard dat youse were sick."

"I was." Amanda lied. "I didn't want Dearest Sallie to catch it. Seeing how she be with chile."

"Did dey know?"

"I 'spect. " She replied. "I tol' Sam to tell'em. Ifen dey don't know, I's here to tell them now."

"I's tell'em youse here."

Caroline left. When she returned she told Amanda that Dearest Sallie would see her in the parlor. Amanda was a little nervous. She had listened when Caroline went to report her return, but Amanda heard no loud or anger voices. Stepping into the parlor, she found Miz Temperance with knitting materials in her lap seated in her rocker, while Dearest Sallie was planted at the piano and Mariah was flipping through a catalogue. All eyes focused on Mandy.

"You need to apologize to Miz Temperance." Sallie demanded.

"I's sorry. Amanda pleaded, "I jest didn't want ya'll to git sick,'specially youse, Dearest Sallie."

"Where did you stay?"

"In Birdtown with my friend Mary Tuskha."

"I'm glad you're home," Miz Sallie said, "I just didn't want to explain this to the Senator." Miz Sallie laughed, "You best go along and see what you can do for Bill. He is in bad shape."

"Yes ma'am."

"Don't do that again."

Amanda curtsied and answered "Yes ma'am,"

Leaving the way she came, Amanda ran out of the house, and on the way back to her cabin. When she got there Bill was awake.

"I's thought I's was dreamin'. It be really you."

"Yeah." She stands akimbo. "Now, wat happen'd to youse. Youse in all these niggers' drawers an' caught somethin'."

"Amanda," he pleaded and begged. "I didn't. Honest."

"Someone poison'd youse or put spell on youse."

Bill could not believe anyone could harm him. He stood there in disbelief. Amanda didn't try to convince him. Perhaps, he needed to go back to Sulphur Springs, but she knew Rozette would be going back. There was no prove, but Amanda felt she was the one.

Chapter 53

Amanda had returned just before Senator Thomas came home for the Presidential Election...for two days after she arrived, the Senator showed up. Cudge was with him and Sam was glad to see him. The long absences between father and son were difficult. There was excitement around the house as the men folks in the county were preparing to vote. Amanda hoped Lincoln would become president and all slaves would be free; however, her hopes were dashed when she overheard a conversation between High Sheriff Duge and Senator Thomas. After seeing all the white folks at the Fourth of July celebration at Webster, Amands had been overwhelmed and convinced that black folks, whether free or slaves, couldn't break that hold.

It was the last week in October and Sheriff Davis had come to Stekoa Fields to see Senator Thomas about the coming election. All Southern states were preparing for a fight to keep their lifestyle alive. Davis and Thomas were seated on the porch when Amanda brought both them a tall glass of lemonade. As she served them, she listened to their conversation.

"Well, that Abe Lincoln has made a name for himself," Davis said.

"Yeah," Senator Thomas agreed and then said, "But the Democratic Party will come out on top. Breckinridge will take the South and some of the Border States."

"Lincoln could get some Southern votes. Ain't he from Kentucky?"

"Yeah," Senator Thomas laughed. "Some around here say he's from right here in the area."

"I heard that rumor. Some say that he was born right here on Mingus Creek."

"Yeah, I remember Mr. Abraham Enloe had a servant girl named Nancy Hanks. She left under suspicious circumstances. It was rumored that Enloe got Tom Lincoln to marry Nancy and take her to Kentucky."

"Married and still sowing some wild oats."

Both men laughed.

"Now that bastard wants to be President of the United States." Davis slapped his left hip and continued to laugh.

"Don't worry;   'cause we ain't gonna put his name on the ballot."

"And nobody can vote for him."

Amanda's heart sank. And yet, if she had to live as a slave, she wanted Bill to share her life. Going back in the house, she put the pitcher on the sideboard and left the house through the back door. She knew Mr. Love was going to come and get Bill to defend his home. If Mariah stayed until Dearest Sallie had her second child, then Rozette would be here. Amanda would be happy as long as Rozette wasn't near Bill.

Bill was up and about after that strange sickness. It seemed that no one really knew what happened to him. Amanda went looking for Bill, hoping to find him in the coach house, but he wasn't there. Being late in the day, he was probably at their quarters. She went there, but the house was empty. Amanda lay across the bed and cried. Perhaps Sam was right, he was just no good.

The next day, the day of the Presidential Election, Mr. Love arrived at Stekoa Fields. He was going to take his family and slaves home and that included Bill. In a few days, the results of the election would be known for now they could telegraph all over the country. Nervously, the South waited. Thomas waited for he would have to go back to the General Assembly, once more leaving his pregnant wife.

Sitting in the parlor, Mr. Love and Senator Thomas talked. Dearest Sallie was upstairs resting and Mariah was with her. Miz Temperance decided she needed to go upstairs also. This left the men folk to discuss the election.

"It's a fact Lincoln didn't get any votes in the Southern states." Thomas said as Amanda served them bourbon.

"That should help us."

"Not much since we had three candidates to choose from.

"Yes," Mr. Love shook his head. "We stabbed our ownselves in the back."

With those words from Thomas and Love, Amanda prayed that indeed Lincoln would be president. Nobody would stop him. Freedom, she said to herself as she glided out of the room. She left by the back door and found Sam at the coach house.

"Sam," Amanda said excitedly. "Lincoln done won."

"How do youse know?"

"Mr. Love and Maser is talkin' 'bout it."

"Jest talk." Sam assured her. "Dey ain't gonna let Lincoln be president."

"Yes dey will."

"South gonna fight to keep us slaves."

"Not ifen the president says no more slaves."

"I's don't know."

Sam pondered the matter. She said that Lincoln was going to be president and all the slaves would be free. As she walked toward the slave quarters, she had to find Bill. She needed to see him before Mr. Love took him back to Waynesville. On entering her quarters, she found Bill sitting by the fire. She went to him and put her hands on his shoulders. He looked up at her and smiled.

"Wat's on yer mind?" he asked.

"You."

"Me?"

"You know dat Mr. Love is here to pick youse up and take youse back to White Sulphur Springs."

"We's have dis moment together." He stood up and carried her to the bed.

It seemed that Lincoln did win the election, but the blacks were still in slavery. Amanda couldn't understand that. He was the boss so therefore they should obey his wishes. At least that was the way it was on Stekoa Fields. Senator Thomas hurried back to Raleigh. Some of the Southern States wanted to leave the Union and Amanda wondered where they would go. It was just pieces of conversations she didn't understand. And then, she heard other things. It seemed that Mr. Love was right, there was going to be a war. She wondered whether it would come to her neck of woods. Who would protect them? Of course the Luftys would keep them safe.

The Christmas season was fast approaching and Mariah wanted to decorate the house. Dearest Sallie wanted a Christmas tree for Little Will and the Yule log for the fireplace. All these tasks were to be performed by the slaves. Sam had the job of going after the Christmas tree and Alfred who always spend the holidays with Flossie and the children will get the Yule log. The slave children made decorations by stringing popcorn for the trimming on the tree. Mariah had Sam take her to Shoal Creek to get some store bought ornaments. Suckey, of course, would cook Christmas dinner. It was a time of happiness and celebration of Christ, but Amanda was alone. Bill was in Waynesville and there had been no mentioned that Mr. Love 'wasn't coming over for the holiday. Even, Master Thomas might not be home for Christmas.

However, life on Stekoa Field would go on as if nothing happened. Amanda got up by the sound of the bell and rushed to the big house. She came in back door and headed up stairs to Miz Temperance's room. Before she got there, she heard the patter of little feet in the nursery. She didn't stop because she knew Flossie was there to take care of Little Will.

When she got to Miz Temperance's room, the elder was still asleep. Amanda did the usually things. She emptied the bed chamber and got fresh water for pitcher. For Amanda the outside world didn't exist. After she had emptied and cleaned the bedchamber, she returned it to Temperance' room. By the time, Amanda returned Miz Temperance was up and waiting for water to wash up.

Leaving Miz Temperance's room, Amanda went to the master bed and did the same for Dearest Sallie. While the ladies were eating breakfast, Amanda continued to clean the upstairs. Everything was routine.

When she finished upstairs, she came downstairs to cleanup. Her first stop was the parlor. She always did that so they could come into the parlor and relax after breakfast. And then she would gather all the dishware and silverware. She would wash them and put them up. By that time, Dearest Sallie, Mariah and Miz Temperance would be in the parlor.

On this first day of December, the ladies gathered in the parlor and talked about the Christmas holiday. It was apparent that Sallie was lonely for Willie, as was Miz Temperance and Mariah missed being home for the holidays.

"Do you think you should travel?" Miz Temperance asked Sallie.

"I'm not due until after Christmas." Sallie said cheerful. I'm fine." She looked over at Mariah. "I know that Mariah would like to get home for Christmas."

"That, I would."

"That's final." Miz Sallie said. "I'll send Sam over to tell father that we're spending the Christmas with him."

Amanda was just around the corner, pretending that she was dusting. She was ecstatic. She knew she would be Miz Temperance's personal servant. It was going to be the greatest Christmas for her.

"Mandy," Miz Sallie called.

Quickly she came into the room. "Yes ma'am."

"Go fetch Sam."

"Yes ma'am."

Amanda did a quick curtsey, and then skipped out of the room. When she got outside, she went to the coach house. She saw him as he leaned against the wall. It seemed as if he was thinking about something.

"Sam," Amanda called, "Dearest Sallie requests yer presence in the parlor."

"Wat does she want?

"Youse seem sad, Sam," Amanda remarked. "I's never seem youse so sad,"

"It's almost Christmas an' Cudge ain't gonna be here."

"I 's so sorry."

Chapter 54

Sam and Amanda walked back to the house. She knew what Miz Sallie wanted, but she didn't want to tell him. Raleigh was still too far away for him to go see his son for Christmas. Amanda kissed Sam on the cheek as they parted.

"I'm sorry about Cudge."

"Thanks, Mandy."

She watched him go into the house, and then she turned and went back toward the slave quarters. When she got there she continued and walked across the unplowed field. Going up the hill, she disappeared into the woods. Looking among the bushes and weeds, she found her mother's gravesite. As she approached it, tears rimmed her eyes. She missed her mother, the only family she knew. Miz Temperance was her grandmother, but it was never spoken in public. Her father was a North Carolina Senator, who was also her Master. She stood there. The noises of Mother Nature were all around. However, the only thing she heard was her mother's voice that whispered in the wind and said "I love you."

Amanda stood there for a long time. She knelt and prayed. Afterward she turned and walked back to Stekoa Field. When she passed the barn, she saw Sam saddling up a horse. She knew he was going over Soco to White Sulphur Springs to inform the Loves that Miz Sallie, Miz Mariah, and Miz Temperance were spending Christmas with them. As she walked into the big house, she saw Caroline. She seemed happy, too.

"We's gonna spend Christmas at White Sulphur Springs.

"Who's we?"

"I believe dat Miz Temperance be goin', too."

"Are youse shore?"

"I tink so."

"I's wonder ifen I's a goin'."

"Miz Temperance been a callin' youse."

"I's guess dat I's in troubl'."

"I told dat youse be rat back."

"I's hope it work'd." Amanda breathed a breath of relief. "Danks."

Amanda climbed the stairs to Miz Temperance' room. When she got there, she found Miz Temperance rumbling through her clothes. She looked up when Amanda came into the room.

"Lord, child, I have nothing to wear," Miz Temperance remarked. "We are going to spend Christmas at Dearest Sallie's childhood home in Sulphur Springs."

"I's know youse are."

"Child, you're going with me." She laughed. "I'm the mother of Senator William Holland Thomas. I must have a personal servant."

"And I's it?"

"Of course. I taught you, didn't I?"

"Yes sum."

When Sam returned to Stekoa Fields to inform Dearest Sallie and Miz Mariah that White Springs Sulphur was waiting for their arrival, everyone began but to pack. Not only did Sam bring them the news, Bill was with him. When Amanda saw Bill, she thought he was going to stay at Stekoa Fields. It just seemed that the Loves and the Thomas's were purposely keeping them apart. Angrily, she ran from the big house and went to her mother's grave. Falling down on her knees, she cried.

"It ain't gonna be, Mama. Dey done did 'gain. Dey gonna separate Bill an' me. Wat is I to do?"

"Run away."

Quickly she turned around and there stood Dave."

Dave smiled, "Run away with me. Ain't nothin here fer us niggers, but killin' ourselv' a workin' fer'em."

"Dave," Amanda replied. "Youse have family rat here. All of them are here. I's have no one. Ifen youse leave, dey mite not ne'er find youse. Don't youse know dat Mr. Lincoln is president and he's gonna free us?"

"How's do youse know?"

"I's heard it from the big house."

"Youse shore?"

"I's shore. I's swear on my mama's grave."

Dave hugged her. "Youse de frien' I e'er had.' He took her hand. "C'mon, let's go back. Someone is a waitin' fer youse."

Hand in hand, Dave and Amanda walked back to the slave quarters. He led her to her cabin. He kissed her on the cheek and walked away. Amanda stood there for a few seconds, and then she went inside. Bill was waiting for her. They rushed into each other's arms.

"Why are you here?" she asked as she moved away from him.

"To take ya'll to White Sulphur Springs."

"Wat?"

"Maser Love say dat Sam shouldn't have to keep a drivin' back and fore. He says dat dat is just too many trips. So's he tells me to to git de big carriage an' bring ya'll o'er."

"Youse mean dat I be goin'." She rushed back into his arms and kissed him.

"We can't stay here." He smiled down at her. "Miz Temperance be a lookin' fer youse."

Without saying another word, Amanda run out of the house and rushed to the big house. She buzzed through the back door and went straight to Miz Temperance room. On her bed were a pile of clothes and Miz Temperance couldn't be found. Just as Amanda started out the door to search for her, she heard voices in the hall.

"Mother," Miz Sallie was consoling Miz Temperance. "Your clothes will do fine."

"But White Sulphur Springs is such an elegant place."

"Wear the one you wore to our wedding."

"Your friends have already seen it,"

"We can change it a little bit and no one will notice. Caroline can do it for you."

"Oh all right," Miz Temperance sighed.

Amanda heard Miz Sallie walk away. Bustling into the room, Miz Temperance saw Amanda and began giving orders. There was an emergence about Miz Temperance, as she made preparations to go to Sulphur Springs for Christmas. Amanda did as the old lady asked her. In less than any hour, Miz Temperance was packed.

"Can's I's go for the evenin'?" Amanda asked.

"Yes," Miz Temperance assured her. "But be here tomorrow morning. Where were you anyway?"

"I was. . ." Amanda hesitated.

"I know." Miz Temperance waved her hand toward the door. "Go ahead."

"I's be here 'fore de bell rings."

Amanda left Miz Temperance's room and headed downstairs. Before, she got to the landing, Miz Sallie called her.

"Yes sum, Dearest Sallie."

"Come to the master bedroom."

"Yes sum" Amanda replied. "I's on my way."

Without any more talk, Amanda made her way to the Master bedroom. Dearest Sallie was seated on the bench that set in front of the vanity. Her personal servant, Caroline was nowhere to be found. Apparently, she had sent Caroline to the nursery to pack Little Will's clothes. Amanda had heard him crying earlier. Flossie was attending to Little Will needs while Caroline was packing his things.

"Yes ma'am."

"I want you to pack my clothes."

"Yes ma'am."

Without asking questions, under Dearest Sallie's instructions, Amanda packed clothes and other personal items for her in the room. She didn't want any conformation with Dearest Sallie. Pregnant women, so Amanda had been told, could be a bit touchy about anything they thought could be going wrong. When Amanda had finished packing Miz Sallie's things, she was dismissed without any complains about Amanda's absence when Miz Temperance attempted to call her earlier.

Amanda knew that Mariah might need help, because, Rozette was needed at Sulphur Springs. Therefore she went to the guest bedroom and knocked on the door.

"Miz Mariah," Amanda called, "Dose youse need any hep with yo' packin'."

"With Rozette not here, I could use you."

"Yes ma'am."

When Amanda entered Mariah had clothes piled on her bed. Immediately, Amanda went to the bed and began to sort things out. Most of Mariah's clothes were summer attire and she wouldn't need them. Hence Amanda placed them back in the wardrobe before she began packing for Mariah's trip home.

After Mariah had selected the items she needed, she left Amanda to pack them. She went downstairs and joined her sister and Miz Temperance in the parlor. As she packed, Amanda heard Dearest Sallie playing "Silent Night." Looking out the window, Amanda realized that the night had caught up with the day. It was apparent that supper had already been served when she returned to the big house and no one said anything to her about it. There had to be some sort of punishment.

After finishing packing Mariah's things, she went downstairs. Before leaving, she stopped at the parlor. As she looked around the room, she saw the entire family was enjoying the holiday season. Little Will was seated on the floor, beating on a drum while his mother played the piano. Of course, Miz Temperance was busy with some needle-work, while Mariah was reading a book. Amanda waited at the door until Dearest Sallie finished playing her song, Foster Stephen's "Willie, We Have Missed You."

"Excuse me," Amanda addressed them all. "It dere anythin' dat I's can do?"

Dearest Sallie turned from the piano and faced her. "No, go your quarters and get some rest."

"Yes ma'am."

"Good night," Miz Temperance said.

"G'night."

Amanda turned and was gone from their presence. Flossie and Caroline were in the pantry area.

"It's 'bout time youse finish'd." Flossie said.

"I 's had to pack all their things."

"Little Will was a handful." Flossie confirmed Amanda's instinct about the situation.

"An' I had to pack Little Will's things." Caroline shook her head. "G'night, girls."

"G'night," Amanda and Flossie said, and went out the door into the night.

The two walked in silence, as the cold night air made them hug themselves. Both were thinking about their man. Alfred would be coming from Shoal Creek to spend Christmas with his family. Amanda was going to White Sulphur Springs with Bill and the big house household to spend the holidays. Tonight, Bill awaited Amanda return to the slave quarters.

The two parted company. Amanda hurried to her cabin. When she opened the door, Bill was asleep. She looked down at him and wanted to awaken him. However, she thought better of it. She would get underdressed and slip into the bed beside him. She secured the lock on the door and banked the fire.

Before they left for White Sulphur Springs, Miz Sallie

asked Andrew to stay at Stekoa Fields until they returned. With Andrew there, Amanda was glad she didn't have to remain. Happiness, she hoped would be at White Sulphur Springs. In the carriage which Mr. Love sent were two seats, and luggage department behind the back seat was big enough for them. Amanda and Caroline were seated in the front, which faced the back. Miz Temperance, Miz Mariah and Miz Sallie were seated in the rear seat, which faced the front. Miz Mariah had Little Will on her lap. Bill was the driver.

They went over Soco Gap, which was rough going. The trails were narrow and muddy. At the very top, they run into snow. Going down the other side of Soco wasn't so bad. Finally they reached the bottom and the going was a much easier.

No one said much of anything and Little Will slept through it all. Amanda was a little frightened, but she prayed everything was going to be all right. She had never been this far away from home in the little valley of Stekoa Fields. White Sulphur Springs was east of Waynesville and she hoped they would get there soon. She was tired and weary. She looked over at Miz Temperance and she saw she was not comfortable either. It was apparent Miz Sallie and Miz Mariah were familiar with the territory.

Finally they arrived at the estate of White Sulphur Springs, a two-story white house with columns. It was twice as big as the modest big house on Stekoa Fields. Bill parked the carriage in the front and jumped down from the driver's seat. He opened the carriage door and helped out Miz Sallie and Miz Mariah.

As they walked toward the door, he turned back and assisted Miz Temperance out. The sleeping Little Will was cuddled in Caroline's lap. Amanda just relaxed by falling back in the seat. Bill reached into the carriage and took Little Will from Caroline. Caroline helped herself out of the vehicle and Bill handed the sleeping two-year-old back to Caroline. As she turned to step on the veranda, the butler had already opened the door for Miz Sallie and Miz Mariah. They walked inside and disappeared, as Caroline followed them to the door. She waited while Miz Temperance slowly entered the house.

Amanda remained in the carriage. She really didn't know where to go. Bill bowed to Amanda and smiled at her.

"Madam, we're here." He reached his hand to her.

Hesitantly, she took his hand and stepped out of the carriage. Looking up at the house, she was speechless. It was a luxurious Greek style plantation house. Across the front were six set of large windows with black shutters encasing all of them. The six white columns were magnificent. Amanda stood transfixed. The steps leading up to the porch were like steps leading up to a palace. This was a fairy tale. It couldn't be the home of the Loves. As she looked at the house, she wondered how Miz Sallie could leave all of this for the little big house at Stekoa Fields. This was gorgeous and completely unbelievable.

Bill came over to her. "Amanda, we hav' to get the luggage out of the carriage."

"Yes, of course," she said. "Of course."

Together, they took the luggage out and it to the house. The front door opened and the butler took the luggage. As she looked in the house, Amanda saw it was very grand with a large entryway. Looking at the tall high ceiling, she couldn't believe the magnificent chandelier. There was a Christmas tree that appeared to reach the high ceiling. It was decorated with all kinds of shining things. Just as the door was closing, she saw a glimpse of a sweeping staircase that led to the upper floor.

When the door closed, she turned and walked with Bill back to carriage. Bill got in the driver seat and she sat in the carriage in the back seat. He took the carriage to coach house and unhooked the horse from the carriage. Meanwhile, Amanda got out and surveyed her surroundings. From the coach house, she could still see the huge house. This time she had a side view, and like the front, there were four set of windows.

"Bill," she whispered. "Dis house is bigg'r tan de Webster Hotel."

"I's know."

"Dat where youse live?" she asked.

"No." Bill laughed. "I live back dere rat now."

"Wat's you mean?" She asked as she went to the carriage and retrieved her personal belongings which were in her head rag tied in a knot.

"I's ain't really conscript'd to Mr. Love likk my brothers."

Bill put up the harnesses and was leading the horses to the barn. He took her hand and the two walked together.

"So youse a free man?"

Bill didn't answer. Instead, he said, "Let me put de horse up an' I's will show youse."

"Shore."

After he had rubbed down the horses, put them in their stall and fed them, they left the barn. He led her down a path to the slave quarters. There were several shabby built huts setting in a row. Amanda was surprised at the shape the huts were in and she forgot Bill might be a free man. With a magnificent house like White Sulphur Springs, the slave quarters were in such shabby shape. Some looked like they would fall down.

It was the Christmas season. That meant the slaves were idle. It was a time to relax or fix up their homes. They could go hunting by setting traps for small animals, such as rabbits. Two young men walked toward them from the slave quarters. They were mulattos, but they didn't walk like a slave. There was something proud about them. When the men came abreast of them, both parties stop.

"So dis is your girl?" He smiled at Amanda and put his hand out for a handshake. "I be George and this be my brother James."

She shook his hand and James. "I's Amanda."

"We knows" James chimed in. "William has tol' us 'bout youse."

"Yes." George said. "Mr. Love has recruit'd us to save his home fro' de North."

"Dat wat Bill say." Amanda frowned. "Why?"

Amanda looked at Bill. She didn't understand anything they were saying. Bill's two brothers were once free, now they were conscripted to Mr. Love to defend his home for a war that hadn't occurred.

"I guess, I's take youse to the big house." Bill replied. "I's see y'all later," he said to his brothers.

Hand in hand, Bill and Amanda walked back to the big house. This time they went to the back door and entered into the pantry area. There was a house slave who ushered them into the main part of the house. Either Bill nor Amanda said anything. She was so fascinated by all the splendor and beauty that she was speechless. Amanda and the house slave looked at each other.

"Dis is Amanda of Stekoa Fields, Miz Sallie's home."

"I's Hattie," she replied. "Wat youse need, child?"

"I's Miz Temperance's person'l servant." Amanda answered. "Where's do I sleep?"

"Miz Sallie's mother-in-law?"

"Yes sum."

"I's 'lieve dat Maser Love tol' me dat youse need'd to stay in the house in her room at night." Hattie shook her. "Lord, child, she needs youse."

"Yes sum."

Hattie laughed. "Child, youse don't hafto say Yes ma'am to me. I's a slave jest likk youse be."

"Yes sum."

Amanda couldn't help it. Hattie took her by the arm and guided to Miz Temperance's bedroom. They left Bill in the pantry area. She looked back to see if he was all right, but she told herself this was Bill's home. Hattie and Amanda went up the backstairs which weren't as elegant as the front stairs. When they got upstairs, Amanda was amazed. There was a long hallway with rooms on each side and one of those rooms was assigned to Miz Temperance. As they went past the doors, Amanda counted them so she could re-member which one was Miz Temperance. It was the second door on the right of the stairs down the hall.

"Miz Temperance," Hattie knocked on the door.

There was no answer. It was apparent that Miz Temperance was still downstairs.

Quietly, Hattie eased open the bedroom door and the two slowly walked in. The room was empty. Hattie entered first and went around to make such everything was in place. Miz Temperance's luggage was on a chest at the foot of the bed. The four-post bed was high off the floor, which re-minded Amanda of Webster Hotel.

Before Hattie left, she informed Amanda of all the things in the room. She opened and closed the wardrobe. Amanda stood there and listened to her ramble on and on. Finally she left Amanda alone in the room to put up Miz Temperance's clothes and set out her personal toiletry.

When Amanda finished, she retraced her steps to the pantry area to find Bill was still there.

"C'mon." he said. "I's show youse the kitchen."

They left the big house as the shadows of the day covered the sun. Walking the short distance from big house, they entered the kitchen. Amanda was introduced to the cook, who was a jolly obese slave named Chloe. After the introduction, Chloe fixed a plate for Amanda and a plate for Bill.

As Chloe set the plate in front of Bill, she busied her-self with keeping the kitchen clean. It was as if they were alone, Bill and Amanda. It was the first time they had sat down and eaten a meal together. All of their other encoun-ters were sexual. Now that they were just eating, did they have anything in common? Bill quickly ate his food and was ready to go. Amanda put her hand over his and he sat down.

"Wat's yer rush?" She took his hand and kissed it. "We's has all night."

"Do we, Amanda?"

"Yes," she said, as she ate. "We's has a lifetime."

"As slaves?"

"Bill, youse ain't no slave."

"Look, Mandy, I was free 'til. . ."

"I know. Youse just wanna be likk yer brother. Don't youse see dat's dey slaves. Youse ain't."

"Look, Mandy," He pleaded. "We's 'lways be 'part."

"No."

"Wat do youse have in mind?"

"Wat about you?"

"Youse knows I wanna marry youse."

"Git 'mission from Miz Sallie?"

"And?"

"Maser Thomas ain't here to stop us. 'Member, Dearest Sallie is in charge. She can give me 'mission to marry you." Amanda got up and walked to the door of the kitchen. "It's 'bout Miz Temperance's bed time."

She blew Bill a kiss and left. With a heavy heart she went to Miz Temperance room and turned in for the night.

Christmas came and it was a merry time. All the slaves were given oranges and red and white striped candy canes. The slaves' dinner was chitterling, wild greens and biscuits with wild tea to drink. Everyone at Sulphur Springs celebrated Christmas. Miz Sallie and Miz Mariah hosted a Christmas party. The house was full of laughter and the sound of Christmas carols. Being Miz Temperance personal servant, she stayed near the excitement.

Now when Miz Temperance bedded down for the night, Amanda slipped away into the night and co-habited with Bill. During the day, they rarely saw each other. And yet even with those nightly stolen interludes, Bill and Mandy still had nothing settled about their lives. However, it was not their decision, but Amanda's owner's choice. On this morning after Christmas, Bill approached Miz Sallie about taking Amanda as his wife. She told Bill it was all right with her, but she couldn't remain at White Sulphur Springs. It was rumored among the slave population that South Carolina had left the Union. Did that mean war? Therefore, Miz Sallie advised him to see Senator Thomas about the matter for he had to make that decision.

Chapter 55

During Christmas, Senator Thomas was still in Raleigh. He was trying to decide whether he should vote for secession or remain in the Union. Although, he wasn't a staunch secessionist, he believed in states' rights. While he was politicking, his second son was born two weeks before New Year's and a week before Christmas. When the General Assembly adjourned on February 25th Thomas journeyed home. He had written his wife many letters about the Union splitting apart, but he thought it would be a friendly revolution.

Meanwhile in White Sulphur Springs, Amanda and Bill saw each other every night. Since she lived in the big house as a personal servant of Miz Temperance, their close encounters were brief. Amanda wasn't happy and Miz Temperance realized this as Amanda went about her work. On the morning of February 27th, Miz Temperance watched Amanda as she brought back the chamber pot. She stared at her, but Amanda paid her no mind. Amanda was thinking about Bill and their relationship. After putting the chamber pot under the bed, she started out the door. She stopped when Miz Temperance called her back.

"Yes sum."

"What's the matter, child?"

"Nothin'."

" I know you miss your mother."

"I's fine."

Amanda turned to go. She didn't want to discuss her

problem with Miz Temperance.

"You know that Senator Thomas is coming home."

"So, I's herd."

"I know about you wanting to jump the broom with Mr. Love's slave."

"He ain't no slave."

After Amanda said that, she realized she shouldn't have said it. She stared at the floor, waiting for Miz Temperance to chastise her. The room was silence with an eeriest feeling about it.

Thoughts shot through her mind. Amanda had listened to the conversation at the dinner table about the Union falling apart. She was waiting to see what Master Thomas had to say about the situation. Slavery was part of the Southern way of life. In the North there was no slavery. Now it appeared Bill and his brothers were going to defend the Southerners right to maintain slavery. At this, she wished she had run away with Power. Now she would be a slave the rest of her life. But...at least, she and Bill could jump the broom. With Thomas coming home, she could ask him if she and Bill could do it.

When Miz Temperance didn't respond, she left the room. Escaping, she made her way outside. It was a sunny day, but there was a chill in the air. The snow had disappeared, but it had left a watery trail to the slave quarters. Sloughing through the mud and water, she knew the mud would end up at the front of the big house. She stopped and listened. It was apparent Master Thomas had arrived at White Sulphur Springs. Quickly, she turned around and dashed through the wet muddy field. Forgetting about the mud that slapped against her, she raced to the house. Desperately, she wanted to hear what Master Thomas had to say.

While Sallie and her family welcomed Master Thomas, she raced into the back entry to the big house. All of Amanda's clothes were dirty and wet. Somehow, she had to find some dry clothing. Being at White Sulphur Springs for almost three months, she knew the ends and outs of the house. Quietly and swiftly, she sneaked into the house where the ragbag was located. Stripping off the muddy dirty clothes and wiping the wet mud off of her legs with her spoiled clothes, she tossed them in a corner. Digging into the ragbag, she found a faded gray dress of Mariah's and slipped it over her head. After hiding her spoiled clothes behind the ragbag, she tiptoed and went upstairs by the back way. As she started upstairs, she heard Miz Temperance call her. She stopped. Listening, she heard Miz Temperance call her again. Then she heard Mariah's voice.

"She's probably out there with that nigger, Bill. I'll help you downstairs to welcome Senator Thomas home. With that nigger Amanda out of the way, he can tell all about what's going on in."

Amanda didn't hear Miz Temperance answer, but she heard the two walk down the sweeping staircase. She prayed she would not be caught. After all the household gathered in the sitting room, she tiptoed and hid in the shadows of the sweeping staircase. From that angle, she anticipated she would be able to hear the conversation. Since Master Thomas would be one doing most of the talking, she knew his baritone voice would echo into her hiding place beneath the stairs.

"What's happening in Raleigh?" Mr. Love asked.

"I've called for a convention. I introduced two resolutions, they ignored them." Master Thomas announced.

"What were the resolutions?" Mr. Love responded.

"One was that the federal government had no power to coerce a seceding state and that the governor could call for a convention of the people to decide whether to secede."

"How did they vote?"

"Many of them had already gone home for Christmas."

"Just as you should have done." Mariah chimed in.

"Ladies," Mr. Love chastised. "This is men's talk."

"Your father is right," Thomas agreed."I'll see you later."

Amanda didn't listen to Sallie's answer, but she knew the women folks would be exiting the sitting room. Quickly she hid herself in a closet under the staircase. Listening, she heard them leave the room. When their voices and foot-steps were no longer heard, she slipped out of the closet and moved closer to the sitting room. As she eavesdropped on Mr. Love and Master Thomas' conversation, she only caught the last of Mr. Love's question. Perhaps Master Thomas' answer would provide her with question.

"Well, sir," Master Thomas replied. "As I told Sallie, we are undoubtedly in the midst of a Revolution."

Amanda pondered about that, but she didn't under-stand it. Perhaps if he would add something to it, she might understand. Desperately, she wanted to know what Lincoln was going to do. He was her ticket to freedom. When free-dom did come, she could jump the broom with Bill. She just didn't like sneaking around.

"James Terrell seems to think that Lincoln will use fed-eral troops to coerce them.

At that moment, Amanda heard her name. It was Miz Temperance. Sighing, she left her hiding place and went to see what she wanted. Tears smarted her eyes as she raced up the back stairs to Miz Temperance' room. Deep down, she realized that Lincoln was going to allow slavery to con-tinue. It just wasn't fair. When she got to the bedroom Miz Temperance occupied, she paused at the door. She wiped her tears with the back of hands and then knocked on the door.

"Come in."

Amanda opened the door and slowly walked in. The two faced each other. Amanda closed the door and leaned against it. Defiantly, she stared at Miz Temperance. For the first time in her life, she didn't cast her eyes to the floor. With her eyes, she challenged her.

"Yes sum?" she questioned her.

"Didn't you know that Senator Thomas was back?"

"I's knowed it."

"Why didn't you answer me when I called you?"

"Didn't hear youse."

"Where were you?"

Amanda just stared and repeated. "Didn't hear youse."

Miz Temperance sighed. "All right, nigger. I know you were with that nigger of Mr. Love. I don't know what's gotten into you. You've been different since yer mama died. I guess you miss her. Remember we are family."

Amanda just stared at her. "Wat's youse want?"

"We'll be going home soon. I want you to pack my bags."

"Yes sum."

Chapter 56

Deep sadness engulfed Amanda's being. She and Bill would be separated...miles apart...miles she couldn't travel and Master Thomas would not allow her to go. All was lost. Rapidly, she packed Miz Temperance's things except her traveling clothes, which were still in the closet and a few personal items for her use. Without asking permission to leave, she ran out of the room and quietly closed the door behind her. She expected to hear Miz Temperance call her back, but no voice echoed through the air. At this moment she was free to do what she wanted. Dashing down the back stairs, she went out of the back door and headed for the coach house. She knew that Bill would be there. When she got there, he was grooming the horse Master Thomas had driven to White Sulphur Springs. With him was Cudge. She had forgotten about her childhood friend. Each had grown in their own way. She looked at Cudge and realized he was worldlier than she was. Her world was just the Smokies, while Cudge had traveled the other end of the state and beyond.

"Cudge!" she said surprisingly. "I's forgot that youse were with Maser Thomas." She ran to him and hugged him. "I know dat yer father is lonely without youse."

"It be good to see youse." Cudge laughed. "I won-der'd where youse be."

"Just hangin' 'round.'"

"Listenin' to wat Maser Thomas had to say."

"Somethin' likk dat."

307

Cudge shook head. "Wat did youse find out?"

"We's ain't neber be free."

"Well, I's hafto go."

Amanda watched as Cudge left the coach house and headed toward the big house. And then she turned her attention to Bill, who was walking the horse to a stall. She walked with him. Together, hand and hand, they bedded the horse down and then they went to an empty stall. Bill took a horse blanket, laid it on top of the hay and invited Amanda to sit down. She sat down and Bill sat beside her. He took another blanket and draped it around her shoulders, drawing her close to him. He kissed her and held her even closer. They heard each other's heartbeat racing through their body. The chill in the air quickly disappeared as their bodies melted the coldness. Gently, he laid her on the blanket and consumed her body. Amanda welcomed him.

This was their courtship. Here at White Sulphur Springs, Bill didn't have a cabin of his own. He was housed in the single men's quarters. So the single male slaves were used for breeding the female slaves. However, Amanda wanted more than that. She wanted to jump the broom with Bill, but it appeared it wasn't going to happen.

Tomorrow William Holland Thomas and his household would be heading back to Stekoa Fields. She was part of that household, but Bill was part of White Sulphur Springs' household. Their romance was over. Master Thomas would decide which single male slave would be her mate. Afterward, Amanda cried. Bill held her. He didn't know what to do. The mountains separated them. She knew Rozette was there at Bill's beckon call. There was nothing she could do.

"I's love youse." Bill insisted.

"I's love youse, too." Amanda put her head on his shoulder. "Our love can't last with youse here an' I's ov'r on Ste"I's come to youse. After all I ain't no slave. My brothers are, I ain't. I's go where I wanna."

"Is da good, Bill?" Amanda asked. "Is we ever gonna be free?

Chapter 57

In a week's time, the Thomas household went back to Stekoa Fields. There was joy among them as they journeyed home. Amanda, however, was saddened. For the last two days, she had not seen Bill. He just disappeared from White Sulphur Springs. She attempted to ask his brothers, but they were too busy preparing for the coming war. Mr. Love and Master Thomas had argued about this pending crisis.

Riding along in the carriage with Miz Temperance, Miz Sallie and her two children and Caroline, Amanda's mind went back to the conversation between Mr. Love and her master as they prepared to leave White Sulphur Springs. Master Thomas was seated in the driver's seat of the carriage, while Cudge sat dutiful beside him.

"James," Master Thomas said, "I don't think there is gonna be a war. Our state rights give us the option of remaining in the Union."

"You don't think that Lincoln is going to allow us to form our own country without a fight." Mr. Love replied.

"Look, Georgia seceded in January." Master Thomas rationalized. "That's two of the four states that border us. I fear that Virginia and Tennessee will join the Confederacy. That means we will be surrounded by foreign states."

"I see your point, Thomas." Mr. Love acknowledged. "I'm ready for'em." He shook Master Thomas's hand firmly. "You need to get ready."

That conversation continued to replay in her mind.

And for Amanda, it meant that slavery would be the way of life for the newly formed country. Lincoln needed to rescue them. Bill was free and she was a slave. He wanted nothing to do with her. As tears fell silently from her eyes, she hid her face from the others.

When they arrived at Stekoa Fields, Amanda was amazed that Mister Andy had begun to ready the fields for planting. The slaves were working like there was no crisis. This made Amanda realized the impending crisis had nothing to do with their status in the scheme of things. Let the white society worry about the situation. And Amanda couldn't help, but worry about herself. She couldn't discuss the situation with Caroline, because she felt that Caroline was happy. However, when she looked over at Caroline, she did detect a sense of sadness. Leaving White Sulphur Springs meant that Caroline was leaving behind her mate, just as she was. They were in the same dilemma. And yet, Caroline surmised that her man would be there.

Before Amanda knew it, everything seemed back to the old routine. Caroline carried the newborn in the nursery with Little Willie toddling behind her. Andrew came out of the house to greet them.

"Pops" he shouted, "It's good to have you back."

"It's good to be back."

The two shook hands. Then Andrew gave Master Thomas some bad news. "Pops, that unruly nigger, Dave just up and left. The paddy rollers couldn't find him."

"Did you ask the Luftys. He might have run there?"

"I haven't had the chance. I've been busy getting the fields ready."

Master Thomas patted Andrew on the back. "That allright."

Master Thomas and Andrew went into the house. Amanda had remained in the carriage as Cudge helped Miz Sallie and Miz Temperance out. Miz Sallie walked swiftly into the house while Cudge assisted Miz Temperance into the house. As Amanda disembarked from the carriage, she thought of Dave. She hoped he was free and well. However, she realized Miz Temperance would require her assistance and she needed to help her. By that time, Cudge returned to the carriage to retrieve the luggage. Together, Cudge and Amanda unloaded the luggage and set them on the porch. Picking up Miz Sallie's and Miz Temperance's bags, Amanda lugged them into the house. Putting Miz Temperance's down, she carried Miz Sallie's to the master bedroom. When she got to Miz Temperance's room, Amanda found her in an anger mood.

"It's about time you got here?" She pointed the cane at her. "You go tell Sam that I need to go to Shoal Creek. Right now!"

"Yes sum."

"Now!"

Amanda dashed out of the door and made a beeline to the back entrance. As she went pass Master Thomas's office, she heard voices. She couldn't stop and listen to the conversation, because Miz Temperance was extremely irate. All she could see was Miz Temperance's cane before her eyes. Running to toward the field, she found Sam, as he stood and watched the other slaves work.

"Sam! Sam!" she called.

Upon hearing his name, he turned to watch Amanda run toward him. When she was abreast of him, she stopped and bent over holding on to her knees. Her breathing was labored, as she attempted to breathe easier.

"Somethin' wrong with Cudge?"

"He be fine."

"Wat?"

"Miz Temperance wants youse to take her home."

Miser Andrew gots me out here crackin' de whip." Sam smiled. "Where be my boy?"

"He be here." Amanda dug her feet in the soft soil. "Wat 'bout Miz Temperance?"

"I's take her in de mornin'."

"Ok." Amanda turned to go back to the house, then she turne back to Sam.

"I's send Cudge to see youse."

"Danks."

Amanda left and slowly went back to the house. After she told Miz Temperance that Sam would take her home tomorrow, the old lady was satisfied. Amanda helped her remove her traveling clothes and put on her comfortable house dress. After helping her downstairs to the parlor, Amanda started outside. On her way, she had to go by Master Thomas's office. She heard voices inside. Stopping, she tried to listen to the conversation. Immediately, she recognized Andy's voice.

"Folks around here are fer Lincoln and they ain't thinking about leaving the Union.

"I know," Master Thomas replied. "I don't anticipate any fighting. Just two separate nations with similar laws with a lifestyle virtually unchanged. I had written Sallie that these mountains would be the center of the Confederacy. This would be the place the Southern people would spend their vacation instead of the North."

"Sounds good." Andy chucked. "But Lincoln ain't goin' let the Southern states leave without a fight."

At that point, Amanda heard footsteps coming from the stairwell. Quickly, she left the house by the back door. She thought about two countries being on this soil. The one up North would be free for black folks, while the one down South would not be free for black folks. And it seemed that she had been born in the wrong section.

Chapter 58

The next morning, Miz Temperance left for Shoal Creek. To Amanda's surprise, Miz Sallie sent her with Miz Temperance. Amanda really didn't want to go, but she had no choice. Therefore, she packed her things and went. In the back of her mind, she surmised that Miz Sallie was sending her away because she eavesdropped on Master Thomas' conversation. The person in the stairwell most had been Miz Sallie and she surely saw her running out of the house.

Now she was in isolation with Miz Temperance. She couldn't talk to Cudge to get the latest news. However, late in March, Sam and Cudge came to Shoal Creek. It seemed that Master Thomas was heading back to Raleigh and Cudge was going with him. Cudge had persuaded his father to allow him to go with him to the store in Shoal Creek to buy some personal items before leaving. On their way back, they stopped by Miz Temperance's.

Miz Temperance was glad to see Sam. The two of them sat on the porch and talked about Stekoa Fields, while Cudge and Amanda ran around the house to chat about the pending crisis.

"Wat's happenin', Cudge?"

"I's herd dat Lincoln got 'nograted. Dat means he's de president now. But there be fightin' in South Carolina. Dey says dat Lincoln be sendin' troops. Maser Thomas is gonna go back to Raleigh fer a 'pecial meetin'."

"Wat 'bout?"

"I's don't know fer sure. It 'pears as if we's be voted out de Union."

"Wat?"

"Dey gonna vote us out of the Union."

"Can dey do dat?"

"I's 'pect dat dey can."

"Cudge," Amanda sighed. "I's wish'd I's listen'd to Power. I's could be up North rat now."

"Maybe." Cudge took her hand. Although, he was younger than Amanda, he thought of himself being wiser. "Maser Thomas hopes it ain't gonna be no war. I's hear'em tell Miz Sallie tat we's can be a separate fro' de North."

"Wat?" Amanda said angrily. "Dat means dat we stay a slave. All'em folks who wants to free us are up North. Ifen, we be separate countries, they can't free us."

At that moment, Sam called Cudge. It was time to go back to Stekoa Fields. Before they left, Cudge reminded Amanda that Master Thomas was a good man. He tried to tell Amanda all the good things he had done for his people. Amanda was sad. Her world had fallen apart.

Late that night, there was a knock on the door. When Amanda answered it, the moonlight shone down on a bedraggled black man, who looked hungry and undernourished. His hair was long and unkempt. While his upper body was bare, he wore tattered soiled, threadbare trousers. He had no shoes on his dirty feet. However, he was carrying some clothes in his arms. It looked as if he had been traveling a long way from home. With, the condition of his clothes, she speculated he must had traveled by night and hiding out doing the day, as he avoided the paddy rollers.

Amanda stared at him, and then she rushed into his arms.

"Bill," she cried. "Bill, my love."

Looking around, she saw no one had spied them. Swiftly, she dragged him into the house, closed and locked the door. Miz Temperance didn't stir in her sleep. Her uneven snoring continued as Amanda sat Bill on the floor. She still was afraid that the paddy rollers might still be following him. Hence she moved the chair and rolled the rug back, which revealed the door to the root cellar. She unlatched and opened it. Going over to Bill, who was in a state of exhaustion, lay there like a rag doll. He appeared to be dead. Gently, she shook him and a groan came from his throat. Frightened, she hugged him tightly. All she could think of he had traveled all the way from Waynesville to see her. Now she had to hide him from the paddy rollers.

"Bill," she whispered in his ear. "I's gotta hide youse."

He struggled to get up. She helped him. With Bill leaning on her shoulder, they slowly made it down to the root cellar. She made him comfortable as she could. Before she left, she cautioned him to be quiet. Although Bill was a free black man, it was dangerous for him to roam around at night. Desperately she wanted to stay with him, but she knew was out of the question. After leaving the root cellar and securing it, she cleaned up the room and went back to bed in the loft. However, sleep avoided her, as she anxiously waited the dawn of the next day. Miz Temperance told her tomorrow would be Easter and she would go to church with her. Amanda had to beg off. She had to be with Bill.

It was Easter morning and Miz Temperance was up and about. Sam had told her that Master Thomas and his family were coming by to take her to church. This was perfect for Amanda. She would pretend she was sick and couldn't attend. Hence, Amanda remained in bed and didn't come down to fix Miz Temperance's breakfast.

"Amanda," she called, "Amanda, its Easter morning. Willie is coming to take me to sunrise service."

'I's not feeling well." Amanda coughed. "I's don't wanna Robert or Little Will to catch wat I's got."

"The children aren't coming." Temperance sighed.

"I feel terrible." Amanda cried. "I's got a bad headache."

"Ok." She answered. "I'll find something to eat. You just be here when I come back, you hear me?"

"Yes ma'am."

Amanda turned over on the pallet. Nervously, she waited for Miz Temperance to leave. Every noise which originated down below, Amanda jumped. If Miz Temperance discovered Bill in the root cellar, she would be in trouble. All she heard was the slow movement of Miz Temperance. Finally, Master Thomas arrived and took his mother to sunrise service.

When she heard the door close, she ascended to the main floor. Peeping out the window, she saw the back of the little buggy stopped about hundred yards from the house. On horseback, she recognized Mr. Charles Bumgarner. The buggy was Master Thomas' with him and his mother inside. Nervously Amanda wondered what they were chatting about. It seemed Mr. Bumgarner looked her way and she ducked down. Peeping through crack in the wall, she saw the buggy and Mr. Bumgarner leave in the same direction.

Amanda wasn't completely satisfied. Deep down, she felt Mr. Bumgarner was going to double back to Miz Temperance's house. Swiftly, she removed the chair and threw back the rug from the root cellar. Quickly she went down the steps and awakened Bill, who lying on the dirt floor. He sat up and looked around at his surrendering.

"Bill," she said. "We's hafto get out of here."

"Where is the old lady?"

"She went to sunrise service."

"We's have the whole house to ourselves."

"Listen to me." Amanda pulled him to his feet. "Did paddy rollers chase youse?"

"Not really?"

"Wat's do youse mean?"

"Mandy," he tried to reassure her. "Dey might have seen my shadow."

"Damn it," She said, "Dey is after youse?"

"I ain't no slave. I's a free man." Bill declared, "I ass my momma ifen I be bond'd to Mr. Love. She tells me I ain't. Jest, James and George. She gave me my freedom papers."

He took a document out of his pocket and showed her. She looked at it, but had no idea what it said. He pointed to word free.

"See tat word. Tat says FREE."

"Free," she repeated the word and handed it back to him.

Together, they made their way up to the main floor. Amanda went to the window and looked out. There was nothing, but the quietness of an Easter morning. When the illumination of the day loomed over the horizon, Bill would be secure. Until then, Amanda was going to keep him impregnable. She knew Miz Temperance was going to spend Easter with Master Thomas and his family. Hence she and Bill could have the whole day to themselves.

When the sun rose over the hill, Amanda felt this was a brand new day. The past was factitious. Boldly she went outside and fetched some water from the well. She had Bill to remove his filthy clothes and bath himself. Pretending she had jumped the broom with Bill and this was their home, she tossed the clothes he wore when he arrived in the hearth and washed his clothes he had carried in his arms. She hung them on the bushes in back of the house with the hoped that the sun would dry them before the end of the day. It being a holiday, it was not uncommon to see blacks walking the roads. Most of the time, the paddy rollers didn't bother them, until darkness covered the day. Amanda prayed this day would be like that. It would be just an ordinary day she and Bill could spend together. Amanda vowed she would ask Master Thomas if she could jump the broom with Bill. Humming a Negro spiritual as she went about fixing Bill some breakfast, Amanda remembered all the good times she had with him. Turning around, she looked at him and laughed. There he was, sitting at the table in worn pair of Miz Temperance's bloomers that Amanda had found in the ragbag.

"Wat's so funny?"

"Youse," she laughed, "In dose bloomers of Miz Temperance."

"My fancy pants!"

"Yer Easter fancy pants."

Amanda and Bill laughed together. . They had not done this in a long time. Their relationship was always one of a secret forbidden love affair that blossomed when darkness covered the day. They wanted more. If their relationship was to advance beyond clandestine meetings, they needed to jump the broom. With Bill's determination to move away from his older brothers, who had conscripted themselves to Mr. Love was an important step. And yet, Bill came to Amanda, a bonded servant of William Holland Thomas to begin his life anew. Amanda was elated he had chosen to come to her. Neither one of them could fathom just what the outcome of the whole situation would be. Freedom was something that Amanda wanted, but it appeared that she would still be a bonded servant and her man would be free. And yet freedom for a black man in Western North Carolina had it limits. Bill had been willing to risk his freedom by coming to her.

By that afternoon, Bill's clothes were almost dry. Therefore, she brought them in the house. As she came in fshe ound Bill in the chair by the fireplace. Amanda placed the clothes on the table and went over to Bill.

"Wat's youse thinkin' 'bout?" She put her arms around his neck.

"'Bout us."

"Wat 'bout us?"

"I be free, but it seems dat youse ain't neber gonna be free."

"Don't seem likk it,"

"I's guess I's thinkin' dat we should jump de broom."

Amanda couldn't believe her ears. It had been her prayer that he would ask her. Now he had said it. Perhaps, he would ask Master Thomas, the deed might be done. Nervously, she hugged him tightly. They had had stolen moments, but it would be great to know Bill was hers. She kissed him and retrieved the irons from the mantle of the fireplace. After sitting the irons on the smothering fire in the fireplace, she asked, "Are youse gonna ask Maser Thomas?"

"Yep." Bill replied. "If'en I has t concrip' myself to Maser Thomas."

"No!" Amanda cried. "No! Youse can't do dat."

"I's love youse. If'en dat de onlee way."

"We's cans runs 'way."

"W'ere to?"

"Jest follow de big dipper.

"I's can't a havin' youse runnin' in all 'rects."

"Den youse go."

"When I git out of dese bloomers an' get dress proper likk a man." He laughed. "I's wait here with youse 'til Mr. Thomas brings Miz Temperance back."

"I gonna git yer shirt an' pants rite now." She said, spontaneously laughing and crying.

Amanda ironed Bill's shirt and pants, while he sat there watching her. As she ironed, moving back and forward to retrieve an iron, she felt like she was robbing Bill of his freedom. Within a short time, she had pressed Bill's clothes and handed them to him. Bill took off the bloomers and tossed them to Amanda, who promptly tossed them in the corner of the room. Turning away from Bill, she took the two irons and placed them back on the mantle. As he dressed, she retrieved the bloomers from the corner and threw them to the ragbag. Standing there, tears slowly ran down her cheeks.

The afternoon went slowly, as the couple talked about the pending crisis and how it was going to affect their lives. Bill felt he had to prove something to Mr. Thomas. Around four, Master Thomas's horse and buggy slowly trotted into the front yard of Miz Temperance's home. Looking out the window, Amanda saw Master Thomas disembark from the buggy, and then he went to the other side to help his mother. Together, they walked to the house. Before Master Thomas opened the door, Amanda did it for them.

"Well," Miz Temperance said. "I see that you're still here?"

"Yes ma'am."

"I need to be getting back," Master Thomas kissed his mother on the cheek and turned to leave.

"Wait!" Amanda cried, "Someone needs to talk to youse."

Bill appeared in the doorway.

"Boy," Master Thomas scolded him. "What are you doing here?"

"Sir, I be free." He handed him his freedom papers.

"I know," Master Thomas sighed. "What do you want?"

"I's wanna jump de broom with Mandy."

"I see."

"I's be willin' to stay rat here." Bill promised. "An' help youse when youse gone."

"Mother," Master Thomas looked to her for advice. "What do you think?"

"Jump the broom?." She pointed at Bill. "How are we going to trust him when you're gone. Only if he gives up his freedom."

"Give up his freedom?" Amanda's heart seemed to stop beating.

"Dat I'right." Bill went over to Amanda and hugged her. "I's be willin' to be conscipt'd to Master Thomas.

"Go ahead and draw up the papers," Miz Temperencee insisted.

Master Thomas shook his head. "All right Mother. I've got more important things to do."

"Cans we have its at Stekoa Fields?" Amanda asked.

"Yes." Master Thomas agreed. "Let's get it done before I have to leave for Raleigh. Boy, hand me your freedom papers."

With the seeds in the ground and the approach of the growing season, just before Master Thomas headed for Raleigh to help decide the fate of North Carolina, Stekoa Fields was a place of celebration. Master Thomas had drawn up the paperwork and Bill signed with an X, while Thomas wrote Bill's name next to it. He and Dearest Miz Sallie gave Amanda permission to jump the broom. The ceremony took place in the front yard of the big house.

Amanda was ecstatic. Everything was ready. Suckey baked the wedding cake and Sam had the broom especially made by Yonaguska's daughter Kanaka. Mary Tuskha and Caroline decorated the oak tree with a variety of colored ribbon. Amanda had Caroline fix her hair. She couldn't have her uncombed kinky, matted, nappy mess. With that wild hair, she couldn't jump the broom with Bill.

After Carolina used an old sheep carding brush to remove the tangles, she rubbed chopped corn in her hair and washed Amanda's hair in rainwater. Then, she rinsed it with dishwater from the kitchen. With kerosene applied to a rag, Caroline rubbed the rag over the strands of Amanda's hair. After each strand was oiled down, Carolina wrapped it with strips of rags. These wraps remained in Amanda's hair until just before the wedding. When the wraps were off, it appeared that Amanda had wavy hair flowing down to her shoulders. With a smile on her face, she looked radiant.

A day of celebration, even some Lufty Cherokees attended the wedding. Having seen and heard about white Christian weddings, she had Sam to give her away. Amanda wore an old dress of Miz Sallie. With Mary's help, they bleached the faded blue dress white. In her arms, she carried a bouquet of wild daisies. Mary tried to get Amanda to wear shoes, but Amanda refused. Being barefooted, Amanda felt free. She and Bill had talked it over and he agreed to jump the broom barefooted, too.

Bill wore knee high dark brown knickers, which were held up with a rope belt and a white mill sack overhead shirt, which was open at the neck. This wedding shirt was Amanda's gift to him. With help from Miz Temperance, Amanda had stitched it. At the opening at the neck was a yoke embroidered with brown thread.

Since it was a slave wedding, a preacher wasn't engaged to perform the ceremony. Master Thomas, a state senator and a lawyer, convinced Bill and Amanda he had the authority to marry slaves. Standing under the decorated oak with Master Thomas, Bill waited for Amanda to join him. Amanda, on the arm of Sam walked toward Bill. She looked over at her fellow slaves and the Lufty Cherokees standing there around and wished her mother was there to witness this blessed event.

When she and Sam got to the oak tree, Sam took Amanda's right hand and offered it to Bill, who took it. Sam stepped back. Now it was time for Master Thomas to perform the ceremony.

With a Bible in his hand, Master Thomas said, "Today we join these two souls together. I join this boy and this girl as one. Let none, but God separate them. I therefore pronounce you both the same. However, keep your name. Now jump the broom."

Hand in hand, Bill and Amanda jumped the broom.

"She belongs to you. Salute your bride."

Master Thomas raised the Bible high in the air. At this signal the slaves started their celebration. Cowbells rang, slaves shouted and even the Luftys gave out a war whoop. The deed had been done; Amanda Thomas and William Hudson Casey had jumped the broom. However, Master Thomas rushed in the house to prepare for the trip to Raleigh, which would change everyone's life forever.

The end of the beginning.

Epilogue

A braham Lincoln was elected President of the United States, although some of the Southern states did not have his name on the ballot. Soon afterward, the Southern states began to secede from the Union, led by South Carolina. The attack on Fort Sumter by rebellious forces on April 12, 1861 marked the beginning of the American Civil War.

On Stekoa Fields, there was some excitement. Sallie's father immediately resigned from the House of Representatives and joined the rebellious troops. A year later, William Holland Thomas resigned his Senate seat and formed the Thomas Legion. His purpose was to defend Western North Carolina from Union forces. Sara's brother Matthew and her uncles' Dillard and John C. Love defended the eastern boundary of Tennessee and the western boundary of North Carolina with now Colonel Thomas.

Cudge, the body servant of Colonel Thomas remained with him throughout the conflict. North Carolina treated him as a civil war veteran and awarded him a pension. As for Amanda Thomas and William Hudson, they remained at Stekoa Field. While their master was gone, they helped keep the homestead going. Like a miracle, Amanda and William Casey had a son in January 1866. They named him Mountville Sherman. Mountville had been conceived just as the Civil War came to a close in April 1865. This was about nine months after the Civil War.

Bill and Amanda continued to live around Thomas' Stekoa Fields. The General Assembly required that all slave couples legalize their marriage. On January 14, 1869, Justice of Peace C. C. Spake married Amanda Thomas and William Hudson Casey.

From this legalized union, Amanda and Bill had five other children. They were James Henry, Cordelia, Delaware, George Power, and Charles Brane. (Born in the late 1870's Amanda's daughters, Cordelia and Delaware, believed they were born in slavery until they grew older.)

In 1892, Amanda and Bill purchased land in the Cullowhee Township. At last they had cut their ties with slavery.

A couple of years after the purchase of the land, Bill left Amanda and went to Murphy. While in Murphy, he met Rosette Hyatt and married her. Making their way back to Jackson County, the couple settled in Webster. (But that's another story for another time.)

After Bill left, Amanda took over the household with the help of her eldest sons, Mountville Sherman and James Henry. The land they owned included woods, minerals, fossils and very good soil. Managing the household and helping in the garden, Amanda canned food that sustained them through the winter months. She raised chickens, gathered eggs, fed and raised hogs and calves that were butchered and canned also.

Her experience as a slave stood her in good sted as this lone woman kept her family together, and gave her children a foothold in life...a foothold in freedom.

My direct lineage comes through Amanda's fifth child, George Power, who was my grandfather.

Passed down through the years, the story of Martha, the child slave, and her daughter Amanda born into slavery, have given all of us, their descendents, a pride that only comes from the realization of stedfast endurance, no matter the odds. Now, we can boldly say..."Sir, I am free."

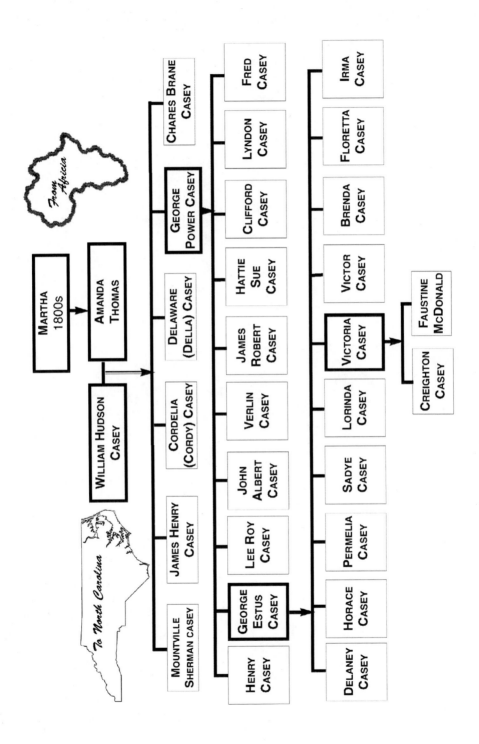

From Africa

To North Carolina

MARTHA 1800s

AMANDA THOMAS

WILLIAM HUDSON CASEY

MOUNTVILLE SHERMAN CASEY

JAMES HENRY CASEY

CORDELIA (CORDY) CASEY

DELAWARE (DELLA) CASEY

GEORGE POWER CASEY

CHARES BRANE CASEY

HENRY CASEY

GEORGE ESTUS CASEY

LEE ROY CASEY

JOHN ALBERT CASEY

VERLIN CASEY

JAMES ROBERT CASEY

HATTIE SUE CASEY

CLIFFORD CASEY

LYNDON CASEY

FRED CASEY

DELANEY CASEY

HORACE CASEY

PERMELIA CASEY

SADYE CASEY

LORINDA CASEY

VICTORIA CASEY

VICTOR CASEY

BRENDA CASEY

FLORETTA CASEY

IRMA CASEY

CREIGHTON CASEY

FAUSTINE MCDONALD

325